The Shining Ones

Jessica Davidson

JesDharma Books

Cover © 2017 Jessica Davidson
Photo by Luiz Claudio

Published by JesDharma Books
Printed by CreateSpace
www.jessicadavidson.co.uk

For Emma – a real life human angel

"O You Who are high in the stars,
You shall never die."

- Akhu Prayer to Nut, *The Ancient Egyptian Prayer Book*

"Someday after we have mastered the winds, the waves, the tides, and gravity, we shall harness the energies of love. And then for the second time in the history of the world, man will have discovered fire."

- Pierre Teilhard de Chardin, *Toward the Future*

Prologue

The camera spun as it descended into the cave, the beam of its light dancing over the rocks like a demented fairy.

William Maxwell dug his hands deeper into the pockets of his parka and squinted at the monitor, waiting for the image to stabilise. He was standing in a bubble of artificial light four hundred miles north of the Arctic Circle on some of the oldest rocks on the planet. Four billion years layered beneath his feet, all the way down to biogenic graphite.

The generator sputtered and the floodlights dimmed. Will glanced at the wall of black rock rising above him, the sky a translucent bruise behind the nunatak. He had always dreamed of exploring this brutal landscape, so different and yet so similar to his native Scotland. Greenland was how he imagined the world was before life took hold, before humans arrived with their mess and madness. Standing on the glacier, listening to it roar and crack, as it had for a hundred thousand years, made him feel like the first man on earth. Or the last.

The lights flickered off and the winch lowering the camera stopped. Will shifted his feet in frustration and looked across the ice to the generator.

'Petar,' he shouted. 'Give the bloody thing a kick.'

In the twilight, the ice sheet gleamed like a carpet of aquamarine beryl. Released from the glare of the lights, Will could see the Milky Way. He tilted his head back, following the shimmering arc of stars, the silent beauty of the vision emptying him of himself. He could disappear in this vastness and never be seen again.

The lights flared and the camera resumed its descent.

Will shook himself and turned back to the screen. The expedition wasn't going well. He blamed the sun. If the sun hadn't tried to kill them all last summer they would have completed their surveys then. That's why he was here now, struggling against the darkness, instead of sitting with his feet up and enjoying the curfew with a bottle of the finest

Glenfiddich. He could be in the Grampians. No pressure, no reports; just him and the mountain.

It was the wrong season for this work. Granted, it was easier to navigate the ice when it was frozen in the winter because there were no melt streams, but they kept running out of time. There literally weren't enough hours in the day up here. They had already delayed the expedition thanks to the superstorm. He didn't understand why they couldn't wait a few more months for the days to lengthen, but the company wanted results. Fast.

In three months of searching he had found nothing. Nothing they could get their hands on without disturbing the wildlife. Greenland National Park was a biosphere reserve so they couldn't just take what they wanted, no matter how much they wanted to. ReSource was a founding member of the ARK consortium, the one group of people he didn't want to cross. They were investing millions in this expedition and their permits were about to expire. If he didn't find something soon ARK would leave him on the ice to freeze. Worse, he might end up indentured to a Work Farm.

Will rammed his crampons deeper into the ice and watched flashes of sandstone and dolomites pirouette over the screen. He wanted to rappel down and get his hands on the rocks, but they had to check the cave out first. Nobody was going anywhere until he had run a full risk assessment.

They had discovered it yesterday, flying over the Ismarken ice sheet in the Twin Otter. The magnetometers had flagged an anomaly, so they had flown in tight circles around the mountain running the radar and gravity gradiometers to build a map of the cave system.

All over Greenland the ice was retreating. The glaciers had shrunk to reveal the virgin land beneath, like gums peeling back from teeth. Melt streams had appeared and thousands of rivers now ran through the ice like varicose veins. One of these melt streams had created a fissure and exposed the cave. A cave no one had ever entered. A cave lost in time.

The camera juddered on the end of its rope. Will pulled off one glove and fiddled with a dial to adjust the light aperture, opening the beam. He held his breath and leaned closer, wishing for the hundredth time that the screen was larger. The light flashed crimson as the beam hit embedded minerals. Was that a ruby seam?

Will stifled a whoop of joy. The other members of his team gathered behind him, jostling for a better look at the monitor.

A collective intake of breath, then silence.

They stood as if engulfed in a sudden ice storm. The camera had come to rest, its light scattering into the vast cavern. It was sixty metres deep and at least twice as long. Will knew it was large, he had expected as much. But standing at the heart of the cave was something impossible. Will stared at the screen in shock.

'What the hell is that?'

1

Mist clung to the city like a security blanket, the river a dark gash through a haze of light. Thousands of glowing beads hung in the air as if defying the darkness of space.

Behind one of those lights, Ana moved between benches administering first aid. She was at the shelter where she volunteered three times a week. It was packed. The earlier rain had driven everyone inside, washing the streets and parks clean. Those who hadn't found a place in one of the numerous squats springing up around the city ended up here in the abandoned church. They squeezed into the pews, fetid steam rising like a storm cloud.

The building was crumbling and wire mesh covered the windows, its oval belly now stuffed with the homeless and desperate. Lines of drying clothes had been strung up between the wooden pillars and several tents nestled against the walls.

Ana dabbed lavender and oregano oil on a dressing and pressed it to the cuts marking a woman's legs. 'Hold this in place.' She waited while the woman placed her shaking fingers over the cotton pad. Ana could feel the woman's fear skittering inside her like disturbed bats.

Another body had been found, crumpled at the foot of a cliff up the coast. There were rumours that the man had been dead before he hit the rocks. Ana knew the rumours were true, but kept what she could see to herself because she didn't want to frighten people any more than they already were.

Somebody was killing the homeless. It made no sense. Most of them were starving to death anyway.

'He used to come here,' said the woman. 'What was he doing in Craster? There's nowt but kippers and kittiwakes up there.'

Ana remembered him. She had tried to fix his broken nose after a fight. He had been a regular at the shelter but no one had seen him in months.

'Are we safe?' continued the woman. 'Here. Would they come here?'

'I don't know. Perhaps.'

The woman's fear intensified. Ana secured the bandage, then gently touched the woman's cheek and watched the flames of fear sputter out. 'Help each other,' she said. 'You're stronger together.'

She gathered up her bottles and dressings, stepped over the bodies filling the aisle and mounted the steps to the altar. It was the only part of the church that hadn't been overrun. A serene Virgin Mary stood at the centre of the stone slab, her face blackened by smoke. She had acquired plastic angel wings that hung from her neck at a wonky angle. A cluster of candles burned at her feet. Mary gazed unblinking into the flames, perhaps waiting for the fire to rise, shred her sapphire robes and curl the paint from her plaster body.

Ana shunted her doctor's bag to one side and leaned across the altar to straighten the statue's wings. She gave the solemn figurine an encouraging smile, then dropped her tincture bottles into their compartment and closed the bag.

Anastasia Wilson wasn't a conventional doctor. She was a herbalist and a healer and had been coming to All Saints since it reopened after the storms. She barely remembered her life before. The old Ana had been vaporised and a serene squatter now gazed at the wreckage of her life through awakened eyes.

Last year the sun had become a dragon, spewing great columns of fire. The earth was hit three times. The first a gentle warning shot, as if translucent wings had enfolded the planet in a protective luminosity.

Then on the cusp of midsummer, emerald and ruby plasma had ripped through the atmosphere as far south as the equator. The earth convulsed like it was under a cosmic defibrillator. Mini quakes shivered through the ground and Britain shook itself like a dog.

By the time the final storm had blown itself out last month, the world had changed, and so had Ana.

She didn't want people to know what she could do; the way her mind could penetrate reality, seemingly of its own accord, like she was practising a long lost skill. Most people didn't respond well to the idea of her poking around inside their heads. One-to-one, she could block their thoughts without much effort, but a person was more than their thoughts and she couldn't block it all.

Not all the time.

She had tried. She had built barricades against others to keep her mind isolated, but it always ended badly. The pain would start small, a slight ache behind her eyes. But if she stayed behind her mental shutters for too long, the pain would increase steadily until she could no longer stand. At Christmas she had managed it for 24 hours before she had collapsed. She had slept for three days and it was a week before she had fully recovered.

Ana closed her eyes and listened to the invisible emotional geometry of other minds as they moved against hers. If she concentrated, she could discern patterns in the noise, follow one thread of thought and find its source. Anxiety hummed through the crowd, a bass note of fear that infected every mind. Except one.

A man was trying to get her attention.

She turned to face the church. The curved wooden pews were filled with people talking in hushed voices. Some warmed their hands on bowls of steaming soup and passed hunks of bread down the line, breaking off a morsel before handing it on. Ana scanned the faces, shadowed by candlelight. Some felt her gaze and glanced up to smile or nod their gratitude.

An old man wormed his way through the crowd towards her. He was wrapped in several coats riddled with holes, his wild hair as deranged as his mind. Ana felt his delirium invade her mental space, forcing itself upon her. A madness of such overwhelming clarity it was almost divine.

There was nothing she could do to help this man. She steadied herself against the altar as he tripped up the shallow steps and stumbled into her arms. The stench of rotting vegetation hit the back of her throat and she tried not to gag.

'Please,' she said. 'Please sit-'

'It's you.' He grinned through his matted beard. 'I knew you would come.'

Ana took his hand and led him slowly down the steps to the nearest pew, nodding silently. Perhaps if she humoured him, he would let her go. She eased him onto the hard bench. 'There now. Have you eaten?'

He touched her long blonde hair with trembling fingers. Ana shuddered involuntarily, but allowed him to stroke her hair. Since the storm people wanted to be near her. She seemed to make them strong. Perhaps it was a cruel joke, but she felt more at home with the homeless.

'You bring the fire?' said the old man, his eyes searching hers. 'You, Akhu... Akhu will come.'

She smiled and gently shook her head. 'It's Ana.'

He gazed at her intently. 'I see the star.'

Ana felt lost. She couldn't understand what she was seeing in his mind. One image dominated: a tattoo of a five-pointed star on a person's wrist. It looked more like a starfish than a star, and she had seen it before. Her friend, Ethne, had the exact same tattoo. Did this man know her friend?

Without warning, he grabbed her left hand and yanked her forward. She almost fell into his lap, but steadied herself and watched his confusion grow. He ran his filthy fingers over her left wrist, searching for something that evidently wasn't there. He looked into her face and frowned. 'Akhu?'

Ethne's tattoo was on her left wrist. It was an obvious case of mistaken identity, but not even a blind man would confuse Ana with Ethne.

Ana smiled and released herself from his grip. 'I'll get you some food.'

She glanced around the church for another helper and waved at the woman dishing up leek and potato soup near the entrance.

Kelly worked at one of the community run City Farms that kept the shelter supplied with vegetables and eggs, and meat when they were lucky. She ladled out a fresh bowl and dispatched it across the church, where it was passed hand to hand until it reached Ana.

The old man's mind was aglow with shimmering figures and huge carved stones. He mumbled the same word to himself, over and over, like a mantra, 'Akhu, Akhu, Akhu...'

Ana touched his shoulder to get his attention. She checked the soup wasn't too hot and then carefully handed it over. He cradled the bowl in his hands and inhaled.

'Stay here tonight,' she said. 'You can get clean, and there might be a better coat for you.'

He gazed up at her like a child. 'The darkness will fight its extinction.'

Ana smiled. 'Yes, I'm sure it will.'

'All is myth,' he said, and slurped his soup. 'All is myth.'

Ana felt his mind disengage from hers and she stepped away. She allowed her mind to travel along the pews, gently probing and checking on people as she went. They were all as content as could be expected; it was time for her to leave. She retrieved her doctor's bag from the altar and squeezed through the crowd to the door.

All Saints stood on the north bank of the river in Newcastle. The north-east city had survived the worst of the storm and the green steel of the Tyne Bridge rose proudly into the sky, lit for the first time in months.

Ana stood at the top of the steps outside the church and peered into the gloom, her breath freezing in the fog. She wrapped her coat tighter and opened her senses to listen. All was still, but then beyond the church she sensed movement: the jumbled fizz of two bored minds.

She walked around the church to the street and found their owners: two men sitting in a black Lexus parked beneath a street lamp. One of them was reading a newspaper, the other played a game on his phone. She listened to the tumble of disjointed thoughts and discovered that the men worked for ARK Security and they were waiting for someone. She told herself it was paranoia to assume they were waiting for her, but made a mental note of the number plate, just in case.

Suddenly, the game playing man glanced up and saw her. Both men panicked when they realised she had been watching them. Fragments of startled thoughts pierced her mind like darts.

It was her. She was Deviant. Dangerous. Call for backup.

Ana hurried past the car into the underpass and forced herself not to run. One of the men had recognised her. Was it a coincidence she had seen them, or were they waiting for her? She could hang around and listen to their thoughts to find out, but it was too risky. She decided not to walk home but to take the Metro instead. She needed to get off the street.

The yellow box of the Metro sign at Monument shone through the fog and Ana sighed in relief. If the light was on it meant the service was running. Few trusted the Metro since the power cuts had begun and only the brave or the foolhardy would risk being stranded underground. Ana was neither. She ran down the steps and through the barriers. It was only two stops, but it was worth it to be safe.

The station was deserted, but she didn't have to wait long for a train. There were two other passengers: a lad in a hood sat near the doors listening to music on his headphones, and opposite was a girl reading a paperback. Ana listened in on the story to distract herself from thinking about the men in the car. It was a tale of doomed love in a dystopian world. The girl was enjoying it, but the story filled Ana with an aching sadness she didn't understand. She shut off the connection and listened instead to the clack of the train on the tracks.

The train slowed and pulled in at Manors station. The girl tucked the paperback into her jacket and stepped off the train. Ana watched her disappear up the escalator. On the platform, the lights began to flicker and a pigeon strutted towards the train. The speaker above Ana's head crackled, 'Stand clear of the doors.' With one hop, the pigeon boarded the train just as the doors hissed shut.

Ana peered down the carriage. The pigeon was trotting towards the lad in the hood. The lights flickered and Ana glanced up in frustration. When she looked back, the pigeon had vanished.

In its place stood a dazzling woman with spiky hair and dove-shaped earrings. Her skin appeared to glow with its own luminescence. She wobbled forward and sat opposite the boy, who hadn't noticed his new companion. The woman watched him for a moment, and then pulled the headphones from his ears.

Brutal beats cascaded into the train and the boy hurried to switch it off. The woman smiled, took his hand and kissed the inside of his left wrist with great reverence and affection. They conferred quietly and the boy nodded eagerly. The lights flickered again, and determined not to miss anything, Ana watched intently. The train jolted and shuddered as it rounded a corner and the lights blinked off. When they came back on, Ana was alone.

She stood, swaying as the train clattered onwards, and walked down the carriage. She searched beneath the seats for the missing passengers and felt foolish. Perhaps she was losing her mind. Pigeons don't generally turn into strange glowing women and then vanish. Just as the train pulled into Byker station, Ana noticed something on the seat where the woman had been sitting.

A single white feather.

She picked it up to stroke its soft edges and was so transfixed she almost missed her stop. She tucked the feather into her pocket and ran up the escalator.

Ana reached the street and checked her phone. She had missed a call from Ethne and a text from Michael. She hurried through the derelict shopping centre towards the main road, past shuttered shops and heaps of rotten garbage, and opened Michael's text.

'Bring E when U come home. Got a surprise 4U.'

'I've had enough surprises for today, thanks Mickey,' she muttered under her breath while broadcasting the thought to Michael. She heard her friend chuckle in reply and decided Ethne's message could wait.

Ana turned to cross the road beside a pile of bin bags and rubbish and then froze. A man's foot protruded from beneath a cardboard box.

She glanced up and down the deserted street and then extended her mind, searching for the man's mental signature. She found nothing. She approached the body and carefully removed one of the bags to reveal his face. She didn't need to check for a pulse to know the man was dead.

Leaning closer, she could see something wasn't right. His clothes were ragged but his fingernails were clean. He looked well fed and his hair had been recently cut. She lifted his shirt and pushed back a sleeve and wasn't surprised to see that he was clean under the rags.

This man wasn't homeless.

She was about to stand when she noticed markings on the man's arm: a line of tiny puncture wounds. The body found on the rocks at Craster had the same marks. She shone her phone torch on them to get a closer look.

Ana shuddered and straightened up. This was another unexplained, and inexplicable, death.

On the edge of her awareness she picked up two minds coming her way. She glanced around, trying to appear casual, but her heart was pounding in her chest. The voices were familiar. She could hear them as clearly as if they were standing right beside her. She hurried away from the abandoned body and crossed the road.

Further up the street, a black Lexus hugged the kerb. She checked the number plate through the glare of the headlamps. It was the same car.

ARK was following her.

She got her keys out of her pocket and doubled her pace, listening to the men argue. Neither of them wanted to be there. They weren't stupid, they assured each other. They knew what had happened, they had worked it out. There had been no storms that day.

Ana began to run.

2

Ethne Godwin was standing outside her therapy practice in China Town, watching the festivities. Red lanterns lined the street, glowing like underworld embers, while sulphur from the New Year firecrackers lingered in the fog. A red and gold arch loomed from the haze, festooned with dragons and flanked by stone lions.

The curfew had been lifted and the street was filling with people. Nobody would be rushing home tonight and the bars would soon be crowded with revellers celebrating the simple pleasure of going for a drink without worrying about being struck by lightning. Or getting caught in a riot.

A gang of men staggered down the middle of the road, arms linked, shouting half-remembered lyrics, all vowels and barely suppressed aggression. Ethne watched them approach and groaned. It was getting rowdy and the last thing she needed was some drunk eejit stumbling in and demanding a massage with a happy ending.

She looked at her watch; Ana should have been back by now. She dropped the latch on the door and ran upstairs to the reception. She checked her mobile as she crossed to the desk and woke the computer. No messages, no emails.

Ethne glowered at the damp patch spreading above the window. She knew Ana would pull a stunt like this. She spent more time at that homeless shelter than she did running her business. The tax return had to be in by the end of the week and Ana had promised to help. Not that Ethne needed help, but this was supposed to be a partnership.

She picked up her phone and dialled. It went to voicemail.

'Where are you? And don't call me back to tell me how much they need you. At this rate we won't be in business anymore and you can give as many treatments away for free as you like.' She paused and closed her eyes. 'Sorry. I'm just...I'm locking up in half an hour. We'll do the accounts tomorrow. Call me.'

She sat at the computer and opened the CogNet search page to check the job bulletins. This summer it would be four years since she had graduated and she still hadn't found a decent job. At least, not one she could keep. Setting up Heaven Scent with Ana had been the perfect solution. The business had kept them both off the Work Farms and had given them a steady income. Until her friend had turned into Mother Teresa.

Ethne was a masseuse, while Ana provided aromatherapy and herbal remedies alongside her newly acquired skills. This meant that in the last few months, all the clients had wanted to see Ana; Ethne was the booby prize. She told herself it was because Ana was a soft touch, but there was more to it than that. Ana's mere presence was healing. Ethne didn't look like she could heal a paper cut. With her nose rings, tattoos, and kohl-darkened eyes, Ethne looked like trouble.

She was an overqualified, over-indebted linguist stuck in two tiny rooms above the Peking Duck watching the paint peel from the walls. Perhaps she would be a masseuse for the rest of her life. The thought made her bilious. The world was falling apart and all she did was give backrubs. Making people feel better was Ana's department. Ethne wanted to do something with her life, something real, something that would change things. But as far as she could see, there would be no future, just a laborious disintegration.

She was surprised by how dull the end of the world was turning out. The apocalypse seemed so dramatic on TV.

She couldn't discuss the future with Ana, not since she had changed. The last time, Ana had been following her around Golden Harvest watching Ethne fill her basket with tins of anaemic vegetables and deformed frozen fish. Not everybody was happy to shop in the Chinese version of Tesco, but Golden Harvest was the only supermarket left after the economy had gone under last year.

'All I'm saying is we need to rethink,' said Ethne, reaching for a carton of long-life milk. 'And maybe relocate. We can't compete with deer penis.'

Ana shrugged. 'Tell me what you want me to do.'

Ethne tucked a stray lock of her raven black bob behind an ear and stomped towards the yoghurts. 'I want you to stop being so bloody nice. Compassion is good. I get that. But it doesn't pay the rent.'

'So we should turn people away if they're poor?'

'Yes,' said Ethne. 'We're not the NHS.'

'Neither is the NHS. Not anymore.'

Ethne spun to face her friend. She didn't want to get into a screaming match in the dairy aisle but couldn't stop herself. 'Has it ever occurred to you that people lie? That they're not actually struggling as much as they claim?'

She knew Ana could read their minds, but that was no excuse as far as she was concerned. Talking to Ana these days was like talking to an especially compassionate brick wall. She continued regardless. 'They come in with their new handbags, their new hairdos and their new shoes, and they give you a sob story about the roof coming in or the boiler packing in or their fucking dog dying, and you-'

'I hear you, Ethne.'

'And?'

Ana shrugged. 'I want to help.'

'So do I,' said Ethne. 'But I don't want to starve to death in the process.'

She had often joked that if she didn't find a proper job she would be forced to sell her own organs. But then she had discovered it was an actual thing people did and it wasn't funny anymore.

There was a simple solution to the lack of cash but she didn't want to take it. She wondered how bad things would get before she relented and swallowed her pride.

Ethne gave up on the job search and shut down the computer. She pulled on her leather jacket, checked the lights were off in the therapy room, then crossed reception to the battered sofa by the door and bent to switch off the water fountain on the coffee table. Nothing happened. Water trickled over the dolphin's back and down the pile of stones to the pool at its base. She didn't know why she had switched it on in the first place. It was supposed to be calming, but the stupid thing made her desperate for a pee. She wanted rid of it, but Ana liked it, so there it stayed.

She hit the button again. It had been playing up since Christmas, probably a dodgy connection. She gave the fountain an aggressive shake and slopped water over the side. 'Shit.'

Her phone buzzed. It was Ana.

'Hey, where are you?' She hit the button again and the fountain stopped. There was a long silence on the other end of the phone. It sounded like Ana was out of breath. 'Are you having an aneurism?'

'Can you come over?' said Ana. 'And bring some food.'

Ethne was walking across the Byker Bridge when the street lights went out. A wave of darkness rippled through the city, followed by a collective groan. Another blackout. She switched on her torch. Everybody carried one these days; the torch was the new umbrella. Better to have one and not need it than be caught in the dark without a source of light.

Before leaving China Town she had picked up a takeaway and the rich aroma was making her stomach growl. She lodged the torch under her arm and snaffled a handful of prawn crackers.

Despite the blackout she could see her destination from the bridge. Ana and Michael lived in a flat at the top of a high-rise in Byker. A faint glow radiated from the window and fairy lights sparkled around the balcony. Michael had built a wind turbine when the power had gone down last year and was now experimenting with other devices. He wanted to generate enough electricity to run the whole building. Unfortunately for Ethne, he had not yet succeeded.

She dragged herself up fifteen floors to find Michael waiting in the darkened hallway. A candle threw deep shadows over his mahogany skin. 'You got in okay?' he said.

'Someone propped the door open. Very considerate. Was that you?'

He nodded and grinned, teeth flashing between dimples in the candlelight. 'Is that Chinese I smell?'

'I ate the prawn crackers,' said Ethne. 'Fuel for the climb.'

'My poor baby.' He ushered her into the warmth of the flat. 'I'll get the plates, or are we going to be savages and eat straight from the trough?'

'I'm hungry enough to eat the plates,' said Ethne, following him into the cramped kitchen. 'So, what's with the summons?'

'It's a surprise,' said Michael, laying out plates on the worktop.

Ana appeared and slipped her arms around his pudgy waist. 'He's being mysterious and it's extremely annoying.'

'No change there then,' said Ethne, piling noodles onto the plates. She glanced over her shoulder at Ana. 'Did you check your messages? Cos you probably shouldn't, I was just shooting my gob off, and-'

'As if you ever do anything else,' said Michael, picking up a plate of chow mien and grabbing a fork.

Ana smiled, took a plate and retreated into the living room. She folded herself into an armchair and rested her plate on her legs.

Michael settled on the sofa beside the coffee table. 'Now you're both here, I want to show you something.'

Ethne perched on the other armchair, her plate on her knees. 'Really, Mickey, don't you have boyfriends for that kind of thing?' She began knotting noodles onto her fork. 'At least let us finish dinner first.'

Michael stuck out his tongue. Ethne picked up a cushion and slung it at him across the table. She had aimed for his head, but it never got there. Instead, the cushion veered away and hung in the air between them, suspended over the table. After a moment, it began to gyrate and twirl until they were both giggling like five year olds.

Ana averted her eyes. 'It's not a party trick, Michael.'

The cushion crash-landed on the table and toppled a pile of CDs onto the floor. Michael shot Ana an apologetic smile and their eyes locked.

Ethne knew they were communicating silently and watched them with a puzzled respect. They had met at university while Ethne was giving massages in the student union bar in exchange for beer. Ana had admired Ethne's numerous tattoos, especially the star on her wrist. Thinking she had found a fellow enthusiast, Ethne had taken her to the tattooist to witness the addition of a soaring eagle across her shoulders, but Ana had almost fainted. Michael had come to the rescue and it hadn't taken Ethne long to realise her new friends were inseparable. If you were friends with Ana, you were friends with Michael: two for the price of one.

Then seven months ago the sun had spewed charged particles into the atmosphere and transformed her friends. They could read minds, move objects with thought, and heal people.

Michael had recorded the development of their new abilities, and once the power grid was back up had posted the videos on his CogNet channel. *The Okeke Gospel* had gone viral within days and Michael had become an official Plasma Pundit. His films catalogued everything from the aurora streaming overhead, to the personal and social aftermath. Ethne had driven him around on her motorbike while he hung off the back and filmed the looting, rioting and general mayhem. She was amazed they were never attacked. Michael seemed to possess a protective aura and they had always emerged unscathed.

She cleared her throat. 'It's rude to talk behind people's backs.'

'Sorry,' said Ana and Michael in unison.

Ethne stared at her noodles and waited for normality to reassert itself. 'So. I'm guessing. Have you made a new film?'

Michael grinned and put his plate on the table. He reached for his laptop and switched it on. 'Not bad for a *Homo sapiens*.'

'I try,' she shrugged. 'Hang on. Are you saying you're not a sap anymore?'

'Patience,' he said. '*The Okeke Gospel* will explain all. Meantime, Ana has something to ask you.'

Ana hastily swallowed a mouthful of noodles and shook her head. 'It's nothing. He's probably just crazy.'

'But what if he isn't?' said Michael. 'Can't hurt to ask.'

Ethne sighed. 'What could I possibly know that you two geniuses don't?'

'You're a Neolithic geek,' said Michael.

'Palaeolinguist.'

'That's what I said.' He winked. 'It's an important puzzle piece, Ana.'

Ana looked at him doubtfully and then shrugged. 'Okay. I met a man today who thought I was you. At least, that's what I think was going on. It was hard to tell. Can you show me your left wrist?'

Ethne shoved her jacket sleeve up to reveal her star tattoo. Ana gazed at it for an age and then nodded decisively.

'That's what I saw in his mind,' she said. 'As clear as you sitting here right now. He kept saying a word, sounded like a sneeze, like Akoo. Akoo.'

'That's what this is called,' said Ethne, tapping her wrist. 'It's an Egyptian star that represents the Akhu, A-K-H-U. In the ancient Egyptian religion, the akh was the spirit, the immortal part of your being. Akhu is the plural form, usually translated as *shining ones*. They were the ancestors, the ones who civilised us, taught us writing, metallurgy, plant medicine, that kind of thing. There are similar myths in other cultures. What exactly did this man say?'

Ana and Michael exchanged a glance.

'What?' said Ethne. 'For the love of-'

'He said the Akhu would come,' said Ana quickly. 'And he wanted to know if I had brought the fire. Does that mean anything to you?'

'They could come, I suppose,' said Ethne. 'I mean, Egyptian civilisation was based on the idea that the pharaoh was a reincarnation of the god Horus. He just kept coming back in different bodies. Like cosmic recycling. The whole point of their religion was to prepare you for death so you could return to the imperishable stars where the gods live, the Shining Ones.'

'So it could mean something?' said Ana.

'Or it could be the ramblings of a crazy person,' said Ethne. 'Then again, there is a legend about a Fire Stone in Egyptian mythology. It was kept in the Mansion of the Phoenix and had names like the benben or the Great Lotus. A mythical serpent was said to have laid it on the Island of the Egg. Might have been a meteorite, but it's never been found. It's a metaphor, obviously, not real. A creation myth about rebirth and regeneration.'

Michael grinned at Ana. 'He thought you were an Akhu and that you'd brought the fire. Sounds reasonable to me. It'll make sense when you see my new masterpiece.' The laptop hooked into the Wi-Fi and he opened CogNet.

Ana sat forward and stared at the computer as if it might explode. 'You promised no more films.'

'This one's different,' said Michael.

'You've already uploaded it?'

Michael frowned at the screen. 'I thought I did.' His fingers flew over the keyboard, searching for the video. 'It's not here.'

'Why did they take it down?' said Ana.

'You didn't upload another film of your arse by mistake, did you?' said Ethne, trying to diffuse the tension.

'I'm serious, it's gone. I only uploaded it this morning.'

Ana put her plate on the table and stood.

'What was it about?'

'Evolution,' said Michael. 'You need to see it, Ana. You both do. ARK call us Deviants but they're wrong. We're going back to the way we're supposed to be. Niloufer showed me. He said it would help if I shared it. I don't understand why they would take it down. I didn't mention the angels or Linnunrata directly.'

Ethne could feel the conversation getting away from her. Michael appeared to be talking nonsense.

'Who took it down?'

Before he could answer a riot of banging shook the front door.

Ana and Michael exchanged a glance, and then spoke in unison. 'ARK.' Michael tripped the switch on his power generator, plunging the flat into darkness and knocking out the computer. He found Ana and took her hands.

'Hide.'

'What about you?' she said.

'Ask Beatrice to take you to Linnunrata.'

'Beatrice?'

'You saw her today,' said Michael. 'On the Metro.'

'I can see a blank bit in your mind. What are you not telling me?'

'I can't show you, Ana. You have to trust me. Hide. Find Beatrice. Go to Linnunrata.'

'Please, Mickey. What's going on?'

Another burst of violent knocking rattled the letterbox.

'Erm, guys?' said Ethne. 'You can argue about who knows what later. Right now there's a big bad wolf outside who wants in.'

Michael spun Ana towards the window. 'I won't let them take you.'

'But-'

'Go.'

Ana retreated reluctantly onto the balcony.

'You too Ethne,' said Michael.

She shook her head. 'I'm not like you. They're not interested in me.' She shone her torch around the room looking for weapons. The only likely objects were items of furniture, everything else was too flimsy or breakable. She didn't want to smash her way through Michael's entire lamp collection or break her torch. Then again, she didn't want to answer the door from behind a raised dining chair either. She wasn't a lion tamer.

A thud cracked against the door and the frame creaked. They were going to kick their way in.

Ethne secreted her keys in her fist and moved closer to Michael. In a fluid motion, he lunged for the door and sprung it open. A huge man fell forward and landed at Ethne's feet. Another man blocked the doorway.

He raised a handheld device, like a large iPhone, and pointed it at Michael.

It beeped.

'Michael Okeke,' confirmed the rugged face behind the device. He was dressed in black fatigues bearing the ARK insignia: red letters over a blue green earth. His taller companion had recovered and looked entirely carved from granite. Neither of them looked friendly.

Rugged pointed his device at Ethne and waited. There was no beep. Standing behind him, Granite pulled a stun gun from its holster.

'You need to come with us, Mr Okeke,' said Rugged.

'Why?' said Ethne. 'You can't just-'

Granite lunged forward and thrust the gun into Michael's ribs. He convulsed violently and staggered back like he had pulled every muscle in his body. He fell to the floor, fighting against the electricity running through his system.

Ethne jumped on Granite and slammed her fists into his back. It was like punching a padded wall. Using her keys, she jabbed a volley of stabs into his ribs. He didn't even flinch.

Strong fingers gripped her neck and pulled. Rugged yanked Ethne backwards and spun her away. She almost went down but corrected her balance and spun back to crack Rugged across the jaw with her keys.

Michael was recovering. He rolled to his feet, struggling for breath, and watched with pride as Ethne kicked and spat, lashing out wildly against both men. With her kohl-lined eyes and elaborate piercings she looked like an enraged Egyptian princess, in jeans.

Granite pulled his hand back, the stun gun raised and aimed at Ethne. While she wondered if being electrocuted would make her incontinent, Michael saw what was coming. He tried to shout a warning, but could only cough and wheeze.

The gun slammed into the side of Ethne's head and she fell to the floor, unconscious.

'Leave her alone,' said Michael, between gasps. 'She's not-' Another shock burned through his body.

Granite holstered the gun with a satisfied grunt. He pulled Michael into an armlock, and pain seared across his shoulders. 'Sorry about your girlfriend,' he said into Michael's ear. He didn't sound sorry.

'Anyone else here?' said Rugged, scanning the dark flat.

Michael shook his head, not trusting himself to speak.

'I have a team downstairs that thinks otherwise,' said Rugged, switching on his torch. He disappeared into the hall.

Michael listened to him searching the other rooms, opening cupboards and slamming doors. He reappeared and shone his torch over the balcony door. It was ajar.

Michael's heart felt tight in his chest. 'There's nothing out there,' he said, hoping his fear didn't show. Whatever happened to him, they couldn't find Ana. He had to keep her safe. He had made a promise.

'She went out,' he said more confidently. 'They must've missed her.'

Rugged crossed to the balcony door and stepped out, then immediately stepped back.

A pigeon flapped at his face like it was trying to rip out his eyes. He swotted at it blindly and stumbled into the coffee table, landing in an explosion of splinters. The pigeon circled the room then fluttered to the balcony and away into the moonlight.

Michael suppressed a smile.

'Stupid damn bird.' Rugged clambered to his feet. 'We'll pick her up when she comes home.'

'Get the stuff,' said Granite. He nudged Ethne's inert form with his boot. 'Should we take Queen Nefertiti too?'

Rugged retrieved Michael's laptop from the wreckage of the coffee table then crossed to the desk. He ran his torch over papers and books, and then flashed the light in Michael's eyes, making him wince. 'Computer back ups?'

'In the cloud,' said Michael.

'Nobody uses that piece of shit anymore.'

Michael thought quickly. Since the networks went down last year, most people relied on physical back ups. You never knew when the power would go off and nobody wanted to lose their stuff. Retro was the new future.

Michael wanted Ana to see the film. She *needed* to see it. If ARK took his discs she would be in the dark.

'In the kitchen,' he said. 'Flash drive. On top of the fridge.'

Rugged disappeared into the kitchen and emerged holding a slim metal box. 'This it?'

Michael nodded and pretended to look suitably crestfallen.

Rugged strode from the flat. Granite followed, pushing Michael in front of him. 'What about Cleopatra?'

'Not a Deviant,' said Rugged. 'Not my problem.'

On the balcony, Ana pressed herself into the corner furthest from the door. The pigeon had saved her. It landed on the handrail and began to pick its way over the fairy lights towards her, cooing and twirling as it came. She watched its solitary dance and the final piece of the puzzle locked into place.

Before Christmas, Michael had vanished from this balcony. He had stepped outside to check the lights and she hadn't seen him for two weeks.

Now she knew how.

She closed her eyes and found his mental signature and followed his progress down the stairs. If she could keep her mind connected with his, she would know where they were taking him.

The men pushed him into the back of a transit van parked outside the tower block. Granite rammed a black hood over his head, and his vision clouded.

Ana could feel Michael reaching out with his other senses, trembling as he listened to the men moving around. For a flash, she caught a glimpse of something that didn't make sense.

Michael had seen this coming. He knew ARK would take him when he posted his video. It was almost as if he had done it deliberately. Ana couldn't understand why he would make himself into a target so willingly.

She stayed close to him, mentally holding his hand and pouring all the reassurance she could into his heart. She spoke directly into his mind, 'I won't leave you, Mickey. D'you hear me?'

Before he could answer, a sharp pain bloomed in his arm and oblivion rose to take him. He was gone. Ana could no longer see him.

3

Ethne woke with a headache. Gentle fingers pressed a cloth to her head and she could hear the murmur of an apology on a loop. She squeezed open her eyes to find herself on the sofa, a cushion behind her head, and Ana bent over her in anguish.

'I'm so sorry, Ethne. I didn't know what to do. Please forgive me, I'm so sorry-'

'Will you stop apologising. It's my fault for picking a fight with a troll. Two trolls.'

Ethne sat up and immediately wished she hadn't. It took all her self-control, and not a little vanity, to prevent her throwing up into her own lap. She took the tea towel from Ana and looked at it. Blood.

'It's just a small cut,' said Ana. 'You'll get a bruise. I'll make a tincture. You need lavender, and I think we've got some lettuce.'

'I'm not walking around with half a lettuce strapped to my skull.'

Ana wandered off and Ethne closed her eyes. The fight had been over in seconds. What had made her think she could stop them? She couldn't just stand there and let them take Michael. A painful bruise was a small price to pay for self-respect.

Ana reappeared with her medical kit and a bottle of lavender oil and set about swabbing Ethne's wounds. Ethne allowed herself to be nursed and scanned the aftermath of the fight. Moonlight bathed the wreckage in a blue glow. Books and CDs littered the floor, a chair and the coffee table had been reduced to firewood.

'We should get out of here,' she said.

'Can you walk?'

'I can try.'

'We'll go to Jack's,' said Ana. 'We'll be safer there.'

'Pity he wasn't here tonight,' said Ethne, standing slowly.

'You read my mind.'

They made it all the way down and out of the building before Ethne was hit by another wave of nausea. She staggered to the bench outside the entrance and sat with her head between her knees. It was a good thing she had walked to Byker this evening, she couldn't handle the Softail in this state.

Ana sat beside her and ran a hand over her back. 'Good thing you're not on your motorcycle.'

Ethne straightened up and gave her friend a sidelong glance. In the last few months she had got used to the telepathy, but often wondered how much Ana picked up. There had been several embarrassing incidents and a couple of blazing rows before they had agreed to be kinder to each other, and Ana had promised to stay out of her head.

Ana's attention drifted across the street to the black Lexus in the parking bay. Ethne had passed it when she arrived. She was always suspicious of men sitting in parked cars, and this pair looked distinctly unsavoury.

Ana stared into the darkness, her expression blank, but Ethne could tell her friend was rattled. She tried to think of something reassuring to say, but the words sounded like bullshit, even to her. She said them anyway.

'They probably only took Michael because of his film. You haven't done anything, so why would they take you, Ana?'

'They're waiting for backup.'

'How d'you know?'

Ana looked at her like she was a prize idiot.

'Oh,' said Ethne. 'I hope you're giving them a thorough probing.'

'They're coming for me because of what I am,' said Ana.

'That'll be the paranoia talking.'

Ana sighed. 'I need to tell you something, Ethne, and you have to promise to listen and not interrupt or make any of your quips or silliness.'

Ethne raised her hands in mock surrender. 'Your wish is my command.'

'Remember the blood tests we did at uni?'

Ethne nodded. 'Phanes BioTech were building that massive DNA database. What happened to it? Did it go under with everything else in the storm last year?'

'ARK bought it.'

'Along with the kitchen sink,' said Ethne. 'Doesn't surprise me.'

'They found a mutation in the DNA. Michael has it and so have I. That's why-'

'That's why you've got superpowers,' grinned Ethne.

Ana looked at her sternly. 'You promised.'

'Sorry. Go on.'

'I heard them talking,' said Ana. 'They call us Deviants. They want to take me to their lab for experimentation.'

Ethne grimaced. 'Don't like the sound of that.'

'I think that's why they've taken Michael too. But there's more.'

'Look, obviously I don't know what's going on,' said Ethne, 'but they can't mistreat Michael, or you. There are protocols and whatnot. I read every word of that privacy and confidentiality agreement thing we had to sign.'

'I know, but Patrick told them things about me.'

'What does your stepdad know about anything? He was a trolley dolly for Speedy Jet. For the love of Thoth, Ana, you haven't done anything wrong, okay? Just because you've got some mutation, doesn't make you a menace. You need to stop worrying. Patrick's dead. Leave him buried. Frankly, I think it's poetic justice he was struck by lightning just after he stabbed you in the back.'

'But-'

Ethne took Ana's hand. 'Listen to me, Anastasia Wilson. You are the kindest, most compassionate person I know. The day you do something diabolical is the day I join the Quakers.'

Ana smiled and squeezed her friend's hand.

'So please don't do anything diabolical,' continued Ethne, 'because I couldn't stand being a Quaker. Or any other God-based nonsense.'

Ana chuckled. 'Ready to move again?'

Ethne nodded and was about to stand when her leather jacket began to vibrate. She retrieved her phone and looked at the caller ID in confusion. She didn't know whether to be pleased or worried or surprised or angry. She tapped answer.

'Ethne?' said a smooth Scottish voice she thought she would never hear again. 'Is that you?'

'William.' She wanted to say more but didn't know where to start. She waited for him to explain himself and give her time to regain her cool.

'Sorry to call like this,' he said. 'But, I need you.'

Anger, she thought. Anger was the correct response. But before she could launch into one of her infamous tirades, he cut her off.

'Don't start, Ethne. Not like that. I have a job for you.'

'Call someone else,' she said, ready to hang up.

'No,' said Will. 'You have to come to Greenland. We've found something and I need you to, well...You need to see this, Ethne.'

She could hear the excitement in his voice and, despite her better judgement, could feel her curiosity rising.

The sound of a car door slamming made her spin round. Another Lexus had turned up. A man was standing beside the car in the darkness, watching them.

Ethne and Ana sprang from the bench. They ducked behind the tower block and started to run.

'This really isn't a good time, Will,' said Ethne as she skirted the burnt out car behind Albion Court. She switched on her torch.

'It's all arranged,' he continued. 'You just have to get to London tonight. There's a charter to bring you over. Are you okay? You sound like you're running.'

'I am running, you infuriating wazzock. I'll call you back.'

'No-'

Ethne and Ana ran between boarded up terraced houses and slipped through a half-collapsed barricade blocking the road. They cut down a back alley, fleeing past stinking heaps of rotting bin bags, before careening into the next street. Jack's street. They slowed to a fast walk, shooting anxious glances over their shoulders.

A car engine sounded behind them. Ethne startled and switched off the torch. She grabbed Ana and hauled her through the gate of the next house. They crouched behind a low brick wall, shielding them from the road, and waited as the headlights passed over them. Ethne held her breath and listened to the noise of the engine. It didn't sound like a Lexus; it was too small. She peered over the wall. A Fiat trundled up the street and out of sight.

She breathed out in relief, then startled again and nearly fell over when her phone rang in her hand. She answered.

'Are you going to explain why a geological expedition intent on raping the earth of all she possesses needs a linguist? I'm assuming it was my language skills you were after and not that your team of barbarians needs a little recreational massage to wind down after a hard day's pillaging.'

Ethne listened to the silence coming down the phone. 'Will?'

'I was just counting to ten,' he said. 'Have you got that out of your system?'

'Probably not. Why d'you want to drag me to the end of the earth? I don't want to come to Greenland.'

'Believe me, you do,' he said. 'You're the only person I trust with this. Ethne, you've been waiting for this moment your whole life. If you don't come, you'll never forgive me for not making you do it.'

She wanted to protest, refuse, hang up and switch off her phone, but something made her pause. Here was an opportunity to do something more challenging than listen to affluent types complain about their so-called problems while she rubbed almond oil into their puffy, overfed skin. Plus, she might not get beaten up again.

Ana was watching her curiously. 'What does he want?'

'He wants me to go to Greenland and look at rocks.' Even as she spoke, it sounded ridiculous. The phone crackled in her hand. She could hear Will breathing and it was making her feel strange, bringing back memories she didn't want to remember.

'Are you still there?' he said.

Ethne heard another car engine heading their way. It was definitely the fake rumble and whine of an electric Lexus. She curled behind the wall and closed her eyes, willing it to drive past.

'Ethne?'

'There's someone chasing us,' she whispered. 'They've already taken Michael, and now they're after Ana.'

The car pulled into the kerb on the other side of the wall and Ethne realised they must be tracking her phone. 'Shit.'

'Ethne, that's Derek,' said Will. 'He's going to drive you to London.'

'Is he fuck.'

'Listen to me. Unless you want to drive down on your bike, you have to go with him, okay? Trust me, Ethne.'

Ana put her hand on Ethne's shoulder and whispered, 'He's telling the truth.'

Ethne peered over the wall at the Lexus and the passenger door opened. 'What's your name?' she shouted.

'Haywood, ma'am,' said the driver.

'Your first name. And don't call me ma'am. It's weird.'

'Derek, ma'am.'

'Great.' Ethne stood in bad grace and returned to the pavement. 'You could've told me,' she said into her phone.

'You hung up,' said Will. 'By the way, ReSource are paying. Six figures.'

'What? That's...What on earth have you found?'

'Get on the plane and you'll see.'

4

Ana watched the glowing tail lights of the Lexus disappear around the corner, leaving her in darkness. She wanted to chase after it and bring Ethne back. She had begged her to stay, but her friend was stubborn and once she got an idea into her head, she wouldn't let it go. So Ana stood and shivered and felt helpless. Michael was gone, and now Ethne.

On the edge of her consciousness, she sensed someone approaching from behind. The footfalls were unusually quiet. Whoever it was, they didn't want her to know they were there. She held her breath until the mind signature drew close and then smiled in relief.

'Hello Jack.'

'Will I ever be able to sneak up on you?'

Ana turned to find Jack standing in a pool of torchlight. He smiled ruefully, his dark hair falling into his eyes and ever-present satchel slung across his broad shoulders. A tumble of images poured from his mind before she could block them. An abandoned office building, a sharp pain to the right shoulder, running in the dark, stalking through rooms and the terror of a man found cowering in the basement.

Jack looked at her sharply. He knew she was reading his mind. 'You promised you wouldn't do that.'

'I know, but it leaks out and I'm tired. What did you do to him?'

'Who?' Jack led the way up the path to his front door and waited for Ana to follow. Her mind felt hopelessly tangled and the tears she had been holding back were gathering. It wouldn't take much for the dam to burst. Jack slipped his arm around her waist as he opened the door, and she began to cry.

'They took Mickey,' she sobbed.

Once inside, Jack held her while she wept and black shadows filled the house with omens. When she had finished crying, Jack listened while she told him all that she had seen that day. He wandered the living room and lit the candles clustered on every surface.

'This changes everything,' he said, dropping the matches onto the coffee table. 'Genome comparison is one thing, but experimentation? What are ARK planning?'

'I don't know, Jack, I'm not all seeing.'

He took her hand and kissed her fingers, trying to tease a smile with charm and distraction, but she was too tired to be bought so easily. She sighed and closed her eyes, wishing she could turn back time. If only they could have met earlier, before the storm, in another life.

'There was another body,' she said. 'In the street. Hidden under the rubbish.'

'Homeless?'

She shrugged. 'He looked clean under the rags. I don't know what killed him.'

'That's what I was doing,' said Jack. 'Not killing people. Don't look at me like that, babes. Found a witness who said he'd seen a body being dumped. Poor guy was terrified, thought I'd come for him. Is that what you saw in my head?'

She squeezed his hand in apology.

Jack continued. 'I was working down my list of empty buildings bought by ARK. Really thought I'd found something this time, but it was just another squat. The witness said he saw two ARK Security guys with the body of a woman in the back of a van. They stripped her, dressed her in old clothes and dumped her in a skip.'

'That explains the body I found,' said Ana. 'Clean, hair neat, no dirt under the nails, and not starving.'

'Injuries?'

'Nothing obvious, but he had the same puncture wounds on his arm as the others.'

Jack nodded. 'There's something else. The witness knew her, the women in the skip. It looks like the others were dressed to look homeless, but she actually was. Just like the guy up at Craster. That's why I scared the witness so bad. He saw ARK take her months ago and thought they'd come back for more.'

'Why her? Was she just unlucky?'

'This is interesting,' he said. 'She was special. That's what he said. Everyone thought so.' He flipped open his notebook and consulted it. 'She was made homeless by the storm but said she'd never been happier.

She was always smiling, always kind. Took care of everyone in the squat. Sound familiar?'

'So she was a nice person. What does that prove? That ARK isn't fussy about who it picks on.'

'Ana. Think about it. ARK are extremely fussy. She said the sun had cured her back problems and even sleeping rough hadn't brought the pain back. I'd put good money on this woman being like you. She had the mutation.'

Ana thought for a moment. 'It makes sense. ARK are doing experiments on us. They've got Michael and now they want me. How many of us d'you think there are?'

'We have five bodies, so far.' He ticked them off on his fingers. 'The two I found before Christmas, yours and the one up at Craster, makes four, plus the woman. All injected multiple times. And two of the men were shot.'

Jack was a freelance journalist for an online news site called *ARK EYE*. The wall surrounding the fireplace was covered with articles and photographs detailing his research into the mergers and dealings of the ARK consortium, as well as the storm and its effects.

Ana crossed the room so she could scan the information.

It had started a year ago. The first solar storm had hardly deserved the title and everybody had enjoyed the lightshow. It had looked pretty but it had also loaded the magnetosphere with plasma, creating the perfect conditions for the mother of all geomagnetic storms when the next flare hit.

The superstorm had arrived in June. It breached the atmosphere and dumped tons of protons and cosmic rays on the defenceless earth. An X-class fireball travelling a thousand miles a second, burning up satellites and taking out power networks. Thankfully, the UK was protected by its cobweb of short transmission lines, so the power had been back on within weeks.

Ana had met Jack two months later. She was helping people made homeless in the aftermath of the storm. He was looking for stories and found her. Ana had been impressed by his articles on Phanes BioTech and the DNA research, and was able to provide more information using her new special skills. Together, they had built a case against the biotechnology firm.

A week after they met, she had joined Jack on a trip to photograph the river. The Tyne had taken to bursting its banks on a regular basis and he was measuring the inexorable rise of the waters. They sat in his battered silver Astra in the abandoned shipyard at Swan Hunter and waited for the rain to stop pummelling the car. The cranes at Jarrow across the river seemed to droop under the relentless downpour, like giant fossilised skeletons of alien insects overcome by the hostile British climate.

Over a shared thermos of tea, Ana told Jack how her life had changed since the sun had erupted. He called it her Storm Story. Like many others, her family was struggling. Her stepfather had lost his job when Speedy Jet went into administration. Unable to find another job, Patrick Wilson ended up on a Work Farm mucking out cowsheds. He was depressed and angry and desperate for money and driving her mother up the wall with frustration.

Meanwhile, Ana was learning to cope with hearing every thought that passed through her parent's heads. The experience had been enlightening, and not in a good way. Her mother was thinking of having an affair and Patrick was finding it hard to accept Ana's powers.

Whenever Ana entered a room he was in, her stepfather would suddenly find a reason to go somewhere else. At first, she thought he was scared, so did her best to be as normal as possible when she was at home. She trained herself to block others' thoughts and tried not to answer questions before they had been asked.

But then she had discovered the truth. Patrick was spying on her and giving the information to Phanes BioTech. It wasn't fear that was driving them apart; it was guilt.

Jack was silent for a long time before reaching across to top up her tea. 'I'm sorry, Ana. It hurts the most when it's someone you love.'

She glanced at him and caught a flash of pain on his face. 'Sounds like bitter experience.'

'Bitter?' He smiled at her with an impish twinkle, and Ana suddenly realised how much the car windows had steamed up. 'Bittersweet, perhaps.'

She didn't want to read it in his mind. She wanted to hear it from his lips. 'What happened?'

'It was long before the storm, when I had a proper job. Worked at one of the majors, don't ask which one, I'd rather not get into it.'

Ana caught the name as he thought it, but kept it to herself. She smiled her encouragement and he continued.

'Anyway, I uncovered a story about the contract awarded to ReSource to mine in the Arctic Alaska Basin, a newly discovered natural gas field off the coast of Siberia. The government said they'd won the contract through tendering, the usual process, blah, blah. But they didn't. I found a source at the MoD who was willing to go on record with evidence that a secret unit was sent out to Siberia to seize the land.'

'They just took it?'

'Yep,' said Jack. 'We were ready to print. It was my big break, it was going to be front page, massive feature with further revelations to come. You know the routine.' He gazed across the wasteland towards the river and ran a hand over his face. 'My dad got wind of it. He knew my source and revealed his identity. The paper spiked the story and I was fired.'

'Why?'

He shrugged. 'The usual cover-up. Shoot the messenger.'

'No, I mean, why did your dad reveal your source? Was he implicated?'

'Not at all,' said Jack. 'But his employer was.'

'Did he know what would happen to you?'

Jack nodded. 'He never liked me being a journalist. I was the biggest disappointment of his life.'

Ana slipped her hand into his. 'I'm sorry.'

'Don't be,' he said. 'If I hadn't lost my job, I wouldn't have started *ARK EYE* and I wouldn't have met you.'

In the dim candlelight, Ana rubbed her eyes. Exhaustion was creeping up on her, but she couldn't rest. Not yet. She scanned the articles covering the wall and sighed. She had to find where they had taken Michael.

Before the storm, Phanes BioTech had amassed the ultimate biobank. It carried the DNA of every person on the planet, except remote tribes far from civilisation. Every school, hospital, surgery, and aid agency had been used to collect the data under the guise of a mass vaccination programme; and if you wanted a passport or driving licence, or needed to claim welfare, your biometrics were required.

The company had started by identifying disease markers in the human genome, running massive comparative studies and cross-referencing billions of DNA samples. Concerned about how the data was being used, Jack had persuaded one of their geneticists to talk, provided he didn't publish specifics about the research. Thomas Lethe had proved to be quite forthcoming. He gave Jack valuable insights into genetics and how the database worked.

Then came the storm and the well of Lethe's knowledge dried up. They knew he worked at the Phanes laboratory; they just didn't know where it was.

Jack joined her to stare at the wall of words and images. 'They've obviously taken Michael to their lab for tests.'

Ana shuddered. 'He's not a guinea pig.'

'He'll have to give informed consent-'

'They didn't ask for his consent before dragging him away. It wasn't like he had a choice, Jack. He was trying to protect me. And now they've got Ethne too.'

'Ethne's fine,' he said, distractedly. 'They can't get to her in Greenland.'

'ReSource is part of ARK. You know that. They have her.'

Jack looked at her sharply. He was trying to understand the connection between mineral extraction in Greenland and genetic research, and failing. She couldn't see it either, but it was there, somewhere.

'You need to call him again,' she said. 'Just try. One more time.'

Jack picked up his phone. 'Don't get your hopes up.' He dialled and waited. 'He probably won't even pick...Oh, Professor Lethe, hey. How are you? We've not spoken for a while. Busy?'

Ana stepped closer and opened her mind so she could hear Lethe clearly.

'Jack Dexter,' said Lethe, warily. 'Still on this, are you?'

'You know me. I'm like the Terminator. So. How are things?'

'What do you want, Jack?'

'Michael Okeke.'

Silence.

'All right,' continued Jack. 'Let's try something else. I know about the Deviants and the mutation.'

More silence.

'And the experiments.'

'What do you know, Jack? Specifically.'

Ana whispered, 'Michael said his film is about evolution.'

'The human race is evolving,' said Jack, improvising, 'and you're doing experiments on this new mutation. So you need people. You can't do it all in a test tube. You need to find out, for instance, what happens if the Deviant gene spreads.'

'It can't spread.'

'Is that so?' Jack glanced at Ana. She frowned and shook her head.

'If we're evolving,' continued Jack, 'then it *has* to spread. The gene must be passed on-'

'Deviants can't breed with normal humans,' said Thomas quickly. 'Only with-'

Ana heard the rest of the sentence play out in Lethe's mind before he bit back the words. Deviants could only breed with each other.

'Ask him about the homeless people,' she whispered.

'One more thing,' said Jack. 'I've been tracking deaths among the homeless. Somebody is killing them, injecting them with something. The police are overwhelmed with all the other crap they have to deal with, and who cares about a few homeless people, right? What can you tell me about it?'

Silence.

Ana could hear another voice speaking to Lethe, urging him to end the call. The voice sounded familiar. It was one of the men who had taken Michael.

'Of course,' continued Jack, 'we both know they're not homeless. The way I see it-'

'You've got nothing.'

The line went dead.

Thomas Lethe switched off his phone, holding it so tight his knuckles turned white with the effort. He glanced at the man sleeping in the bed. It wouldn't be long before they got ahead of him, and then he would be redundant. All his years of work and research, for what? So he could be superseded by a kid who had never read a single book on genetics in his life.

Behind him, someone aggressively jangled the keys, and he turned away from the bed.

Robson watched him impatiently, his solid bulk filling the doorway. 'He'll be out of it till morning.'

Thomas nodded. There was a commotion in the stairwell and an imperious voice demanded entry to the room. The lawyer had arrived. There was something about the man that enraged Thomas. He wasn't a violent man by nature, but Christian Gregori triggered something primitive in his soul, and it twitched into life whenever he spent more than five minutes in his company.

Gregori had an army of underlings to do his bidding and yet he always came himself. He was ARK's lawyer, overseeing all seven companies, and couldn't possibly be everywhere at once, and yet he seemed to manage it with ease. Thomas saw too much of him at any rate. One glimpse of the perfect suit and the immaculate blond hair was enough to push his blood pressure up a couple of points.

Then there was his smile. Thomas shuddered. God protect me from that man's smile, he thought.

'Excuse me,' said a supercilious voice from the stairwell. Robson moved aside and Gregori squeezed past him into the room. 'Most kind.'

The lawyer approached the bed and gazed at the sleeping man with the intensity of a hungry lion. For one awful moment, Thomas thought he might actually climb into the bed. He cleared his throat and Gregori snapped out of his strange trance.

'I can't wait to meet him either,' said Thomas, uneasily.

Gregori turned to look at him. 'I have arranged for an increased security presence, and tranquilliser guns will be issued to all security personnel.'

'Isn't that overkill? I mean, there's only one of him.'

'And I suggest you lock him in,' said Gregori, making for the door.

Thomas followed the lawyer into the stairwell. 'He's not a prisoner. Our guests stay here voluntarily.'

Gregori trotted down the spiral staircase, his footsteps echoing around the stone walls.

'Mr Okeke did not arrive voluntarily. How do you think he will react when he awakes?'

Thomas followed the lawyer down the stairs, frowning at the bulletproof gold helmet of hair. 'He wants people to understand what's happening. I assume that's why he made the film.'

Gregori stopped and Thomas almost walked into him. The lawyer turned, moved up a step and fixed him with his ice blue eyes, standing close enough to kiss.

'You're an intelligent man, Lethe. Don't disappoint me now.'

Thomas fought the urge to step back. 'Once I've explained the research and shown him what we're doing here, I'm sure he'll-'

'He'll what?' Gregori smiled.

Thomas felt a sudden attack of vertigo and looked away quickly.

The lawyer continued down the stairs. 'Cooperate?'

'Perhaps.'

They reached the bottom of the stairwell and the lawyer stopped again. 'You've seen his films, professor?'

Thomas nodded.

'Then you know of what Mr Okeke is capable.'

'Yes, but-'

'You look tired Thomas. Are you getting enough rest?'

How could he rest? Thomas was convinced he would never sleep again. He dragged his fingers through his unkempt hair, willing the day to be over. He couldn't remember the last time he had shaved or had a proper shower. He took a deep breath and tried to summon the strength to argue with the lawyer. The rising wail of a sob caught him off guard. He coughed and pulled himself together enough to look Gregori in the eye.

Gregori smiled. 'Lock the door, Tom.'

Thomas stared at the floor. The damnable lawyer always got his own way. He sighed and nodded his assent.

5

Ethne snuggled into her insulated down jacket and listened to the reassuring purr of the twin propellers. She had the plane to herself, aside from the two pilots squeezed into the cockpit. ReSource had provided everything she needed for her visit to the ice sheet. There was no door between the cockpit and cabin so the pilots had studiously ignored her while she got changed. She was now wearing more layers than a black forest gateau.

The charter flight to Reykjavik had been uneventful and she had slept, but since clambering aboard the Twin Otter she had been too excited, despite herself. She glanced out of the window to be greeted by her own eager face peering back. The only signs of life had come when they had passed Ittoqqortoormitt, the nearest town to the wilderness into which they were heading. According to the pilot, they were now over the Stauning Alps and flying deeper into the polar night. It would be many hours before twilight and even then the sun would scarcely graze the horizon. Ethne dug through the layers and located her watch: six o'clock.

A flurry of green luminescence rippled through the darkness beyond the wingtip. Ethne watched with a curious mix of delight and dread. She told herself, firmly, that the storms were finished. This was normal, bog-standard aurora. The plane wasn't about to be struck by lightning, or turned into an electromagnetic oven reducing the occupants to quivering cancer-riven wrecks. All things considered, she wasn't surprised most of the airlines had gone bust.

The floodlights of the ReSource base camp appeared on the skyline, and over the sound of the engine came the whirr and clunk of the ski hydraulics locking into position. She grinned at herself in the dark reflection of the window: they were going to land on the glacier. She wanted to jump and shout with the thrill of it, but stayed in her seat and composed herself. She didn't want Will thinking her enthusiasm was directed at him.

The plane rumbled to a standstill and Ethne jumped down and gave the pilots a grateful wave. The polar wind stiffened against her skin, ice biting her ears and fingers. She fumbled with her gloves and yanked her fur lined arctic hat down as far as it would go. At least it hid the gnarly bruise rising on the side of her forehead.

Up ahead was a sheer black wall of jagged rock, runnels of ice marking its crevices and crags. As the plane taxied away, Ethne gazed across the ice sheet, astonished by its unnatural vivid blueness. It looked as if someone had spilled an industrial amount of toilet cleaner onto the ice.

On the edge of the ice sheet, the floodlights blazed over a cluster of tents and snowmobiles, and a knot of people checking equipment. One of the men left the group and approached.

It was Will. He walked towards her, boots crunching on the shimmering blue ice.

He looked inordinately pleased to see her.

'Howdy, stranger.' He beamed beneath his hood. Ice particles clung to several days of ginger stubble on his chin. 'Did I get the right clothes size?'

She nodded grudgingly. 'Flying me out in the company jet? Plying me with expensive togs? All this special treatment feels like an inducement, but it won't work.'

'Is that right?' He led her across the ice to the cave opening. 'Not ready to prostitute yourself to the Corporate God, your Lord and Master?'

'No, but I will be keeping this rather lovely hat.'

'It's good to see you too,' said Will, grinning at her over his shoulder.

'So, what's down there?' said Ethne, barely able to hide her curiosity. 'I still don't get why I'm here.'

'All in good time.' He held out a tangle of rope and metal hooks. 'Your carriage awaits.'

Ethne rolled her eyes and snatched the harness from his hands. She had been rock climbing and abseiling with Will a hundred times. Dragging her up and down mountains was his idea of a romantic date, but he invariably got distracted by petrology and would subject her to fascinating soliloquies, though she hated to admit it, on how the rock from which they were dangling had come to be.

Ethne got herself strapped in and double-checked the belay. 'What are you plundering anyway?'

'The usual. Rare earth elements, minerals, cool rocks. Y'know.' He grinned.

'No oil?'

'Oil is always on the agenda,' said Will. 'If I find oil the company will love me forever and have my babies, but it's unlikely. Most of the hydrocarbons are offshore.'

'How do they feel about you working outside your brief?'

'We had to send pictures to calm them down,' he said. 'The directors got quite excited once they'd seen them, but the lawyer was something else. It's the archaeological find of the century, and he wanted us to ignore it. Concentrate on making us money, he said. Even ordered us to cease and desist. Can you believe that?'

'No curiosity these lawyers,' she said, and jumped into the abyss.

Ethne rappelled into the cave, carefully feeding the rope through her gloved hands. More floodlights were rigged around the cavern below, and she cautiously lowered herself into their glare. She emerged from the narrow entrance and got her first glimpse of what lay beneath.

In the centre of the cavern was a collection of six standing stones around another that had fallen. They weren't arranged in the traditional circle, but she couldn't discern the pattern. Around the stones were more scientists uploading and logging data, huddled over crates packed with high-tech equipment.

All caution gone, Ethne doubled her speed. Her feet touched rock and she unhooked the carabiner. Will landed in a flurry of rope and dust, and smirked at her dumbfounded expression.

'Try not to get yourself fired this time,' he said.

She ignored him and wandered towards the stones, transfixed. They were six to seven feet in height and covered in carved symbols. Finally, she understood why she was here.

Ethne had become a linguist so she could track the earliest languages. She wanted to find the roots of civilisation. It was an obsession driven by a dream. From the age of thirteen she had been haunted by hieroglyphs and couldn't sleep without dreaming of an ankh: a cross with a loop at the top. It was the Egyptian symbol of eternal life, and for a reason she couldn't fathom, it was following her around. She had even bought herself an ankh pendant and wore it every day in an attempt to break the spell. It hadn't worked.

Will stood back and watched as she walked around the stones, marvelling at the writing. It didn't look like any known language.

Each stone had a different rough-hewn shape, reminding Ethne of Callanish in the Outer Hebrides. One side of each stone was sculpted and polished to a flat surface. These smooth faces all pointed inwards and the symbols were carved into the polished surfaces.

In the centre was a different type of stone, conical and smooth, like a narrow inverted egg. It lay at an angle, having slipped from its trench at some point over the years. Ethne crouched beside it and carefully brushed some of the dust from its polished face. It looked like black glass.

'Obsidian,' said Will, answering her unasked question. 'Volcanic glass. Traditionally used for daggers and mirrors, that kind of thing. Rare to find such a large piece and remarkable it's still intact. See those layers of colour?'

Swirls of red and green reflected in the glow of the floodlights, reminding Ethne of rainbows shimmering in diesel and oil.

'That tells us it's fire obsidian,' he continued. 'Extremely rare. Nanometric crystals of magnetite give it that beautiful reflective quality. It's only found in one place on the planet and it's not local.'

Ethne looked up. 'Iceland?'

He shook his head. 'Glass Buttes, Oregon. Three thousand miles away. Kind of unbelievable, if you ask me.'

Ethne stood. 'What are the others?'

'The menhirs are red granite,' he said. 'Igneous, so volcanic in origin again, but these could be locally sourced. They have high levels of quartz and are rich in iron, which is what gives them this wonderful deep rust colour.'

He ran a gloved hand over the stone. 'Have you spotted the configuration?'

She shook her head. No doubt it would be obvious as soon as Will pointed it out. He picked up his laptop from a nearby crate and flipped it open. She joined him and watched as images of the stones plotted onto a graph appeared on the screen.

'It's a spiral,' he said. 'Taking the obsidian as the centre, using a polar graph we can plot the positions of the six menhirs and it gives us the phi ratio.'

'The Golden Section,' said Ethne, in recognition.

'Beautiful.'

The Golden Section was found everywhere in nature: the spirals in seashells and galaxies, the dimensions of the human face and body, and in the structure of the most important molecule on the planet: DNA. Phi was fundamental to life, and now here it was in a collection of impossible stone megaliths.

Will was scrutinising the data on his computer, looking up periodically to frown at the obsidian block on the cave floor.

'I think there's a stone missing,' he said. 'We'll have to lift the obsidian to be sure. There should be another hole hidden beneath it.'

'So it's unfinished?'

'Looks like it,' he said. 'We'll get some ropes around it and haul it up. But in the meantime, Ethne, can you translate the text?'

She slipped off one glove and ran her hand over the nearest stone. Her fingers slid into the indentations that formed the letters, feeling the serrated edges where ancient chisels had worked the stone. Some of the shapes were familiar now she could see them up close: circles, crosses, wavy lines. It looked like a combination of Neolithic rock art with its spirals and stick men, and a proto-cuneiform similar to early Sumerian. Here and there were shapes that made her heart jump with shock: symbols that could have been lifted straight from an Egyptian tomb.

She stopped at a five-pointed star and gazed at it for an age before pulling back the layers of her sleeve to reveal the tattoo on her left wrist. It was the same symbol, etched into her skin with blood and ink: an Akhu star, the mark of the Shining Ones.

Will cleared his throat. 'Well?'

'You're assuming it is a text,' she said. 'We've got no context, no cultural markers. It could say anything. Or nothing. Where would I start?'

Will rubbed a hand over his beard. 'The earliest Greenlandic culture was Neolithic. The Saqqaq. Hunter-gatherers, Palaeo-Eskimo. They came across the Arctic from Siberia around three thousand five hundred BCE, but there's no evidence they built megalithic structures or had a written language.'

'Have you dated the stones?' said Ethne. 'If we can work out who made them, that might give me something to go on.'

Will looked at his feet. 'Well...'

'Spit it out.'

'You know we can't date rocks, right?' he said. 'You can only tell how old they are from the depth at which they're found. Stone circles are usually dated using artefacts found on site, like pottery, burials, food remains. There is evidence of a fire in one of the alcoves near the entrance. It would've taken them a wee while to get these stones in place and no doubt they stopped for a spot of lunch at some point. Then again, that fire could've been set many years before the stones.'

'Or many years after,' said Ethne.

'Precisely,' agreed Will. 'There is something else though. OHD. Obsidian hydration dating. Obsidian absorbs water when exposed to air, so in theory, if you can determine the level of hydration, or how much water has been absorbed by the stone, you can determine the date the obsidian was extracted.'

'In theory?'

'Temperature effects the hydration process, and although we know the temperature of this cave, we can't be sure where the obsidian was sourced. We would have to control for the geochemical signature-'

'Spare me the hardcore science, Will. How old d'you think these stones are?'

He took a deep breath. There was a mischievous light dancing in his eyes that told her he was enjoying this, drawing her in, making her wait.

'If we take Glass Buttes as the source of the obsidian,' he said, 'although I have no idea how they transported it this far, and if it wasn't sitting in front of me I'd tell you it was impossible – that gives us a preliminary date which is also confirmed by what we know of the ice floes and climatic changes on Greenland over the last several thousand years.'

He stopped and gave Ethne another drum roll accompanied look. This was the worst foreplay ever. 'Get to the damn point,' she said.

'The carbon dating on the fire also confirms the dates, but as I say, we can't be sure-'

'For the love of Thoth,' said Ethne.

'Okay,' he grinned. 'The OHD and the ice records give us a date of between eleven thousand and nine thousand BCE.'

Ethne suddenly felt light-headed. She reached for the nearest stone and steadied herself against it.

'Whichever way you look at it,' continued Will, 'nobody could've got into this cave before or since then. At the end of the Ice Age the climate was going wild, temperatures going up and down, ice melting then refreezing. There was one window of opportunity to get in here, and that was ten thousand BCE. Give or take.'

'Why didn't you tell me this on the phone?'

'It's better this way,' he said. 'I get to watch.'

Ethne leaned heavily against the stone. Her journey backwards through time via the languages of the ancient world had come to a frustrating impasse. Last year she had got a place on the spring dig at Gobekli Tepe in Turkey so she could see the Neolithic temples for herself. The hunter-gatherers who had built them, around ten thousand BCE, didn't even use pottery, never mind the written word. Instead, the stones were carved with a multitude of ancient creatures: foxes and boars rubbed shoulders with serpents, lions and birds.

After two thousand years of continuous use, the temples had been buried and abandoned. Nobody knew why.

Ethne had wanted to see if she could find a pattern or some clue that would tell her more about the people who had built them and how they related to the earliest civilisations. But her enthusiasm had backfired.

Security had been tight and she wasn't allowed near the stones during the day. So one night, she had sneaked into the site armed with a torch and a notebook to stand before one of the colossal T-shaped pillars. Its head tilted down as if to gaze into her eyes, and she ran her fingers over the stone, wishing it could speak and share its secrets. She had been caught by a guard and thrown out, escorted to the airport and sent home.

As far as anyone knew, the oldest known languages were Egyptian hieroglyphs and Sumerian cuneiform, but they were only six thousand years old. There were older Neolithic scripts and even older Palaeolithic symbols, but none had been successfully translated.

All Ethne had were the myths. Every civilisation on every continent had stories about beings called Shining Ones who had shared their wisdom with mankind. They were the gods and angels who had taught the locals how to build megaliths and follow the stars, how to grow crops, and how to write.

Ethne knew there was no such thing as a god or an angel. The Shining Ones were flesh and blood men and women who were ahead of the curve. Every culture had its leaders, and the Shining Ones came from a lost culture that existed during the Ice Age. It was wiped out in the floods when the ice melted, leaving a trail of clues scattered through the megaliths and myths of the ancient world.

If Ethne wanted to find the roots of civilisation, she needed to get into the heads of the Shining Ones, and to do that she needed words. She ran her fingers over the characters etched into the granite. Was this the voice of the lost culture speaking to her across time? The marks were so fresh they could have been made last week. She could be looking at the oldest language ever discovered. A language and a culture hidden for thousands of years under the ice.

6

Ana woke in the night and lay in the darkness fretting about ARK. It hadn't taken them long to find her, despite switching off her phone. Jack had said it wouldn't stop them, and he was right. ARK had become her shadow.

She had spent the evening searching for Michael, to no avail. She had pushed her mind to its limit until she was exhausted and in danger of crying again, so Jack had ordered her to bed. She listened to him sleeping now so peacefully, as if the world wasn't ending around him, as if it was just another day.

Unable to sleep, she got up and checked the street. The Lexus was still there, its huge mesh grill glinting in the moonlight like the yawning mouth of a demon. She perched on a stool and watched through a gap in the curtains. She could do it with her eyes closed, but it didn't seem right to use her powers for such a trivial reason. A cigarette glowed intermittently in the heart of the car. She watched until it burnt out, shivering in one of Jack's T-shirts and wondering why ARK hadn't come for her yet.

Jack stirred in the bed and found her gone. She felt his momentary anxiety and turned to smile at him through the darkness.

'I've been thinking,' she said.

'Uh oh.'

'We need to disappear.'

'Is that one of your superpowers?' he said sleepily.

Ana got back into bed. 'Don't be silly.' She snuggled close to Jack, knotting her cold limbs with his until she felt the warmth returning. He began sinking into sleep, so she ran her fingers over his skin until he responded and almost pushed the plan from her mind.

She sat up, ignoring his protests. 'And we need to watch Michael's film.'

'I agree, now come here.'

They made their escape plan over breakfast. They would retrieve Michael's backup discs and then slip under ARK's radar and away. Jack said they must do everything exactly as if it were a normal day so ARK wouldn't be alerted to their plan. He would go for his usual early morning run, and then they would leave.

Ana waited in the hallway, anxious to get going. Footsteps sounded on the path outside and she grabbed her coat from the hook. Jack stumbled through the door fiddling with his phone. It looked like he was changing the SIM, and he startled when he saw her. 'Oh, hey, ready to go already?'

'Got a problem with your phone?'

'Nah, just dropped it. Back came off, stupid thing. Give me a sec.'

He vanished up the stairs and after a moment Ana heard the shower running. She pulled on her coat and resisted the urge to read his mind. She had promised to stay out of her friend's heads as a matter of courtesy, but she didn't have to be psychic to know something was wrong. Simple instinct told her Jack had lied. The frozen look on his face, like he was caught doing something he knew he shouldn't. But what?

Half an hour later they emerged from the lift outside Ana's flat, grateful the power had been restored. She slipped her key into the lock, but Jack stepped ahead of her.

'Wait here,' he said, and went inside.

Ana surveyed the chaos from the doorway while Jack moved from room to room like a cop in a detective film, checking for uninvited guests. She inched over the threshold. He reappeared from her bedroom and motioned for her to stop. She froze, and he slipped onto the balcony.

This was absurd. She knew there was nobody else present. She had scanned the flat with her mind, but Jack was Being A Man. She waited while he satisfied himself they were alone.

He reappeared. 'Nothing but a pigeon.'

Ana smiled. 'She's still here.'

'Probably not the same bird, babes.' He ran his eyes over the wreckage and whistled. 'Quite a fight.' He pulled his phone from his leather satchel and started taking photographs.

'What are you doing?' said Ana. 'We have to find the discs.'

'Evidence,' he said, taking another snap. 'Need to make a record.'

Ana went to the desk to search the drawers while Jack finished documenting the mess. She knew the discs were here somewhere; she had seen Michael using them earlier in the week.

'Try the wardrobe,' said Jack, distractedly. 'It's where people usually hide stuff.'

Ana crossed the flat and made a mental note to check Jack's wardrobe for a stash of secrets before they left the city for good.

Michael's room was eerily tidy. She stared at the neat pile of books and the freshly made bed and felt nothing but confusion. Michael never made his bed, and he was usually too busy reading to keep his shelves in order. His glasses lay on the bedside table, unused and unneeded since the superstorm. Ana stood with her hand on the doorknob, the horrible scenes of last night playing in her mind, and forced herself to believe he was safe.

She had met him in the playground at school when they were eleven. Michael had been curled in a defensive ball against the missiles of dirt and daffodil bulbs exploding over his back. Ana had put herself between Michael and the pack of runts tormenting him and screamed in a fury so righteous that two of the boys had burst into tears before running away. They hated Michael because he was Nigerian, but they hated him more because he was sensitive and the girls liked him.

As Jack had predicted, the plastic box filled with DVD backups was hidden under a pile of old jeans at the back of the wardrobe. She took it into the living room and sat on the sofa to check the contents. She was flicking through the discs when her scalp began to prickle, as if the air in the room had become electrically charged. She scratched her head absently until a shift in the light made her look up.

A woman with spiky hair and dove earrings stepped from the balcony looking as striking as she had on the Metro yesterday.

Jack stared at her as if she were a ghost. 'Where did you spring from?'

'The balcony,' said the woman, laughter dancing in her eyes.

'But I, I looked, I...there was no one there,' spluttered Jack.

The woman smiled at Ana and took her hand. She raised it to her lips and kissed the inside of her wrist.

'It is an honour to meet you at last, Anastasia.'

'Um...likewise,' said Ana, bewildered.

The woman turned to Jack, who looked like he wanted to run from the room. She went through the same routine and pressed a kiss to the inside of his left wrist. She let go and he clutched at his hand, his mouth working with the avalanche of questions filling his head.

'Who are you?' he managed.

'You may call me Beatrice,' she said, and held out her hand. 'Give me your computer.'

The commanding note in her voice made him obey without thinking. He opened his satchel and produced his laptop. It contained vital information about ARK so he always carried it with him. Beatrice took it, placed her hand on the closed screen and waited. After a moment, she handed it back.

Jack looked at it with suspicion, and then switched it on. 'What did you do?' The computer booted and seemed fine. He checked his document folder. It was empty. He searched his other folders. All his files were gone. All his research. All his work. She had wiped his hard drive. 'What the fuck?'

'Do you have data stored anywhere else?' said Beatrice.

'No,' he said, clutching his laptop like a life raft.

'Don't lie to me Jack.'

She gave him the same look his mum used when he was trying to pretend it wasn't him who had broken his bike or lost his school books or eaten all the biscuits. He decided to reason with her.

'Look, there's no point in wiping my data. I can download it from the server at work, and you can't wipe that so you're wasting your time. You're not going to stop me posting this story.'

Beatrice watched Jack as if she was deciding whether to let him live, and he realised there wasn't a thing he could do if she decided against it. He shivered involuntarily, but held her gaze.

'I see,' said Beatrice. 'Then you must make me a promise.'

'A promise?'

'Don't post the story.'

'Are you working for ARK?' said Jack, his temper rising. 'That's it, isn't it?'

'I do not work for ARK.'

'Why should I believe you?'

'If you are not willing to believe me, why did you ask the question?'

Jack frowned at her and tried to speak but found he didn't know what to say. His mind was going in slow motion and he was having trouble thinking.

Ana touched his arm and spoke to him as if he were a child. 'Jack, it's all right. I told you what happened. Think about it. She was the pigeon. She stopped ARK from finding me last night. She's here to protect us.'

Beatrice smiled and the room brightened. Jack felt lightheaded and tried to blink away the extra light. The mysterious woman appeared to have translucent skin, as if it shone with its own light, and it seemed fresh, like she was newly born. But her eyes held depths of wisdom and knowledge only achieved after eons of existence. He doubted anything could surprise her.

Since the storm Jack thought he had got used to strange things happening, but this situation had slipped out of his control so fast. He wanted to sit down and put his head between his knees, but didn't want to look weak. He needed more information.

'Why can't I post this story?' he said.

'For your protection,' said Beatrice. 'Timing is everything. If this story, as you call it, were to be told too soon, it could jeopardise everything we've worked-'

'Did you take Michael's film down?' interrupted Jack.

'We did.'

Ana gasped as the truth dawned. 'You were trying to protect him from ARK.'

Beatrice nodded and smiled sadly. 'Too late.'

'But that's why we should expose them,' said Jack. 'If we keep this hidden, it leaves ARK free to operate from the shadows, and when they're ready with whatever it is they're planning, it'll be too late for us to fight back. We need to get ahead of them.'

'You would attack the Hydra with nothing but a candle?' said Beatrice.

'What?' said Jack testily.

'What you say is true,' continued Beatrice. 'ARK cannot be trusted with the future. That is why I am here. I know you understand the power of truth, Jack. And the power of lies. You must act only when you understand the difference.'

'The difference is obvious.'

Beatrice smiled as if Jack had told a bad joke. 'Gather the information, by all means. I applaud your desire to understand. But you must not go public. Not yet.'

Jack shoved his laptop into his satchel. 'It would be harder for ARK to snatch people from their homes and experiment on them if the world knew what they were doing.'

'The world would not believe what they are doing,' said Beatrice. 'Michael was given a choice to reveal the truth or not. I asked him to wait. He knew the consequences of not doing so and acted anyway.'

'Where is he?' said Ana. 'Is he all right?'

Beatrice placed her hand on Ana's shoulder. 'Do not concern yourself. You must not worry about Michael. Do you understand?'

'Yes, but-'

'He is with ARK, as you know. He is impatient for the future. He sees more than most and it is painful for him, I think.'

'Could you bring him back?' said Ana. 'Find him and, I don't know, take him somewhere safe?'

Beatrice took Ana's hands in hers. 'It is as it should be.'

'So you won't help him.'

'He has help,' said Beatrice gently. 'You are my concern, Ana.'

'Will you take me to Linnunrata?'

Beatrice gazed deep into her eyes. 'Michael told you to ask?'

She nodded.

'We will take you there at the earliest opportunity, but you must be patient. The timing is most important.'

'If you want to keep me safe, surely that's the best place,' said Ana. 'Why don't you just take me there now?'

Beatrice glanced at Jack. 'It is not time. But your instinct is good. I see your plan. You must hide. Keep yourself safe, Ana. I will come when needed.'

With that, she walked to the balcony and beamed at them over her shoulder. In a flash of ice blue light, Beatrice transformed into a pigeon. She fluttered briefly, as if saying goodbye, and then was gone.

7

Michael lay across the middle of the bed, the soft pillows enveloped his head like the bosom of an immense goddess. Half asleep, he stretched out, luxuriating in the comfort and warmth. Subdued birdsong drifted through the window, as if the bird was concerned not to wake him. He hadn't slept this well in years.

The memory of his abduction the night before slowly returned. He opened his eyes to find his hosts hadn't bothered to undress him. He threw back the covers, frowned at the intricate pattern of roses on the sheets, and then looked around. For a moment he thought he was at a posh hotel. The plush bedroom had ivory coloured wood panelling and thick ornate curtains. From the cushion-loaded double bed he could see a wardrobe, a small table and chair, and a door leading to a gleaming en suite.

He slipped off the bed and padded across the thick carpet to the door. It was locked. Wherever he was, it was a five-star prison.

He checked the wardrobe and found a selection of clothes, then crossed to the window and pulled back the drapes. The hand-stitched embroidery was of too high a quality for these to be called mere curtains. He ran his fingers over the fabric and gazed out of the window. A long gravel drive stretched away from the building into an expanse of fields shrouded in mist. ARK had brought him into the middle of nowhere.

Michael returned to the bed and propped himself up on the pillows. He extended his mind beyond the locked door and discovered a labyrinth of stone corridors and spiral staircases. He wanted to explore further, but sensed someone approaching the room.

Keys fumbled at the lock and a man entered carrying a laptop. Michael's laptop. The man was smart but dishevelled, and exuded an air of exhausted intensity. 'Ah, you're awake.' He turned the chair and sat, and began to scrutinise Michael as if he were an animal in a zoo.

Michael returned his stare. 'If you think I'm about to sprout wings and fly away, you're going to be disappointed.'

The man smiled weakly. 'I'm sorry, Michael, for the manner in which you were brought here last night, but we can't be too careful.'

Michael smiled. 'It wouldn't do to treat people like human beings, would it?'

The man shifted awkwardly and stared at the laptop on his knees.

'Where am I?' said Michael.

'Can't tell you that, I'm afraid. Not with your abilities.'

'Worried I might call the cavalry?'

'Something like that.'

'I might anyway,' said Michael, sounding braver than he felt. 'Who are you?'

'Professor Lethe. Thomas. Head of Genetics for Phanes BioTech.'

'Did you take my film down?'

The professor looked confused.

'Someone took the video down off CogNet,' explained Michael. 'I just thought, maybe...'

'No, that wasn't...I wasn't aware it was gone. We were lucky to see it when we did, then.'

'Lucky, right.'

'Listen, Michael. I want you to understand, I didn't want to lock you in. I'm as unhappy about this situation as you are, but my hands are tied.'

'You're forgetting something,' said Michael. 'I can read your mind.'

The blood drained from the professor's face and his fingers gripped the laptop turning his knuckles white. Michael listened to the tumble of fear and confusion roiling around Lethe's mind and plucked the essential details from the noise.

'You believe I'm a charlatan,' he said, 'and that all I've done is memorise textbooks on genetics and used special effects in my films. Correct?'

'Have you?'

Michael laughed. 'You won't believe it until you see it.'

'Where did you get the information in your film?'

'From the horse's mouth, so to speak.'

'What does that mean?'

'The DNA told me.'

Thomas stood. 'I have studied my subject for three decades. A kid who got a second in computer science and almost got thrown off the course, is not going to advise me on genetics.'

Michael smiled. 'Gregori's got you by the balls.'

Thomas sat. 'What do you know about that?'

'I told you,' said Michael, tapping his head. 'See, I know you're thinking about locking that door and leaving me in here to rot. I don't blame you. I'd feel the same in your situation. But then you'll have to answer to this Gregori. Who is he, by the way?'

'The lawyer.'

Michael nodded. 'Figures.'

'Gregori found the film,' explained Thomas. 'He suggested you be brought in to assist in our research.'

'Putting you in this awkward position. I sympathise, professor, and I'm happy to help. I have no desire to step on your toes or undermine your work. I'm at your disposal. Well, I would be, if you were willing to believe me and I wasn't stuck behind a locked door.'

'The door is locked for our safety.'

'What am I going to do?' grinned Michael. 'Run amok?'

Thomas opened the laptop, hit a few keys and turned the machine around. One of Michael's videos was playing, showing his experiments with the light he had found pouring from his fingers. Two spheres of clear blue light hovered above his upturned palms. Sparks flew back and forth as he tried to form a third ball above the others to see if he could juggle, just for fun. But the sparks ignited the cuffs of his shirt and in a flash his arms were ablaze.

'You think I'm a fire hazard?' chuckled Michael.

On the screen, he grabbed a damp towel and swotted out the flames before turning to grin at the camera.

Thomas snapped the laptop shut. 'I don't know what to believe, Michael. Aside from a few lucky guesses as to what I might be thinking, you seem rather ordinary. I have no reason to believe your claims. I shall tell Gregori that you refused to cooperate.'

'And then what?'

Thomas stood. 'He would decide. But Gregori is not a man I would want to have control over my fate.' The professor tucked the laptop under his arm and strode to the door.

Michael smiled to himself and concentrated. Two fizzing balls of light sprung to life in his hands. He let them hang there for a moment before conjuring a third.

'Okay, professor,' he said. 'You win. I admit it. I'm a total faker.'

Thomas turned. Michael was juggling with three sparkling balls. He swung his legs off the bed and stood, the lights gyrating in the air around him.

Thomas froze, transfixed by what he was seeing.

'You want to check I'm not faking it?' said Michael, grinning.

Thomas shook his head slowly. The lights stopped dancing and morphed into one glowing ball that hung in the air between the two men. Thomas gazed at it like he was hypnotised.

'Now I have your attention,' said Michael, 'perhaps we can come to an arrangement.'

Thomas nodded dumbly. Michael allowed the light to fade until it flickered into the void. Thomas blinked, his attention back on Michael.

'You have my help if you want it, professor. Does it matter how I get my information?'

'I am a scientist. I do not operate on hunches, guesswork or whatever it is you do.' Thomas returned to the door and took out the keys.

Michael laughed. 'You're still going to lock me in?'

'Someone will bring you down to the lab shortly,' said Thomas, opening the door.

'If you leave the door unlocked, I promise to behave.'

Thomas smiled sadly, 'You have no idea where you are, Michael,' and locked the door behind him.

8

Ethne glanced around the cavern. The floodlights threw twisted shadows over the rocks, like ghosts seeping into the cave from a hidden dimension beyond. The dry air buzzed with the murmur of voices. For a moment, she imagined they came from the stones themselves, igniting the ancient language in her mind. Then the words broke through and the spell was broken. It was just Will's team working around her, drilling into the bedrock and running endless figures and calculations through handheld computers.

On the flight to Greenland she had been given a non-disclosure agreement and was ordered to sign. Thinking nothing of it, she had done so. But now, standing beside evidence of an advanced ancient culture, evidence that was irrefutable and would turn the history of human civilisation on its head, she couldn't help but wonder what ReSource were planning. Would they share this with the rest of the world, or keep it for themselves?

It all depended on what the stones said. It was up to her to make them speak, to bring this long forgotten world back to life. She pulled out her phone and glanced around to be sure nobody was watching. When she was certain she was alone, she began taking photographs. Working methodically around the spiral, starting at the centre, she built a mosaic of images she could use to reconstruct the text later, if necessary. Unfortunately, there was no mobile signal in the cave. She would have to send the files to her computer later, or as soon as she could get her hands on a satellite phone without causing too much suspicion.

'Magnificent, aren't they?' said a woman's voice.

Ethne startled and almost dropped her phone. She turned, and tried to look as innocent as possible.

The owner of the voice was a small woman swamped by an enormous arctic jacket. She ran her fingers over the text carved into the stone with an attitude Ethne could only describe as reverent. She was also the only person in the cave not wearing a hat. Perhaps she couldn't find one to fit, because she had the largest blonde afro Ethne had ever seen. She stared at it, stupefied. It resembled a halo and even seemed to glow. It was a moment before she realised the hair was caught in the beam of a floodlight.

The woman turned and smiled. Light poured from her mouth, as if she were breathing starlight and showering Ethne in a dazzling grace.

Ethne blinked and time seemed to slow. She told herself it was the glare from the lights, but there was something otherworldly about this woman and Ethne was having trouble thinking. Aware she was gawping like her brain had been removed, she tried to shake herself out of the trance, but only succeeded in stumbling over her own feet. What on earth was going on?

'Sorry Ethne,' said the woman, taking her arm and turning her around. 'You're getting blinded by the lights there.'

Out of the glare, Ethne could see the woman clearly. At a glance she seemed young, but there was a depth to her eyes that indicated she had seen everything imaginable, and then more. Under the stupendous mound of hair, the woman emitted an ethereal beauty so profound Ethne took to staring at her all over again, as if she had lost control of her will.

The woman chuckled. A beautiful, musical laugh that made Ethne want to laugh too. She had to pull herself together. How did this uncanny woman know her name? Before she could find out, the woman took her left hand and lifted it to her mouth as if she were a gallant knight declaring his intentions. But instead of kissing her hand in the usual way, she turned it and planted a delicate kiss on Ethne's wrist.

'I'm Lucy.' She ran her fingers over the Akhu tattoo on Ethne's wrist and smiled. 'You have no idea how good it is to meet you, Ethne Godwin.'

'How d'you know my name?'

'Will told me,' said Lucy, waving vaguely in the direction of the other scientists.

Will was supervising preparations to raise the obsidian block in the centre of the spiral. A rope had been secured around the stone and attached to a winch powered by a snowmobile outside the cave. Will wandered across from the entrance and steered everyone away from the stones.

'Clear,' he said into his walkie-talkie.

The rope tautened and the dark mass of volcanic glass slowly began to rise. Will and two other men guided the stone into its trench using hastily improvised wooden props. Ethne watched, anxiety mounting, until she realised she was holding her breath. Just as the stone was about to slide upright into the trench, Lucy gripped her arm and held on so tight Ethne was convinced she would get another bruise.

The towering obsidian stone finally locked into position in a cloud of dust. Will removed the ropes and crouched to check it was securely in place. Lucy relaxed her grip and Ethne went to get a closer look.

The stone stood eight feet high, a broad column of black glass, wider at the top and polished to an opaque sheen. It was unmistakably phallic, a great swirl of flame rising through it, as if entwined by a burning serpent. It reminded Ethne of a Hindu lingam, associated with Shiva and his endless cosmic dance of regeneration.

Transfixed, she found herself intoning an ancient Egyptian text under her breath: 'This is the sealed thing, which is in darkness, with fire about it, which contains the efflux of Osiris, and it is put in Rostau. It has been hidden since it fell from him.' And she knew what she had found.

It was the Fire Stone.

So much for metaphor, she thought. The stone that contained the secrets of the Shining Ones didn't appear to be a meteorite or mythical. The legend of the Fire Stone was real.

Dust clung to its surface. She gently brushed this away to reveal rainbow swirls of colour reflected in the lights, as if a raging fire was trapped inside the stone. As her hand touched the glass she sensed this fire, just beyond her fingertips. If the stone were to be broken, the fire would burst forth and consume the world.

She snapped her hand back and gazed at the Fire Stone in awe. She could see her own reflection in silhouette, the rainbow flames licked around her form, burning away all that she was and could never be again. As if she had stepped inside the stone, the fire entered her. A warm fizzing rose through her legs, pooled at her pelvis and abdomen, and bathed her internal organs in a glowing heat. She closed her eyes and luxuriated in the sensation. It was like being hugged from the inside.

Without warning, the gentle warmth strengthened into a furnace. Lightning blasts shot down her arms and up her spine, jerking her head back with the force. Flames flickered through her body, dissolving all obstacles in their fury. A fireball exploded in her heart and made her cry out.

She couldn't see. The world was light. She was light.

As suddenly as it began, it was over. Ethne opened her eyes. The opaque volcanic monolith stood before her, the fire dormant. It was just a bit of old rock. The reflection showed another person standing beside her.

Ethne turned to find Lucy watching her with a rapt expression, hands clasped in prayer at her chin.

'How do you feel?' said Lucy.

'Fine,' shrugged Ethne. 'How are you?'

Lucy grinned and clapped her hands like she was five years old. 'It works.'

Ethne turned back to the obsidian. Her head felt strange and the bruise on her forehead was aching. She removed her fur hat and ran her fingers over the cut, or what she thought was the cut. She couldn't find it. She felt around her forehead, even checking the other side, despite knowing the cut had never been there. The swelling had gone down and the cut had vanished. That was impossible. Had the stone healed her wound?

Lucy was smiling at her with undisguised devotion. She placed both hands on Ethne's shoulders and looked deep into her eyes.

'Do not concern yourself, Ethne,' she said. 'Whatever happens, you are safe. Do you understand?'

Ethne gazed into those ancient eyes and knew the truth of Lucy's statement. She also knew she didn't have time to get her head around what had just happened because the cave was about to be attacked.

In a heartbeat, the floodlights died and the cavern was plunged into absolute darkness.

9

Jack fought his way up the steps to the police station, pushing against the tide of bodies cramming the entrance. Nobody was moving. He couldn't tell if they were entering or leaving and found himself caught in a Gordian knot of frantic and enraged people.

Ana watched from the pavement. Stone griffins glared at her from each corner of the towering grey edifice. Everything about the building was designed to intimidate, but the flagpole above the entrance stood empty and the blue lamps on either side of the door were smashed. Abusive graffiti had been washed off and reapplied so many times that the stone cladding had taken on a garish mottled appearance, as if the police had commissioned a new work from an especially edgy artist.

Jack craned his neck and encouraged Ana to follow. The plan had seemed simple. Before breaking free of ARK they would visit the police and find out what they could about the homeless deaths. Jack had a source at the station and they had helped each other out on numerous occasions, but on this story his friend was yet to share. The plan was that Ana would read his mind and extract the details they needed. But first they had to find him.

Ana watched the scrum for an opening. It was impossible. She shook her head at Jack, but he nodded urgently and mouthed: use your powers.

She glanced up the street. The black Lexus was parked beyond the Magistrate's Court where another scrum of people filled the pavement. The police were processing misdemeanours as fast as they could, but the system was on the brink of collapse. Most crimes now went unacknowledged and unpunished, unless the victim was willing to pay ARK for the privilege of justice.

Ana felt her hands become warm. There was a simple way to clear a path to the door, but she would have to be careful not to hurt anyone. With one eye on the Lexus, she approached the knot of people on the steps. She raised her hands and sent ripples of electromagnetism into the air around her. The people closest began to move, turning in search of the source of their discomfort.

Ana's cheeks burnt in embarrassment. She apologised as she walked through the crowd and up the steps to the heavy wooden doors. She reached Jack and took his hand. He recoiled as the static charge grounded itself through his body, and he clutched at his arm. 'Careful, babes.'

'Sorry,' she said. 'Let's find him and get out of here.'

Once inside they were greeted with more of the same. The foyer was crammed with bodies. People clawed their way to the reception desk between two giant pillars. Police officers shouted from behind the glass, trying to impose order.

Ana drove a path through the mayhem to the desk and dragged Jack with her. He slammed his press pass against the glass.

'Lucas. I need to speak to him.'

The officer behind the glass looked at him impassively. Exhaustion exuded from every pore of his being, as if the only thing holding him up were strings attached to an unseen controller who drove him mercilessly onwards. He shook his head slowly and repeated what he was saying to everyone who made it to the desk.

'If it's not an emergency, we can't help, sir.'

'I have information,' said Jack, 'about a body found last night. Ana-'

'If it's not an emergency, we can't-'

Jack hit the glass with his fist. The officer didn't even flinch. He opened his mouth to speak, but before he could repeat himself again, Ana leaned across and smiled. She poured out as much empathy and compassion as she could muster, soothing the man's battered soul with understanding. He relaxed a fraction and Ana felt a sob catch in his throat. If it weren't for the glass, she would climb over the desk and hug him.

'You're doing a great job,' she said, 'under the circumstances. We'll get out of your way.'

She pushed Jack back into the scrum and another irate citizen took her place at the window. Behind her, the officer repeated his mantra.

Lines of tension were running along Jack's jaw. She had to calm him down before he started a fight. She touched his cheek. 'This isn't going to work.'

He turned his head, searching for an escape route. Across the foyer a door opened and a man's head poked out.

'Dexter?' he shouted. 'Jack Dexter?'

Jack started towards him, pulling Ana behind him.

'Lucas,' said Jack, taking his hand. 'It's like a zombie feeding frenzy in here.'

'Tell me about it,' said Lucas. 'Saw you on the monitors. Where's the fire?'

'Can we go somewhere quieter?'

Lucas shook his head. 'Sorry mate. We're using interview rooms as cells now. This is as good as it gets.'

Detective Chief Inspector Lucas was a gaunt man with greying hair in need of a trim. It looked like he had slept in his clothes for several days. He took Jack by the arm and steered him to the corner behind a pillar. Ana stayed close and did her best to focus as Jack began probing for information. As they had feared, DCI Lucas was unforthcoming with new facts.

'Case is closed,' he said.

'Five bodies are found, all with the same injuries-'

'Eight.'

'Eight bodies? You don't know what happened to them, and you close the case?'

Lucas shrugged. 'Out of my hands, Jack.'

'So you didn't close it?'

'Edict from on high,' said Lucas, his eyes clouding.

'ARK,' said Jack.

'Careful, Jacky boy. If they don't want you looking, you don't look.'

'But-'

'Take my advice,' said Lucas, leaning close. 'Let it go.'

Jack turned to Ana and gave her a meaningful look. She nodded, thanked Lucas with one of her smiles and led Jack from the station. Once they were back on the pavement, he turned to her. 'And?'

'Not here.'

'Good thinking, Wonder Woman. Let's go shopping.'

'Why?'

'Exactly,' said Jack. 'No suspicious activity, remember? We're in town, so we go shopping.'

'And then what?'

'Then we run.'

Ana browsed the sale racks of jumpers and tops and slung a selection over her arm. She had already stocked up on toiletries and was now buying enough clothes to last a couple of weeks. She put them on her card, rather than using cash. They had each taken as much from the bank as they were allowed. It wouldn't last long, but it was a start.

Jack was waiting for her on the pavement. She emerged from the shop and handed over some of her bags.

'Three o'clock,' he said.

Ana glanced at her mobile. 'It's only two thirty, what are you talking about?'

'Black Lexus, to your right. It's been around the block once.'

She checked the road. The car was sitting at the traffic lights, indicator blinking to turn right. 'What do we do?'

'Keep shopping,' said Jack. He strolled casually down the street. 'We'll do it next time round.'

'Do what?'

'Make the switch.'

The Lexus took the turn and disappeared. Ana breathed out in relief. They still hadn't tried to grab her. Perhaps she had misunderstood what she had overheard yesterday, after all, how long did it take to arrange backup?

Jack stopped to look in the window of a bakery. On the pavement beside him was a fractious baby in a pushchair surrounded by a group of people arguing. The buggy was laden with shopping bags. Ana watched the child crying fitfully and wanted to scoop it up and comfort it, but Jack grabbed her arm.

'Give me your phone.'

'Why?'

'False trail.'

Ana glanced down the street. The Lexus had turned back into the street and was coming their way.

She moved behind the bickering throng so it shielded her from the road and slipped her phone into Jack's hand. He checked it was switched on then sidled up to the pushchair.

68

He checked the road. A bus was heading towards his location and would block ARK's view of the pavement when it passed. He waited.

The Lexus threaded through the slow moving traffic. Jack watched it approach reflected in the bakery window. The bus drew parallel with him.

With a flick of his wrist, he dropped Ana's phone into one of the shopping bags on the pushchair.

The bus moved on. The Lexus slid past.

Jack put his arm around Ana's shoulders and planted a kiss in her hair. 'As soon as they turn, we run. Ready?'

Ana turned to smile at him. 'Ready.'

The Lexus turned to make another circuit. Jack took Ana's hand, spun her around and began to run. They ducked down a side street and raced to the next turning. Once clear of the high street, they slowed to a fast walk.

'What about your phone?' said Ana.

'It's a stealth phone.'

She pressed for more, but he didn't want to discuss it in the street. They took the indirect route back to his house, cutting down lanes and alleyways to be sure they weren't followed on foot.

When they arrived, Jack moved his car from the street and parked it in the yard behind his house, while Ana closed all the curtains. It wouldn't take ARK long to realise they were tailing the wrong person and return to this house to stake it out. But Jack didn't plan to hang around. He and Ana would be long gone before then. While they prepared to leave, he explained.

As Ana had suspected, he did have secrets hidden in his wardrobe. She sat on the bed and watched him empty the contents of a locked tin onto the duvet between them: loops of wire and circuit boards, old mobile phones, and several biometric IDs.

'Do you trust me?' he said in a small voice.

Ana nodded, her stomach clenched in anxiety. He handed over an ID card, used as a passport and driving licence. She opened it and looked at the picture. It was Jack, but the name read: Joshua King.

'Why do you have a fake ID?'

'Emergencies,' he said. 'I have others. Different names.'

'Jack?' She shook her head in disbelief. 'Why? How did you get them?'

'Friend of a friend,' he said, taking it back and slipping it into his jacket. 'I know how it looks, but they're useful, especially for dealing with organisations like ARK. If I need to disappear, this is how I do it. This is how I stay ahead of them.'

'And the phone?'

He pulled his phone from a pocket. 'It's untraceable. Changes the IMEI code automatically every time you use it. Makes it practically invisible. Plus it spoofs your GPS so they don't know where you are.'

'So where are we going?'

'My dad's old place up the coast,' said Jack. He stood and returned the tin to the wardrobe. 'It's mine now, of course. Haven't been since...' He trailed off and stood with his back to Ana and pretended to tidy his clothes.

A stab of grief penetrated her heart from his, and then he turned with a mangled smile on his face. He brandished two car number plates he had pulled from the wardrobe. 'I'll change these, then we'll get going.'

Ana sat on the steps at the back door and watched him work. He had only mentioned his father once before. It was the day their friendship had blossomed into love, sitting in his car at Wallsend watching the rain and sharing stories. When Jack had told her about his father's betrayal, she had seen how it had broken his heart and knew she could trust him. Long after the rain had stopped, they emerged from the car and he had taken his photos of the swollen river and revealed the final twist in the tale.

His father had died shortly after the storm. As an officer in the Territorial Army, Jack senior had been called upon to keep the peace and rebuild the infrastructure of the country. He had survived fire-fights and snipers on the streets of London, raging wild fires across the south-east, and treacherous floodwaters in Wales. But when 21 SAS had been called to rebuild a collapsed bridge in Cumbria, his luck had run out.

Jack was proud of his dad, despite failing to win his approval. He knew there was no way to redeem himself now, and to add further salt to the wound, Jack senior had been awarded the George Cross after his death.

Jack was quiet on the drive north. Careful to avoid being spotted by the CCTV network, he took the B roads and byways, threading through villages and remote farms as the sun set.

The cottage was on the coast overlooking the North Sea near Howick, in the shadow of the ruins of Dunstanburgh Castle. It had been his father's bolt-hole and safe house, bought for cash and hidden from everyone except his family. Every Christmas and school holiday had been spent at the cottage. It was here Jack had learned to shoot. His dad had balanced tins and bottles on the rocks, and Jack would clamber over the boulders and scree with an old Enfield revolver, firing lead slugs into the sea. He had earned a pound for every direct hit and soon had enough to buy his own computer.

Not long after that, his father had caught him writing. The shock and dismay on his face couldn't have been worse if he had caught Jack watching porn. There had been no more shooting lessons, and the Browning semi-automatic his father had promised to bequeath him had been locked away and forgotten.

Jack began to relax when the distant waves drew close and the scent of the sea filled the car. Ana leaned across and placed her hand on his thigh. 'Okay?'

He smiled, but kept his eyes on the darkening road. 'There's something I meant to ask.'

'Mmm?'

'Linnunrata,' he said. 'What is that? A town?'

Ana withdrew her hand and stared out of the window. Clouds were gathering on the horizon, the line between sky and sea blurring to an ominous smudge. A storm was coming.

10

Ethne stood in the darkness of the cave and held her breath. She was sure an attack was imminent; she had seen it clearly in her mind's eye. Could she have imagined it? The others were irritable rather than scared. Voices called out for the generator to be fixed while people searched for sources of light. A faint glow came from the entrance high above their heads. Then around the cavern points of light appeared as torches and headband lights were switched on.

Ethne scanned the cave, searching for Will. She spotted him near the wall of jagged rock that soared over their heads to the mouth of the cave. He was using the light strapped to his head to scan the ropes. He grabbed one and pulled. It was slack. He pulled again. This time it fell and coiled around his feet like a dead snake. He peered into the darkness above his head and raised his walkie-talkie. 'Petar? Come in.'

Ethne crossed the cave towards him, careful not to collide with any stones or people. Will worked along the ropes, feeding them through his hands to find the ends. Every rope had been cut. Static poured from the radio. He looked up and cupped his hands.

'Petar!' he shouted. 'What's going on?'

Ethne reached him. She put a hand on his shoulder making him jump in surprise. He turned, blinding her with his headlamp.

She shielded her eyes. 'We're under attack.'

Will stared at her in confusion.

'We have to get out of here,' she said as calmly as she could manage.

He blinked, registered what she was saying, and then nodded. The rest of his team were gathered behind Ethne, silently waiting for his orders.

'Okay,' said Will. 'Get your kit together. We're climbing out. There are bolts and camming devices in my bag.'

'What about the equipment?' said a man's voice from behind a torch.

'Leave the gear, Marcus,' said Will. 'We'll come back for it as soon as we know what's going on.'

Gunshots echoed around the entrance. As one, they looked up in shock. An explosion shook the mountain, showering rocks and dust into the cavern.

Ethne fled for the stones, surrounded by a frenzy of panic. Several people scrambled up the rock face without equipment, while others screamed, hid in alcoves or ran aimlessly around the cavern.

Ethne scanned the mayhem looking for Will. Where was he?

More gunshots cracked around the narrow entrance. One of the men trying to climb out fell back. He landed on the cave floor in a crumpled heap so twisted it could only mean one thing. Ethne stared in numb shock. Who was doing this? Ana had warned her. She had stood on the pavement with tears in her eyes, pleading with her not to go. It was a trap, she had said. ARK would take her, just like they had taken Michael.

Ethne looked at the impossible stones with their enigmatic script. She watched the terror erupting around her. None of it made sense. Why would ARK give the go ahead to catalogue the stones, pay her a ridiculous sum to decipher the writing, and then attack their own people? Somebody else wanted these stones to remain hidden.

A movement to her right gave her a jolt. Lucy was searching the crates around the stones, oblivious to the chaos. She didn't have a torch; she didn't need one. A faint glow emanated from her skin, lighting her way. Ethne stared in disbelief.

Lucy bent over a crate and picked something up. A laptop. In one swift movement it vanished into her oversized jacket. She looked at Ethne, eyes loaded with meaning. Ethne frowned in reply and mouthed: what are you doing?

Lucy flashed a devilish grin and winked. 'Get ready to run.'

Another explosion shook the cavern and pellets of rock rained down through the dust filled shadows. Ethne threw her hands over her head and crouched against a granite menhir. More blasts reverberated through the stone, humming and buzzing around the spiral. She wanted to wrap her arms around the entire monument and protect the ancient legacy from the destructive insanity being unleashed around her.

Strong arms pulled at her shoulders. Lucy was trying to tear her away from the stones, from *her* stones. How could she leave them here to be blown to pieces by lunatics?

'We must leave,' said Lucy into her ear.

Ethne staggered towards the forbidding wall of rock that stood between her and escape. A feeble twilight glowed at the entrance, sixty metres above her head.

Bodies lay at the foot of the jagged slope. Ethne searched frantically for Will, kneeling beside a man who looked the right size in the gloom. She turned his head and jumped back in horror. Her fingers felt slick with blood. The man's face was unrecognisable, his brain visible between bony splinters. It wasn't Will, but whoever it was, had a bullet through his skull.

'Ethne,' shouted Lucy. 'Now.'

She turned, trying to wipe the blood from her hands, fingers shaking. 'If we climb they'll shoot us.'

'We're not climbing.' Lucy hooked her arms around Ethne's waist. 'Hold on.'

Without thinking, she obeyed and gravity seemed to fail. She wasn't flying, but falling upwards, as if the laws of physics had become inverted. The rock face blurred as she flew past, and an eerie silence filled her ears. The daylight grew stronger as they approached the mouth of the cave. She could taste the ice and the crispness of the air. They surfaced and the silence ended with a roar as the mountainside erupted around them. Boulders and ash smashed into the ice and tumbled into the cave.

Lucy deposited Ethne onto the ice. She wobbled and turned on the spot to survey the carnage. The tents were torn, flapping and burning in the wind, the snowmobiles a tangle of charred metal. The cave entrance was strewn with bodies, dark blood vivid red against the ice. She ran between them to check for signs of life. She found none.

At the edge of the camp she found snowmobile tracks etched into the ice, leading away onto the glacier. Whoever had cut the ropes and fired the shots that killed these men, was long gone.

'Ethne,' shouted Lucy. 'Jump on.'

She spun round. On the glacier stood a sledge pulled by ten Greenland huskies yipping and hopping from paw to paw, desperate to be moving. Lucy was standing on the sledge, beaming like a queen who has just been given the day off.

Overhead, Ethne heard the distant thrum of an engine. It didn't sound like the whirring blades of a helicopter or the propellers of the Twin Otter in which she had arrived. It was something else. The whine of a fat wasp. She looked into the limitless sky searching for the source of the incessant noise.

The sun had hauled itself over the horizon but was barely visible. It hugged the line of rocks and ice, throwing the primordial landscape into a shimmering dawn so beautiful it almost made Ethne forget the horrors around her.

The buzzing wasp grew louder. Ethne ran for the sledge, glancing back to see what she thought was a large toy aeroplane flying towards her over the nunatak. It was only once she had clambered aboard the sledge that she realised what it was: a Predator drone.

Lucy set the dogs running with a shout as if she had done it a million times before, and the sledge took off over the ice sheet. Ethne lurched and grabbed the side to stop herself falling out. The ice rumbled past in a cold blur as the dogs powered over the glacier, barking with happiness. She pulled a fur blanket over her knees and watched Lucy guide the dogs. The mystifying woman seemed to know where she was going. Or perhaps the dogs did.

The whirr of the drone followed them. Ethne looked up and had the distinct feeling they were about to be fired upon. Lucy was an oasis of calm, as if she was just taking her dogs for a morning run.

'They're not going to let us get away,' said Ethne. 'Not alive, at any rate.'

As she spoke, the glacier in front of them exploded in a cloud of ice shards and rock. Ethne screamed and dug her fingers into the side of the sledge. A chasm had opened in the ice. At their current speed they didn't have time to steer around it, they would be on it in seconds.

'Hold on,' shouted Lucy.

Ethne obeyed, crouching as low as she could. Lucy shouted and whipped the reins, goading the dogs to run faster. They hit the edge of the chasm. The dogs took off and the sledge lifted from the ice.

For a blissful moment they were suspended in silence, and the sun glinted from a million ice crystals.

A crash, and the sledge jolted violently as they landed. The dogs continued to run. Ethne sat up. She looked back at the fast retreating chasm, amazed they were still going, and laughed with relief.

Overhead, the drone circled and flew away. Ethne watched and prayed with feverish hope that the attack was over. Perhaps they had run out of missiles and had to return to base, wherever that was. But she was wrong. The drone looped around and flew straight for them. It wouldn't miss a second time.

Lucy had seen it. She gave Ethne a look so fierce it terrified her more than the Predator flying towards them.

'Get under the blanket,' said Lucy. 'You must cover your eyes.'

Ethne stared at her stupidly. A blanket wasn't going to stop her getting blown to pieces.

'Blanket,' shouted Lucy, making Ethne jump. 'Now!'

'What are you going to do?'

Lucy grabbed the fur blanket and threw it over Ethne's head. 'Close your eyes. Do not look under any circumstances. Do you understand?'

Ethne nodded and began to tremble. She curled into a ball under the blanket and squeezed her eyes shut. Her heart was beating so hard she thought it would dislodge the blanket, so she clutched at it until her fingers ached. What was this crazy woman about to do?

The sledge powered onwards. She listened to the hypnotic swish of the runners cutting over the ice. Overhead, the scream of the Predator as it plunged down. She had been right about one thing: they had run out of missiles. They were going to crash the drone straight into the sledge. The burr of the engine filled her ears. She held her breath.

Ethne's mind filled with the image of blue eyes and a crooked smile. Ice crystals glinting in ginger stubble. Will. He was trapped in the cave. She didn't even know if he was alive.

From under the blanket, through closed eyes, she sensed an immense light, as if the sun had come unhinged and fallen directly onto the glacier. An explosion roared through the air and a searing heat penetrated her fur shield. The dogs barked like it was the end of the world, but the sledge kept moving.

'Okay,' shouted Lucy.

Ethne threw off the blanket, the sledge swerving in a wide arc. The Predator drone lay in a burning mangled heap on the ice. Columns of fire and smoke rose into the air. Ethne stared at the wreckage in dumb surprise.

'What the-' she said, as a wing dropped off the drone and burst into flames. 'How did you do that?'

'Are you hurt?' said Lucy, looking her over with concern.

Ethne shook her head. Physically she was fine, she was great. She was better than great. She was alive. She just had a few questions. A few million questions.

'What are you?' she said.

Lucy laughed. 'You'll see.'

11

Jack rolled the Astra to a stop and peered through the windshield. The secluded cottage was nestled behind a grass bank and overlooked slabs of craggy rocks that tilted into the sea. A cove of sand curved to the south, while to the north, the ruins of Dunstanburgh Castle blurred into the sky with the gathering storm. Waves exploded over the rocks, hailing spray against the low wall running around the front of the cottage. The chimney pots stood stark against the smudge of dusk, like tank gun barrels aimed straight up in a standoff with God.

They unpacked the car, running back and forth between the stone porch and the boot while the wind tugged at their clothes. They had stopped for food supplies on the way, driving an extra fifty miles in the wrong direction just in case. While Ana filled the kitchen cupboards, Jack checked the wood store and was relieved to find it was still full. The cottage felt neglected and damp. He loaded the inglenook with logs and got a fire going in the stove. It would take hours to warm through enough to banish the ghosts he could feel loitering in the alcoves and seeping out of the stone.

He watched Ana put the kettle on, and then slipped into the hallway to unlock the cupboard under the stairs. He knelt and pressed his fingers to the wood panel at the back of the cupboard. It eased open to reveal a black holdall. Jack breathed out in relief. His father's arsenal was still there. He would clean and oil the guns later while Ana slept.

The living room was freezing so they huddled at the kitchen table with mugs of hot chocolate and powered up the laptop. Jack opened Michael's box of discs. They were neatly labelled in black marker with the date each film had appeared on *The Okeke Gospel*. According to the comments on CogNet, most of the viewers believed Michael had used special effects. Jack would think the same if he hadn't seen it for himself.

His favourites were the videos that featured Ana.

When her powers had first manifested, she had struggled to control them. Over time and with much practice, she had gained mastery, but only so she could hide her powers. She just wanted to be normal. Jack couldn't understand it. Admittedly, some of things he had seen were extreme, and not all of it had been captured on camera, much to Ana's relief.

Lights had danced about her head, as if she were being followed around by fairies. Electrical equipment spat sparks when she stood too close. Rose petals fell in waves from the air above her head and cascaded into heaps at her feet. And one heartbreaking day, Jack had arrived at the flat to find Ana floating a foot off the floor. Tears poured down her cheeks as she pleaded with Michael to pull her down, to make it stop.

Jack was glad the mutation had passed him by.

'Can we watch that one where you and Mike play catch with your minds?' he said, flicking through the discs.

'Don't be silly.' Ana reached into the box, pulled out the most recent disc and quickly loaded it into the computer.

A gust cracked against the window making her jump. She opened her mind into the desolate land surrounding the cottage to search for other minds. She found none. They were alone, at last.

While the film played, the storm rumbled in across the sea, providing a dramatic and ominous soundtrack to the images on the screen.

Intercut with simple shots of Michael talking in a wood-lined room, were animations he had created to illustrate his work. Great swirls of colour danced over the screen. The images were drawn from shamanic and aboriginal art: bold, earthy tones mixed with dazzling splashes of primary colour, sinuous curves and explosions of dots, breathtaking fractals and spirals. It was a visual feast.

Through it all, Michael explained what he had discovered about the mutation. Using his new gifts, he had developed an understanding of genetics and consciousness, subjects he had never formally studied. He knew things now that he couldn't have imagined just six months ago, setting out ideas Ana could barely follow.

She grasped this much: human beings were evolving. The mutation had triggered a leap in development equivalent to the shift from *Homo erectus* to *Homo sapiens*. The next step would make us smarter and healthier. Michael explained how short-sighted he was before the storm, how he couldn't see without his glasses. But within days of the mutation switching on, he had perfect sight.

But that wasn't all.

The real change was a shift in consciousness which allowed the new humans to see how everyone was connected and the whole of life pulsed with an inner light. They weren't really a new species but an enhanced version of the old one: brilliant and compassionate and impossible to control.

Michael christened the new humans Homo Angelus, or Human Angels, and then delivered his final bombshell. The mutation would spread.

The image of a fat, throbbing chrysalis filled the screen and Michael's voice explained what was happening to the caterpillar wrapped inside.

'The transformation begins in the cells. The change is triggered by imaginal cells, which are so different from the caterpillar's normal cells that the body attacks them. The immune system treats the imaginal cells like an invading army and tries to destroy them.

'In response, the imaginal cells fight back. They multiply and spread. They cluster together and begin to resonate at a higher frequency than the normal cells. They grow stronger and their numbers increase.

'Finally, overwhelmed by the imaginal cells, the normal cells stop attacking. They stop resisting. They begin to resonate at the same frequency as the imaginal cells. They begin to sing the same song.

'The caterpillar's transformation is complete. He has become a butterfly.'

Michael's ecstatic face filled the screen. 'We are the future. We are Human Angels and we're coming for you!'

The screen went black.

Ana stared at the computer, her own stunned face reflected in the monitor. Jack stood and went to the fireplace to poke the smouldering logs. He glanced at Ana sitting immobile at the kitchen table, staring into space.

'No wonder ARK wanted him,' he said. 'It's a declaration of war.'

She spun to face him. 'That's ridiculous.'

'You really think they're going to sit back and hand their power over to...well, you, Ana? You and every other Deviant.'

She winced. 'Please don't use that word.'

'Sorry,' said Jack. 'But think about it. If the gene spreads the way Michael says it will, how long before-'

'I don't want to start a war, Jack. I'm not interested in power or being in charge or whatever, and Michael isn't either. That's not what he's saying.'

'It isn't how they'll see it,' he said. 'It doesn't matter what the truth is. What matters is what they *believe* is happening. If ARK think you're trying to take over, they will try to stop you.'

Ana joined Jack by the fire and perched on the edge of one of the sofas flanking the fireplace. She stared into the flames licking around the wood.

Jack grabbed a blanket and sat beside her, throwing it over their knees. 'What did you get from Lucas?'

'They're experimenting on them.'

'Is that why they've been injected?'

Ana nodded and closed her eyes and tried to block the disturbing images pouring into her mind. 'Only two were shot, but they all had the puncture wounds, and they'd all been injected multiple times. The forensic reports couldn't identity why. They were all healthy.'

Jack sighed. 'Not very helpful.'

'There's more,' said Ana. 'The reports found traces of barbiturates in all the victims except the two who were shot. And the DNA profiles show an unknown mutation.'

'I think we can guess what that is.'

'Phanes obviously hasn't shared their research, because the forensic lab suggests the mutation occurred as a result of illegal gene therapy, hence the multiple injections.'

'Interesting,' said Jack. 'Any data on the other bodies, the ones we didn't find?'

Ana nodded. 'The first was a man, found in October. The other two were more recent, a man and a woman. All with the same injuries. But there's one more thing. The woman you found a couple of weeks ago. She was pregnant.'

'Is that significant?'

'The lab was confused by this and it was flagged to be checked, but the foetus had the mutation too. What kind of experiments are they doing on these people, Jack?'

'Let's think it through,' he said. 'We know ARK have been studying this mutation since at least September because that's when Lethe stopped talking to me, and you picked it out of his head. So they've known about the powers for five months, and the health benefits.'

Jack got up and retrieved his computer from the kitchen, then rejoined Ana on the sofa. Before they left, he had accessed his backups on the server at work and replaced the files Beatrice had wiped. He opened everything he had on the storm and the mutation and scanned them for salient facts.

'Gamma rays are emitted during solar storms,' he continued. 'High energy, short wavelength, ionising radiation which can cause damage to the structure of DNA. So that might be what triggered the mutation, but no one is sure. Michael said it will spread, but short of another storm, I don't see how that could happen, unless we all start breeding like bunnies. Except now, thanks to Lethe, we know they can only breed with each other.'

'Maybe that's why they took him,' said Ana.

'To breed? Like a stud farm?'

'They won't get far with Mickey. No, they want his help.'

'To understand the genetics and do what?'

'He said there were two effects from the mutation,' said Ana. 'The health aspects and the consciousness aspects. So perhaps they *are* working on a gene therapy, but not for the reason in the forensic report.'

Jack nodded. 'Michael got perfect vision from it, there's probably other benefits too. If they could develop a vaccine that cured all diseases-'

'Like an elixir.'

'Yes, but the pharmaceutical companies wouldn't be happy about that. Their profits would vanish overnight. They'd all go bust. No, ARK aren't interested in humanitarian causes.'

'But they might want the benefits for themselves,' said Ana.

'What do people in power always want?' said Jack.

'More power.'

'And they don't like to share,' continued Jack. 'Perhaps they want to control the mutation. Switch it on or off. That way, they can choose who has the power and who doesn't. So maybe they want Michael to help them put the genie back in the bottle. Would he cooperate with something like that?'

'Not willingly,' said Ana. 'And what if it can't be stopped? Michael said it will spread spontaneously. ARK won't like that.'

'We need to find this lab and stop them before-'

'They wouldn't kill him, would they?' said Ana in a tiny voice. 'I mean, if he refused-'

'He's smarter than them,' said Jack. 'He has powers, remember. Let's concentrate on finding the lab and then we'll get him out.'

Jack pulled up all the details he had on Phanes BioTech. He had been following ARK for years, watching as they pooled their resources and pushed back against government regulations.

Before the storm, the world had already been falling apart. In Britain unemployment had been rising, power cuts were normal and petrol was rationed. All available plots in and around cities had been ploughed and returned to farmland. The unemployed were put to work milking, planting, and harvesting so the country could be more self-sufficient and import less food. Global transport and trade were breaking down due to energy shortages and endemic conflict.

ARK had helped to keep the lights on and the wheels turning. Then two days before the storm hit, they had moved their satellites. Nobody understood why. ARK had claimed it was a malfunction.

Then the sun had erupted. It had taken everyone by surprise, but ARK had recovered first and their competition had been wiped out. While world leaders bickered over how to respond, ARK had stepped into the breach. By the time people realised what had happened, ARK had quietly taken over.

In his darker moments, Jack would look at the unfolding saga and convince himself ARK had planned the whole thing. It was absurd, of course. Everybody knew solar storms were impossible to predict, and not even ARK were powerful enough to create one.

The consortium had begun with the three companies that gave them their acronym: Amrit Securities, ReSource Industries, and Kali Defence Systems, or KDS.

Amrit provided asset management and financial services. CEO Ian Goldsmith had presided over the largest series of mergers in the history of banking, gobbling up assets as the remaining banks failed.

Meanwhile, ReSource had conducted the biggest land grab since the spread of the British Empire, driven by Sebastian Coburn's evangelical belief that the earth would deliver the future into his hands. They had invested heavily in technological innovation, and pushed mining operations deep into previously protected landscapes, such as the Arctic.

Finally, KDS defended ARK's wealth. Kali was run by Akash Devan, a military strategist and engineer. He had personally designed many of the planes, tanks and guns being used to subjugate populations all over the world under the banner of ARK Security.

From the start they had positioned themselves to take over key areas of production and economic activity, and in time were joined by another three corporations. These were the Chinese agribusiness and food company, Golden Harvest, run by Wei Zhou; American internet and communications giant CogNet, run by Richard Franklin who had recently bought several TV networks around the world; and Phanes BioTech, the pharmaceutical and biotechnology firm that had cracked the mutation's code under the guidance of Fredrik Thorsen.

Jack had also detected the presence of another company but it seemed to be a silent partner. Numerous references to an organisation called Pinecone Freeholdings came up in relation to properties owned by ARK, but aside from that, he couldn't decipher their function. He had been tracking the properties on their list in the hope that one would turn out to be the laboratory run by Phanes, but so far he had drawn a blank.

Finding Thomas Lethe had been a breakthrough that, in the end, had led nowhere. He was no further forward than he had been six months ago and it didn't leave them with many options. He fired up the Wi-Fi and loaded the Phanes website. There was little point in looking at it; none of the important stuff was displayed up front. Early on in the investigation he had engaged the services of a hacker who was only able to tell him what he had already guessed.

Phanes kept all their important data locked down on a server impossible to access from the outside. They had their own data centre with dedicated generators and backups, and the only way to get at it was by going there in person. Phanes HQ was also protected by multiple passwords and biometric ID systems. There was only one way he was going to find the information they needed. He would have to visit their headquarters himself.

He loaded the media page to double-check the name of the press officer only to find himself confronted by an image of Ana smiling back at him. A closer look revealed his mistake: it was Evangeline Wilson, Ana's mother.

He glanced at Ana sitting beside him staring into the flickering fire. 'Babes?'

'Mmm.'

'Didn't you say your mum worked for the NHS?'

'Press officer, yes. Why?'

'I think she got a new job.'

Ana looked at the screen in confusion.

It had been Christmas Eve when the truth about her stepfather's betrayal had finally come out. Ana had kept the secret for months. Perhaps it was selfish, but she didn't want to be the unwitting cause of the breakdown of her parent's marriage. Even after Patrick's foolish romantic gesture, she had still tried to protect their feelings by pretending she didn't know.

She should have told the truth from the start. Maybe things would have been different. Maybe Patrick would still be alive.

He had taken the family out for Christmas dinner in town, and with great fanfare had produced his own homemade crackers stuffed with lame jokes and novelty toys. Evangeline's cheeks had been flushed with happiness as she ripped open the belly of the final cracker to find her toy.

She had pulled out a diamond ring.

Her happiness had turned to suspicion, and she had demanded to know where Patrick had got the money for such an extravagant gift. He said a friend had finally settled an old debt, giving him the opportunity to thank her for putting up with him. He knew he had been a pain, but from now on, he would be a better man.

It was a lie well told, and Evangeline had wanted to believe it as much as Patrick needed her to. Replete with turkey and mince pies, and a little drunk on brandy, the family had ambled home through the snow. Ana linked arms with her mother and they sauntered along, talking of this and that, while Patrick went ahead up the street.

They caught him hiding behind the bins at the Work Farm, talking to his friend on the phone and pleading with him to back up his story. Evangeline tore the ring from her finger and threw it at him, along with some carefully chosen words.

Only then had Ana revealed the truth. The money had come from Phanes BioTech, and now her mother worked for them too.

'Is this why you two aren't speaking?' said Jack.

'I don't...I didn't...' she shook her head, unable to process this new betrayal.

'What's her problem?'

'She thinks I'm a monster.'

'Has she met you?'

'She said I was a freak of nature. Not out loud, but I heard...'

Jack put the laptop on the floor then scooped Ana into an embrace and spoke into her hair. 'You're not a monster. Or a freak. Your mum is wrong.'

12

Ethne huddled beneath her fur blanket and watched the unforgiving landscape roll by. She was numb with shock and her tears froze in rigid lines on her cheeks. She told herself she was crying because of the icy wind, but she knew that wasn't true. She hadn't expected to feel this way. It had been nine months. She thought she was over him, and now Will was probably dead.

Lucy drove the huskies relentlessly over the ice. The sun retreated behind them as they rode east, sinking beneath the horizon and taking the little warmth it offered with it. If they didn't find shelter soon they would freeze to death on the ice sheet, unless Lucy could make an igloo magically appear out of the wilderness, as she had with the sledge and huskies.

Through the dying light, as if in answer to a prayer, Ethne spotted a Danish flag fluttering against a pole. The flagpole stood outside a wooden hut with small white windows and red frames. Smoke escaped from a narrow chimney and a pair of white antlers vaulted over the door. Laid out on the ground around the hut were sledges in various stages of repair, and a fearsome barking came from an enclosure to one side.

As they approached, a man emerged from the hut, a bolt-action rifle raised and ready to fire. His aggressive stance contrasted with his raggedy thick beard and large woolly jumper. It was like being threatened by a pissed off teddy bear.

'Hoooole!' shouted Lucy, and the dogs slowed.

The sledge stopped outside the hut. Lucy jumped down and approached the man, oblivious to the gun. The man hesitated a fraction, then lowered his rifle and ran to Lucy, beaming through his beard. They embraced like old friends and launched into a frenzied discussion in high-speed Danish.

Ethne eased off the sledge, willing her frozen limbs to move, and tried to follow the conversation. Danish wasn't a language with which she was familiar, but there was enough overlap with other Scandinavian tongues that she was able to pick up the gist.

The gun toting teddy bear was called Jorgen and was a member of the Sirius Sledge Patrol, the Danish military unit stationed on Greenland. Underneath all the hair and the jumper, he was about the same age as Ethne. The Sirius insignia on his sleeve looked familiar: a red circle with a husky in a white six-pointed star. Some of the men around the entrance to the cave had had the same insignia on their coats. Jorgen had been following events on his radio, listening to his colleagues as they fought an unknown enemy.

It was clear they weren't used to combat situations. Polar bears were their usual foe.

Jorgen greeted his dogs with great affection and busied himself unhooking them from their harnesses, taking them into the fenced area beside the hut.

Ethne stood on the compacted snow and watched him work, struggling to understand all she had seen that day.

Lucy leant on the doorframe of the hut, watching her. 'You have many questions.'

'No shit,' said Ethne.

'Come inside and get warm.'

Ethne looked at this impossible woman with her ridiculous hair and decided she wasn't going anywhere until she got an explanation. She shoved her hands into her pockets and fixed Lucy with a look she hoped conveyed total determination.

'What just happened?' she said. 'We get out of the cave without ropes. A convenient dog sledge just happens to be waiting for us. You blow a drone out of the sky with, what? Perhaps you have a rocket launcher hidden inside your massive coat. We arrive here, and you two know each other, and well by the looks of it. Did you borrow his dogs? Did you know all this was going to happen? And why are you grinning at me like that? This is serious.'

'The world is not as you think it is,' said Lucy.

'Oh, really, well, thanks for that,' said Ethne. 'That's much clearer.'

Jorgen had finished with the huskies and was watching this exchange with amusement, his gun resting against his shoulder.

'Jorgen will explain,' said Lucy and disappeared inside the hut.

'Always with the weaving and the ducking,' said Jorgen, turning to Ethne and taking her hand. He gave it a firm shake and smiled at her like she was a long-lost friend. 'Jorgen. Good to meet you...'

'Ethne,' she said. 'Are your colleagues all right? I don't know Danish, but I understood they were involved in the firefight. And I saw, um, bodies. They had the same insignia.'

Jorgen nodded and steered Ethne towards the hut. 'Thank you, Ethne. They were fighting, yes. We lost some.'

'I'm sorry.'

'Others are in pursuit. We will find them. Whoever they are.'

Inside the cabin the space was divided into areas: a tiny but practical kitchen, a radio station with headphones and satellite equipment, a cache of weapons, and a water desalination unit. Everything needed to survive in one of the last wildernesses on the planet. An oil burner warmed the cosy space with room for several well-worn armchairs. A screen separated the sleeping area from the rest of the hut.

Ethne sank into one of the armchairs still wearing her arctic gear. 'So, Jorgen, how d'you know Lucy?'

'She saved my life,' he said with a casual shrug. 'Last year, during the storm.'

'You were out here then?'

'Best place. Is no problem to me if the power goes off, yes?'

'Point,' said Ethne. 'So, what happened?'

'One of the dogs was sick at night,' said Jorgen. 'I went to check on him. I was foolish, sleepy. I left my Glock. A polar bear came looking for food. She was very thin, starving. Poor creature. She thought I looked pretty tasty. Next, there is a light and the bear is gone, and Lucy is there.'

'Did you lend her your sledge today?' said Ethne.

He nodded. 'We made a deal the night of the bear. She told me a day would come when she needs my help. That day was today.'

Ethne looked at Lucy who was smiling benignly at them from beneath her insane blonde afro. She had removed her oversized jacket to reveal a fluffy jumper covered in an intricate pattern of peacock feathers. She couldn't be what Ethne thought she was, because what she thought Lucy was didn't exist. As far as she knew.

'Are you an angel?' she said, feeling idiotic.

Lucy giggled like a joyful child. 'Something like that.'

Ethne shook her head, not in disbelief but to dislodge the objections she could feel rising to the surface. She considered herself an empiricist. Show her the evidence and if it checked out, she accepted it. Angels, fairies, goblins, and the like, were for kids. They were stories, nothing more. How could she accept that the woman sitting opposite was an angel? But then how else could she explain their escape from the cave?

Lucy would say no more on the subject, and Jorgen disappeared into the kitchen to make them something to eat. After the mayhem and destruction in the cave, the peace pervading the homely cabin was a welcome relief, and Ethne slowly relaxed. She feasted on dumplings, wriggling her toes as they thawed, the stew working its magic on her frozen body.

Flames crackled in the wood burner and from behind a screen came the low monologue of Jorgen talking over the radio, tracking the progress of the Sirius Patrol. He had no trouble accepting the reality of angels. Jorgen was a man selected after rigorous psychological and physical testing to be rock solid in the face of this overwhelming and hostile environment. He may be more park ranger than military soldier, but he was not weak-minded.

Ethne cupped her hands around a mug of steaming hot chocolate. She blew on the dark liquid and watched Lucy over the rim.

The angel was frowning at the laptop she had stolen during the attack. After fumbling with the catch, she had finally got it open, and was now randomly pressing keys, turning it around and upside down, trying to switch it on. A musical bong sounded from the machine and she nearly dropped it in surprise. Lucy stared at the screen as it lit up, her frown deepening.

'Um...Password?' She looked at Ethne. 'I think this is your department.'

Ethne took the computer and rested it on her knees. The screen showed a tiny circular photograph of a familiar face and a flashing cursor waiting for a password. This was Will's machine. She buried the avalanche of confused feelings bubbling in her heart, and concentrated. She could crack Will's password. She knew him better than anyone else.

She tried some of his favourite mountain routes, the climbs he was always raving about. Nothing. After three failures, a hint flashed up. It said: Ethne.

She stared at her name, her eyes clouding with tears, and desperately pushed against the hollow ache filling her chest.

'What is it?' said Lucy, her voice soft with compassion.

Ethne looked up and a tear escaped and trickled down her cheek. She quickly wiped it away and shook her head, turning her attention back to the screen.

'The password is connected to me in some way,' she said, hoping she sounded businesslike and in control.

'The day you met, perhaps,' said Jorgen, sitting down in the other armchair. He swigged from a mug of tea. 'Your first kiss? Men are romantic.'

Ethne raised a sardonic eyebrow in his direction. She could think of many exceptions to that rule. But it was worth a try. The day she met Will they were in the student union bar at university. She had been giving her usual massages and he was hanging around, pretending to ignore her, even though she could tell he wanted to come over. Most guys just wanted an excuse to strip and show off their beer bellies, but he had seemed genuinely interested. Not in getting a massage, but in her. He was a year ahead of her on his course, and in the end, she had approached him.

She typed in the date. It didn't work. Neither did their first kiss nor the first time they had climbed together. By now the computer was having a mini panic attack and suggesting she reset her password using her CogNet ID, but since she didn't know that either it wasn't going to help. She was amazed she hadn't been locked out of the machine.

There was one more date she could try before she would have to give up. She typed it in. The screen sprang to life and Will's desktop appeared.

Her own face smiled up at her, sitting atop Ben Nevis, thermos of tea raised in a toast. A moment captured in time. He had taken this picture, put away the camera, and then stayed on his knees. When he had asked the impossible question, she didn't know what to say. She had just looked at him, aghast.

'What was it?' said Jorgen.

Ethne looked up and her face flushed. 'Um...the day he asked me to marry him.'

Jorgen smiled as if that was the most obvious answer she could have given. 'He is in the cave?'

She nodded. 'Can your people get him out? Did they find the attackers?'

'Yes,' he said, looking grim. 'We will check the cave, don't worry. They tracked the attackers across Ismarken. Helicopters were waiting. There was more fighting, some of the attackers were shot. They had no ID, nothing on them. Helicopters the same, no markings, no identity.'

'So were they ARK?' said Ethne.

Jorgen shrugged. 'It might be Special Forces. But what country, I do not know.'

Ethne turned to the computer and opened all the photographs of the stones and tiled them over the screen. Someone powerful wanted to suppress these incredible relics. The way she saw it, there were two options. Either they knew what the stones said, which was impossible. Or they were moving against ARK for some mysterious reason. Only by translating the text could she work out why ARK were so keen to have these stones, and why the unknown attackers, were so keen to stop them.

Ethne scanned the photographs looking for repeating patterns that would indicate some sort of linguistic structure, word groupings or grammar. She didn't see how she could translate it without a key, like the Rosetta Stone.

That gift to ancient languages had been discovered in 1799. It contained the same piece of text in three different scripts: Egyptian hieroglyphs, which were unreadable at the time; Demotic script, a simplified version of hieroglyphs; and the well-known ancient Greek. Starting with the Greek, they had been able to decipher hieroglyphs for the first time. Without something similar, she was groping in the dark.

Lucy sat on the floor beside Ethne's feet and watched the images flash across the screen. Ethne stopped at a photograph of the Fire Stone lying on the cave floor. Will had said there should be another granite menhir, and that the hole was hidden under this stone. She searched for more photographs, eventually finding a few hasty snaps taken just after the raising of the fire obsidian. Sure enough, there was the hole.

'I wonder what happened to the missing stone,' she said. 'Maybe they dropped it. Or it got lost somewhere on the mountain under the glacier.

Or it could've been carried out to sea, travelling along the ice as it moved down the valley over the centuries. Is that why they didn't finish the monument? Because they lost the stone. Or did something else stop them?'

'They did finish it,' said Lucy.

'How d'you know?' said Ethne. 'You weren't there.'

'How do you know?'

Ethne looked down at the mass of blonde curls framing Lucy's head and frowned. Dealing with an angel was going to take some getting used to. Lucy looked up and grinned.

'Sorry,' said Ethne. 'I forgot. Angel, right?'

Lucy inclined her head in a mock bow.

'Why don't you save us some time and explain it to me,' said Ethne.

'Where would be the fun in that?' said Lucy. 'Besides, that's not my job. I'm here to help. But I'm not doing it for you, Ethne.'

'You can't interfere with my free will?'

'Correct.'

'What can you do?'

'I can advise,' said Lucy. 'For instance, I would suggest you look at the backs of the stones.'

'There's nothing on the backs,' said Ethne, searching for more photos. 'All the markings are on the smooth front surfaces.'

She stopped at a shot of the back of the second stone in the spiral. Close to the ground, etched into the granite, were markings. She zoomed in. It looked like a plan of the design, a template for the layout of the stones, except in place of the Fire Stone was a depiction of flames. Splaying out from the little fire were six circles, one for each stone. Where the seventh stone should have been, there was a gap. A line ran from the gap right down to the base of the stone.

'It's a map,' said Lucy.

At the base was carved another symbol. A cross surmounted with a loop. Ethne stared at the screen in shock, her hand groping at her throat to locate her pendant. She pulled it from under her jumper and held it between her fingers.

An ankh. The pendant she had worn everyday since she was thirteen. After years of recurring dreams, here it was again.

'The key of life,' she said, stunned.

'Only in this context,' said Lucy, 'it represents the Key Stone. The stone you need to find in order to translate the text.'

'Like a Rosetta Stone?' said Ethne. 'But where is it?'

'Look at the angle of the line,' said Jorgen, leaning over Ethne to point at the screen. 'South-south-east. From here, that could be Iceland or Scotland or further down.'

'Are you saying this missing stone could be anywhere along that line?' said Ethne. 'We'll never find it.'

'You already did,' said Lucy.

They both turned to look at the angel. She was sitting cross-legged on the floor, beaming up at them with an impish twinkle in her eyes.

'Funny how things turn out,' she said. 'The Key Stone was meant to be found first. And indeed it was. Too soon. But that's free will for you. Makes things so much more exciting, don't you think?'

13

Michael lay on the doctor's couch and watched Thomas Lethe tap a syringe. A drop of clear fluid escaped from the needle and Michael shivered. He didn't want this injection. He knew it wouldn't do any good, but that wasn't the reason. He didn't want the professor to see his arms. People always reacted when they saw the scars and Michael wasn't in the mood to explain.

It hadn't taken him long to acquaint himself with his prison. After a late breakfast in his room, he had showered and tried some of his new clothes. They weren't what he would have chosen for himself, but they did fit. He pulled on a shirt that made him look like a bank manager and then sat on the bed to explore the building with his mind.

All three floors were watched by cameras blinking in corners and linked to an array of screens in a room downstairs. The guards he encountered on his remote patrol were dressed in the standard black uniform of ARK security. They were tense and restless, but he couldn't decide if they were bored or scared.

One of them came to his door an hour later. Michael stepped into the stone stairwell and found another guard waiting for him; each had a gun cradled across his chest. They marched him down the steps, one in front and one behind, descending the spiral into an oak panelled lounge stuffed with cosy armchairs. An aromatic fire flickered in the grate.

'How many people are staying here?' said Michael.

'Keep moving,' said the guard behind him.

Michael knew the answer. Only two of the bedrooms were occupied. His and the one used by the professor on the floor below. What had happened to the other guests? He felt sure the guards wouldn't tell him.

The stone steps continued down in another spiral, but the guards turned into a hallway with a carpet the colour of blood and took him past the other empty bedrooms instead. Michael extended his mind to see what lay at the bottom of the stairwell and found a reception desk complete with two more armed guards.

Halfway along the hallway, the guard in front dropped into another spiral stairwell. Michael followed and trotted down the stone steps to emerge into a long banqueting hall with a heavy wooden table stretching the length of the room. Two iron candelabras filled with unlit candles stood beyond the table, and a fire blazed in an enormous stone fireplace. The same rich burgundy carpet covered the floor and paintings hung at intervals depicting long dead ancestors in ruffs and wigs.

At the far end of the room Michael could hear sounds of cooking coming from behind a door. He sent his mind into the room and found preparations for lunch in full swing.

'What is this place?' he said. 'Some sort of castle?'

His escorts ignored him so he stopped walking and the guard behind lurched into him. 'Keep moving or we'll carry you down.'

Michael turned to face him and smiled. 'Answer my question first.'

The guard stared at him blankly. Michael continued to smile and the guard's resolve slowly crumpled. Panic flashed through his mind and he began to finger his gun nervously. Michael caught a glimpse of one of the earlier guests dropping a CCTV camera on the guard's head in an explosion of sparks. It was clear the guards were more frightened of the Deviants than the Deviants had been of them.

'I'm not here to hurt you,' said Michael carefully. 'I just want to know what this place is.'

The guard swallowed. 'C...castle, like you said. Used to belong to Pemberton-Smythe-something-or-other.'

'I heard he went bankrupt,' said the other guard. 'Follow me.' He disappeared down more steps in a tight spiral, and Michael followed.

Why was ARK running a lab in an old stately home? It wasn't an obvious place for a genetics laboratory, and perhaps that was the point. It was easier to stay hidden. Nobody outside would suspect what lay within these walls.

The lab was in the cellar. ARK had converted the basement by lining the ancient stone walls with glass panels and steel to create an airtight room running the length of the building. At the far end were smaller, enclosed spaces containing doctor's couches. Michael now lay in one of these glass cubicles, a camera watching him from the corner.

He had spent most of the day in this room, doing tests and running through the professor's experiments so boxes could be ticked and his general level of health could be confirmed. Thomas was working on a therapy, delivered via vaccine, which switched off the mutation. It worked in the lab, but so far had failed in every living subject. This version was yet to be tested.

'Raise your left sleeve, please,' said Thomas.

Michael did so, and held his breath. There was a pause as Thomas took in the lines scored into Michael's flesh, and then it began. Not a word came out of the professor's mouth, but Michael heard it all. The sympathy mixed with revulsion, confusion, fear, and finally hollow grief.

Michael had been nine when he had first cut himself. It was better to feel something than to feel nothing. The welts on his arms were a reminder that he was alive. If he could bleed, then he could feel. Ana had put a stop to it when she found out.

Things had improved when he left home and went to university. He had moved in with Ana and they had watched the world from their perch on the highest balcony. He found new friends and his love life blossomed and gave him the confidence to tell his family the truth. But they didn't want to hear that their son was gay.

Ana had found him soaking in a warm bath, the water turning red with his blood. He owed her his life.

Thomas covered the puncture wound with a small round plaster and disposed of the needle. Michael watched him from the couch. He sat up and swung his legs to the floor. Thomas was avoiding his gaze and Michael could feel an emotional avalanche threatening to erupt from the professor's mind.

'How long does it take?' he said.

Thomas turned, his eyes glassy with tears. 'Pardon?'

'The gene therapy,' said Michael. 'How long-'

'We can test you tomorrow.'

'Are you okay?'

Thomas smiled, but it looked forced. 'Of course.'

'You sure?'

Thomas dropped a steel dish and it clattered to the floor. He stooped to retrieve it, but his hands were shaking. He slung the dish into the sink in the corner and gazed at his right hand where his own scar sliced across his palm. He ran his fingers along the familiar ridge of skin and closed his eyes.

From the couch, Michael noticed the scar. 'What happened?'

Thomas looked at him sharply, as if he had forgotten Michael was there, and took a long moment before answering. He gazed unseeing at his hands as he spoke.

'It was twenty years ago. The day I met my wife. She was a nurse and I was an idiot. Got drunk on my birthday and broke a glass.' He raised his hand to show Michael the scar, then continued. 'Lucky for me, Sarah was on duty that evening in A & E. She sowed me up and by the time she had finished, I was in love.'

He smiled sadly. 'She's gone now.'

'I'm sorry,' said Michael.

'My fault, of course,' continued Thomas, as if Michael hadn't spoken. 'She left me, before the storms. I was working too much and she was...I'm sorry, I don't normally...'

Michael wasn't sure what to do. Thomas was clearly upset, but he was also mortally embarrassed by the fact and Michael didn't want to do anything that might shut the professor down. He wondered if he should try to comfort him, draw him out and encourage him to talk. If Ana were here, she would know exactly what to do.

Thomas wiped his eyes quickly and gave Michael another forced smile. 'I killed her.'

Michael almost fell off the couch. 'You what?'

'I only found out recently,' said Thomas, staring at his hands again. 'She drowned in one of the floods last year. If I'd still been around, I could've...I could've saved her. But I was here. Working...'

Michael crossed the room and put his arm around the professor's shoulders. A tumble of images and emotions poured into his mind and it took a moment for Michael to understand what he was seeing.

Thomas had lowered his guard and in a wordless confession, Michael saw the horror of what had been done. In that moment, he knew they would never let him leave.

14

Ana sat on the window seat in the living room with her eyes closed. Rain pelted the glass in wild gusts. There was no point in trying to see out, there was nothing to see. Nothing except the endless raging ocean and the darkness.

Jack had gone. A new plan was forming in his mind and she had been unable to talk him out of it. Visiting her mother was a bad idea, but he was adamant. She had wanted to go with him, promising to stay in the car and keep out of sight, but he had vetoed that too.

'You can't be seen,' he said, pulling on his coat. 'You're safe here.'

'What if they come for me while you're gone? What if they're just waiting for the right moment?'

'ARK don't know you're here,' he said, and kissed her lightly. 'Nobody does. And look.' He gestured towards the window.

A pigeon was sitting on the sill, eyeing them through the glass.

'Your guardian angel is watching over you,' he said, and slipped out the door.

Ana listened to the roar of the sea churning in the storm. It seemed as if the whole world was in commotion. She opened her eyes and glanced at the clock. Jack had been gone a long time.

She peered into the night. Rivulets of water poured over her reflection. Looking down, she noticed the hunched pigeon, its feathers puffed out and drenched. Rain dripped from its beak.

Ana opened the window and leaned out. 'Do you want to come inside?'

The pigeon cocked its head one way, then another. For an awkward moment, Ana thought she had invited an ordinary pigeon into the house, but then it hopped towards her. She stepped back and the pigeon flew through the window, spraying water over the curtains.

She turned to find Beatrice scrunching her fingers through her sodden hair. Ana glanced at Jack's luggage piled by the door. She had thrown everything they might need into his suitcases but hadn't unpacked yet, despite having nothing better to do. Unpacking seemed like defeat. She didn't want this dank cottage to become her home. She flipped open a case, retrieved a towel, and handed it over.

'Nice weather for ducks,' said Beatrice, rubbing her hair with the towel.

'Let's get you warmed up.' Ana steered Beatrice around the sofa and stood her in front of the fireplace. Then she fussed about making drinks and offered to cook something.

Beatrice watched her with affection. 'Ana, this isn't necessary.'

'Don't be silly. It's the least I can do.'

'I don't eat or drink,' said Beatrice. 'I don't need nutritional sustenance.'

'Oh.' Ana looked at the two steaming mugs of hot chocolate in her hands and felt foolish. She put them on the kitchen table and wandered through to the living room, embarrassed to meet the angel's eye.

'It is my job to look after you,' said Beatrice. 'Not the other way around.'

Ana perched on the edge of the sofa and stared into the fire. The frustration of being stuck in this house was making her cranky, and she had only been here a few hours. What would happen if she had to stay here for weeks? Months? Longer? She shuddered and looked at Beatrice, still warming herself by the fireplace.

'How long will I have to stay here?'

'It is for your protection.'

'I should be healing people, not hiding.'

'I agree,' said Beatrice. 'Some of us wanted to spread the word to prepare the Human Angels for what is to come. Others of us, myself included, believed this would make you into targets. We could not agree, so the choice was given to Michael.'

'Is that fair?'

'Perhaps not, but he reasoned it was worth the risk. After all, you can defend yourself more effectively if you know who, and what, you are, which is why he made his film. And ARK will come for you whether you know who you are or not. I argued that we needed more time, but then Michael's actions escalated events and put you in danger.'

'He wouldn't do that,' said Ana. 'He must have his reasons.'

'He knows how strong you are.' Beatrice smiled, pouring infinite love into the room. Ana shifted in her seat and stared self-consciously at her hands. It felt as if every part of her was visible. She could hide nothing from Beatrice.

'Jack loves you, Ana. Remember that.'

Ana looked up. 'What's that supposed to mean?'

Beatrice stuttered an apology, then unfolded and refolded the towel in her hands before placing it carefully on the sofa beside Ana.

'Do not concern yourself,' she said. 'I meant nothing by it. Just that no matter what happens, you can trust in his love for you, that is all. I am sorry if I alarmed you, please forgive me.'

Ana was stunned. She assumed an angel would always be in perfect control of herself, but Beatrice seemed genuinely flustered.

'Are you really an angel?' she said.

'It is a good enough word.'

'If Ethne was here, she'd take you apart over that statement.'

Beatrice chuckled. 'Words are prisons, indeed.'

'And you can transport people?' said Ana. 'I mean, before Christmas Michael disappeared from the balcony. He went outside to check the lights and I didn't see him for two weeks. Then I saw you take that boy from the Metro, so I thought, maybe...'

'We can teleport, yes, but I didn't take Michael. That was Niloufer.'

'How many of you are there?'

Beatrice laughed. 'More than you can imagine.'

'Could you teleport me to where Michael is?'

Beatrice stopped laughing.

'Ana, please trust us. He is where he needs to be. Besides, travel by angel is no picnic, as you say. It must be done only when there is no alternative.'

'What did you see about Jack?'

Beatrice turned to the fire and shook her head.

'Please,' said Ana. 'I know you can see parts of the future. I've seen it, sometimes, in flashes. There are potential futures, like offshoots from the present moment, and until a person makes a choice, all options are available. But then they choose, and it narrows to one thing. You saw something in Jack's future and then you back-pedalled.'

'I should not have spoken,' said Beatrice. 'It remains true, but I should have realised you would ask questions. I am only young, in what you might call Angel Years, but I have already forgotten much about being human.'

'You were human? I didn't think...'

'Some of us were human,' said Beatrice, joining Ana on the sofa. 'Some never were. The first human ascended to the angelic realm at the end of the Age of Ice. It wasn't attempted again for some time.'

'Why?'

'There were, how do you say it? Teething problems?'

Ana nodded and grinned. 'What about you?'

'I was recruited due to the manner of my death. In 1482, or thereabouts, I find it hard to remember exactly. I worked as you do, Ana. I healed. I knew the seasons and the moons. I knew which plants were given to cure disease. I treated people with kindness and respect, and so I was burnt as a witch.'

Ana placed her hand on the angel's arm. 'I'm sorry.'

Beatrice placed her hand over Ana's, and then continued. 'The Celestial Council thought I had potential so I was apprenticed, first to Niloufer, and thence to my Teacher, one of the Great Ones. My apprenticeship lasted 500 years, so you see, I still have much to learn.'

Ana's mind reeled. Her problems felt trivial in the face of this information. If an angel with 500 years' practice could still make mistakes, what hope did she have of getting it right? There were so many questions she wanted to ask, she didn't know where to start.

'If I ask you things will you tell me?' she said.

'Ask away,' said Beatrice. 'There's nothing else to do. You may as well have your answers, if I can give them.'

'Why a pigeon?'

Beatrice erupted into a fit of giggles and looked at Ana out of the corner of one eye. 'That's your first question? I give you carte blanche and you want to talk Columbidae.'

Ana shrugged. 'I'm just curious how it works.'

'All right,' said Beatrice. 'We are Light Beings. Technically, we have no form. We are all forms. To interact with you, I take this form. We disguise ourselves as pigeons most often because they are ubiquitous. Nobody is ever surprised to see a pigeon. It means we can watch you without your knowledge.'

'Pigeon reconnaissance,' said Ana. 'Very sneaky.'

'Some of us take other bird forms. My Teacher, the Great One, uses an eagle. We take human form when there is work to be done. It is easier to interact and intervene when you can talk face to face.'

'Can you intervene when you're not in any form?'

Beatrice nodded. 'But some humans don't hear us. They get their signals confused or choose to ignore us. Humans have an infuriating habit of not believing something unless it is standing in front of them.'

'If you don't have form, how do you learn?' said Ana. 'I mean, you had an apprenticeship. You don't go from human to angel just like that.' She snapped her fingers. 'The angelic intelligence or consciousness or whatever it is, must organise itself somehow. It must have a structure.'

The angel smiled. 'You are thinking concretely. The mind cannot conceive of these things. To interact with you, to take any form, my being must be downsized, as it were. But you are correct. There is a sense in which it could be said that I have a true form.'

'What is it?'

'I cannot show you,' said Beatrice, solemnly. 'It is forbidden. It would kill you. Or paralyse you. Or destroy your nervous system. At the very least, you would go insane. What we are is a vortex of pure energy and intelligence. We take form to complete a task, but otherwise, we are outside form, beyond time and space. Ageless. Always forever, everywhere and nowhere.'

Ana shook her head and grinned. 'All of that squashed into one tiny pigeon.'

Beatrice exploded into infectious giggling again, and Ana soon forgot to worry about what the angel had seen in Jack's future.

At that moment Jack was driving north, returning to the cottage with a heavy heart. He had found a way to gain access to Phanes' headquarters, but the risks were extreme and he wasn't sure how Ana would react. The meeting with her mother hadn't exactly gone to plan.

Evangeline Wilson lived in a truncated terrace opposite the Angel of the North in Gateshead. Jack took the turn off the western bypass and pulled into the car park for the Angel. His was the only car so he left the Astra at the far end, hidden from view behind some scraggy bushes. From habit more than need, he grabbed his torch from the glove box and set off down the path. The light from the street lamps provided enough glow through the winter trees, but he felt happier with his own source of light, just in case.

He knew he should go straight to the house, but couldn't resist a peek at the giant sculpture. It seemed to be calling to him, drawing him close. He strode up the mound to the base of the statue.

The Angel rose into the evening darkness, its steel wings thrust across the sky, silhouetted against the stars. Jack stood at the Angel's feet and gazed at its head twenty metres above him.

A great silence spread through his being, as if infinity were contained within him. The Angel leaned over and wrapped its stiff wings around his body, powerful and yet gentle. Jack closed his eyes and a tear escaped. Joy exploded through his veins like a narcotic and he began to laugh. In the darkness of his DNA, a light sparked into life. All of the universe was alive with the fire of starlight and the flapping of angel wings.

As suddenly as it began, the spell broke. Jack opened his eyes to find himself standing with his arms stretched around the base of the sculpture, tears pouring down his cheeks and a big stupid grin on his face. He stepped back sheepishly, as if he had been caught doing something shameful, and wiped his tears on his sleeve. He glanced around, checking there were no witnesses to his delirium, then made his way back to the road.

The house was on the end of a short line of three terraced houses on the other side of the dual carriageway, hidden behind messy hedges. A track led around the side to the rear of the buildings, and beyond lay the fields of one of the Work Farms. Jack walked up the path to the front door and knocked. While he waited, he pulled out his press pass, took a deep breath and got into character.

The door opened and an older version of Ana stood framed in the doorway. The hall light shone through the mound of blonde hair piled on top of her head. For a moment, Jack felt like he was looking into the future. He stared helplessly until Evangeline spoke and shook him from his reverie.

'What do you want? If you're collecting for charity, you should know I don't give to cold callers.'

'Very sensible, Mrs Wilson,' he said. 'Jack Dexter. Journalist. I write for *ARK EYE*, perhaps you've seen-'

'No.'

He flashed his press pass and smiled his best smile. 'I'd really like to talk to you about Phanes BioTech. You're their press officer, is that correct?'

'Contact me at work, Mr Dexter.'

'Under normal circumstances I would, but I was just passing. You're on my list, so I thought, why not? I understand your late husband worked for Phanes too.'

'No.'

'Oh?' said Jack, feigning confusion. 'Perhaps you'd like to clarify the details for me. I want to get my facts straight.'

'I have nothing to say to you.'

'I understand. Why did you leave your job with the NHS?'

Evangeline looked like she was about to close the door, so Jack stepped forward as subtly as he could and slipped his foot over the doorstep.

'What does my CV have to do with anything?' she said.

He smiled. 'Perhaps I could come in?'

'No.'

'All right. What does Phanes offer that the NHS couldn't? Did you get your own office? More money?'

'There is more to life than money, Mr Dexter.'

'Call me Jack.'

'Well, Jack,' said Evangeline stiffly. 'Let me tell you something your readers, if you have any, need to understand. Phanes BioTech are working tirelessly to protect us from the ultimate threat to our existence.'

'And what would that be?'

'The Deviants.'

'Deviants?'

Evangeline looked flustered for a second. He had pushed her into admitting they were working on the mutation. That information wasn't in the public domain, something he was keen to change, but he had to be careful or she would shut him down completely and he'd get no more out of her.

'I already know about the mutation, Evangeline. I just needed to check. You understand.'

She gave him a terse nod.

'You're right, y'know,' he continued carefully. 'People have no idea what's coming. I've seen what the Deviants can do. People need to be warned. Perhaps they would rest a little easier if they understood what Phanes is working so hard to achieve. I'll keep your name out of it, if you'll answer some of my questions.'

Another terse nod.

'Can I come in?'

'Don't push your luck, son.'

Jack peered into the hallway. On a small table at the foot of the stairs were a telephone and a pile of papers, folders and assorted work paraphernalia. On top of the pile he could see Evangeline's ID badge for the office and the details of his plan began to form.

'What was Patrick Wilson's association with Phanes BioTech?' he said.

'He provided them with valuable information.'

'So he was a spy?'

She bristled at that and turned away, her eyes clouding. Jack braced himself for a door in his face. 'Sorry, Evangeline, but I'm just trying to-'

'Patrick did his duty. To protect his family. To protect me.' Her voice broke with emotion. 'I didn't understand that until it was too late, you see.'

Jack placed a hand on Evangeline's arm. 'Perhaps a cup of tea.'

'After he died I realised the danger we were in,' she continued, 'and that something needed to be done to stop them.'

'The Deviants?'

She nodded emphatically.

'But isn't your own daughter a Deviant?' he said lightly.

'How do you know that?'

'I was doing a story on homelessness and she was working at one of the shelters. She was helping people. She didn't seem dangerous to me.'

'That's because you don't know her, Jack.'

'I spent some time with her,' he continued. 'She seemed kind, caring. The mutation changes how the ego works-'

'Get out.'

'But-'

Evangeline placed a hand on his chest and pushed, propelling him off the doorstep and onto the path. 'How dare you. She put you up to this.'

'No. Really, she didn't. She tried to talk me out of it.'

'If I see you again I will call ARK,' she said, and slammed the door.

Jack stood on the path for a stunned moment, then walked back to the pavement and ducked behind the hedge. What had Ana done to turn her mother against her so vehemently? Evangeline Wilson seemed to connect the death of her husband with her daughter. To Jack, the idea sounded preposterous.

While he brooded upon the implications, he wandered up the track that led behind the houses. He flicked on the torch, careful not to shine it on any windows, and searched for another way in. He had to get Evangeline's ID pass. Without it, his plan wouldn't work.

A high wall enclosed the small gardens behind the row of houses. Since Evangeline's house was at the end it would have been simple enough to climb over the wall, except for one thing. Short rusty spikes and barbed wire were fixed along the top making access impossible. The other houses were less security conscious. He would have to climb in from next door.

Now would be the perfect moment for a power cut he mused as he scaled the wall. He dropped silently into the garden, but not quietly enough. A square headed brown pit bull exploded from the patio, growling and spitting at him like it was trying to win a contest for Most Angry Dog. Jack crouched and slunk back into the darkness. He stayed low, keeping his head down and his eyes lowered. The dog was on a chain so it couldn't reach him, but the noise would attract unwanted attention.

Sure enough, a light went on in the kitchen, followed by a blinding halogen on the patio. The entire garden burst into daylight. Jack pressed himself into the foliage at the base of the wall and held his breath. A man's face appeared in the kitchen window. He was holding a cricket bat.

The dog was going ballistic. Jack closed his eyes and willed the infernal beast to be quiet. He chastised himself for not thinking to bring a juicy steak or treats laced with strychnine or something equally nasty. Where was *his* guardian angel when he needed it?

Maybe it was magic, an answer to a prayer, or a lucky coincidence, but at that moment the dog whimpered and stopped barking. Jack opened his eyes. The man in the kitchen glowered and shook his cricket bat. Before the lights went out, Jack saw him mouth the words: damn cats.

Jack waited a moment and watched the pit bull closely. The dog rolled onto its side and fell asleep. It wouldn't stay that way for long. He bolted from the shrubbery and threw himself over the wall in one fluid movement. He landed in Evangeline's garden to the sound of more frenzied barking behind him. He would have to leave by the front door, whether he liked it or not.

He put the torch in his pocket and waited by the wall to watch for movement within the house. If necessary, he would wait until Evangeline went to bed. He checked his watch and sighed. Seven o'clock. It could be a long night.

In due course, a light went on behind a small frosted window above the back door. Jack guessed this was the bathroom. He watched as the window slowly steamed up. Evangeline was in the bath. This was the best opportunity he would have unless he wanted to be stuck out here half the night. He went to the back door and pulled out his lock picks. Two seconds of careful fiddling and he was in.

Jack eased the door open a fraction and slipped through the gap, closing it silently behind him. He stood for a moment, listening to the house. A squeak came from upstairs, the sound of Evangeline's body moving against the ceramic tub. He switched on the torch and moved through the kitchen to the hallway. He located the table with the telephone.

The pile of papers and the ID badge were gone.

He wheeled around. The door to the living room was open. He stepped through and shone the torch around the furniture. Sofa and armchairs, an empty coffee table, shelves stuffed with books. A noise upstairs made him startle.

She was draining the bath.

Jack's heart rate tripled and he fought to keep the torch steady. At the far end of the room was the dining table. A single empty plate had been pushed to one side and papers were spread over the table. Evangeline had been working over dinner. He crossed to the table.

Upstairs, the bathroom door opened.

He couldn't see the ID badge. Where had she put it? He ran the torch over the rest of the room. A dresser stood against the wall. On it was Evangeline's handbag and the pass.

He snatched it up and shoved it in his pocket. He was about to switch off the torch when something caught his eye on the table. In amongst the papers were sketches of Ana, sheet after sheet depicting her in various scenarios. In one, she was surrounded by hundreds of colourful butterflies, hair splayed out around her head like a halo.

Jack was stunned. Evangeline may have turned against her daughter, but these pictures showed something more: she was obsessed. One of the drawings was particularly vivid: Ana was standing in a devastated landscape with golden eyes, and a huge round belly. He stared at it, transfixed, until a noise above his head nearly made him drop the torch. Evangeline was moving around upstairs. He pocketed the drawing, switched off the torch, and moved silently to the front door through the darkness.

A creak on the landing upstairs made him freeze. He turned, expecting to see Evangeline coming down the stairs, but there was no one. A shift in the light against the wall told him she had returned to the bedroom. He continued to the front door and slipped through.

Once outside, he waited on the doorstep and kept his head low in case she looked out of the window upstairs. He didn't want her to see him walking down the path. When he heard footsteps on the other side of the door he bolted for the street. He didn't allow himself to relax until he was back in the Astra.

The plan was insane, he knew it was, but it was the only one he had. Jack pulled up outside the cottage. The rain had stopped but the sea was still exploding over the rocks. He tasted the salt in the spray as he let himself in. Laughter drifted from the living room. He found Ana and Beatrice sitting side by side on one of the sofas laughing so hard they were crying.

'Bea, Bea,' said Ana, between cackles. 'Tell Jack about the time you tried to teach that man how to make electricity and he nearly burnt his house down.'

Jack stood in front of the fireplace and watched the pair of them hooting and giggling like lunatics. He pulled Evangeline's ID badge from his pocket and dangled it in front of Ana like he was trying to hypnotise her.

Beatrice stopped laughing abruptly and got up. 'I'll leave you two be,' she said, heading for the window.

Ana wiped the tears from her cheeks and beamed at Jack like she was drunk. He wasn't in the mood for this. He frowned and waited for her to calm down. Slowly, a corresponding frown spread over her face and she gazed at him in confusion.

'Why have you got twigs in your hair?'

Jack checked his hair and removed a piece of hedge. A giggle formed in his belly, slowly rising until it popped and he began to laugh. He sat beside Ana and they chuckled together over nothing for a few minutes, until Ana stopped and reached for the plastic badge in his hand.

'You did it,' she said.

He nodded, still smiling. 'Can you make yourself look like your mother?'

Ana began to laugh again and Jack joined in. Outside, a pigeon watched from the window sill, a tiny smile forming in its soul.

15

Ethne stamped her feet against the freezing concrete of the runway. They called it a runway, but it was just a strip of land cleared of snow and ice at Constable Point, not far from Ittoqqortoormitt. High-powered floodlights picked out the rust coloured hangars and a row of yellow diggers parked outside. Jorgen had offered to fly her to Iceland. He needed to collect some supplies and it provided a perfect opportunity for her to begin the long trek back to the UK. She had a Key Stone to find.

The dinky Cessna Caravan taxied out of the hangar and trundled into the middle of the runway. This would be her second trip in a private jet in as many days; she didn't want to get used to it. A flash of blue light startled her, and Lucy appeared by her side.

'Last chance to fly the angel highway,' she said.

Ethne smiled and tried to look grateful for the offer, but deep down she was still adjusting to the idea of angels even existing, never mind allowing them to zap her from one location to another like some sort of personal teleportation service. The very thought of it made her brain fizz with vertigo.

'I really need to get some sleep, Lucy.'

'See you back in Blighty, then.'

'You could come with me. Give me a chance to pick your brains.'

Lucy shook her head. 'Passports are a problem. Technically, I don't exist.'

'Right,' said Ethne, like that made any kind of sense. 'You know you're going to have to explain all this at some point. I'm not going to let you get away with, as Jorgen puts it, weaving and ducking.'

Lucy grinned. 'I know. See you.' And she was gone.

Ethne tried to sleep on the flight back but the stones and their mysterious writing wouldn't let her rest. By the time she arrived at Heathrow she had covered several sheets of paper with symbols, trying out different combinations, looking for patterns. There was no way she could decipher this language without the key. She had to find that missing stone.

Lucy said she had already found it, but Ethne couldn't remember so that wasn't much use. Standing stones had been the bane of her childhood. While her friends were drinking cider and passing out in the town square, she had been charging about the countryside mapping stone circles. If the angel was correct, there was only one man who could help. Her father. She didn't want to go home, but she didn't have a choice.

Ethne finally slept on the train back to Newcastle and nearly missed her stop. An old gentleman in a tweed jacket prodded her with his umbrella, muttering darkly about people singing in their sleep. He jolted her from a dream in which she was a priestess wearing a long cloak of feathers. She was floating a massive piece of red granite across the choppy sea in a boat, while a tempest surged and swirled around her.

Thankfully her flat wasn't far from the station. She sleepwalked down to Grey Street and stumbled up the road to her front door. As she slid her key into the lock, she glanced down the road.

A sleek black car was turning into the street. A Lexus.

Ethne froze, her key still in the door, and waited. She watched over her shoulder as the car drove slowly past. The men were pretending to look for a parking spot, and as they drew level, she recognised them. The driver was the overgrown ape who had tried to crack her skull open with his stun gun.

The Lexus turned down the street beside the Theatre Royal and disappeared from view. Ethne breathed out in relief.

Was she a target now? ARK only followed Deviants, so perhaps there was another reason. She still didn't know who was responsible for the attack on the cave. Whoever it was would want the photographs and data on the computer in her bag, and on her phone. And in her head. She had to get away.

A flash of light made her jump and drop her keys. Lucy appeared beside the door, staring up the street at the retreating Lexus.

'Will you stop doing that?' said Ethne.

'Friends of yours?'

'Hardly,' said Ethne. 'Come in quick, before they decide to abduct me.'

'Not going to happen,' said Lucy casually. 'Not on my watch.'

Ethne led the angel up the endless stairs to her flat, perched at the top of the Georgian façade on the grandest sweep of buildings in Newcastle. Outside it appeared elegant, but inside it was dank and boxy. The windows didn't let in much light because they were covered with nets to stop the local kittiwakes shitting on the listed stonework. The alleyway at the rear told the true story of this neighbourhood: a warren of fire escapes, perpetually full wheelie bins, and a thriving lap dancing club. The stench of stale beer, vomit and sex had seeped into the concrete. Sometimes Ethne believed that every tramp who ever died in this city, did so right here, under her bedroom window.

The flat was sparsely furnished and what she had was falling to bits: one small and sagging sofa, a beanbag which tended to explode and spill its guts if you sat on it, a low table piled with history books, and a TV that wasn't even plugged in. The rest of her books were stacked against the walls since she had never got round to getting any shelves, and over the years her library had mushroomed. She suspected the books were breeding when she wasn't looking.

Lucy surveyed the living room in horror. 'Were you robbed?'

Ethne ignored her and ran from room to room, gathering up supplies. She had lived here for seven years and it had never felt like home. For a brief moment last year she had contemplated moving in with Will. She spent more time at his place than her own flat, and it had made sense at the time. But then he had asked the question that couldn't be unasked, and she had bolted.

Ethne caught sight of herself in the bathroom mirror and decided to have a shower and change her clothes. If ARK were after her, she might not get another chance for a while. When she emerged clean and steaming, with fresh kohl lines around her eyes, Lucy was peering through the mesh over one of the front windows. 'They could come up and get you but they're not moving. They must be awaiting orders.'

Ethne joined her at the window. The Lexus was parked opposite her front door. She finished packing, wrapped up her tent and stuffed some clothes into a rucksack. She grabbed her keys and picked up her spare helmet. Lucy was still at the window.

'Such a shame they're not capable of independent thought,' she said wistfully. 'But that's humans for you. Never make an effort to think unless it's absolutely necessary.'

'Thanks.'

'It wasn't a judgement. It was an observation.' Lucy beamed at her. 'And I wasn't talking about you. Are we leaving?'

'We'll have to go out the back,' said Ethne, 'and try to be as inconspicuous as possible.'

Lucy looked appalled, as if being inconspicuous was the worst thing imaginable. They left via the fire escape. Ethne lowered the steps, and then picked her way through the bins to the gate on the other side on the alleyway, holding her breath against the reek of death. Beyond the gate, she unlocked her garage space and rolled up the metal shutter.

Lucy gasped in admiration when she saw what stood inside. 'This is what you call being inconspicuous?'

Ethne gazed at the gleaming Harley Davidson, and grinned. Her heart was already racing with the joy of riding again. It had been too long. She pushed her rucksack and tent into the two leather saddlebags, pulled on her helmet, swung a leg over the seat, fired up the ignition and rolled out of the garage. She left the Softail idling while she locked up.

Lucy was still admiring the bike. 'It makes sense now. You live in squalor so you can afford this.'

'Shut up and put this on,' said Ethne, handing the spare helmet to Lucy.

Lucy looked at the gold open face helmet in her hands, a small frown on her beautiful face. She shook her head firmly and handed the helmet back. 'I don't need this.'

'You do if the traffic police say you do,' said Ethne. 'Besides, it's a classic.'

'But my hair,' said Lucy, patting her afro like a pet.

Ethne raised the helmet over the angel's head. 'Do I have to do it for you?'

Lucy snatched the helmet from Ethne's hands. She shoved it gracelessly over her hair, flattening the mass of frizz so it poked out the bottom like the stuffing coming out of a chair. 'Where are we going anyway?' she sulked.

Ethne got onto the bike, and Lucy climbed up behind her.

'To see a man about some stones,' said Ethne. 'But first, I need a decent breakfast.'

The Broken Cup was deserted. It was too late for the breakfast crowd and too early for lunch. Ethne leaned back in the orange plastic seat and swigged down the last of her coffee. Lucy was still eating. Ethne had never seen anyone devour so much in one sitting. She had started with the usual: eggs, bacon, toast. But then came the waffles and pancakes with maple syrup. Then more eggs. And chips.

Aside from Ethne and the voracious angel, there was one other customer. A desolate man sat by the window staring into the street nursing a mug of tea. The proprietress kept refilling his cup, but he was too preoccupied to notice.

'I thought angels didn't have to eat,' said Ethne, as Lucy crammed a handful of chips soaked in egg yolk into her mouth.

'You thought angels didn't exist,' said Lucy through a mouthful of potato.

While she ploughed through the entire menu, Lucy had been explaining angel lore and metaphysics. Ethne got the impression she was being patronised and was convinced the angel was dumbing it down. Then again, she doubted she would understand the truth if it unfurled itself before her eyes and did a dance.

She shrugged and continued her interrogation. 'So let me get this straight. You're a being of light and have no real form to speak of. But you can take any form you like in order to do a job.'

'Correct.'

'So you chose that hair.'

'Correct.'

Ethne watched for signs of an ironic twinkle and when none came realised, not for the first time, that she was out of her depth. She had never encountered such absolute sincerity. The only time Lucy avoided a direct answer was in relation to what she was. Now that Ethne was coming to terms with the fact of angels, she assumed their existence would be straightforward, but apparently it wasn't. Existence in general was a rather hazy subject. As Lucy seemed fond of saying: reality was not what she thought it was.

There were so many questions crowding her mind Ethne didn't know where to start, so she began with the obvious: 'Angels are usually shown as male or kind of androgynous hippies. All wings, halos and shapeless frocks. But that's obviously wrong. Do you ever take the form of a man?'

Lucy beamed. 'I'm so glad you asked.'

Ethne watched in fascination as Lucy's jaw strengthened, her eyebrow ridges lowered and her shoulders broadened. She (he?) still looked like Lucy, but a male version. He was rather magnificent. Beautiful and elegant, but strong and magisterial. Ethne wanted to run her fingers over his luminous skin and...

She blushed and stared furiously at her empty plate. 'Okay, that's enough. Go back.'

She risked a look but Lucy was still resplendent in her male form, beaming at Ethne with such a depth of affection it took every ounce of self-control not to lunge at him across the table and tear off his clothes.

'Please Lucy,' she said through gritted teeth. 'For the love of Thoth.'

In a flash, the old female Lucy was back, complete with ridiculous hair, grinning in triumph. 'And that, Ethne Godwin, is why I manifested as female for this task.'

'Very wise,' said Ethne, her heart still beating a little too fast for comfort. 'Out of curiosity, and I'm just asking, have you ever, y'know...with a human?'

Lucy exploded in joyous laughter. 'Y'know? My, my, Ethne, I didn't realise you were such an old maid.'

Ethne looked at her plate again. 'Yeah, well, I don't know. I didn't want to offend.'

Lucy patted her hand. 'That's impossible. And for the record: I don't have to eat. I don't *need* food, I just enjoy eating. Sex? Well, it's frowned upon, as it were. We have rules. We are not to fraternise with our charges, but it happens. On occasion.'

Ethne stared at the angel in disbelief and pushed the tumble of unspeakable but delicious thoughts she was having out of her mind. She had to focus.

'When you blasted the drone out of the sky, did you take your true form?'

'Correct.'

'Which is why you made me cover my eyes.'

'Correct.'

'But the dogs were fine. Surely a massive dose of electromagnetism would fry even the hardiest husky.'

'You ask a lot of questions,' said Lucy, mopping the last of the egg from her plate with a lone chip.

'Would you rather I accepted things on faith?'

Lucy grinned. 'I like you. I like the way your mind works.'

'Are you going to explain it?'

Lucy took a breath. 'Well. It's not just electromagnetism. That's how you would see it because that's how you're attuned, shall we say. The huskies have a different consciousness. To a husky, it's nothing. For you to see that light too soon and in too great a quantity could be dangerous. When you are ready, you will see.'

Ethne nodded. She didn't understand but knew it was the best explanation she was going to get. Now for the serious question.

'Was that the Fire Stone? In the cave.'

'Of course.'

'The one in the legends? Guarded by snakes in the dark on the Island of the Egg? In Rostau?'

'That's the one,' said Lucy, and swallowed her last chip.

'Rostau is the ancient name for Giza,' said Ethne. 'I don't know if you've checked a map recently, but that's in Egypt. What's the Fire Stone doing in Greenland?'

'Good question.'

'The Fire Stone contains the secrets of the Shining Ones,' said Ethne, thinking out loud. 'The Shining Ones were a bunch of shamans or priests at the end of the Ice Age, so what's the secret? Is that what the text explains? Do the stones carry instructions for using the Fire Stone, like a manual? Does it explain why it's in Greenland?'

Lucy gazed longingly at her empty plate and ran her finger across a smudge of egg, then licked it clean.

'Are you listening to me?' said Ethne.

'It's a prophecy.'

'What is?'

'Now who isn't listening?'

Ethne sighed. 'The text on the stones is a prophecy.'

'Correct.'

'Written by the Shining Ones?'

'Let me tell you a story,' said Lucy, shoving the plates to one side. 'The legend begins before time. It is a tale told many ways by many peoples, but for you, Ethne, I will give it to you straight. A great experiment was devised to discover the limits of life. It was dangerous and carried great risk, but there was no other way. So the Great Light fell into darkness. The light was brought into the darkness of matter through the process of evolution. This experiment was to be overseen by the Guardians of Light. They go by many names, but you know them as the Shining Ones.'

Ethne nodded eagerly. She pulled back the sleeve of her leather jacket to reveal her left wrist and pointed at her tattoo. 'The Akhu star of the Shining Ones, but that's just the Egyptian version. There's the Seven Sages in India, Viracocha in the Andes, Quetzalcoatl in Mexico, the Abgal in Sumer, the Tuatha De Danann in Ireland. It's like a universal obsession of the ancient world. They all claimed the roots of their civilisation came from gods or angels who taught them how to be civilised. Anunnaki, Nephilim, Watchers, Devas, Angels. And that was you, wasn't it?'

Lucy waived a dismissive hand. 'I merely provided assistance.'

'But if you're not one of the Guardians of Light, then who is?'

'Allow me to finish my tale, Ethne. There will be time enough for your questions later. During the Age of Ice a great cataclysm was foretold. The Guardians were to withdraw and their knowledge would be hidden. The prophecy was created. Seshat found a way to pass her wisdom to the one who would return at the time of the Great Awakening. The Prophecy and the Fire Stone were placed in a cave in the far west of Thule to protect them from the coming destruction. Fire filled the skies and the world slept.'

Lucy pierced Ethne with a look so intense she had to look away. The names Seshat and Thule were ringing so many bells inside her head she was having trouble thinking.

'Only Seshat's chosen scribe can find the Key Stone,' continued Lucy. She reached across the table to point at Ethne's ankh pendant. 'Only she can unlock the secret knowledge.'

Ethne placed her own fingers over the ankh at her throat. 'Seshat? She's the daughter of Thoth.'

Lucy smiled sadly. 'Alas, that is what many have come to believe. She has many names, of course. In the end, it is the wisdom that matters, not the name.'

'She came first, didn't she?' said Ethne. 'It was Seshat who invented writing and taught architecture and astronomy. Later, when the patriarchy took over, the moon god Thoth usurped her power. Seshat was demoted. Now people think she was Thoth's daughter or his wife, or both. But she started it. It was always her.'

Lucy nodded. 'It was foreseen. Civilisation came from the Goddess, Ethne. And now she is to return.'

'Is that what the Great Awakening is?'

Lucy smiled. 'You'll see.'

'And Thule? I thought that was northern Europe: Norway, Doggerland, now under the sea, and Scotland. So I guess Greenland was part of it too, making it the far west of Thule. What was the fire filling the sky? Was there another plasma event, a solar storm like we've just had?'

'Correct.'

'So, to summarise,' said Ethne. 'At the end of the Ice Age there was a destructive solar storm. To protect their culture and preserve it for the future, the guys in charge-'

'Priesthood,' interrupted Lucy, a twinkle in her eye.

'Priestess-hood, surely,' said Ethne, grinning. 'Anyway, they stow the prophecy and the Fire Stone somewhere they know it'll be safe, planning to return at the right time. Which is now. So we need to find out who this Seshat is, because it'll be her who needs to unlock the prophecy, right?'

Lucy chuckled softly.

'What?'

'Are you being deliberately obtuse? What is that hanging around your neck?'

Ethne touched her pendant again, the light slowly dawning. She stared at the angel in shock. 'But it can't be me. I'm not...one of them. I don't have the mutation. I'm not Deviant. I can't be one of the Shining Ones.'

'The Fire Stone activated your mutation,' said Lucy. 'That is what the Fire Stone does. The Fire Stone in turn can only be activated by the Prophet.'

Ethne felt dizzy. She remembered the fire entering her body while she stood before the obsidian lingam, and the world dissolving into light. She thought it was just a vision.

'But...me?' she said in a small voice.

Lucy smiled. 'You will remember soon.'

'You said I found the Key Stone already, but too early. Did I mess up?'

'No, no, that was not your doing. The stone is keen to be found. And besides, the timing is always a little off. You did write the prophecy twelve thousand years ago. You can't be expected to get every detail right.'

'*I* wrote the...' Ethne shook her head and ran her hands over her face. She suddenly felt unbearably old.

16

Robson shifted in his seat. He had been sitting in this damn car for what felt like his entire life. When the fleet of Lexus LC-EV coupes had first arrived, his crew had gone wild, tearing down empty motorways and burning through the tyres; breaking them in, they said. He wasn't too hard on them. He knew there was going to be a lot of waiting around and not a lot of action. Better to let them get it out of their systems. When he had first got the keys it had felt like he was piloting a spaceship, but even that got old. The most elegant and comfortable seat becomes unbearable if you sit in it long enough.

They were parked up the street from the Broken Cup. Nobody had been in or out in an hour. If he didn't have the BIR-D, he would be worried they would lose her again. The Biometric Identity Reader allowed them to track the Deviants as long as the target had a phone; switched on or off, it made no difference. Every crew had a portable BIR-D. If they encountered a subject, they could scan their biometrics into the system and in seconds the database would confirm their DNA status.

The database had flagged Ethne Godwin as soon as her passport had cleared customs. She had turned; the mutation was active. Robson had told them it was a glitch, made them double and triple check, but it was true. Somehow, between their encounter two days ago and her return to the UK, she had become Deviant. It wasn't possible, everybody knew that.

Outside her flat, they had secured the wiretap so now they could follow her wherever she went, even if she slipped out on them, as she had tried earlier. It took all the anxiety out of a shadow operation, and all of the fun.

Robson glanced at his partner sitting behind the wheel. It was a wonder the man fit in the car. Stan was over six feet tall and made of pure muscle. His love of tasering first and asking questions later had earned him the name Stunner, but behind his back they called him The Wall. He was ploughing through endless sausage rolls and salt and vinegar crisps, tossing the empty packets and spraying pastry crumbs over the seat until it looked like he was sitting at the epicentre of an explosion in a Greggs bakery. He belched softly and reached for another pasty.

'What is wrong with you?' said Robson.

Stan looked at him, a cold sausage roll rammed in his mouth, eyes framing a question.

'Don't you ever clean up after yourself?' said Robson.

'Um 'ungry,' said Stan, a spurt of pastry flying towards the windscreen.

Robson reached across and started scrunching the detritus into his hands, ready to throw it out the window. 'It's like working with a chimp.'

'Why can't we just go and have a proper lunch?' said Stan, nodding at the café. 'I could murder a fry-up.'

'Because she'll recognise us, knob-end.'

Stan grunted and continued to eat. Robson knew what the others called him behind his back. He had caught them at it once and had pretended to laugh with them, but he wasn't happy about it. Robson and Stunner were called Laurel and Hardy, with him being the fat one. He wasn't even overweight. Or that stupid. He hit the button to open his window and dropped Stan's mess into the gutter.

'When are you going to call HRH?' said Stan, brushing the crumbs from his shirt.

'Don't call him that.'

'He thinks he is,' said Stan. 'His Royal Haughtiness more like.'

'We need to ID the other woman first.'

Robson had never seen the woman with Ethne Godwin before, and he knew most of the Deviants in this region by sight. There was no way he would forget a hairdo like that.

There was movement inside the café. 'Look lively.'

Stan started the car and the door to the café opened.

Christian Gregori stood at the feet of the Angel and tilted his head back. The sun shone weakly behind the giant steel head giving the sculpture a golden corona and making him squint. He shielded his eyes and ran them along the length of the great wings, sticking out like the wings on a plane.

'Preposterous,' he said under his breath.

He circled the base of the statue one more time. He was waiting. He hated waiting. He pulled out his phone and checked the screen. They should have called by now. He tried to understand when people let him down but he needed the patience of an angel to deal with his latest collection of reprobates, hooligans and murderers. It would be so much easier if he could do things himself, at least that way he could control the outcome, but he had to work within these ridiculous constraints.

He had been forced to amputate one arm of his security team for severe dereliction of duty. They had lost Anastasia Wilson. She had vanished along with her bothersome boyfriend, the so-called journalist. It had taken them two hours to realise they were following an irate single mother with three petulant children, who had led them around the city centre buying cheap clothes and Pampers before she clocked them. She marched up to them in the middle of Eldon Square, aiming her pushchair at them like a missile, and demanded an explanation for their behaviour. They were shamed into retreating and were now suspended without pay and as far as Gregori was concerned they could go to hell.

So he had taken matters into his own hands. He was wandering aimlessly around this ridiculous piece of public art, called the Gateshead Flasher by the locals amusingly enough, because he was on his way to see Evangeline Wilson. If anyone knew where Ms Wilson had gone, it would be her mother. But first, he needed an update from Robson, and he was late.

Gregori checked his phone again. He wanted to see Evangeline in her own home because it was neutral territory, and she would be leaving for work soon. The conversation he was envisioning would run smoother if his subject were not distracted by the usual hustle and pantomime of the office environment. He needed absolute focus for his method to work.

He was about to leave the Angel of the North and abandon all hope of ever receiving this call, when his phone buzzed in his hand. He fought the desire to answer it immediately, instead taking a few more steps along the path back to the statue. He let it ring and made them wait.

'Robson,' he said finally. 'This is good news, I hope.'

'Good news and bad,' said Robson.

Gregori sighed and looked heavenward, the bulk of the Angel filling his vision. 'Just tell me.'

'No sign of Anastasia Wilson. Sorry, sir.'

'She must be found. She cannot be allowed to roam free now that the Fire Stone has been activated.'

'Fire Stone?'

'No concern of yours, Robson. It has been retrieved and will soon be deactivated, but in the meantime, we have a potential escalation on our hands. Ms Wilson must be brought in.'

'About that. I'm having trouble finding anyone willing to-'

'I am aware of your team's myriad failures,' interrupted Gregori. 'They are cowards to a man, are they not?'

'Yes, sir.'

'Well, then let us find a way in which we might repair the damage. You must do this job yourself, Robson. You will, of course, need more men. I will leave that in your capable hands. Ms Wilson is not to be harmed. Just remember, she is extremely dangerous. Do not underestimate her.'

'Will do. I mean, I won't,' spluttered Robson.

'And the good news?'

'We've located Ethne Godwin. She's turned, and she's with another woman, and we don't...I mean, we can't find out who she is. She's not on the database.'

'Can you describe this woman, Robson? Or perhaps one of you had the foresight to take a photograph?'

'Yes, yes I did,' said Robson, sounding absurdly happy with himself. 'I'll send it now, shall I?'

'If you would be so kind,' said Gregori.

He waited a second for his phone to beep, and then opened the image. A blurry shot filled the screen, but the form of the woman was unmistakable. He raised the phone to his ear, his hand shaking imperceptibly.

'Robson, listen to me very carefully,' he said. 'Follow Ms Godwin. Watch her, but keep your distance. She has protection. Do you understand?'

'Yes, sir.'

'She will be travelling and it shouldn't be too difficult for your team to keep up. However, if she gets close to the Key Stone, she will have to be sacrificed.'

'Right,' said Robson. 'Got it. Keep our distance but don't let her near this... What is it?'

'You'll know it when you see it.'

'Sir, can I clarify? By sacrificed, you mean?'

'She must not touch the Key Stone. Take all necessary measures.'

He hung up.

Now for Evangeline Wilson. Gregori crossed the dual carriageway, strode up the path to the front door and knocked briskly. Muted swearing drifted from the other side of the door, then it was flung open.

'What do *you* want?' said Evangeline.

'Good morning to you too,' said Gregori. 'May I come in?'

Evangeline Wilson was a raddled version of her daughter, her frizzy mass of blonde hair piled on top of her head like a haystack. They had been introduced, at his behest, when Evangeline joined Phanes BioTech three weeks ago. He had been curious: she was the mother of the most dangerous woman on the planet, but had turned out to be a disappointment. Evangeline Wilson was unremarkable in a way that, to his amusement, he found remarkable.

She glowered at him, clearly in no mood for a chat. 'I'm about to leave and I'm late as it is.'

'It won't take a moment.' With his immaculate hair and tailored suit, Gregori looked like the kind of expensive lawyer no mere individual could afford. He held her gaze and let his dominance work its intimidating magic, before hitting her with his coup de grace: his smile.

Evangeline blinked, dazzled by his brilliance. She fumbled with her jacket and blushed under her hurriedly applied makeup. Gregori knew his smile transformed him from Upmarket Lawyer to Nordic God, and he relished these moments of exquisite confusion. Carefully orchestrated disorientation was his stock-in-trade.

'Please, come in,' swooned Evangeline, pulling open the door. She led him to the living room, fussing with her hair all the way. 'I'm sorry I can't offer you a drink, Christian. It's been one of those mornings, I'm afraid.'

'That is quite all right, Evan. May I call you Evan? I've noticed your friends at work call you thus, and I would like to think we could be friends.'

She blushed an even deeper shade of vermillion, nodding like a hormonal schoolgirl. 'Of course, you can call me whatever you like.' She chuckled and was then suddenly mortified. 'Oh, Lord, I mean, I didn't...um...'

Gregori smiled. Not his blazing, compete with the sun smile, but a cold, shrivel your internal organs smile. Evangeline took a step back, a small frown gathering on her forehead.

'Perhaps we could sit down, Evan.'

It wasn't a suggestion. Evangeline sat on the edge of the sofa, her eyes anxiously scanning the lawyer's face. He remained standing and cast a weary glance around the room. The reality of his being there had finally sunk in, and she was getting worried. A visit from your employer's lawyer was an occasion for concern, and he allowed the tension in the room to build. He could feel the questions she wanted to ask fill the space between them, piling up and spilling over each other like rubbish in a landfill.

Finally, he turned his gaze upon his subject and gave her a smile laced with the merest whisper of charisma. Its stupefying effects must be carefully controlled. It did no good to binge on such a narcotic, and he needed her compos mentis.

'What-' she began, but he held up a hand to silence her.

'I need to speak with you about your daughter, Evan. It is most urgent.'

He was expecting her to be shocked, concerned for her daughter's well-being, or even just a little curious, but for the first time since they had met, Evangeline Wilson surprised him.

She grunted and stood. 'I have nothing to say.' She walked across to the dining area and began rifling through stacks of papers on the table.

Gregori was stunned. He watched her for a moment, unsure how to proceed. It wasn't a sensation with which he was familiar, and he didn't enjoy it. Perhaps he should be more direct. 'Where is Anastasia?'

Evangeline spun to face him, her cheeks flushed with frustration. 'I don't know where she is and I don't care. Now will you help me find my ID badge?'

Gregori approached the table. 'Where did you have it last?'

'There,' she said, pointing aggressively at the dresser. 'I've looked everywhere. I've looked in places I would never put the bloody thing. It's gone.'

The lawyer listlessly picked up a sheaf of paper from the table, making a play of helping. 'Are you sure you didn't leave it at work, Evan?'

'I'm not an idiot, Chris.'

Gregori took a deep breath. He hated it when they called him that. If Evangeline saw the look on his face she would wilt in a fit of terror. He turned away and pretended to search for her stupid work pass.

'I don't understand your attitude towards your daughter,' he said lightly. 'We know she is Deviant, of course, but-'

Gregori's heart stuttered and he stared in wonder at the vision before him. Laid out on the table were a series of colourful drawings of Anastasia, rendered expertly in pencil and watercolour. Evangeline Wilson had succeeded in surprising him for a second time. He picked one up to get a closer look, marvelling at the artistry. 'Did you-'

Evangeline snatched the picture from his hands and began to gather the others together. 'They are none of your concern.'

'No, no,' he said. 'Please. Let me see. They are exquisite.'

She froze and looked at him warily. He smiled, not too much, and allowed some warmth to light the space between them. Evangeline relaxed and handed over the drawings. 'They're just doodles, really.'

'Nonsense,' he said, looking them over one by one, his heart racing with exhilaration. 'You have a rare talent, Evangeline. These are remarkable, truly remarkable.'

She blushed. 'They're dreams. I mean, I have dreams and then I paint them.'

'Fascinating.'

'It's nothing,' she said. 'I mean, I've always drawn, y'know. Doodles, little pictures, this and that. But then, with the storm, I don't know what happened, really. These dreams...just sort of...'

Gregori nodded. 'You were inspired.' He placed a hand on her arm and looked directly into her eyes. 'Thank you, so much, for sharing these with me.'

Evangeline smiled shyly and looked away.

'I wish you had shown me earlier,' he continued. 'You have no idea how important these drawings may prove to be. And, I have to say, they underscore the importance of my finding your daughter, Evangeline. If you have any knowledge at all of her whereabouts, I would be forever grateful if you would consent to share it with me, humbled as I am before your rare and precious gifts.'

Evangeline gazed at him, perplexed by his abrupt change in attitude. Finally, she shrugged and removed the pictures from his hands and stuffed them into a folder.

'I don't know where she is. I'd tell you if I knew, believe me.'

'I do, I do,' said Gregori.

The lawyer sighed. He was rapidly running out of options. He watched as Evangeline finished gathering together her papers.

'I will vouch for you at work,' he said. 'And we'll arrange for a new pass. Do not concern yourself, Evangeline.'

She flashed him a quick smile and picked up her handbag. 'Actually, you're the second person to ask about Ana. There was a journalist here last night, fishing for information.' She froze and stared at Gregori like he was a ghost.

'What is it?' he said, his senses tingling.

'He took it.'

'Who?'

'The little bugger,' said Evangeline, marching towards the front door. 'He must've broken in and taken it. I knew I shouldn't have left it lying around.' She led the lawyer out of the house and turned to lock up.

'Who? Evangeline. Who took your ID?'

'Jack Dexter.'

Gregori stood on the doorstep and smiled. He need not have worried. Anastasia Wilson was about to walk back into his open arms.

17

The Phanes BioTech headquarters was a purpose built complex on the edge of Killingworth on the outskirts of Newcastle. Jack parked the Astra as close to the entrance as he dared. The car park was riddled with cameras and security guards patrolled the grounds in pairs.

He glanced at Ana sitting beside him hunched over the laptop. She had backcombed her hair and padded out her clothes until she looked more like her mother. Carefully applied makeup had completed the illusion of middle age. It worked from a distance, but close up she looked like a drag queen. Pointing that fact out over breakfast was a mistake he wouldn't be making again. She had had to start from scratch, once she had stopped crying and throwing the contents of her makeup bag at him.

'The trick is confidence,' said Jack, trying to sound upbeat. 'Walk in like you're meant to be there.'

Ana's fingers shook as she scrolled through the floor plan of the building. Jack had found it on the architect's online archive while she had been reapplying her warpaint, and now she was trying to memorise it. The plan seemed simple enough. She would walk in as Evangeline and find the location of the laboratory or anything else that would help them find Michael. Neither of them was happy with the plan, but it was the best they had.

Ana closed the laptop and looked at the entrance across the tarmac and close cut lawns. The glass and white brick office complex was arranged in a square around a central courtyard. But the visible building was the tip of a vast high-tech iceberg. A row of giant towers of liquid nitrogen stood down one side. These fed into the basement and lower floors of the building which were all underground and spread out beneath them. There were acres of cryogenic storage held in steel tanks: a library of blood, saliva, and urine, containing data on the entire population of the planet.

It wasn't just incubators of tissues samples and frozen vials of purified DNA that were stockpiled. The biobank was matched with surveillance data from CogNet and the Security Services. Phanes BioTech had everything. They didn't just know your eye colour and whether you were susceptible to heart disease or mental illness. They knew what you spent your money on and where, who your friends were, what you liked and what you fantasised about. Your plans, desires, hopes and dreams. Your fears and obsessions. Your weaknesses.

Phanes knew the identity of every Deviant. They had found the mutation and now they wanted to control it.

'Ready?' said Jack.

Ana nodded and placed her mother's ID badge around her neck. She watched the security patrol walk past the entrance and stroll down the path that would take them around the building.

'Let's go,' she said, and opened the door.

They walked towards the imposing entrance. Two white pillars supported a wall of glass from which hung the gleaming bronze company logo: Phanes, the Orphic god, suspended in flight. Ana gazed at the figure in awe.

Phanes was a sinewy golden winged hermaphrodite with a serpent coiled around his naked form. He was the first being to be born from the World Egg, a primeval god of creation, also known as the Shining One. An ancient hymn, quoted on the company website, described how Phanes scattered the darkness and brought light by spinning and whirring. He battled chaos and through this ancient dance, birds had been created.

A year ago, Ana would have dismissed this tale as mere mythology. But having met Beatrice, she wasn't so sure.

As they neared the entrance, Ana hung back. She glanced at Jack. He seemed calm and looked like he was enjoying himself. She took a deep breath and tried to empty her mind. She was about to walk into the headquarters of the organisation that was trying to abduct her and wasn't convinced her disguise would work for long. All she had to do was work out how to get past the biometric security. She may look like her mother, but her DNA was different. She didn't want to think about what would happen if they found a Deviant on the loose, running around inside their offices.

Jack swept through the automatic doors ahead of her and strode to the enormous front desk. The reception area was spacious with deep leather sofas and leafy plants arranged around the walls. Glass panels behind the reception desk revealed the inner courtyard where a fountain sprayed water into a pool surrounded by Japanese style gravel paths.

Ana calculated her options. She had to get into the offices on the floors above and to do that she needed access to the lifts. These were on the other side of the door to the right of the reception desk. A door with a rather large security guard standing directly in front of it.

The guard had his eyes on Jack, so Ana carefully moved towards the wall. She rummaged in her handbag, pretending to look for something, all the while inching closer to the door. She leaned against the wall behind a large potted palm and waited.

From there she could see the lock mechanism on the door: a fingerprint scanner, which also took a pinprick of blood, above a keypad and a handle. To gain access she needed her mother's blood and thumbprint, as well as a numerical code, which thanks to the website, she knew changed every day. She would have to wait until someone came through from the other side. Thankfully, Jack had this part of the plan covered.

He flashed his press pass at the ultra neat woman behind the reception desk and explained he was doing a story on genetic databases and wanted to speak to someone for a statement. The receptionist seemed reluctant to bite and pointed out, quite reasonably, that he could've achieved that with a phone call. Jack pulled out his phone and started taking photographs and making a lot of noise about allegations of misuse of data. The security guard at the door bristled, moved towards Jack and called for backup with his earpiece.

The door was now clear.

Ana slid along the wall and held her breath. She had to time this perfectly. Through the glass panel in the door she saw a man in a suit running towards reception. She pressed herself to the wall beside the door and waited.

The door flew open and the suited man burst through. As the door closed slowly behind him, Ana slipped through. She was in.

She walked purposely towards the lifts and scanned the list of department names displayed on the wall above the buttons. She had to decide who was most likely to know the whereabouts of the laboratory.

The obvious place to try would be the lower floors and basement where the genetic data was held, but the area was so vast she was worried if she ended up down there she may never find her way back out. Plus she doubted her mother's pass would grant her access to that department.

She pressed the button for the lifts and waited. The IT department might know, since they would be dealing with all the data coming from the lab. Or perhaps the Evolutionary Research department was a safer bet. They were on opposite sides of the building, so she decided to try the research offices first since they were closest, and stepped into the lift.

Her strategy was risky. All she had to do was wander around and listen to the chatter in people's heads. Sooner or later, someone would give something away and she would be able to dig for more details. If somebody blew her cover, she would have to run.

Just as the doors were closing, the besuited guard appeared and thrust his arm between the doors. Ana took a deep breath and smiled as he stepped in beside her, trying to remember to act like her mother. He acknowledged her with a nod and Ana sensed recognition in his eyes.

'Trouble?' she said, as casually as she could manage.

'Damn journalists,' he said gruffly. 'No offence, Evan.'

'None taken.'

The guard turned to look at Ana more closely. She smiled again, a little nervously this time. His ID badge had twisted itself round, so she couldn't see his name. Had he seen through the disguise already?

'Looking good, Evan,' he said. 'Have you lost weight?'

Ana turned away from his gaze and pretended to look embarrassed. How would her mother respond? She patted her hair and giggled softly. At the same time, she opened her mind and gently probed his, searching out his name.

'Now, now, Kevin. Less of that nonsense.'

Kevin chuckled and gave her a gentle shove.

The lift deposited them on the third floor and Kevin waved Ana out of the lift ahead of him. 'Where you off to, Evan?'

'Research.'

He looked surprised. 'I would've thought they'd want you in the main conference room.'

Ana rummaged desperately through Kevin's thoughts looking for clarification but it was no use. His mind was firmly fixed on Evangeline's breasts. He just wanted to keep her talking while he fantasised in the most graphic way. It was all Ana could do to stop herself gagging at the images pouring into her head. She shut off the connection and gave Kevin a steely look. 'Perhaps you should concentrate on doing your job and leave me to do mine.'

'Easy tiger,' he said, blocking her path. 'What's up?'

Ana took a deep breath. 'Nothing is up, Kevin. I'm just busy. So if you don't mind.'

She tried to walk around him but he kept moving to block her way. After a minute or so of this inelegant dance, Ana was ready to zap him with a burst of static electricity. She turned away and got a grip on her temper. If she lost it, she didn't know what would happen. Her powers became erratic if she didn't keep her mind focused. 'Please, Kevin. I'm sure you have more important things to be doing this morning.'

'I've always got time for a tango with my favourite lass.'

She wanted to scream. Who was this idiot? Did he always behave this way with her mother? Perhaps the images she had seen weren't fantasy, but reality. Sometimes it was hard to tell the difference.

Kevin smirked. 'But, since it's you.' He stepped to one side.

'Thank you.'

Ana walked towards the doors at the end of the hallway. To her horror, Kevin followed. He jumped in front of her to open the door and swiped his card through the electronic slot at the side. As she stepped through into the corridor beyond, Kevin tapped her lightly on the backside, a chuckle sounding deep in his throat.

Ana gritted her teeth. She had no idea what her mother's relationship was with this man and she had no desire to find out. He continued to dog her all the way to the Research department, prattling away about various work colleagues and their gossip-worthy activities. Ana listened and nodded, making what she hoped were appropriate noises and interjections at the right moments. They reached the door and Kevin leaned against it, blocking access to the entry system.

'What's wrong, Evan?' he said, looking worried.

Ana smiled and tried to stay calm. 'Nothing.'

'You seem, I don't know. Different.'

'I'm just tired, that's all.'

Kevin nodded. 'I heard you lost your pass.' He flicked the ID badge around Ana's neck with a finger. 'Where'd you find it?'

Ana's heart rate tripled. He must have realised something was wrong. She smiled again, but it felt forced. 'Hidden at the bottom of my bag. Silly of me.'

'A load of fuss over nothing.'

Ana nodded and shrugged. Kevin's eyes had gone cold and he was staring at her in the most disconcerting way. Her heart was doing somersaults.

'What happened?' he said flatly.

'I don't know what you mean,' she said. 'Kevin, I really need-'

'I should've known this would happen. It was too soon. I can see that now.'

Ana stared at him in disbelief. She allowed her mind to open again and received a flood of images: her mother laughing with Kevin in a bar, a drunken kiss in a taxi, and one night of frenzied passion.

Ana was stunned. Her stepfather had only been dead a month. She knew her mother had been thinking about having an affair, but so soon? Ana probed a little deeper and saw her mother turning away from Kevin, sadness in her eyes. She saw him calling her. Crying after the call ended.

'I'm sorry,' said Ana, placing a hand on Kevin's arm. 'I just need more time.'

Kevin nodded and looked at his shoes. He sniffed loudly.

'Will you wait for me?' said Ana.

He looked up, hope in his eyes. 'You said it would never work. What changed your mind?'

'Life's too short to be alone, Kev.'

He beamed and moved towards her. For a horrible moment, Ana thought he might try to kiss her. She took a step back and placed a hand against his chest. 'Not here.'

Kevin nodded, a blush running up his neck.

'Are you going to let me through this door,' said Ana, 'or do I have to call security?'

He chuckled and stood aside, then swiped his pass through the slot. Ana stepped into the office. Kevin was still standing in the doorway, gazing at her like she was the Mona Lisa. 'There's no reason why it couldn't work, Evan. I know you're better than me. You're smarter, more talented, your drawings are awesome, and you're a damn sight more bonny too-'

'Kevin-'

'Howay, Evan. I want to say it. You're too good for me. But I love you and if that's enough for you then, well...' He drifted off and looked at his shoes again.

Ana wanted to hug him, but also realised she had got her mother into enough trouble already. Kevin looked up sheepishly and she smiled at him.

'Later kidda,' he said and closed the door.

Ana breathed out in relief and turned to survey the office. The open plan space was lined with desks overflowing with computers and stacks of paperwork. A large oval meeting table surrounded by chairs overlooked the central courtyard, and several whiteboards were clustered against the back wall covered in hastily scrawled lists, arrows and diagrams. The one thing missing was people. She hadn't expected that. Perhaps they were in the conference room, as Kevin had suggested.

She picked up a folder from the nearest desk so she could look the part, and started pacing the office. She searched every surface, scanning for anything connected with the laboratory or the research being conducted there. She found a list of telephone extensions and ran a finger down the numbers, searching for the lab or Thomas Lethe, but they appeared to be internal numbers only. The white boards at the end of the office were no help and all the computers were switched off.

Ana turned on the spot feeling helpless. She needed minds to probe. Where was everyone?

She glanced down at the folder in her hands. It was marked with one word: Siddhis. Frowning in confusion, she flipped it open and skimmed the contents. It was filled with reports on the historical records of apparently supernatural powers demonstrated by spiritual masters, mainly from India and Tibet, some from South America. The word was Sanskrit and meant perfection or attainment. The siddhis listed in the folder included all the obvious powers like clairvoyance, clairaudience and telepathy, as well as stranger abilities like becoming smaller than the smallest particle, and even teleportation.

Ana knew there was nothing supernatural about any of these powers. It was simply a matter of knowing how to use your mind. Michael had been experimenting with some of these powers in his videos on *The Okeke Gospel*. Perhaps this was how he had developed such an advanced understanding of genetics: he shrank his consciousness down to the molecular level, which allowed him to see the DNA in action, so to speak.

She skimmed through the reports. There were accounts of miraculous healings, the bringing of rain or stopping of a deluge, and even the old Jesus trick of walking on water. Some of the stories sounded like urban myths; little old men putting one over on people who disrespected them.

There was an Indian yogi, bent double with age, who wanted to travel on a particular train. Unfortunately he couldn't pay and the stationmaster refused to let him on board. So the yogi sat on the platform and waited. When it was time for the train to leave, it wouldn't start. Engineers were called. They tried everything to get it going but nothing would work. Finally, somebody pointed out the yogi sitting serenely on the platform. Realising the cause of the problem, the stationmaster changed his mind and allowed the yogi to travel for free. At that moment, the train engine started and the yogi happily climbed aboard.

Ana chuckled and was about to close the folder when something caught her eye: a warning.

There were tales of yogis and shamans who had abused their power. Terrible things had happened as a result, and their powers had deserted them. The literature on this subject was filled with exhortations against using your powers, and when you did use them it must only be for good and never for yourself. There were dire consequences that could not be avoided.

Nature would always seek to bring life back into balance. If you saved a life or made rain or stopped a storm, ripples were sent out from that moment, changing everything in an unstoppable cascade. Bringing rain to one location meant shifting weather patterns around the globe. The tiniest change in one place could have devastating repercussions. Everything was interconnected, so every thought created a ripple, every action more so.

Ana shivered. The unease in her soul sent a wave of white-hot prickles across her scalp and shimmering down her spine, like she was standing in an ice cold shower. What events had she set in motion with her unthinking actions? It did no good to claim ignorance. The transgression stuck whether you meant it or not.

A shadow fell across the pages in her hands and she looked up. A woman was frowning at her.

Ana noted the name on the pass hanging around her neck, and then quickly scanned her mind. She saw the image of a cat but sensed sadness around it; perhaps it was ill or dying. The woman was becoming suspicious. Ana had to act fast. 'Hi, Yvonne. So sorry to hear about your cat.'

The woman's eyes filled with tears. 'Thanks, Evan. It was over quickly at least.'

Ana placed a hand on Yvonne's arm in sympathy. She pushed past the images of a cat spinning around the wheel of a truck, to search for details about the laboratory. 'Where is everyone?'

'Emergency meeting,' said Yvonne, her wariness returning. 'Shouldn't you be there?'

'I am,' said Ana, waving a hand distractedly. 'Just needed to grab some info. Having trouble finding it though. Don't suppose you know where the Michael Okeke stuff is? There was a computer and videos with all the crazy siddhis on them.'

'Is that the new guy helping out?'

Ana nodded and tried to stay calm. 'He's at the lab.'

Yvonne nodded and appeared to be thinking. Ana searched through the jumble of images and fragmented sentences circling Yvonne's mind. She knew nothing useful but was trying her best to help. 'You could try IT,' she said hopefully. 'Dave's the lead on the lab stuff. If there's a computer, he'll have it, but you know what he's like. Probably lost it under a mountain of Monster Munch and Jelly Babies by now.'

Ana rolled her eyes and sighed. 'Thanks Yvonne. Sorry again, about, y'know. If there's anything I can do.'

'Thanks Evan.' Yvonne wrapped Ana in tight hug and clung to her. Finally, she let go and stepped back, and gave her an appraising look. 'That diet's working. What's your secret?'

Ana shrugged and patted her hair. She turned towards the door, desperate to get away before Yvonne became too friendly. Behind her, Yvonne giggled. 'I know what it is. It's big and muscular and soppy and starts with the letter K.'

Ana opened the door and resisted the urge to flee. She turned and gave Yvonne a cheeky wink. 'Don't tell.'

Yvonne shrieked with glee and clapped her hands. 'I knew it.'

Ana slipped into the corridor and took a deep breath. She wasn't sure how much more of this she could take. The IT department was on the other side of the courtyard on the next floor down. She followed the hallway round to the stairwell and was about to head down the steps when she felt pulled in the opposite direction.

Behind her, a short corridor led off the main hallway and ended in wooden double-doors with a brass plaque that read: Conference Room One. As she approached, she sensed a large group of people gathered in the room beyond. This must be the emergency meeting.

She stood beside the doors and sent her mind into the room. There were at least a hundred people and it took a moment for the cacophony of voices to settle into something intelligible, as she sorted the spoken phrases from what people were thinking in the privacy of their minds. She listened for a while, hunting through the fragments, and gradually pieced together the details of the emergency.

Six stone megaliths covered in an ancient script had been found in Greenland. The script was awaiting translation, but in the meantime various staff members had been tasked with compiling all the relevant data on the legends of pre-history connected with the Shining Ones. An earnest man was explaining how these gods of antiquity were believed to be the bringers of civilisation.

So this was why ARK needed Ethne in Greenland. Did they have her locked away somewhere working on the translation of this script? Ana pressed herself to the door, desperate to hear all she could of Ethne's fate. Somebody must know what had happened to her. She probed the minds sitting in rows and found no thought of her friend. Nobody was thinking about the laboratory either.

A familiar mind signature made Ana jump in surprise. Her mother was sitting at the front of the room, typing ferociously into a laptop. Losing her ID badge hadn't stopped her coming to work.

Ana was about to move onto the next mind when a stray thought caught her attention. It was a flash of conversation between Evangeline and a tall, absurdly handsome man with immaculate blond hair. Her mother had many confused emotions surrounding this man. He was called Gregori and seemed important, like a spider at the centre of an elaborate web. Perhaps he was part of the management team. They were in a car and he was giving her a head start on some classified information and making her promise not to tell anyone else. Soon they would have to act, and act fast, and he needed her to be prepared.

Ana probed deeper to find the nugget Gregori had shared. A torrent of information poured from her mother's mind. It seemed to contain something Evangeline had been unable to process or accept because Ana couldn't make sense of it. Her mother had simply pushed much of it away and slammed it behind an internal door. The only detail she could see clearly was that the mutation was spreading, but Ana already knew that.

Something else had happened in the cave in Greenland that had unsettled Gregori, and it was connected with her. He saw Ana as the epicentre of a disease, which if left unchecked, would destroy humanity. Shaken by this revelation, she was about to break off the connection when a man's voice spoke directly into her mind.

'Hello Ana.'

She jumped back from the door in shock. Somebody knew she was here. Had her cover been blown? Did they have Deviants working for them? She had to get out, but she still hadn't found the location of the lab. She ran down the stairs, careened into the hallway and almost collided with the door into the IT department. This was her last chance to find Michael.

She swiped her mother's card through the entry system. Nothing happened. She tried again. Nothing. Her heart began to flip over itself as she realised her mother must have deactivated her ID badge as soon as she had lost it. How could she have been so stupid not to see that possibility? Now she was stuck on the wrong side of a locked door.

She stared at the electronic strip and wondered if she could knock and brazen her way in. The thought made her go weak at the knees, but then she realised it was only a magnetic strip. Maybe she could fool it with some electromagnetism of her own. She placed her hand over the device and concentrated, letting lines of magnetism run down her fingers as if they were a card in the machine. The lock clicked open.

Everyone ignored her as she entered. She made her way down the central aisle and scanned the desks, looking for the messiest. Sitting in the corner was a young man emptying a packet of crisps into his mouth. His desk was a riot of half-eaten snacks and sweets. An army of Jelly Babies were lined up along the top of his computer screen.

Ana approached. He glanced up as he dropped the empty crisp packet into the overflowing bin beside the desk.

'Hi Dave,' she said, smiling.

'You can't have one, so don't even ask.'

Ana fumbled in confusion and peered into his head for clarification. He was talking about his candy army. 'Don't worry, wouldn't dream of it. I just need the Okeke computer.'

'Why?'

'You know who wants it,' she said, hoping Dave would fill in the gaps for her.

'Gregori?'

She nodded and smiled apologetically. 'You know how he is.'

He grunted and continued to stare at her with indifference. 'He's an idiot.'

'Well, yes, but-'

'I don't have it,' said Dave. 'Gregori knows that.'

'Right,' said Ana, her mind skidding all over the place.

'Computer's at the lab,' he continued. 'Lethe needed it. I just uploaded the drive to the server. Like I always do.'

Ana pushed into Dave's mind, searching out the location of the lab, but it was no use. He didn't know. Clearly, Phanes BioTech kept their employees on a strict need to know diet of information.

'Why are you really here?' he said. 'Has he sent you to spy on me?'

'What? No. He probably just forgot. Too busy dealing with this Greenland thing.'

'What Greenland thing?'

'Never mind,' said Ana, heading back to the door. 'Thanks anyway.'

'Gregori doesn't forget,' shouted Dave, reaching for the telephone on his desk.

Ana left the office as quickly as she dared. Behind her, Dave had called security. She was still clutching the Siddhis folder from the research department and her luck had run out. A mass of voices echoed down the stairs. The conference room was emptying. She had to get out.

She ran down the rest of the stairs and hurried along the corridor, looking for the exit while trying to remember the floor plan. Where was she? The inner courtyard seemed to have vanished. Her stomach hollowed out in dread as she realised her mistake. She had descended too far. She was in the labyrinthine basement.

She ran through the warren of bare corridors, past lines of identical doors, each marked with meaningless numbers and letters. The hum of the harsh strip lighting buzzed overhead. She turned a corner and found herself back at the stairwell leading to the IT department. Upstairs, the sound of agitated voices and running grew louder.

She was trapped. The only other exit on this side of the building was accessed through the biobank. She ran past the stairs and round the corner, and turned into a short passage ending in double-doors. They were sealed behind the same entry system as reception: fingerprint scan, DNA sample and numerical keypad. There was no way she could fool this lock into opening with a little electromagnetic wizardry. She would have to use the stairs.

Ana returned to the corridor and sent her mind out ahead as an early warning system. She rounded the corner and stopped abruptly. Somebody else had entered the basement: a mind she recognised. The one person she did not want to run into.

Her mother.

Ana spun on the spot. She was cornered.

'I'm surprised you lasted this long,' said Evangeline, coldly.

Ana turned, and held the Siddhis folder to her chest like a shield. Evangeline looked her up and down, and then snorted. 'I suppose I should be flattered.'

'Mum, I'm sorry-'

'Save your breath, Ana.'

'I need your help.'

Evangeline glared at her with such ferocity it made Ana step back in shock.

'Do you really think breaking into my home, stealing my pass and then running around my workplace impersonating me is the right way to go about achieving that?'

Ana looked at the floor and shook her head. 'I'm sorry.'

'For someone who is supposed to be better than the average person, you do seem to spend an inordinate amount of time apologising for yourself, Anastasia. Can you explain that?'

Ana looked up. 'I'm not better than anyone. I never said I was.'

Evangeline snorted and turned away.

Ana started desperately towards her mother. 'They have Michael. They took him to the lab. They're going to kill him.'

Evangeline turned to face Ana, battling to hide her shock.

'Please, I have to find him,' continued Ana. 'Where's the lab?'

Evangeline shook her head slowly. 'They won't kill him. They're looking for a cure.'

'Is that what Gregori told you?'

Evangeline nodded. 'Michael's helping them. He volunteered.'

'I was there when they took him. He definitely didn't volunteer. And it's not an illness, you know that. The Homo Angelus are healthier, we don't need a cure.'

'Homo what?' said Evangeline. 'I do believe the power has gone to your head.'

'Mum, please-' Footsteps sounded on the stairs behind them. She was out of time.

Ana thrust the Siddhis folder at her mother, who took it without argument. 'Kevin loves you, by the way.'

Evangeline's mouth dropped open and for a moment her eyes softened. Ana felt a pang of compassion and wanted to embrace her mother, but two security guards had just rounded the corner. She turned and fled.

She skidded around the corner into the passageway leading to the biobank and raised her hands. A ball of kinetic energy formed between them. She focused on the entry system and released the energy.

The doors exploded open. An alarm pierced the air and a red light pulsed above the door as she ran through. One of the doors hung precariously from its hinges. She had used too much power. She made a mental note to be more careful next time and plunged into the room.

The space was vast and filled with bulbous steel tanks. Beyond these, on the other side of a metal fence, stood endless rows of computer servers. Lights blinked in sequence and wires trailed between the modules like noodles. At the far end was a fire exit.

Ana ran for the computers. A shot rang out. She ducked and ploughed on, and ran for the gate in the fence.

Behind her, security guards moved between the tanks with guns raised, their voices echoing around the cavernous space. 'Don't hit the cryo tanks!'

Ana collided with the fence as another shot pinged off the metal frame above her head. The six foot high wire mesh ran the length of the room. Ana yanked at the gate. It was locked.

She glanced over her shoulder and a gun appeared from behind a tank, searching for a target. The guards were closing in. She began to climb.

Another shot.

The air beside Ana's head fizzed as a bullet whipped past. She reached the top, flung herself over and jumped down to land on the other side. She scrambled behind a stack of humming servers and crouched to watch the men advance towards the fence. If she ran for the door, would they shoot her in the back? She decided they would, but she had to risk it.

A guard was unlocking the gate.

The exit was one hundred yards away. Calculating carefully, Ana built a force field of energy around her body. She closed her eyes and ran for the exit, and sent the force field out behind her. She didn't know if it would stop bullets, but it was the only chance she had.

She hit the bar on the fire door and careened into an enclosed stairwell. Before running up the steps, she glanced back. The security guards had vanished. None of them had made it past the fence. A ripple of fear ran through her. Had she used too much power again? Were they still alive?

She ran up the steps to another fire door and burst through into piercing daylight.

She turned on the spot to catch her bearings. The nitrogen towers were lined up along the wall beside her. She wheeled around and took off towards the car park.

Jack had already seen her explode from the fire door. The Astra screeched to a halt in front of Ana and the passenger door flew open. She dove in and Jack hit the accelerator.

'Holy shit, Ana. What did you do?'

Ana struggled to get her breath back, her body fizzing with adrenaline. She opened her mind backwards, like having eyes in the back of her head, to see if the guards were all right. She had to push all the way back into the biobank where the security team were picking themselves up off the floor. Her force field had knocked them down, but it wouldn't take them long to catch up.

Jack drove like a stunt driver. The car rumbled across a roundabout and powered into a housing estate in Killingworth.

Ana frowned as rows of boxy houses whizzed past. 'Where are we going?'

'They're following,' he said. 'Got to lose them.'

They drove in silence, the engine screaming in protest as Jack pushed the Astra to its limits.

'What happened?' said Ana, eventually. 'Did you find the lab?'

'No. They threw me out. You?'

'I ran into a problem.'

'I noticed.' Jack shot her a grin. 'What problem?'

'Somebody identified me.'

'Blew your cover?'

She shook her head. 'They didn't see me face to face. It was someone capable of reading my mind.'

18

Ethne eased the Harley through the Newcastle traffic, patiently waiting for a long stretch of clear road. Lucy was perched behind her, beaming at curious onlookers, waving at children and dogs, and generally drawing too much attention to herself.

The Softail purred happily as they hit the bypass and sailed past the airport into the Northumbrian countryside. Ethne's grin broadened as her speed increased. Her riding time had been cruelly curtailed in recent years thanks to a combination of spiralling fuel prices and rationing. There was nothing worse than having the ultimate freedom machine locked in a garage going arthritic from neglect. But then last week she had dreamt of empty roads and the blur of trees, and woke determined to make the dream real. Still in pyjamas, she had run through her maintenance routine, changing the oil and checking the tyres. She had even cleaned the battery connections.

The spruce and pine trees of Redesdale Forest morphed into a tunnel of emerald and asphalt as she powered through the Cheviot Hills and out of England. The last time Ethne had travelled down this road she was eighteen and heading in the opposite direction, vowing never to return. She slowed as they passed the hill fort that loomed over the clutch of houses by the river, and took the turning, her heart tight in her chest. The Jed Water shimmered in the morning sunshine as if welcoming her home.

The Georgian house was hidden from the road down a long drive, a red sandstone cube surrounded by trees. Ethne parked at the front door and cut the engine. She sat for a moment and listened to the silence, broken only by the river bubbling at the bottom of the garden.

As a child she would come out here to find peace when relentless screaming and door slamming had filled the house. With her feet dangling over the bank, she had given her worries to the water and asked the river to make it stop. But the day after her thirteenth birthday it had stopped, and she had found the silence and her father's slow implosion worse. All the drama left with her mother, packed into two bags with no forwarding address.

She got off the bike and gazed around the garden. Hidden in a corner near the trees was a mound of earth and rocks. A stone entrance carved with spirals made the burial chamber look ancient, but it was only twelve years old. Ethne sighed and looked up at the house.

A face peered from the downstairs window, and then vanished. The sharp ache in her heart intensified as the front door opened.

'Ethne?' said a cracked voice through a bedraggled beard.

'Hi Dad.'

Conor Godwin was an expert in megaliths, standing stones and Druidic culture. If there was a menhir he didn't know about, it didn't exist. After making absurd amounts of money in the City, he had retired to the Scottish Borders to pursue his Neolithic hobbyhorse, even renaming the family home Newgrange House, much to Ethne's chagrin. As obsessive about ancient British history as he was about derivatives and stock options, he spent so long buried in musty books that he often forgot to eat.

Ethne looked at the gaunt dishevelled figure standing on the front step. He had aged, his black hair now streaked with white. His piercing grey eyes were the same, but they seemed vacant, like he was being slowly erased from existence.

Ethne suddenly didn't know what to say or how to explain why she was there, so she stood on the gravel feeling helpless and idiotic. A sharp cough reminded her of the angel's presence.

'Oh, Lucy, sorry. This is my...Conor Godwin.'

Lucy bounced forward and took his hand. 'So you're the stone expert.' She lifted his hand to her mouth, flipped it over and kissed the inside of his wrist in one flowing movement.

Conor looked baffled. 'Friend of yours, Ethne?'

Ethne scuffed her boot along the bottom step. She wanted to push past this awkwardness and get down to business. Fortunately, she had the perfect way to bridge the chasm, opened by years of mutual neglect, on the laptop in her bag.

'Can I come in?' she said. 'I have something you need to see.'

Conor led them into the sitting room, and then disappeared to have words about tea with Irene, the housekeeper. Lucy curled herself into a ball in an armchair while Ethne gazed at the book-lined walls looming from all sides.

One of her recurring childhood nightmares had always ended the same way. She would be trying to reach something hidden on one of the top shelves, although it was never clear what. She had climbed, carefully placing her feet on the edges of the shelves as she heaved herself up. But then the room had started to shake and she fell. She had landed on the floor as the shelves gave way and buried her under an avalanche of books.

Conor shuffled back into the room and looked at her expectantly. She moved a small table in front of the sofa, then sat and opened the laptop. Conor hesitated. She could feel his eyes on her, no doubt taking in the ear and nose rings, and wandering what she had been up to in the years she had been absent from his life. His attention would be diverted soon enough.

Ethne opened a set of photographs showing the spiral of stones inside the cave. 'These were found recently in Greenland. They conform to the Golden Section.'

Conor sat and leaned towards the screen. He groped blindly for his glasses and put them on at a wonky angle.

'Alignments?'

'Don't know,' she shrugged. 'We didn't get that far. But it's unlikely to be aligned to any constellations and it's not a calendar. Nothing like Stonehenge or Avebury. This cave is deep inside a mountain. These stones have never seen daylight. At least, not since they were carved.'

'What are they? Granite?'

'Red granite for the menhirs. And then there's this.' She pulled up an image of the raised Fire Stone. 'Fire obsidian.'

'Remarkable,' said Conor. 'Both of these are volcanic, which gives them a positive, masculine polarity. I assume the surrounding stone of the cave is mainly sandstone and limestone, which gives a negative, feminine polarity. This is a classic temple design. Gothic cathedrals are based on the same principle, as are the pyramids at Giza in your beloved Egypt, Ethne.'

She nodded. 'The outer casing stones of the Great Pyramid are limestone or sandstone, but inside they used red granite. What's your point?'

147

'It creates a circuit, an electrical charge,' he said eagerly. 'The red granite contains high levels of quartz making it an excellent transmitter, like an old-fashioned crystal radio. The human body-'

'It has iron too,' she interrupted.

'Exactly. Your bones contain quartz as silica and your blood carries iron. The ancients chose these stones not just to reflect the human form, but to connect us to the cosmos, to transmit and receive information. It's an ancient communications technology.'

Ethne could feel a lecture coming on so quickly pulled up another set of photographs. These showed the mysterious writing on the smooth inner surfaces of the stones.

'This could be the earliest written language. If I can translate it.'

Conor looked at her, his eyes drilling into hers. A torrent of questions was about to tumble from his mouth. She had to get him onto the point of why she was here or this could take all day.

'I don't have time to discuss this in detail,' she said quickly. 'I need to pick your brains.'

'At least give me the dates,' he said, removing his glasses.

'Ten thousand BCE. Well, between eleven and nine thousand, but the end of the Ice Age. Same age as parts of the Gobekli Tepe temples in Turkey. The oldest known megaliths in the northern hemisphere, for sure.'

Conor gaped at the screen in amazement and Ethne suppressed a satisfied smile. She had made his day.

Behind him, the door eased open and Irene teetered through balancing a laden tea tray. She had become the family housekeeper a year before the abrupt departure of Mrs Godwin, and her name was often spat with fury in the arguments that had zipped about the house. Irene was the same age as Conor, but the idea of there being a secret tryst between them, Ethne found laughable. Her father was only interested in one thing and it wasn't women.

Irene squeezed past the sofa and Lucy jumped up to help, whisking the tray away as if it weighed no more than a feather. Irene looked a little put out, but soon brightened when Lucy asked if she had any cakes.

'You just had a massive breakfast,' said Ethne. 'Several breakfasts.'

Lucy shrugged. 'There's always room for cake.'

While the angel stuffed herself with Victoria sponge, Ethne took Conor through the essential details of the stones and their discovery. She showed him the map on the base of the second stone depicting the Key Stone.

'I need to find this stone,' she said. 'It's the only way I can translate the text. Perhaps it's like the Rosetta Stone. It might contain this language and another, possibly hieroglyphs. There are one or two Egyptian style hieroglyphs on the stones, and the Key Stone itself is shown as an ankh.'

Conor nodded and enlarged the photograph showing the map of the Key Stone. 'Where are you expecting to find this stone?'

Ethne decided it was too complicated to explain Lucy's claim that she had already found it. Better to keep it simple. 'It might be somewhere in Scotland,' she said, glancing at the angel who had jam smeared around her perfect mouth. 'Have you come across anything that might fit the bill?'

Conor leaned back on the sofa and closed his eyes. It looked like he was asleep or dead, but this was his way of accessing information from his own internal internet. While Ethne waited, she got up and paced the bookshelves. She ran her eyes over the spines and cast the occasional glance in his direction. He could do this for hours, and she resisted the urge to shake him. This ability to disappear into his own world had driven her insane with frustration as a child. In the end, she had learnt to ignore him, until sharing the same house had become impossible.

She hadn't meant to leave the way she did. As soon as her trust fund had been released into her control on her eighteenth birthday, she had bought the Softail and fled. She hadn't touched a penny of his money since, even when she desperately needed it. She was too proud, and too ashamed.

Perhaps wheeling the Harley inside the house had been a deliberate provocation. It had certainly got his attention. She had parked the Softail in the centre of the reception area directly under the crystal chandelier at the bottom of the stairs. The sun had moved behind the house and this was the only place she could get enough light to see what she was doing. Spread over the floor were sheets of old newspaper covered with engine parts and her tool kit.

She worked methodically through the parts, cleaning and returning them to the Twin Cam engine. She was almost finished when the door to the sitting room opened and her father appeared, frowning at her over his glasses.

She ignored him and picked up a rag to rub the chrome headlamp and remove a splodge of oil.

'What's all this?' he said.

'You said I could buy whatever I wanted.' She gazed hungrily at the gleaming bike. 'I wanted this.'

'So you thought you'd turn the house into a damn grease pit.'

'There's better light in here.'

'This is a Baroque reception room,' said Conor. 'Not Brands Hatch.'

'I was going to clean up.'

'No. You do it right this minute, young lady.'

'I have to finish putting-'

'Now!'

Ethne stood and glowered at her father. In his mind she was a perpetual thirteen year old, a motherless child requiring endless supervision and interference. He hated having to deal with her. Childcare was demeaning, a distraction, an irritant. He hated anything impinging on his precious solitude.

'Right. I'll go,' she said, flinging the rag to the floor. 'That's what you want, isn't it? That's how you prefer it.'

'No, that's not what-'

'That's why she left,' said Ethne. 'She probably thought you wouldn't even notice she was gone. And you didn't, did you? You just built that ridiculous fucking Neolithic bunker in the back garden and pranced around like you're fricking Gandalf. But I noticed, Dad. I noticed she was gone.'

'Ethne...'

She turned away and furiously suppressed the tears burning her eyes. Her mother had sent a postcard from New York six months after leaving them. There was no explanation, no apology. She had never asked for any money. Technically, her parents were still married, although that meant nothing and probably never had, as far as Ethne could tell. For years she had blamed herself. If she had been a better daughter maybe her mum would have stayed.

She had finished cleaning the motorcycle, channelling her rage into removing every last drop of dirt and oil, and the bike shone like a star. The next morning she had driven away from the house and vowed never to return.

Ethne sat on the sofa now and watched her father for signs that he might be ready to re-engage with the world. He stirred, opened his eyes and gazed out of the window, still deep in thought. Ethne couldn't take anymore.

'Well?' she said impatiently.

'There's one possibility,' he said slowly. 'There's nothing as you describe with several languages, but there is something else. You remember the legend of the Wandering Giant?'

She shook her head.

'There are many tales of stones that move,' said Conor. 'The diamond stone at Avebury, for instance, is said to cross the road at midnight. Countless others are said to flip themselves over either at midnight or when a cock crows. St Olan's Cap in County Cork is said to have healing properties and will teleport itself back if removed from its site. The whole country is awash with stones wandering about, dancing, or drinking from rivers.'

'What's special about the Wandering Giant, then?'

'It's not native. There have been sightings, or encounters, with the Wandering Giant, but nobody can pin it down. It's never been found in the same place twice. Some say it doesn't exist. There have been sightings from Orkney down to the Grampians.'

'That's one restless stone,' said Ethne. 'What did you mean, it's not native?'

'The legend says that a giant visited these isles from a far off land but was unable to return home. He got trapped here, turned into a stone by either the devil or a witch, depending on who is telling the story. He was condemned to roam the land, searching for his lost lover who will, one day, finally release him.'

'Sweet,' said Ethne. 'Why did people think it was from a far off land? Is it a type of stone not usually found here?'

'No. It's red granite, which is found in Scotland. That's not the issue. It's what they called it, Ethne. The far off land was Khemit, or the Land of Khem, and the stone was sometimes known as the Egyptian Giant.'

Ethne nodded. 'Khemit is ancient Egypt.'

Her father was looking at her with a curious intensity. There was obviously more to this story. She was sure this Wandering Giant was the stone she needed to find, but with a search area covering most of Scotland, it was an impossible task. She ran a hand through her hair and tried to think.

'Stones don't wander about,' she said. 'There must have been more sightings of this Egyptian Giant in one particular location. Where did the story first originate?'

'That's the peculiar thing,' said Conor. 'It seems to have started in Orkney and then spread south.' He stood and gave her another meaningful look. 'You don't remember, do you?'

'What?'

Lucy beamed at Ethne from the armchair. 'I told you.'

Conor rushed from the room. In a little while, he returned carrying an armful of photo albums and sat back on the sofa. He rifled through the pages then pulled two photographs from their slots, handing one to Ethne. It showed her sulking in a field with bad hair, shivering in the biting wind. To her left were the remains of a lightning blasted sycamore tree, and to her right towered a block of red granite which leaned slightly towards her.

'What am I looking at?' she said.

'That's you,' said Conor.

'I can see that. Are you saying this is the Wandering Giant?'

'We returned the following day. I wanted to take some more pictures, get some close ups of the stone and take some more measurements, but...' He placed the second photograph into Ethne's hands. 'It was gone.'

Ethne stared dumbly at the picture, her expression mirrored by her thirteen year old self in the photograph, pointing at the empty space in the field where the stone should have been. Behind her stood the dead sycamore, its blackened branches stark against the grey sky.

She shuffled the photos back and forth, then finally laid them side by side on the table beside the laptop. She remembered now. It was a week after her birthday and her father had insisted they go menhir hunting. She was angry and shaken by her mother's departure and in no mood to traipse around Scotland looking at old rocks; they barely spoke. But then they had stumbled across a mystery and it had changed them both.

That night, curled in her sleeping bag, she had begun to dream. The stone came for her and would not release her. Awake, she remembered nothing, but her dreams were lucid and filled with indecipherable scripts and floating stones.

Ethne touched a finger to the ankh pendant around her neck. The past was returning, joined to the future through the secrets she held in the darkness of her memories.

19

The silver Astra flew down the backstreets towards the city, following lines of abandoned houses and empty shops. Jack had been unable to lose the two cars tailing him, so had decided to lead them into a trap: the Newcastle one-way system. He floored the accelerator and raced down side streets and barricaded lanes, doubling back on himself and creating a tangled trail. By the time he entered the city centre he had lost one Lexus. Despite the traffic, it wouldn't take them long to catch up. He would have to ditch the car.

Jack checked the rear view mirror and saw the black glint of the Lexus several cars back. He stopped at the lights by St Nicholas Square and ran through his options. He would have to do this fast. If ARK saw him take the turn, he would be cornered.

He looked up at the wrecked Job Centre on his left. Every window had been smashed, and then the boards over the broken windows had been burned. Incredibly, the building was still in use; a line of desultory people snaked out of the door and up the street. Opposite the Job Centre was the Cathedral with its red and gold clock, and behind that, a hidden car park and their escape route.

Jack glanced at Ana in the passenger seat. 'Ready to run?'

She nodded, her attention riveted on the traffic lights in front of them.

Jack eased off the brakes. The lights turned orange. He shot past the Job Centre. Slalomed right, then left, and flew down the narrow back lane behind the church. As they careened around the corner, he checked the mirror. The Lexus was stranded at the lights. Stuck on red.

'Did you do that?' he said, pulling into the car park.

'What?' said Ana, the picture of innocence.

Jack grabbed his satchel from the back seat and jumped out of the car. Ana followed. He took her hand and they ran, plunging down the steps to Dean Street below.

'You switched the lights,' he said, as they hit the pavement. They hurtled down the steep hill towards the colossal stone arch of the railway bridge. Then dodged across the cobbles to enter the narrow passage of Dog Leap Stairs to climb the bank beside the bridge.

Breathing hard, Jack powered up the precipitous steps, pulling Ana behind him. Halfway up, she had to stop to catch her breath. Jack slipped his arm around her shoulders. 'I've never seen traffic lights change back to red so fast.'

'Don't Jack.'

'What?'

She shrugged his arm away. 'It makes me feel bad.'

'It hurts when you use your powers?'

She shook her head and continued to trot up the steps.

'What then?' he said, following.

'I feel guilty,' she said, looking embarrassed. 'It's like cheating.'

Jack laughed, and then stopped abruptly when he caught the look on her face. He cautiously replaced his arm around her shoulders and planted a kiss in her hair. 'Well, I think it's fantastic. You're a real life superhero. Only without a cape.'

'Now you're just being silly,' she said, but she was smiling again.

They emerged into the grounds of the Castle, its ruins carved in two by the railway bridge, the square turrets of the Keep just visible above the stone arches to their left. Jack considered making a dash for the road over the grassy banks and tumbled down walls of the ruin, but didn't want to run into ARK by mistake. So he took Ana's hand and led her over the wooden walkway into the renovated gatehouse and stopped at the entrance to scan the street.

He pulled Ana close and slid to the edge of the archway to peer through the winter branches of the cherry trees beside the road.

The traffic lights at the junction of St Nicholas Square were clear. There was no sign of the Lexus.

'How are we going to get back?' said Ana.

'We need to get to the station and get a train to Alnmouth and then it's a two hour hike. We'll have to leave the car.'

Ana considered for a moment. 'I could ask Beatrice to bring it back.'

'Do angels drive?'

'She probably wouldn't need to.'

Jack frowned. His head hurt to think about these things, so he pushed it to the back of his mind and concentrated on getting them home safely.

'Ready for more running, babes?'

Ana squeezed his hand in reply and they set off across the street to run along Westgate Road, following the direction of the traffic to the station. Jack spun his head to watch every car as it passed, until he felt dizzy and almost fell over his own feet.

'We're okay,' said Ana. 'Just run. I'll know if they're coming.'

They ran past piles of bin bags and rotting waste that littered the street, to arrive at the main road. The huge portico of the station entrance was further down the street, but Jack veered left into a tunnel and pulled Ana with him.

They climbed the ramp into a car park and threaded between rows of abandoned cars with broken windows and flat tyres, making for the gate into the station concourse.

The roof girders vaulted overhead like a giant triple ribcage. The train tracks curved away to the left, while on the right were shops and bars and the ticket office hidden behind a line of stone arches.

'Stay close,' said Jack, sweeping the concourse with his eyes.

The station was busy. Everywhere he looked, people hurried between the ticket machines and the turnstiles, or watched the destination boards. He scanned the faces, looking for anomalies, for people who didn't fit. Everything seemed routine.

'We need two sets of tickets,' he said. 'Normally, I'd say we split up, but I'm not letting you out of my sight.'

Ana put her arm around his waist. 'More false trails?'

He nodded. 'We'll get tickets going south at the machine using my card, then we'll have to risk going to the counter to pay cash for the Alnmouth tickets.'

'Or we could get them on the train.'

Jack turned to grin at Ana. 'See, that's why I love you.'

She kissed him lightly on the lips, then froze, her eyes fixed on something over his shoulder. 'They're here.'

'You see them?'

She nodded. 'One of the men who took Michael. He's on the phone, standing by the boards with his back to us. Big guy, like a cube with legs, cropped hair.'

Jack spun on the spot and found the man. 'Can you read his mind? What's he saying?'

'They've found the car,' said Ana. 'This man, Robson, he's the boss. He thought we might be heading out of the city so he came here. The others are on their way.'

'Damn it.'

Jack took Ana's hand and pulled her towards the shops beside the station entrance. 'Plan C.'

They ducked into the newsagent, running past stacks of magazines and sweets, and then out between the stone arches to the street. Traffic was heavy and slowed to a crawl.

A flash of gleaming black metal caught Jack's eye. A Lexus, stuck between a bus and several taxis. It wasn't going anywhere soon, but that wouldn't stop the men inside it.

Jack swerved through the cars and Ana followed. They ran up Pink Lane, dodged down an alleyway into another lane, weaving through the warren of narrow passages that crisscrossed the city centre.

'They're following,' shouted Ana, as they neared the next street.

Jack stopped at the end of the lane and surveyed the street from the corner. 'Which way, babes?'

Ana focused, sending her mind out into the surrounding area and found the men. 'They're running up the main road, coming this way. Robson thinks we're heading for the bus station.'

'I hate that guy,' said Jack.

'Are we heading for the bus station?'

'We *were*.'

'So what's Plan D?'

He nodded at the entrance to the shopping centre opposite. 'Lose them in Eldon Square then steal a car.' He glanced at Ana. She clearly wasn't happy with the plan, but they were running out of options. He took her hand and they ran across the street and through the open doors into the mall.

They pelted up the escalator and skidded into the main concourse. Jack spun on the spot to catch his bearings. Further down the mall, over the heads of the crowds, he saw two ARK Security guards coming their way.

Ana tugged on his hand, pulling him in the other direction. They zipped between the shoppers and wove their way to the multi-storey department store at the end of the mall.

The men followed, causing gasps of shock and screams as they shouldered through the crowds.

The man in front pulled a gun.

Jack ran into the store and scanned the shop floor. Ana stood beside him, growing more frantic by the second as she watched ARK approach. He took her hand. 'Trust me?'

She nodded. He waited until their pursuers entered the shop. He wanted to be sure he was seen heading down the escalator. When ARK were as close as he dared, he pushed his way down the escalator, squeezing past tutting shoppers.

At the bottom, Jack pulled Ana towards the lifts and hit the button to take them back up. While they waited for it to arrive, he dodged behind a rack of winter coats and Ana crouched beside him to watch the escalators.

Behind them, the lift doors opened.

The ARK security men arrived at the bottom of the escalator and scanned for their target. They saw the empty lift and took the next escalator down. As soon as their backs were turned, Jack dove into the lift and held the door for Ana.

They went back up to the mall and ran through the concourse, making for the fire exit at the back of the complex. Jack was about to hit the metal bar to take them into the stairwell, when he realised Ana wasn't with him.

He turned and frantically scanned the mall, and found her talking with a distressed middle-aged woman. Ana hugged the woman, then held onto her hands and looked deep into her eyes. On her face was a look of concentrated compassion. Jack knew that look. She was reading the woman's soul, divining the solution to her problems. They didn't have time for this.

He whistled high and loud, and Ana looked up. She frowned at him as if to say: not now. Jack glanced up the mall and scanned for signs of ARK. It wouldn't take the men long to realise their mistake. He had to get Ana out.

He marched across and took her arm. 'We need to go.'

'Christine needs my help, Jack. I can't just abandon her.'

He smiled coldly at Christine. 'Another time.' He pulled Ana towards the exit, but she twisted free of his grip.

'I need to do this,' she said. 'If I don't-'

'I'm sure she'll manage without you, babes.'

'No, Jack. It hurts me.'

'You said it didn't.'

'It hurts if I *don't* use my powers,' said Ana. 'If I block them or don't share them when they're needed, it's like my energy drains.'

'Well then, you can just be tired. Come on.'

Jack tried to take her arm, but she moved out of reach before he had even finished thinking about it. 'Don't start getting in my head, Ana. We don't have time for this.'

'I'm telling you. I *have* to do this. It's like a tsunami. The energy drain is just the start, like the tide going way, way out. Then the wave comes back and it's unstoppable. I have to keep letting it out, a little at a time, or it's too much for me. Do you see? Please.'

He gazed at her in confusion. 'But you can just let it out later.'

'It's too risky to wait.'

'It's too risky to stay here,' shouted Jack.

Ana stepped forward and gently placed her hand on his arm. 'We can take her to Heaven Scent. We can hide out there.'

'Are you crazy? That's the first place they'll look for you.'

Ana shook her head firmly. 'They'll assume I would never go there because it's obvious. So they won't go there. It's the last place they'll look. So that's where we'll go.'

'That's nuts.'

'Listen,' said Ana. 'You have to trust me. Robson is convinced we're trying to get out, so he won't expect us to sit tight. It hasn't even occurred to them to check where I work.'

Jack watched in disbelief as Ana led a gushing and grateful Christine down the stairwell and into the street. He followed like an obedient dog and decided he needed his head examined.

20

Ethne folded the map and slid it into the saddlebag on the Softail. It was now the middle of the afternoon and it wouldn't be long before the sun began to set. She was anxious to hit the road and begin her search, but her father had persuaded them to stay for lunch. Not that Lucy had needed much convincing.

While the angel had devoured soup and sandwiches, Conor had marked Ethne's map with little crosses to show the sightings of the Wandering Giant. There was a definite pattern, if looked at chronologically. The stone was dancing its way south. All she had to do was drive north and meet it halfway.

She zipped up her leather jacket and suppressed a smile. Lucy was wrestling with her helmet, trying to find a way to wear it without disturbing her plentiful hair.

The front door opened and Conor appeared with several Tupperware boxes balanced in a tower in his hands.

'Food for the journey,' he said as he crossed the gravel drive. 'Can't have my little girl going hungry.'

Ethne took the boxes with a grateful smile. 'Less of the little.'

Conor looked mortified. 'Sorry. I didn't mean...forgive me, Ethne.'

She laughed and shook her head, and squeezed the boxes into the second saddlebag. 'Very thoughtful of you, thanks Dad.'

He rubbed his head sheepishly. 'Actually, it was Irene's idea.'

Ethne smiled, full of surprise at herself. Something deep inside was changing. Where was her righteous anger? The rage that had fuelled her adolescence seemed to have evaporated. 'Doesn't matter,' she shrugged.

Conor smiled and looked a decade younger than when she had arrived. 'Don't stay away so long next time.'

Ethne went to her father and opened her arms. They embraced and the years fell away, the river burbling happily beyond the trees. Lucy watched, her smile irradiating the air with warmth.

Ethne was about to step away when a shard of light pierced her mind and opened her head like a sardine can. Into the gap poured images, emotions, thoughts. Unbidden and overwhelming, they filled her mind with heartrending revelations of the truth of her father's soul. She saw his heartbreak at the loss of his wife, and then again at the loss of his daughter. His joy at her return. His love for Irene.

Ethne pulled back. Her heart burned as if an unseen force had opened her chest, poured petrol into the cavity and set it alight. She felt arms around her shoulders and heard the soft murmur of an angelic voice in her ears, soothing and calming. Slowly the fire subsided and she could breathe again.

'That's going to take some practice,' said Lucy, kindly.

Ethne took a couple of long, deep breaths. Conor was watching her, stricken with worry. She wanted to go to him, reassure him, but feared one more touch would blow her head off and burn her heart away for good. She had just experienced what Ana and Michael must go through every day simply walking down the street. Her *Homo angelus* gene was kicking in.

'I'm okay,' she said, but her voice was shaking. 'I will be okay, won't I?'

Lucy nodded and ran a tender hand over Ethne's hair. 'You appear to be a Touch Empath. Your friends are different. I'll talk you through how to control it.'

'Thanks, Lucy.'

'You can't drive like that,' said Conor. 'Stay the night, please.'

Ethne gathered her strength; she had wasted too much time already. She picked up her helmet. 'I'm fine. Driving will help.'

'I'll look after her, Conor,' said Lucy with a smile.

Ethne sat on the bike and fired up the engine. Lucy clambered aboard and gave Ethne's shoulder a squeeze.

'Before I go, Dad, promise me one thing?'

Conor nodded.

'Tell her.'

He looked confused and opened his mouth to speak, but Ethne cut him off. 'Irene.'

He blushed and scratched at his beard. 'I will. Take care.'

'Will do,' said Ethne. 'Oh, and if anyone from ARK turns up looking for me, you never saw me, I was never here, and you know nothing, okay?'

He nodded. 'Good luck.'

'You too,' she winked, and turned the bike towards the drive. As she drove away, she saw her father running after her in the mirrors, waving frantically and shouting her name. She stopped and waited for him to catch up and get his breath back.

'I just remembered,' he said, panting. 'It might be nothing, but I just thought with all the strange goings on. Looks like old Pemberton finally sold up.'

'Who?'

'Queer bird, used to own Jedhirst Castle, liked shooting things. Last time I was up that way, I noticed something peculiar. There were guards patrolling the grounds and I think I saw the name ARK. You saying it just now jogged my memory. They were armed, Ethne. Like they were expecting a war.'

She nodded. 'We'll check it out. Thanks.'

'Be careful.'

She waved goodbye and watched him get smaller in the mirror until she turned the corner and he was gone.

Jedhirst Castle was on their way into Scotland. It would be easy to drive past and see what was happening, if anything. The castle stood in its own woodland on the banks of the Jed Water, a mile and a half from Jedburgh. The fortalice was built at the dawn of the Renaissance, and since falling into the hands of Pemberton-Smythe-Burns in the 1990s had styled itself as a hub for all things Scottish. He had hired it out for banquets, ceilidh, and bagpipe lessons, and Ethne could remember sulking her way through several falconry displays in her teens. She had wanted to have a go at the archery.

Ethne drove into the valley towards the river, the engine purring happily beneath her like a metal lion. As they approached the castle, all she could see from the road were trees and the odd turret. To get a closer look, she would have to drive round and cross the river.

She took the turn and eased down the lane to the castle grounds, passing a handful of cottages, before arriving at the driveway.

The grounds were surrounded by a four foot high stone wall with access via an open gate. It looked deserted. She turned off the engine and dismounted; Lucy followed.

Ethne scanned the grounds. All the visitor signs had been taken down. She wandered over to the squat cottage that used to be the visitor centre and peered through the window. It had been gutted. All the displays and history lessons were gone, leaving a battered table and scuffed floorboards.

She stood on the gravel driveway and stared up at the windows of the castle. It was a curious building. From the front it looked like an imposing fortress complete with pointed turrets, but at the back she remembered a thatched cottage that clung to the thick stone walls like an overfed baby.

There were no armed security guards, no cars, no signs of any activity whatsoever.

'Why don't you try doing your thing?' said Lucy.

'What thing?'

'See inside. It doesn't just work on people, y'know.'

'By touching the stone?'

Lucy nodded eagerly. Ethne hesitated, reluctant to open her mind to whatever memories these stones may be harbouring. Wars had been fought on this soil. People had died here. She didn't know if she could handle seeing that. She walked across to the castle wall and placed one hand on the stone. She closed her eyes and waited and ran her fingers over the rough, pitted surface.

Nothing happened.

She took a step back and gazed up at the line of windows staring blankly back at her. 'It's not working. There's nothing here.'

'You're blocking it,' said Lucy. 'Try again and don't be scared. You can handle it. You're a tough old thing. Just remember: you control what you see by directing your attention.'

'What happened to my free will, angel?'

'Stop making excuses, Ethne. Just do it.'

Ethne returned to the wall in bad grace and put both hands against the stone. She breathed deeply and let the sensations prickling her fingers amplify and fill her mind. Images started to form, faint echoes. Someone was in there, she could feel them moving around, but it was too diffuse. She stepped back.

'I need to get closer. You wait with the bike.'

She left Lucy on the driveway and wandered towards the archway. The entrance was around the back. There were doors on this side of the castle, but they were boarded up and looked like they hadn't been used in years. Most of the human traffic seemed to come this way, if her fingers were telling the truth.

She walked slowly through the archway, running her hand along the stone as she passed. The sensations were growing in strength and fully formed images began to pour into her mind: A white van pulled up, its brakes screeching. A bundle carried down the steps. A body bag. It's heavy and the men almost dropped it. They shouted at one another and the back of the van was flung open.

'What do you want?'

Ethne looked up with a start. A security guard was staring at her with evident hostility, the ARK insignia on his black uniform. He was holding an assault rifle, and although it wasn't pointed at her, Ethne didn't need to read his mind to know he was thinking about doing so.

She smiled and tried to stay calm, but her heart was hammering against her ribs. 'Just admiring the stonework. This place used to be open to the public. What happened?'

The guard began walking towards her, forcing her to walk backwards through the archway. He definitely didn't want her there.

'It closed,' he said. 'Now it's a holiday home for a wealthy property developer who doesn't appreciate trespassers.'

'Oh?' said Ethne, eyeing the monstrous gun. 'What's the name of this property developer?'

The guard stared blankly at her for a second, then blurted. 'Fred.'

'Fred who?' her voice wavered.

'Frederick...You ask too many questions.' He fingered the trigger on his rifle.

Ethne raised her hands and backed off towards the gate where Lucy was standing, hands on her hips and a small frown gathering on her forehead.

'I'm going, okay?' said Ethne. 'Sorry I ruined your day.'

The guard watched her leave, and was still standing there, gun at the ready, when she powered up the Softail and scrambled down the lane, the castle retreating in her mirrors.

21

Jack pressed himself against the wall beside the window in Heaven Scent and craned his neck to look into the street below. A couple strolled the pavement, stopping to check the menu in the window of a restaurant and reading lists of ailments displayed outside the Chinese herbalists and acupuncturists. There was no sign of ARK.

Soft music and the tinkling of wind chimes drifted through from the treatment room on the other side of the reception area. He was anxious to get back to the safety of the cottage, but Ana had said she needed at least an hour to deal with Christine's emotional crisis, maybe longer. He looked at the damp patch spreading from the corner above his head and sighed. They could be stuck here for hours.

He crossed the room looking for a distraction. An indoor water fountain sat on the low table between the desk and the threadbare sofa. A dolphin teetered absurdly atop a pile of precariously balanced stones surrounded by a pool of water. He hit the switch on the base. Nothing happened. He crouched to get a closer look and tried the switch again, toggling it back and forth.

Finally, he picked it up, carefully lifting the base to peer beneath. Perhaps he could fix it while he waited. A curious sight greeted him. Taped to the underside of the fountain was a DVD in a clear plastic envelope. He yanked at the tape to release the disk, and then plonked the fountain back onto the small table. Water began to pour from the hole in the top of the dolphin's head and cascade into the pool below. Jack ignored it, his attention on the DVD in his hand. He flipped it over, searching for a label.

It was blank. Why was a DVD hidden under the fountain in Heaven Scent? Did Ana know it was there?

Jack retrieved his laptop from his bag. While waiting for it to boot, he plugged it in to give it a charge, since you never knew when the power would go off these days. He sat at the desk, and with one eye on the door to the treatment room, loaded the disc.

It contained one file with no name. He opened it and hit play.

It started with blurred shots of snow and a man talking on a mobile phone. A date stamp in the corner said it was 21:37 on Christmas Eve, and the high angle told Jack he was looking at CCTV footage. He could hear the murmur of the man's voice and a low hiss.

Glancing again at the door, Jack reached for his satchel. He grabbed his earphones, quickly plugged them in and cranked up the sound.

The man circled around beneath the camera in a highly agitated state. He was asking someone for a favour but the conversation wasn't going well. 'Please, mate,' he said. 'Just back me up. You only have to do it if she asks.'

Jack marvelled at the piles of snow lining the alleyway and heaped over the wheelie bins. So much had happened since Christmas that he had forgotten about the weeks of icy weather. He had thought it would never end.

The man's face came into view and Jack recognised him. It was Patrick Wilson, Ana's stepfather. He had died on Christmas Eve. According to the official autopsy report, he had suffered a catastrophic heart attack after being struck by lightning. It must have happened shortly after this video had been shot. Was that why Ana had kept it? But then why was it hidden under the fountain?

Jack paused the video and zoomed in on one of the bins to read the logo: a smiling man holding a hoe and the letters GWF: Feeding the Nation. Patrick was outside one of the Government Work Farms. Jack zoomed back out and hit play.

Fat flakes of snow drifted in slow motion, hypnotic and relentless. Patrick continued to plead, and then abruptly turned and lowered the phone. Into the shot walked Ana and her mother, arm in arm.

Evangeline shouted at Patrick, 'You lied to me.'

'A white lie,' said Patrick.

'Where did you get the money?' she said.

'Does it matter?'

A fizzing ball of light shot across the screen so fast that Jack wasn't sure where it had come from. It hovered in front of Patrick's face and he inched away from it, terrified. Ana stepped forward and the light closed in on Patrick forcing him to walk backwards until he was pinned against a wheelie bin, the light hanging between his eyes.

'You know you can't lie to me,' said Ana. 'Tell her.'

'Please...' said Patrick, his hands raised and shaking. He stared at the light burning inches from his face, too scared to speak.

'He got it from Phanes,' said Ana, and the light vanished. 'He's been spying on me.'

Evangeline stalked towards her husband. 'Is this true?'

Patrick nodded and Evangeline lunged at him, battering her fists against his chest. He grabbed her wrists, yanking them apart, but she wriggled free. Patrick stepped clear of his wife. It looked like he was thinking of making a run for it, but she pushed him. He stumbled, and then slapped Evangeline hard across the face sending her spinning.

Jack turned his attention to Ana. She stood motionless, watching her parents fight. The snow evaporated above her head as if she was encased in a force field that slowly expanded until the snow hardly touched her at all. Lights sparked from her fingers and her hair fanned out around her head, glowing gold against the snow. Her attention was riveted on Patrick.

He took Evangeline in his arms and hugged her close, but she resisted. He clamped his hands either side of her face and lowered his mouth to kiss her forehead.

Slowly, he slid his hands down to her throat.

The curtain of snow thickened momentarily and came down harder.

Jack leaned towards the screen. He couldn't see clearly, the snow obscured his vision. Was he choking her?

Suddenly, Ana moved. She stepped forward and raised her hands. Patrick's hands were still at Evangeline's throat. He turned to face Ana and froze when he saw the look on her face.

A force field erupted from Ana's palms and ripped through the air. The snow fizzed and swirled in its wake.

It slammed into Patrick and lifted him from his feet.

The screen went black.

Jack stared at his own horrified reflection in the laptop. He was paralysed, numb. Ana had killed her stepfather. The truth of it ran around inside his mind like a demented streaker. He had underestimated her.

Finally, Evangeline's attitude towards Ana made sense. She was terrified of her own daughter.

A noise from the treatment room made him jump. The music had stopped. She was coming out. Jack ripped out his earphones, slammed the laptop shut and leaned back in the chair, pulling his face into what he hoped was a calm, relaxed and normal looking shape.

The door opened and a beaming Christine emerged, babbling happily to Ana who followed her into the reception area. Jack's heart flipped over itself. He didn't know how to act. He was terrified to even think. What if she read his mind? He tried to push everything he had just seen out of his head. Should he turn her in? Should he run? Would she kill him if she found out that he knew?

'What's the matter?'

Jack looked up. Ana was staring at him, a small frown on her forehead. Christine had gone. They were alone.

'Nothing's the matter. Just charging the laptop.'

'Should we try to leave now?'

He managed to nod and slowly stood, amazed he still had command of his legs. He wobbled to the window and gave a cursory glance up and down the street. It seemed clear. He turned to find Ana watching him.

'You look pale,' she said, kindly. 'Are you hungry? We didn't get lunch, did we?'

Jack thought he would throw up if he tried to eat something. 'I'm fine. Let's get out of here.' He unplugged the laptop and stowed it in his bag. He was about to lean down and switch off the dolphin fountain when Ana beat him to it.

'Why is this on?' She hit the switch and pulled the plug from the wall.

Jack shouldered his bag and turned to the door. Ana was still watching him closely. He mustn't think. He filled his head with images of their earlier encounter with ARK and hoped she kept her promise not to pry. But how could he trust her now? How could he be sure she hadn't already seen everything he carried around inside his head, every dark, twisted little secret.

'You really don't look well, Jack.'

He tried to smile. 'Perhaps I am hungry.' His voice shook. He had to get himself under control. If she suspected anything she would kill him. She could just stand there and do it. No weapons, no guns, no knives, no fists. Just whatever it was she had inside her.

Jack imagined a steel door crashing down between them, sealing Ana out. It sucked the air from his lungs and pushed her beyond reach. He could never touch her again. He had to cut her off. He had no choice, even if it felt like his heart had been ripped from his chest.

Ana led him from Heaven Scent and locked the door while he waited in the street. He scanned for signs of ambush, but his heart wasn't in it. Perhaps he should let ARK take her. She would then be their problem, not his. There was only one problem with that scenario. He had a job to do and he couldn't do it without her.

They walked down Stowell Street, aiming to cut through the back lane at Blackfriars. It was the middle of the afternoon and the office workers in the surrounding buildings were safely trapped behind their desks for another couple of hours so the place was deserted. When two ARK Security men appeared in the street ahead of them, standing side by side in the middle of the road like gunslingers in a bad movie, Jack almost laughed.

Ana grabbed his hand and pulled him towards the oriental arch bridging the opposite end of the street.

A black Lexus skidded across and blocked the street beneath the arch. Two more men got out and stood, guns in their hands, red and gold dragons dancing over their heads.

Jack spun on the spot. They were cornered. The men behind them were advancing. There was nowhere left to run.

He dropped his bag into the gutter, and then moved close to Ana. She gazed at him, desperate and afraid, and his heart melted. How could he abandon her now?

The four ARK security men closed in.

'Time to come with us, Ms Wilson.'

Ana kept her eyes on Jack. He was standing abnormally still and there was a look on his face she didn't recognise. He gazed at her with such intensity she thought he might burst into flames.

'I'm sorry,' he said.

Why was he apologising? It was her fault ARK had found them.

She recognised Robson and Stan, the huge man who had knocked Ethne out and taken Michael. Stan stepped forward and dropped his hand heavily onto her shoulder.

She didn't think. There was no calculation, no knowledge of what she was about to do. It simply happened.

His hand shot back as if repelled by a violent force, and sent him sprawling into the road.

When Stan hit the ground, Jack exploded into action. He cracked his left elbow into one stunned face. Spun and smashed a fist into the next. The air erupted with fists and feet crunching against spines, jaws and noses.

Ana backed away from the mayhem in shock. She had never seen Jack move so fast or with such brutal ferocity. He anticipated every move, every punch, as if playing a game of violent and bloody chess. She watched, mesmerised, as he destroyed two of the men, leaving them battered and unconscious on the ground.

Only Robson and Stan remained. Jack barrelled into Robson, knocking the gun from his hand. Meanwhile, Stan scrambled to his feet and approached Ana. He inched towards her like she was a wild animal liable to savage him at any moment.

Ana watched in amazement as the force field around her crackled and fizzed. Stan lunged and grabbed her arm, but then recoiled as if he had been stung. He stumbled back and fell over his own feet.

Ana knew he wasn't going to give up. She had witnessed his brutality towards her friends. He was an unthinking thug in a uniform and he wouldn't stop until he had done his job. She raised her hands. Lines of light forked through the air, sparking against the asphalt in tiny explosions.

Stan stood and pulled his taser from its holster. He aimed it at her chest, his hands shaking.

'Back off,' said Ana, moving away from him.

But he kept coming, his hands growing steadier.

'Please,' said Ana. 'I don't want to hurt you.'

He barked out a joyless laugh.

She could feel the energy building in her hands. She knew she couldn't control it. Her mind was already clouded with too much fear. She glanced at Jack, hoping for help. He was locked in a savage embrace, fists flying, his nose ruptured, one eye closed and bloody. She took another step backwards. If she blasted this man now, she would kill him.

'Jack!' she shouted desperately.

He fought on, oblivious. She was on her own. Stan kept coming and she kept walking backwards until she felt the Lexus behind her. She was stuck, pinned against the car beneath the arch. She kept her hands raised. Great arcs of light danced between her palms.

Stan's eyes opened wide in awe and fear. The taser began to shake.

'Back off!' she shouted. 'Please.'

His finger tightened on the trigger. 'Time for some of your own medicine.'

It happened too fast. There was a moment, a terrible pause when Ana knew what to do, but her hands would not obey. The force field gathered itself and rose within her. She felt it surging down her arms. But she couldn't act.

A shot rang out.

Stan fell to his knees then slumped to the ground. Jack stood behind him, a gun in his hand, pointed at her, Robson unconscious in the road at his feet.

Ana stared at him, sickened and confused. Blood poured from his nose and one eye was swollen shut. He stood firm, the gun aimed at her like she was the enemy. She kept her hands raised. Light danced between her fingers, cascading and spilling out into the air around her.

'Stand down!' shouted Jack.

Ana couldn't move. What was he doing?

He opened his mind, and lowered the steel door he had placed between them. She saw it all. The truth about who he was and what he had to do.

'Stand down,' he said gently.

Ana lowered her hands, and the light and power discharged harmlessly into the ground at her feet. She searched his eyes, trying to understand, but found herself confronting a stranger. He wasn't even called Jack.

He was a government agent. His Majesty's Secret Intelligence Service was using her to gather information on ARK and the mutation. His name was Joshua King and their entire relationship was a lie.

'I'm sorry,' he said. 'It wasn't meant to happen like this.'

There was a tiny pop, like a miniature bottle of wine being uncorked, and the flutter of wings intruded into the space between them.

Joshua ducked as a pigeon dive-bombed his head and made him drop the gun. A flash of blue light and Beatrice stood between them, hands on her hips. She did not look pleased. She fixed Ana with a soul-shrivelling glare. 'I told you to stay hidden.'

Ana looked at her feet and mumbled an apology.

'Look at this mess,' continued the angel, pacing back and forth between them.

Joshua opened his mouth to speak but stopped when Beatrice turned her glare on him.

'I could heal your face but I won't,' she said. 'It'll do you good to walk around looking like that for a few weeks. And you.' She turned back to Ana.

'I can't just leave Michael-'

'Silence.'

Ana lowered her eyes. 'Tell me what to do.'

Beatrice placed a hand on Ana's shoulder and gently lifted her face to gaze into her eyes. She smiled and smoothed a hand over Ana's hair. 'You are too precious. Please understand. I am not angry with you. I am tasked with your protection, but my goodness, you don't make it easy.'

Ana smiled. 'Sorry.'

Beatrice clapped her hands once. 'Right. You will go to Linnunrata. At least there we can keep an eye on you. Take Joshua with you.'

'But-'

'It is as it should be,' said Beatrice.

Ana eyed the interloper with suspicion. She wanted nothing more to do with him. She certainly didn't want to go all the way to Linnunrata with him, wherever that was. Beatrice paced up and down between them, deep in thought. Finally she stopped, and looked at them each in turn.

'I could take you the quick way,' she said. 'But I won't. Go here.'

She flicked her fingers at Joshua and his phone pinged. He retrieved it and peered at the screen. 'Finland?'

Ana's heart sank. Beatrice had explained how the angels could move people from place to place. It wasn't an easy mode of travel for humans, but she would rather be teleported, despite the dizziness and the headache. The thought of spending hours stuck on a plane with Joshua, whoever he was, filled her with dread, but Beatrice was adamant.

'You have things you need to discuss,' she said.
And with that, she vanished.

22

Michael wandered the benches in the laboratory and watched the professor across the room. Thomas was preparing for the next stage in their experiment and was busy doing something technical with a circular booth that looked like an old diving bell. Michael rubbed absently at the puncture wound on his arm and gazed at all the equipment. There were desktop freeze dryers, automated pipetting machines, thermocyclers and DNA microarrays. He stopped at the huge real-time PCR System. He didn't even know what a PCR System was, but it looked impressive and he was desperate to start pressing buttons to figure out how it worked, but Thomas caught him and warned him off.

'Right,' he said, opening the hatch into the diving bell. 'In you pop.'

Michael climbed inside and sat on the stool. The booth was hermetically sealed against light and contained a photomultiplier that counted biophotons, the light emitted by DNA. If the vaccine worked he should be emitting less coherent light. In the lab, the vaccine appeared to switch off the *Homo angelus* gene. It was time to find out if it worked in real life.

Thomas closed the hatch and sealed Michael into darkness. A small speaker in the wall behind Michael's head crackled and the professor's voice came through, tinny and bright.

'Okay, Michael. Just relax. Try to hold still. It won't hurt. Switching on in five, four, three, two...'

Half an hour later, Michael emerged from the dark canister and stepped back into the lab.

Thomas sat at the computer and stared intently at the lines of numbers scrolling down the screen as the system processed the data. Michael could tell it wasn't going well. He could've told Thomas the vaccine hadn't worked yesterday. He could feel it. He didn't need a machine to tell him what was going on inside him.

'It hasn't worked, has it?' he said.

Thomas leaned back in his chair and rubbed his eyes. 'There must be something in the person either switching the gene back on after the vaccine has switched it off, or preventing the vaccine from working in the first place.'

Michael sat in a swivel chair and rolled himself across the floor to join the professor at the computer. They had watched his film together and Michael had done his best to explain the details, but it was like they were talking different languages.

'Let's try again,' he said patiently. 'Talk me through it once more.'

Thomas sat up straight. 'All right. From the beginning, so there's no confusion.'

Michael nodded. 'Explain it like I'm a kid.'

Thomas looked at him sharply and Michael distinctly heard him think, 'You are a kid.' The professor grunted and turned to the computer. He opened a new window and filled the screen with gyrating images of DNA molecules.

'Our DNA is made up of coding sections and non-coding sections,' began Thomas. 'They're jumbled up, but the coding sections build proteins, the basic building blocks of all living things. When it was first discovered, we thought the coding sections would make up the vast majority of our DNA, but we were wrong.'

'These coding segments are A, C, G, and T, right?' said Michael.

'Correct,' said Thomas. 'Those are the four chemical bases: adenine, cytosine, guanine, and thymine. They pair up to form an incredibly stable structure: the famous double helix.' He tapped the screen and the image zoomed in. 'All of life shares the same DNA. Humans are 99 percent the same as chimps, 97 percent the same as mice, and 50 percent the same as cabbage. What makes a species unique are the non-coding segments. These used to be called junk, basically because we didn't know what it did. But in humans the so-called junk DNA makes up to 98 percent of the total.'

'That's a lot of junk,' said Michael.

'It is,' said Thomas. 'Your genes, the coding segments that build the proteins, are dotted around here and there, surrounded by a vast sea of non-coding, seemingly random stuff. The interesting thing is that the more complex an organism is, the more non-coding DNA they have. Humans, being the most complex organism, have the most junk.'

'So the mutation was found in the non-coding DNA?' said Michael.

'In the alu transposons,' nodded Thomas. 'That's where we find big differences between us and chimps, for example. The DNA is transposed, or moved around within the genome, and this changes its behaviour. Which is what can produce a speciation event: the emergence of a whole new species.'

'But this isn't really a new species, is it?'

'Not exactly. It appears to be an epigenetic change, meaning the mutation changes the way the genome is expressed. You're still human, Michael, but the mutation seems to be rewiring and supercharging your DNA. It's making it work more efficiently and making the photon emissions from your DNA so much more coherent than normal.'

'Photons being light,' said Michael.

'Correct, although technically we're talking here about biophotons.'

'So how many people have the mutation?'

'At this point, it's about two percent of the population,' said Thomas. 'But the potential for this new gene is there in everyone, hidden in the retro-transposons.'

'The *Homo angelus* gene has always been there?'

Thomas nodded. 'It would seem so. This change is latent in everyone. If I can understand what caused the mutation to activate in one individual but not in another, I can control it. How did you know your gene had activated, Michael?'

'I used to need glasses. Couldn't read stuff right under my nose. Then I had a dream and woke up feeling kind of new, like something had shifted inside. It's hard to explain. Like my mind was a closed fist before, but now it's open. There's more space. In here.' He tapped his head.

'What was the dream?'

'I woke, in the dream, to find the room full of flies. I got up and battled through them. It was horrible. There were hundreds of them, all flying about, filling the air. I reached the window and opened the curtain, and it was only then that I saw they weren't flies. They were butterflies. I opened the window and they flew away.'

'When was this exactly?'

'During the blackouts,' said Michael. 'Near the end of June. Over the next few days I began to notice I didn't need my glasses anymore. The world was suddenly in focus.'

Thomas nodded eagerly. 'I've seen cases of spontaneous cures for diabetes, heart disease, even cancer. Think what we could achieve if I can isolate the health benefits of this gene.'

'You don't need to,' said Michael. 'That's what I've been saying.'

'Listen to me. The mutation cannot spread. We've been over this. The mutation makes it impossible for someone with it to breed with someone who doesn't have it. As far as I can tell, people who have the mutation can breed with each other, but with such small numbers affected, I can't see it spreading far. That's why I must find a way to control the mutation.'

'What d'you think triggered it in the first place?'

'The solar storm. The gamma rays in the solar flares-'

'Correlation doesn't equal cause, professor.'

'Don't lecture me on the scientific method,' said Thomas testily.

'Okay, but think about it. Is there a pattern to who has the new gene? Are we seeing more Homo Angelus at certain latitudes?'

'No,' Thomas frowned. 'Fair point. What's curious about this mutation is its uniformity. We're seeing it across the world, even in places least affected by the plasma storms. That's how I knew it was dormant in everyone.'

'Others have switched this gene on in the past,' said Michael. 'The likes of Siddhartha Gautama and Yeshua. Or Buddha and Jesus, to you. They didn't need to wait for a solar storm.'

'That's a leap, Michael. We don't have access to their DNA. It's pure conjecture.'

'Fair enough.'

'So what did trigger the mutation?' said Thomas. 'Since you're the fount of all knowledge.'

'The solar storm was like a cosmic alarm clock,' said Michael. 'The gene was dormant, like a sleeper cell waiting to be activated. The alarm goes off and wakes some of us up. The gene is triggered and those woken by the alarm are transformed from *Homo sapiens* to *Homo angelus*. It's the same method used down the centuries by all those spiritual masters and yogis and shamans and crazy alchemists.'

'What method?'

'It's in the light.'

'The gamma rays-'

'No,' interrupted Michael. 'Not the electromagnetic spectrum. There's more to light than what we can see or measure. It's nonlocal, quantum. The information that triggered this mutation is encoded in the light and is directed by consciousness. *We* are making this happen, professor, using our own minds. How else d'you explain how you discovered the mutation in the first place?'

Phanes had billions of genomes on file; every chromosome, every letter had been mapped using the world's most powerful quantum computer. After the storms, the system had flagged a change in a small percentage of samples. At first they thought it was a computer malfunction, a virus, or even a hack. They ran and re-ran all the protocols, and found nothing amiss. They retook samples and ran the programmes again. The mutation was confirmed.

Somehow, the DNA in the frozen blood samples had changed. When the individual's *Homo angelus* gene switched on their body, it also switched on in the blood samples. This was true even if the person was on the other side of the world. It was a nonlocal effect, a holographic connection between the parts and the whole.

'You have to understand this,' continued Michael. 'The key to this mutation is in our consciousness. That's why your stupid experiment isn't working. You will never control the mutation like this. How many more people will Gregori have you kill to protect ARK? You have to stop.'

Thomas sighed. 'I can't just take your word for this. You understand that, don't you?'

'Call HQ,' said Michael. 'Ask them to check the database. Run the protocols again. Ask them if there have been any spontaneous changes.'

'That's not poss-'

Michael held up a hand. 'Just do it, Thomas. Ask them if any more people have turned Homo Angelus.'

Thomas shrugged. They could only say no.

23

Scotland's mountains and lochs swallowed the buzzing motorcycle like it was fly. Ethne drove steadily, her eyes scanning the landscape, her heart captivated by a fresh revelation of beauty every time she turned a corner. She stuck to the byways and tracks and avoided built-up areas in the belief that the Wandering Giant would do the same. The stone was waiting to be found by one particular person: herself. She drove north, cruising forests and valleys, but taking the high roads as often as possible. From the tops she could see further, the world laid out at her feet.

Lucy whispered encouragement as they drove and marked the map every time they stopped. Ethne found the angel curiously good company, when she wasn't making judgemental pronouncements about her life choices or complaining about humans not thinking properly. They fell into an easy rhythm of work and mutual understanding that seemed to be built on a longstanding rapport. Ethne became convinced she had met Lucy somewhere before, but was equally convinced she would have remembered if she had.

As the light began to fade and the Wandering Giant remained unfound, Ethne grew irritable. Lucy directed her to a picnic area beside a glistening loch and watched over her as she ate the cheese and pickle sandwiches provided by Irene and her father.

For once, Lucy ate nothing. They sat side by side at the wooden table and gazed over the dark mirror of the lake as the sun sank and the water glowed deep orange.

'Better?' said Lucy.

Ethne nodded and cleared her mess from the picnic table. 'It's not dark yet. Let's crack on.'

'You're the boss.'

They returned to the Softail where Lucy gave Ethne a firm look and thrust the helmet into her hands. 'I want to fly.'

Ethne stowed the helmet and thought it was about time the angel unfurled her wings. She turned in time to see Lucy transform, but not into the shape she was expecting.

In a flash of ice blue light, Lucy morphed into the form of a golden eagle. She flapped her enormous wings and took off, climbing into the air, soaring high over the loch before circling back. She perched on the picnic table and folded her wings and eyed Ethne over her razor-sharp beak.

'Show off,' said Ethne.

She climbed onto the motorbike and set off. Lucy followed, flying beside the bike and then taking off into the hills. She returned frequently and performed a quick change into human form to report her findings. With the superior vision of an eagle, they were able to cover more ground in the fading light than Ethne could have hoped for.

On her final report, Lucy returned with bad news. On the edge of a scruffy patch of woodland, they got together to agree where to camp for the night. Ethne sat on the bike and waited as the eagle flew into the wood. Lucy emerged from the trees looking troubled. 'We have company.'

Ethne jumped off the bike and looked up the road but couldn't see anything beyond the brow of the hill.

'A black Lexus,' said Lucy.

'ARK?'

'It's parked a way back,' continued the angel. 'I've spotted it a couple of times. They're keeping their distance. I suspect they know about me.'

Ethne pulled out her mobile phone. She had switched if off before they left, thinking that would stop ARK from tracking it. Clearly, she had been wrong.

'Are you going to tell me not to concern myself?'

'It had crossed my mind,' grinned Lucy.

'It doesn't make sense,' said Ethne, returning to the bike. 'I mean, why hire me to translate the prophecy and then try to stop me? Unless they're making sure whoever attacked us in Greenland doesn't get to me? Or have they changed their minds about decoding it? I wish I knew what was going on.'

'Let's just do our job and let them do theirs,' said Lucy. 'Their motivation will become clear soon enough.'

Ethne gazed beyond the trees into the darkening sky. 'We'll camp further up, away from the road.'

They found a spot on the edge of the woodland, hidden behind a tumbledown stone wall and scrubby hedge. Now it was properly dark, Ethne was getting jumpy. She was seeing ominous shapes in the trees and imagining terrible things. Lucy took pity on her and tried to help with the tent but only succeeded in making things worse. It took an hour of jostling and strong words to get it nailed into the ground.

Ethne jumped up for the hundredth time to check the road, listening for the sound of an engine or stealthy footfall.

'Sit down and stop fretting,' said Lucy, piling up sticks to make a fire.

'What if they've been waiting all day for us to stop so they can creep up on me while I'm asleep and slit my throat?'

'They're not going to do that.'

'And you know that because?'

'Because I'm watching over you,' said Lucy. 'You sleep. I watch.'

Ethne sat and wrapped her arms around her legs. Lucy moved one hand slowly over her little pile of sticks and a spark ignited. Within seconds they had a blazing campfire.

'I wish I could do that,' said Ethne, gazing into the flames.

Lucy gave her a devilish wink. 'Be careful what you wish for.'

The house was in darkness again. Whenever the power went off, Conor took his oil lamp and decamped to his passage tomb in the back garden. It made more sense for him to be out here in the dark, than rattling around in the house waiting for the lights to come back on. He could spend hours crouched in the chamber, working the stone. Time passed differently within these walls, morphing and bending back on itself, transporting him to another world. Over the years he had covered the walls with the spirals and swirls of Neolithic design in the belief that their meaning would be revealed through their creation.

A noise outside the passage made him still the flint tool in its groove on the wall to listen. Someone had entered the tomb. The footsteps shuffled closer and he relaxed. It was Irene, probably bringing him some food.

'Just put it down there,' he said, as she entered the chamber. 'Thank you, Renie. What would I do without you?'

Irene placed the tray, loaded with vegetable soup, bread rolls and cheese, on the smooth sandstone floor, and then straightened up. There was just enough height in the chamber for her to stand. She watched Conor making his strange markings and sighed. 'You'll catch your death out here, Con. I've got the wood burner on. Come back inside.'

He continued to scrape the flint against the rock, lost in his ancient world. Irene turned and stooped to enter the passage. The sound of a car pulling up outside the house made her stop. 'Are you expecting someone?' she said.

'No,' said Conor, lowering the flint. 'Stay here, Renie.'

'Is it those men?' she said, returning to the chamber. 'The ones Ethne warned you about?'

'More than likely.'

Irene gingerly lowered herself to the cold stone floor and pulled her legs to her chest. Conor dropped his flint and moved to sit beside her.

'I left the back door open,' said Irene in a tiny, fearful voice.

Conor took her hand and gave it a squeeze. They sat in silence and listened to the sounds of men walking around outside the house. Hushed voices gave way to shouts and consternation. It appeared the men were having trouble getting into the house, despite the wide open door. Conor and Irene exchanged a baffled glance, the lamp burning steadily between them.

The men left the house, their voices carrying through the garden and echoing off the trees. Footsteps approached the tomb and stopped outside the passage entrance.

Conor extinguished the lamp.

24

Michael leaned back in the stiff chair and glanced around the dining room. Candlelight flickered over the oil paintings lining the walls, and the stone fireplace crackled with heat from the fire. His stomach grumbled in response to the rich aromas drifting from the kitchen. This was the first time he had been allowed to eat in the banqueting hall. He and Thomas had been brought from their rooms and told to wait. They sat opposite each other halfway down the enormous oak table where places had been set. Another was set at the head of the table, leading Michael to speculate as to who might be joining them.

Thomas poured two glasses of red wine from the carafe and pushed one across to Michael. 'It'll be the damn lawyer. They never send anyone else.'

'Did you ask about the mutation spreading?'

Thomas nodded.

'And?'

'We'll find out shortly,' said the professor. 'Although I don't know why they couldn't just tell me over the phone. Why we need all this-'

The doors at the end of the room were flung open and Gregori strode through. He stood beside the fire for a moment to absorb its warmth and ignored the two men staring at him expectantly.

'I do love a good fire,' he said, gazing into the flames.

Michael watched the lawyer closely, disturbed by the peculiar prickling sensation running all over his body. There was something abnormal about the man, as if everything he did was for show. The expensive suit, the immaculate hair, the perfect teeth, the shoes so shiny you could see your face in them. They were all distractions, but from what? Michael tried to probe, to get behind the mask, but he hit a brick wall. It was as if the lawyer had taken out an injunction against the world. Perhaps he was just being careful in the company of a known Homo Angelus, but Thomas didn't seem to like him much either.

Gregori made his way down the table to his place at the head. He stopped at Michael's chair and looked down his nose at him.

'I don't believe I've had the privilege,' he said, offering his hand. 'It is good to meet you at last, Michael. You have caused us much excitement.'

Michael played along with the charade and smiled, allowing his hand to be shaken and feigning meekness. It wouldn't do any harm to let the lawyer think he was taken in by the power play.

Gregori flashed his teeth at both men, and then sat. He clicked his fingers and two kitchen staff appeared carrying tureens and plates piled high with bread. Gregori watched as they carefully dished up the soup, growing more impatient by the second. 'Bring out everything, would you?' he said, at last. 'And then leave us be. I do not wish to be interrupted.'

The kitchen staff scuttled back and forth, filling the table with roast lamb and vegetables, and a bowl piled with a creamy looking confection that Michael wanted to sink his face into and inhale. Finally, the three men were left to eat at their leisure and it was some time before the conversation turned to the matter in hand.

Gregori leaned back in his chair and dabbed delicately at his mouth with a napkin. 'I am so glad you called, Thomas.'

The professor looked up from his plate and swallowed. 'Is it spreading?'

'It is,' said Gregori. 'Our protégé here was correct. Spontaneous mutations have been found. The gene is spreading.'

'How?' said Thomas. 'We need to study it. I'll need to work out the mechanism. Why has the gene switched on in these individuals? What was the trigger? How can we help it to spread further?'

'We need to find the epigenetic switch,' agreed Michael. 'How does it normally work?'

Thomas shoved his plate to one side and topped up his wine. 'Epigenetics looks at the way factors outside the genome can influence how DNA is expressed. So things like the food we eat, the chemicals we're exposed to, how much we exercise, even the nature of our social environment, all affect our DNA. If a person has the genetic marker for heart disease, for instance, they can switch it off by eating a healthier diet. Even better, that epigenetic change can then be passed on to the next generation.'

Michael nodded. 'So in this case, something in the light has triggered the change, but it's directed by our consciousness.'

'I checked the studies and published papers,' said Thomas. 'There's a clear link between a person's thoughts and feelings, and the expression of their DNA. Positive thoughts lead to lowered stress levels, which makes the body more efficient at healing. But how that works, exactly...'

'It depends on how you see consciousness,' said Michael. 'Most people assume the brain creates consciousness, but consciousness isn't just inside your head. It's in every living thing. Not just the ones that have brains. A plant has a kind of consciousness, an intelligence. They learn and communicate.'

'What's your point?' said Thomas.

'If you want to anchor consciousness in living things, you don't do it using brains. You do it through DNA. The brain is important, don't get me wrong. The brain directs consciousness, organises and filters it. But consciousness comes first and DNA acts as an antenna. It's like a crystal in a radio that transduces the signal. Consciousness is encoded via the light-'

'Yes!' Thomas leapt from his seat and began to pace in an erratic circle behind his chair. 'DNA emits photons. Of course! At the molecular level, all interactions are electrical. All of life is really a sea of light. Michael, you are brilliant, I'm sorry it took me so long to listen to you. The photons act as switches but consciousness is the key. We have to *want* to change. It's all in the intention.'

A polite cough from the head of the table made Thomas spin round. Gregori was examining his fingernails. 'No doubt, this is fascinating, professor. But please sit down, your whirling is making me dizzy.'

Thomas returned to his seat. 'Tell me about the people who've changed. If we know more about them, we'll be able to see how this is working in vivo.'

'As you wish,' said Gregori. 'The first was Ethne Godwin.'

Michael gasped. 'Is she all right?'

Gregori waved a dismissive hand. 'I am about to tell you something that will not leave this room. Do you understand?'

Both men nodded and shared a wary glance.

'You will want to know how I can know such things,' continued the lawyer. 'Suffice to say, I have my methods, but be assured, I will not lie to you. There will be many questions, of that I am sure. Answers, however, will be few. You will be satisfied with what I give you.'

Thomas scoffed. 'For goodness sake, man-'

'Now,' snapped Gregori. 'Ethne Godwin. She is responsible for the situation in which we find ourselves. It is thanks to her sterling efforts that we now must, as they say, play catch up. Yesterday in Greenland, Ms Godwin activated the Fire Stone. This in turn activated her *Homo angelus* mutation.'

'Fire Stone?' said Michael. 'I remember her talking about that. It's her thing. She's got a tattoo. Something about the Akhu? Ancient Egypt and a long lost culture. She got herself in trouble last year searching for it in Turkey. But she said the Fire Stone was a legend. Are you saying it's real?'

'Oh yes, very real.'

'What is it?' said Thomas. 'How does it activate the mutation?'

Gregori gave the professor a look of such withering scorn, Thomas almost slid from his chair to the floor.

'The ancients were an advanced people, in many ways,' said Gregori. 'The Fire Stone is the oldest soul technology. And now that it is active, the mutation is free to spread. Anybody who has sustained contact with a Homo Angelus could find their mutation is switched on.'

'Could?' said Thomas. 'It's not certain then.'

Gregori shook his head. 'You said it yourself, professor. Intention is the key. They have to want to change. It may not even be a conscious wish, but it is there nonetheless.'

'Well, I've been with Michael for a couple of days. Have I changed?'

'You have not.'

'So it takes longer-'

'It takes love,' said Gregori.

'Where are you getting this information?' said Thomas. 'How am I supposed to use this? I can't introduce love into the lab.'

'You don't need to,' said Michael. 'ARK don't want the gene to spread. Not willy-nilly. They don't want any old person to have access to this. Do you?'

Gregori smiled like a shark.

'But you can't put the genie back in the bottle,' continued Michael. 'Once the *Homo angelus* gene is switched on, it stays on. That's why your vaccine doesn't work. You're fighting a losing battle. Right now, out there somewhere is the most powerful weapon you can imagine. She doesn't know it yet, but when Ana realises who she is, she'll be unstoppable, and-'

A ripple of fear and rage passed through Michael's body. He was certain it came from Gregori in reaction to Ana's name. He scrutinised the lawyer's face but the imperious mask was still in place.

Gregori met Michael's eye, his smile gone. 'It was foreseen. We have been preparing for this day for longer than you can imagine. The efforts of your friends will come to nothing, Mr Okeke, and you will be unable to assist them in any event. Your services will no longer be required, Dr Lethe.'

He stood and flicked an invisible speck of dust from his suit. The doors at the end of the hall were flung open and four security guards entered. Michael and Thomas exchanged a fearful glance.

'Evidently,' said Gregori, 'you will not be allowed to leave.'

Michael sprang from his seat. Before he could turn towards the advancing guards and ready himself to fight, a sharp pain exploded in his shoulder. He glanced down, his vision already hazy, to see a tranquiliser dart embedded in his arm. He pulled it free and stared at it until his knees crumpled and the darkness engulfed his consciousness once more.

25

Ethne knew she was dreaming because what she was seeing didn't make sense. She was in the boat in her feather cape, floating the menhir up a river. The stone hovered over the deck, and to keep it afloat, she sang. Icy mountains towered on either side of the valley, reflecting the song, amplifying the line of the melody until it harmonised with itself in a glorious echoing chorus. The stone was carried up the mountain on cushions of resonance, and she sang it into the cave.

Ethne wriggled in her sleeping bag, turning over and trying to free herself from the absurdity of the dream. The vision shifted abruptly to another landscape. A great valley carved by a glacier, a river meandered like a shimmering serpent between two immense crags. In the heart of the valley beside the water, stood a giant. Alone for centuries, awaiting the return of his love. He watched as an elegant golden eagle circled overhead and smiled in response to its call. Around his neck hung a pendant, the mirror of that worn by the one he loves and the one he awaits.

Ethne woke, her hand finding its way to the ankh at her throat. She felt its reassuring shape in her fingers and closed her eyes. It was a moment before she realised she had the answer she had been searching for, and rubbed her head to keep herself awake. The cold air was finding its way into every gap in her sleeping bag. She needed to get up and find the map before she forgot the dream. She manoeuvred towards the tent opening and peered out.

Strange lights zipped across the sky as if the stars had fallen and were dancing. Transfixed, she crawled from the tent and stood. A glow on the horizon seemed to be the focal point of the light display. Great bands of plasma moved through the air, morphing into fantastical shapes: a two-headed snake, a phoenix, a fire-breathing dragon.

As if a cosmic switch had been flipped, the sky plunged into darkness and the glow on the horizon vanished. A flash at her side made her jump and Lucy appeared.

'Didn't I ask you not to do that?' said Ethne, shivering slightly. 'Was that you just now. In the sky?'

Lucy grinned. 'It feels good to let rip occasionally.'

'Gave the ARK minions something to think about.'

'They're asleep.'

'Useless.'

'Indeed.'

'Lucy, can you, I mean...is it possible to make stones float? In the air.'

'Anything is possible,' said the angel.

'Anything?'

Lucy nodded. 'You just have to understand the rules.'

'But surely singing to a stone isn't enough to move it.'

Lucy searched Ethne's eyes, staring at her for so long and so thoroughly that Ethne had to look away. She shrank before the angel's gaze and squatted beside the dying embers of the fire, now shivering in earnest.

'It is returning,' said Lucy. 'Soon you will remember.'

Lucy flicked her hand over the fire and the flames grew. She added more sticks and poked at the glowing wood, deep in thought.

Ethne watched her for a while, wondering which of her many questions she should ask first. She felt like she was standing on the edge of a precipice. Any second now, Lucy would say or do something, and she would fall, tumbling into madness and chaos.

'I don't understand anything,' she said. 'All the rules seem to be broken.'

'You never knew the rules, Ethne. What you have been taught, the way you are made to think, if I can even use that word in this context, distorts the truth. To understand, you must forget everything you ever learnt.'

'Right,' said Ethne, trying to wipe her mind clean. 'So, let's start at the beginning. What is the Great Light?'

Lucy draped a blanket over Ethne's shoulders. 'You like the tough questions don't you? But you're right, the Great Light is where it all starts. All arise from the Great Light.'

'Do you mean God?'

'Come on now, Ethne. You know better than to ask a question like that.'

'Yeah, I know,' she shrugged. 'Words point to other words. You can't describe reality in words, you can only point in its general direction and grunt. Language is a hall of mirrors, but it's all we have, so you'll have to humour me.'

Lucy smiled and her eyes blazed with a fearsome love of such intensity that Ethne didn't know where to look. She stared into the fire and watched the flames dance along the wood, reducing it to hot ash.

'To be honest,' said Lucy, 'I don't know. About God, that is.'

'But you're an angel. How could you not know?'

'I'm not omniscient, Ethne. I can only see so far. Undoubtedly further than you can see. For now, at least.'

'What does that mean? That I'll be able to see God?'

'Humans are in a much better position to understand the nature of God. That is the entire point of this enterprise. It is why we are all here, spinning on this little rock through space.'

'To understand the nature of God?'

'If you wish to use that word,' said Lucy. 'Yes.'

'Would you be happier if I called it the Great Light?'

Lucy shrugged. 'It is of no importance what you call it. It is what it is.'

'Okay, let's park that,' said Ethne. She had no desire to get into an endless semantic argument with anyone, never mind an angel. 'Next question: is there anything that isn't in the Great Light?'

'No.'

'What about darkness?'

Lucy grinned. 'I like you.'

'You said.'

'Darkness is ignorance,' said Lucy. 'It is not really the absence of light, merely the inability, or unwillingness, to perceive it.'

'And this Great Light fell into darkness, into ignorance. Why?'

'Imagine: You are the Great Light. In potential, you are everything that could ever exist, it's all contained within your being. But in reality you are none of these things. All you are is a state of potential. Anything could happen, but nothing ever does. Nothing ever really is. It just *could* be. How dull is that? How boring! No change, no life, no point. What does ignorance provide?'

'The potential for knowledge?' said Ethne, feeling like she was back in school. 'If you don't know something, you want to find out. It makes you curious. You want to solve the mystery.'

'Correct,' said Lucy. 'And that creates movement and change and life. Only by appearing to separate from itself, by creating darkness, could the Great Light begin to know itself.'

'That's the experiment you mentioned. The evolution of life. So evolution is about self-knowledge? The Great Light is trying to understand itself, discover the answer to its own mystery.'

'Correct. And the only way it can achieve this is through a very particular type of mind. It lives and evolves through myriad forms in search of that mind. A mind capable of carrying both sides of creation: the darkness and the light. The purpose of evolution is to give birth to such individuals. It took aeons, Ethne. You can't imagine how long we have been working towards this moment, how many interventions we made, but we were finally gifted with a being capable of self-knowledge: the human being.'

'Did the Guardians of Light guide evolution?'

'No, that is my humble task,' said Lucy. 'I was one of the Great Beings of Light tasked with overseeing evolution. The Guardians protect the knowledge here on earth. The Guardians are human.'

'Got it,' said Ethne. 'So the Great Beings of Light are the angels.'

'You're doing it again. Throwing words around like they mean something.'

'So you're not an angel?'

Lucy sighed. 'I am light. You call us angels. It is a word. It is not reality. As the Great Light fell, she spun herself into form. I am one of the First Ones. First to be created. First to fall.'

'There are others like you?'

Lucy nodded. 'We have been called many things through time and I have appeared under many names. You would recognise us as archangels, but I never much liked that word.'

Ethne gazed into the fire and searched her memory for an archangel called Lucy. She could remember the obvious ones like Michael, Gabriel, and Raphael, but they were from the Judeo-Christian tradition and she was sure Lucy was older than that. Perhaps she took her name from another culture. Ethne repeated the name under her breath like a mantra, waiting for inspiration.

The truth sprang upon her like a ravenous lion. The woman sitting by the fire smiling at her with such warmth and affection, who had saved her life more than once, who was an archangel, who had fallen. Why hadn't she seen it sooner?

She wanted to run, but found her legs wouldn't move. Her body seemed to be liquefying and turning to stone simultaneously. Ethne stared at Lucy in horror and disbelief and thought she might be sick. She must have misunderstood.

'But you can't be...Lucifer?'

The angel's reaction was a surprise. She groaned and rolled her eyes, like she had seen this a million times and was bored to the roots of her ridiculous hair with it. 'Here we go.'

'I don't know what to think,' said Ethne, her voice wavering. 'How can I believe anything you've told me? I could be stuck out here in the arse end of nowhere running around after a stupid stone that probably doesn't even exist just to please your sick sense of humour, or boost your angelic ego, or whatever psychiatric condition you have.'

'I cannot lie,' said Lucy softly.

'Says the liar.' Ethne stood. She backed away from the fire and clutched the blanket tight around her shoulders.

'Ethne-'

'A few days ago, if someone had told me Lucifer existed I would've laughed in their face. I never believed in any of this. I'm not a God person, let alone an angel person. And then you turn up and pull me out of that cave and destroy that drone and tell me all this stuff about the Great Light falling into darkness and a prophecy and how I have this role to play, and I'm having insane dreams and my head is full of stuff I don't understand. And now you tell me you're this rebel angel who told God to go fuck himself, even though you claim you don't know if God exists, and I don't know what to believe anymore.'

'I understand,' said Lucy, smiling benignly. 'Please try to remember, Ethne. All the stories you have been told are untrue.'

'You...you never rebelled against God?'

'Those who tell these tales do not understand the nature of reality, Ethne. Please sit down. You'll catch cold away from the fire. I will try to explain.'

Ethne reluctantly returned to her perch on a log beside the campfire.

She gazed into the flames and sighed. 'See, now I have a problem. Even if you explain, I won't know if I can believe you.'

'You would have to take it on faith,' said Lucy, with a devilish twinkle.

'I can't do that.'

Lucy smiled. 'Just one of the many reasons I love you.'

Ethne laughed cynically. 'Now I think you're trying to sweet-talk me.'

'Here is my proposal,' said Lucy. 'I will tell you the truth, as I am unable to do otherwise, and you can take it or leave it. I won't ask you to believe.'

'Why can't you lie?' said Ethne. 'Would you spontaneously combust or something?'

Lucy chuckled. 'No. I am light. I have only fallen a fraction from the Great Light. I can only do what I was created to do. You, Ethne, have a choice. You can think for yourself, you can doubt and question. That is your purpose. If I try to think for myself, I see nothing but my own reflection multiplied. All I can do is serve the light. I cannot turn away from that light because there is nothing but light for me. So you see.'

Ethne smiled apologetically.

'Perhaps I could use a different name,' continued Lucy. 'Would you be more comfortable calling me Mātariśvan?'

'Who?'

'Or perhaps Māui, or a whole menagerie of Native American animals. Or Melek Taus, Loki, Thoth, or of course, Prometheus. There are many more. All fire-bringers and teachers of mankind in their own way. We are a large family.'

Ethne hid behind her hands and cringed. 'I'm so sorry, Lucy. I should've thought it through. I'm such an idiot.'

'Don't be so hard on yourself,' said Lucy. 'We are often misunderstood. Humans often react badly when encouraged to think for themselves.'

'Is that why they made you a scapegoat? Saying you rebelled and then throwing you out of heaven.'

'Nothing to do with me, Ethne. It's all in the human mind. You do so love your stories. But this was one of the risks of evolution: That the darkness would overtake humanity and ignorance would triumph over consciousness. It was foreseen and there is no reason for concern.'

'All part of the plan, huh?'

Lucy grinned and shrugged modestly.

'So what's next?' said Ethne. 'Poor old Prometheus stole fire from the gods to give to us and got chained to a rock for his trouble. If that wasn't enough, an eagle came every day to feast on his liver. That's the price we pay for being conscious, which is why most of us don't bother. It's easier to be ignorant.'

'Oh Ethne, no. No, no, no, a million times no.'

'What?'

'These stories are lies told to keep you chained,' said Lucy, her eyes shining. 'That was the reason my name was used to cast doubt and sow fear. I bring the light and it is rejected and the story is perverted. Humans must not challenge God, humans must not think for themselves, humans are children, humans are sheep. Lies, lies, lies.'

'I suppose you had nothing to do with tempting Adam and Eve in the Garden of Eden either?'

'Oh yes, that was me,' said Lucy proudly. 'But again, the story was perverted.'

'It's a half-remembered myth from earlier shamanic cultures, isn't it?' said Ethne. 'The tree, the maiden, the serpent. Three of the most ancient symbols ever created.'

Lucy barked out a laugh. 'You think *you* created them? My, my, someone has an ego.'

'Yeah, all right,' said Ethne, picking up a stick to poke the fire. 'There's no need to rub my ignorance in my face. Why don't you enlighten me?'

'You want the fruit?'

Ethne gazed at the angel through the fire. 'Are you tempting me?'

'It is not temptation if it is in your nature to want to know,' said Lucy. 'But there are consequences to knowledge. What is seen cannot be unseen. However, there are also consequences to remaining in the dark. It is not a happy state of affairs. The pitiful course of human history stands in testament to that.'

'Prometheus wasn't chained to his rock forever, was he?' said Ethne. 'He was set free.'

Lucy grinned. 'I really do like you. Did I mention that?'

Ethne laughed. 'Once or twice.' She gazed at the angel in wonder. Despite all the lies told in her name, she didn't seem sad or even angry about it. 'You still love us. I mean, after everything we've done, the way we cast you out when all you wanted to do was help. You still think humans are worth saving?'

'Yes.'

'Then you'll be pleased to hear I know where the Wandering Giant is.'

Lucy jumped up and rushed around the fire and wrapped Ethne in a fierce hug. 'Why didn't you say? Oh, Ethne, I knew I could count on you. You'll see it all soon. You shall remember and the world shall awaken.'

26

Joshua drove through the night while Ana slept. He had been awake for over 24 hours and fatigue was creeping up on him like a bad cold. They had arrived at Rovaniemi in Finland and had crossed the Arctic Circle by ten p.m. last night, but Linnunrata was another two hundred miles north. Six hours of relentless darkness and ice. The snow chains on the hired BMW gripped the road effortlessly, but Joshua kept his speed steady. He had never driven in conditions like this and had no intention of ending up in a ditch.

The flight to Finland had been difficult for them both. Ana had done her best to ignore him while he fidgeted and squeezed his long limbs into the cramped space. They had hardly spoken since ARK caught up with them in China Town and Beatrice had ordered them to Linnunrata.

'We can't do this,' said Joshua.

Ana gazed out of the tiny window and watched the patchwork of Newcastle shrink into a haze of clouds. After catching an early flight, they had one more change to make at Helsinki. The plane was almost empty; not many could afford to fly these days. Further down the narrow cabin, a group of loud-mouthed businessmen were playing musical chairs, spreading themselves out over the seats and making pointed remarks about value for money. Hundreds of airlines had gone into administration after the storms, and those remaining had hiked their prices to cover the spiralling costs of keeping the fleets in the air.

'Ana,' said Joshua. 'You can't ignore me.'

'I'm not ignoring you. I'm just not talking to you.'

'Right.'

Ana sighed and closed her eyes. Joshua continued to fidget. She wanted to yell at him and hurt him, but knew she couldn't do it without getting upset.

She didn't want to give him an excuse to be kind to her. She might end up forgiving him by mistake.

Joshua cleared his throat. He was trying to get her attention. She could feel him tugging at her awareness, willing her to look at him, so she clamped her eyes shut even tighter.

'I'm sorry,' said Joshua softly.

'You said.'

'Please can we talk about this.'

'There's nothing to say. You lied from the start. You let me think you were called Jack Dexter. This whole relationship is a lie, so why should I pretend it's real by talking to you.'

'It is real.'

Ana turned to face him. 'I don't even know who you are. For all I know, your name isn't even Joshua King. It's one of those other names you have in one of your many fake passports.'

'Shhhh, not so loud,' hissed Joshua. 'I promise you. Joshua King is the name on my birth certificate.'

'You sure?' she said, sarcastically. 'You haven't got yourself confused with somebody else? Joshua King isn't some dead child whose identity you've stolen so you can pretend you don't exist?'

Ana turned away. She could feel him burning holes in the back of her head but she refused to face him.

'Ana, look at me.'

She ignored him. Joshua sighed the saddest sigh Ana had ever heard. He gently turned her face to his. 'Let me show you.' She glared defiantly into his eyes. Joshua gazed back and opened his mind and heart to hers.

Ana pushed past his memories of the ambush by ARK and skimmed over recent history to find the beginning. It was clear Joshua had been censoring himself since the day they had met, lying to himself as well as to her.

'So you really are a journalist?'

Joshua nodded.

'And your dad really got you fired?'

'All of that's true, Ana. MI6 got in touch when I uncovered the story about ReSource in Siberia. Kendrick was impressed and recruited me to Operation Phoenix.' He paused and glanced at Ana warily. 'You mustn't tell anyone I told you that, okay?'

'What's Operation Phoenix?'

197

'More secret than secret,' said Joshua. 'I don't even know all the details. I just go where I'm told and bring back the intel.'

'You could've told me.'

'I wanted to,' he said. 'Normally it's not that hard being undercover. As long as you don't say the wrong thing or mess up your body language, you're safe. If they can't see you or hear you, you can't get burnt. But with you, Ana, you're amazing. I had to be careful *all* the time. I couldn't drop my guard for a second. I wasn't even safe inside my own head.'

'What do you want, an award? A medal? A standing ovation?'

'Every time I had to lie to you it killed me,' he said sadly. 'I was going to tell you. Even rehearsed it, had a whole speech and everything, but the right moment never seemed to come up.'

'You pretended to be my friend,' said Ana. 'You pretended you cared. You reassured me. You seduced me, told me you loved me, just so you could, what? Spy on me? Find out if I was a threat to national security? Am I a terrorist to you people?'

'I didn't pretend, Ana.'

She turned back to the window and folded her arms in protest.

'Do you even want to believe me?'

'No,' she lied.

Joshua sighed. 'I didn't expect to fall in love with you.'

'Occupational hazard, I guess,' said Ana, heavy on the sarcasm.

Rage exploded in Joshua's belly and he punched the headrest in front, making Ana jump. He leaned across the armrest and pushed his face close to hers, blocking her into the seat with his arm.

'It may have escaped your notice,' he hissed, 'but I saved your life back there. ARK was going to take you. I could've let them. Easily. Or you could've killed them. Either way, you would've been fucked. And, oh yes, I watched the video on the disc. I know you killed your stepfather. I'm not the only one who's been keeping secrets, Anastasia.'

He sat back and stared straight ahead. Ana watched him nervously. What was he planning to do with her? The video was damning. Michael had helped her to hide the evidence. He had returned home from Linnunrata that night to find Ana distraught. He had stepped from the balcony as if he had just come back from the shop, but she was too scared to notice. It had taken an hour for her to calm down enough to explain what had happened.

After the attack, she had stood in the snow and stared at Patrick's lifeless body knowing she had the power to kill and it had sickened her. She wanted to take it back, to turn back time and erase her mistake. She gazed at her hands as if they belonged to somebody else, frozen to her bones and lost to herself.

Slowly she realised Evangeline was running in circles around her, and Ana thought her mother had lost her mind with grief. Evangeline shoved Ana away from the body and continued to run through the snow creating a mess of footprints.

Finally, Ana understood what she was doing and joined in, but her mother pushed her away again.

'Go home. Tell no one.'

'Mum, I'm sorry...'

Evangeline couldn't look at her. 'Just go. I'll deal with it.'

Ana walked home alone and the snow continued to fall. When Michael appeared at her side, she collapsed into his arms and wept. He had tried to read her mind, but the images and emotions were so fragmented and jumbled that he couldn't make sense of it. Finally, he had hacked into the security system at the Work Farm to retrieve the CCTV footage and wipe the hard drive.

Ana had wanted to turn herself in, but Michael had said there was no point, nobody would believe her anyway. Her blast of energy had fried the camera. The farm had assumed it was a lightning strike and didn't investigate further. The autopsy on Patrick had ruled the same. There was nothing else that could produce that level of static shock. She was in the clear.

She knew she should destroy the video but her conscience wouldn't allow it.

Patrick had sold her to ARK. The only father she had known was willing to give her away in exchange for a few thousand pounds. It was the worst betrayal and she could never forgive him for it.

Now a second man had betrayed her. Joshua stared resolutely ahead, tension running along his jaw. She had to make him understand. She had to tell the truth.

'He had a heart problem,' she said desperately. 'I didn't know. It was an accident. I didn't mean for it to happen.'

'Occupational hazard,' said Joshua.

'He was hurting Mum,' she pleaded. 'I just wanted to get him away from her, to stop him, push them apart. I didn't think he would die. I didn't know-'

'I believe you, Ana.'

'Don't.'

'What?' he said. 'You think I'm still pretending?'

'So you admit you were pretending before?'

'No. Look.' Joshua sighed and ran a hand over his face. 'The way I see it, you have no choice but to trust me. Right now, I'm your best hope if you want to stay safe. It really doesn't matter if you believe me or not, but will you please let me help you?'

She reluctantly agreed, although her consent was beside the point. Officially she was under the protective custody of His Majesty's Government Secret Intelligence Service. Neither of them was happy about it.

Joshua glanced at Ana sleeping so peacefully beside him now. White dusted pine trees lined the road, illuminated in the glare of the headlights. Millions of ice crystals glinted as they passed. The snow fell in sheets, thick fat flakes hurling themselves against the windshield in a suicidal frenzy. It was crazy to drive through this blizzard, but he had to reach the cabins tonight.

It turned out Linnunrata wasn't the name of a town; it was a cabin complex near Inari in Lapland. Linnunrata meant the Bird's Way and was the Finnish term for the Milky Way. Ana had explained what Beatrice had told her about angels and birds. The Milky Way was a bridge between worlds, the route taken by souls leaving this world and angels entering it. Not long ago, Joshua would have dismissed this as fantasy, but since meeting Beatrice, he couldn't rule anything out.

A dark shape moved in the road up ahead. Joshua slowed and peered through the curtains of snow. A moose was standing in the middle of the road, snow lining the curve of its antlers. Joshua stopped the car. The headlamps bathed the beast in an ethereal glow. Joshua hit the horn.

The moose ignored him.

Ana opened her eyes. 'Whas goin' on?' she said sleepily.

'Moose.'

'Huh?' She rubbed her eyes and peered into the arctic gloom.

Joshua hit the horn again, making her jump.

'Stop that,' she said. 'You'll scare him.'

'That's the idea. Unless you've got a better one.'

Ana gazed at the moose as it slowly turned to face the SUV. It returned her gaze, radiating pure power. Ana's heart quickened. She wanted to leap from the car and throw her arms around his beautiful neck, but stayed in her seat. She doubted the moose would appreciate the gesture, and she would freeze in seconds. She smiled to herself and chuckled. She had fallen in love with a moose. The majestic antlers lowered as the beast dipped its head, as if in greeting.

'Uh oh,' said Joshua. 'Is he going to charge us?'

Ana gripped his arm and shushed him, her eyes fixed on the animal in the road. She opened her mind wide and absorbed herself into the snow covered landscape and trees. This was the moose's home, his territory. She silently asked for permission to continue on their way, promising to treat his land with respect. She lowered her eyes to a spot on the ground, and waited.

Time seemed to slow and the flakes fell in silent slow motion. Then through the icy air came an almighty bellow. The moose raised its massive head and thundered its dominance. Slowly, it turned and strode like a king towards the side of the road. Ana watched in wonderment, almost sorry to see it leave.

Joshua breathed out in relief and eased the BMW forward, continuing their solitary drive north. A mile or two passed before they spoke.

'You did that, didn't you?' he said. 'Some sort of Jedi mind trick.'

Ana shrugged. 'Might be a coincidence. I just asked him if we could go on, that's all.'

'I didn't know you spoke moose.'

She laughed and turned to smile at Joshua, but then remembered she was supposed to be angry with him, so turned away again and glared out of the window. 'I suppose MI6 know where we are.'

Joshua sighed and drove on in silence.

'You could've not told them,' she continued. 'We could've had one moment alone, away from them and from ARK. Look at this place. We could've disappeared.'

'They would know we were in Finland anyway,' said Joshua. 'They're tracking the passports.'

'But if you wanted to, you could disappear?'

'If I wanted to.'

'So you don't want to. Your job is more important than anything else. Than me.'

'You are my job.'

'Right, I forgot. You're just pretending to love me.'

'That's not what...I didn't mean it like that.'

'Then explain it to me,' said Ana. 'What is your job? What's your mission? And don't say you can't tell me. I could pin you down and rip it out of your head if I wanted to, and don't think for a moment that I won't.'

'I believe you, babes.'

'So tell me.'

'I was following ARK long before the storms,' said Joshua, 'long before the mutation. They were consolidating, building an empire. I mean, these giant international corporations have the government in their pocket, no matter how they try to spin it otherwise. Through the lobbies and trade deals they more or less have control of the country, and not everyone is happy about that.'

'What does that have to do with me?'

'I'm coming to that,' he said. 'It's the age-old question: who has the power? Corporations have undermined democracy, and politicians have colluded in the demolition of their own power. And then comes the solar storm.'

'And the mutation.'

'I was following Phanes BioTech,' continued Joshua, 'trying to find out what they were doing with the DNA database they were building. That's when I got in touch with Lethe. I wanted to recruit him, but he was way too careful and he probably doesn't have the full picture, anyway. Neither Phanes nor ARK have told their staff what they're up to, as you discovered, which makes it doubly worrying.

'Anyway, when the mutation showed up, I don't think they were concerned at first. It was just a weird anomaly, a bunch of people curing themselves of various diseases and getting healthy. Big whoop. But then they started getting powers, and that's when Lethe stopped talking to me. And then there's you.'

'What was so different about me?' said Ana. 'There are plenty of other people with these powers. Why are they fixating on me?'

'That's what I had to find out,' said Joshua. 'Kendrick sent me to make contact with you. If we could understand why Anastasia Wilson was so important to ARK, we could figure out what they were planning.'

'And what are they planning?'

He shrugged. 'And now there's this find in Greenland. The standing stones and mysterious ancient writing.'

'Ethne is supposed to be translating the text,' said Ana. 'They said it was a prophecy. Something to do with an ancient myth about the Shining Ones. Ethne could tell us more. Shall I call her? Is that safe? Could I use your phone?'

'They'll be watching her,' said Joshua. 'You don't want to do anything to endanger her life, but then again, we need that information.'

'Maybe someone at Linnunrata will know. I hope Ethne's all right, Jack.'

An uneasy silence filled the car and Ana stared at her hands. 'Sorry, I meant...'

Joshua glanced at her warily. 'Don't apologise. I don't mind what you call me so long as you talk to me, Ana.'

He drove on in silence and waited for the bad air to clear before picking up the thread again. 'If ARK want this prophecy they'll make sure Ethne translates it, so they'll look after her until she does.'

'And then what? What happens to her once she's translated it?'

Another shrug from Joshua.

Ana unplugged his phone from the charger and stared at it, trying to decide what to do.

If only there was a way to contact Ethne directly, mind to mind. But Ethne was normal; she wasn't a Homo Angelus. Ana could reach out to Ethne in her mind as much as she liked but it would go unheeded. She sighed and plugged the phone back into the charger.

'Joshua?' she said tentatively. 'Promise you'll tell me the truth?'

'Sure, babes.'

'What does MI6 plan to do with the Homo Angelus? Long term. Assuming you can stop ARK doing whatever it is they're doing, there's still going to be all these people running around with, for want of a better word, superpowers. They won't just let that go, will they?'

Joshua shifted in his seat. Ana was watching him. He could feel her mind pressing against his. The answer was logical enough, and she already knew it. He didn't want to talk about it. He didn't even want to think about it.

'Long term, I don't know,' he said. 'They don't tell me that stuff. For me to do my job, I don't need to know what they're planning down the road. But-'

'But?'

'But...' Joshua sighed. 'They'll either get you working for them like Ingo Swann and Uri Gellar, or...'

Ana stared into the blizzard swirling around the car as they drove north, deep beyond the Arctic Circle. Perhaps she could go on the run, take up with the Sami tribesmen, become a reindeer herder.

'Would you come with me?' she said quietly. 'If I had to run away. Would you help me disappear?'

Joshua glanced at her with a sad smile. 'Sure, babes.'

The sun was yet to rise when the BMW turned off the main road. The sign to Linnunrata was obscured by snow but Joshua knew he was in the right place. There wasn't another town, or even a house, for miles around. He drove carefully down the long winding track through a dense pine forest, searching for the cabins. The snow had finally stopped falling, and the land was stilled in deathless sleep.

They emerged from the forest to find a cluster of wooden cabins arranged around a central square, with more trees scattered around the perimeter. All the shutters were closed. There didn't seem to be a soul in the place. Joshua drove into the centre of the square and parked next to another vehicle heaped with snow. He shut off the headlights, plunging them into darkness.

Into the Stygian gloom came a shaft of light. Someone had opened a door in the cabin ahead of them. Ana and Joshua watched as two figures approached the car, clearing a path through the snow as they came. They didn't have shovels, but appeared to be doing the work solely with their minds, raising the snow into high banks on either side of the path.

As the figures moved closer, Ana gasped in recognition. Beatrice waved and another mound of snow flew through the air to land, perfectly packed on one side. Ana leapt from the car into the freezing air.

'You made it,' said Beatrice, wrapping Ana in a warm embrace.

'Sorry it took so long,' said Ana.

'Nonsense,' said the angel, stepping back and smiling broadly.

Joshua climbed from the BMW and joined Ana. Beatrice embraced him too, and Joshua suffered an awkward moment while he decided what to do with his hands, finally opting to return the angel's hug. Beatrice chuckled. She stepped back to look into his face.

'That eye is already healing,' she said. 'Good. Now then, Ana, Joshua, I'd like to introduce you both to Niloufer.'

A refined gentleman stepped forward and bowed slightly to the humans. He appeared to be in his fifties and his caramel skin glowed with the characteristic angelic luminescence. Niloufer took Ana's hand and delicately kissed her wrist.

'Lovely to see you, Ana dear.'

He repeated the same greeting with Joshua, planting a kiss on the inside of his wrist. Joshua frowned fiercely and looked hopelessly lost.

Beatrice giggled and beamed at him. 'Perhaps we should explain.'

'Yes, please do,' said Joshua, trying to regain his cool.

'Our greeting is a blessing,' said Beatrice. 'The wrist is a pulse point. It delivers our love directly to your heart. We would kiss you on the carotid artery in your neck, but that might seem too intimate, especially on first meeting.'

'And you know humans,' said Niloufer, with a wink. 'If we went for the neck, you would think we were vampires.' He raised his hands and bared his teeth in a bad impression of Nosferatu.

'Does that answer your questions?' said Beatrice.

Joshua tried to smile. 'Some of them.'

'We are very pleased you are here,' said Niloufer. 'The others are most excited to meet you both.'

'What is this place?' said Joshua.

'I like to think of it as an Angel Boot Camp,' grinned Niloufer. 'Please. Come inside and warm your bodies. The others will be up soon. In the meantime, I think some food and a little nap. How does that sound?'

'Good,' said Ana, and followed the angels up the perfectly cleared path to the cabin.

Joshua lagged behind. It all seemed cosy and welcoming, and the angels were undoubtedly goodness personified, but at the mention of the words 'boot camp', his hackles had gone up. Perhaps he was being paranoid. He had spent too long inserting himself into battles between sworn enemies, looking for ways to bend the outcome to the greater good. People rarely lived up to their higher ideals and circumstances inevitably got messy, sooner or later. You couldn't trust anyone, especially if they used the words 'boot camp'.

They were not the words of a peaceful organisation. They were the words of someone planning a war.

27

In Scotland, a small round tent quivered in the breeze. Naked trees danced and entwined their branches in a prickly embrace. High above, soaring in great circles, an eagle surveyed the landscape. The sun crept across the horizon in orange and pink tendrils, and a gelatinous mist hung low, clinging to the pines and obscuring the mountains.

From her vantage point beyond the mountain peaks, Lucy watched Ethne sleep, her dreams turbid and convoluted. She was connecting the dots of her past, recombining everything she had once known. There would soon be more to incorporate. She would awaken a new person.

Ethne stirred. Lucy descended and stood silently outside the tent. A tousled head emerged. Ethne rubbed her eyes and peered up at the angel.

'Morning,' she said groggily.

'Sleep well?'

Ethne grunted and crawled from the tent. After a breakfast of cereal bars, she packed away the tent, loaded the Softail and drove north once more. She had marked the map, guided by her dream, and under directions from Lucy, navigated through the sticky air, careful not to drive off the road into the mire.

As the sun began to burn through the mist, Ethne descended into a basin between two rocky outcrops. A river meandered in great loops through the marshy ground. This was the spot. She stopped the motorcycle and gazed over the landscape just as the clouds parted. Sunlight blazed gold against the wall of rock on the opposite side of the valley. Beside the river stood a stone, leaning slightly towards the water as if about to drink. It was massive, at least eight feet tall.

'There he is,' said Ethne. 'Our Egyptian Giant, or Wandering Giant, or Big Ass Stone, depending on your viewpoint.'

'The Key Stone,' said Lucy, her voice wobbling with excitement.

They clambered from the bike and stowed their helmets. Ethne was anxious to run down to the riverbank, but Lucy grabbed her arm and gave her a stern look.

'Do not touch the stone until I am beside you,' she said. 'I need to ground you. Understand?'

Ethne nodded and grinned, then took off down the slope. She ran for the stone but the boggy ground kept throwing her off balance and it forced her to slow down. She swallowed her impatience and proceeded with more care.

Lucy watched for a moment then checked the road. A Lexus had pulled up and was parked on the brow of the hill. Two men in black fatigues got out, their eyes on Ethne striding carefully down the bank.

Ethne glanced back, expecting to find Lucy behind her, but the angel was still beside the bike. She was staring up the road with her hands on her hips and didn't look happy. Ethne followed her gaze: two ARK Security men were marching down the bank towards her. One of them pulled a gun.

A shot echoed around the valley.

An inferno erupted in Ethne's shoulder. She stumbled and fell to her knees, gasping in pain. She pressed her hand to the wound then stared dumbly at her blood soaked fingers.

Another shot rang out.

Ethne ducked instinctively. The air beside her head boiled as a bullet fizzed past. She pulled herself upright. She couldn't let them stop her. She had to get to the stone, she had to touch it. The giant had waited centuries for her return. She couldn't fail him now. She lurched forward, the stone ahead of her, swaying in her vision as she staggered forward.

The men reached the riverbank and ran for the stone, firing off shots as they closed in on Ethne. Without warning, the man in the lead fell backwards as if he had run into an invisible brick wall. The second man shouted at him to get up, but then suffered the same fate. Both clambered to their feet and tried to move forward, but the air was impenetrable. They were stuck.

The first man raised his gun. Ethne was almost at the stone. He aimed carefully and pulled the trigger. Nothing happened.

Lucy walked slowly down the bank, concentrating on the men. She had thickened the air between ARK and Ethne, creating a force field that no human could walk through. She strode past the men and ignored their shouts and their fists pounding against the solid air. Ethne was nearing the stone.

'Do not touch it,' shouted Lucy. 'Wait for me.'

But Ethne wasn't listening. The pain in her shoulder had grown and was now so intense it had pushed all other thoughts from her mind. She stood before the stone, panting with the effort of staying upright. She was losing a lot of blood. If she didn't act now, she would never complete her mission.

The Key Stone towered over her. There was only one symbol etched into the red granite. It was worn and eroded by rain and time, but it was unmistakable.

An ankh.

She touched the pendant at her throat with bloody fingers. Without knowing it, she had been waiting for this moment her whole life. She reached out to the stone and ran her fingers along the lines of the ankh. How was this supposed to help her decode the prophecy? There was no key, no clue as to how she should translate the text.

Perhaps it was her imagination, but the stone seemed to reach out and pull her into an embrace longed for over aeons. Heat built in her fingertips. A violent fizzing set her hand vibrating, as if she were holding it in a furnace. Before she could pull away, an explosive force more violent than a hundred gunshots erupted from the stone and penetrated her body.

Ethne was catapulted from the stone in a wide graceful arc. She landed less gracefully, twisted and bleeding in the marshy grass, unconscious and lost to this world.

28

Ana stood at the cabin window and peered into the darkness. The nights were long and cruel up here, and the days short. It would be several hours before the sun broached the horizon. Joshua was sprawled across the bed behind her, snoring loudly. He had eaten an enormous breakfast and then crashed out.

The cabin was all shiny metal surfaces and pale polished wood. There were six cabins in the complex, each sleeping up to ten people, except for one that had been converted into a communal meeting area with smaller workshop spaces upstairs. This was where Niloufer, Beatrice and other angels inducted the Homo Angelus into their new identities. They took around fifty guests at a time, each staying for a week or two, sometimes longer. The angels had processed thousands already. Linnunrata wasn't the only training centre. There were more dotted around the world, hidden in remote corners under the radar of ARK and curious governments alike.

Niloufer had explained all this to them over breakfast and promised more details once the others were up. While Joshua had wolfed down heaps of smoked mackerel, Ana had struggled with a bowl of porridge sweetened with cloudberries. She felt queasy but didn't know why. Although the food was tasty, she found her appetite had abandoned her.

Niloufer watched over her solicitously and poured more hot chocolate when her cup was drained. It was unnerving to be observed so closely, the way a mother watches her baby, delighting in every twitch and inexplicable facial expression. She could hide nothing from him.

'You are tormenting yourself,' he said kindly.

Ana pushed her empty bowl to one side. 'I'm just feeling a bit sick, that's all.'

'I speak of the terrible injustice that befell your family,' said Niloufer. 'I so wish it could have been prevented, but alas, it was not to be.'

'It was my fault,' said Ana. 'I killed Patrick, even if it was an accident.'

'You must not blame yourself, Ana. You had not yet received training. You were newborn, innocent. How could you have understood the power you wielded, or more importantly, controlled what was happening to you?'

'Well, it's nice of you to say so,' said Ana, and sipped her drink.

'I'm not being nice, Ana. I am not saying this to ease your conscience or to make you feel better. It is simply the truth. We bring the Human Angels together here to train them because the powers only manifest when you are with at least one other angel, human or otherwise. It is even better when there are many. Your powers manifested because you were with Michael. You were unguided. You were not to blame. One of us should have been with you, and for that I am deeply sorry.'

She listened now to the strangely soothing noises coming from Joshua's sleeping form and wondered if she had been too hard on herself. The angels were ready to forgive her, but she knew she couldn't escape the consequences of her actions. Perhaps ARK and her mother were right. She didn't deserve such power if she couldn't control it.

Ana decided to leave Joshua sleeping and crept downstairs. She carefully placed her feet at the edges of the wooden steps to avoid creaking and waking the others. Niloufer had told her there were another five people lodged in this cabin, who were all keen to meet her. They were due to leave the complex soon and continue their work in the outside world.

As she reached the bottom of the stairs she heard someone moving around in the kitchen. A tall blonde woman in a fluffy dressing gown was pouring milk into a bowl, her back to Ana. Wondering how to introduce herself, Ana stood for a moment, watching as the woman returned the milk to the fridge. She was about to speak when the woman beat her to it.

'Hello Ana,' she said, turning to smile at her. 'How was your trip?'

'Um...fine, good thanks. Sorry, I didn't...did I wake you?'

The woman laughed and shook her head. She picked up her bowl and shovelled muesli into her mouth, then walked past Ana and sunk onto one of the sofas beyond the dining table at the bottom of the stairs.

'I'm Freja,' she said between mouthfuls. 'It's good to meet you. Beatrice told us all about you.'

'Really?' Ana sat on the other sofa and tucked up her feet. 'I don't understand why everyone is so interested in me all of a sudden. I'm no more special than you, Freja. Or anyone who's been through this place.'

Freja chewed thoughtfully for a minute, her eyes on Ana. 'You don't know, do you?'

'Know what?'

'Not for me to say, but there's a prophecy and you're in it.'

'Me?' Ana was flabbergasted.

A door banged upstairs and Freja looked up. She seemed to go inwards into herself for a moment, and then turned to Ana and smiled. 'Seth is up. He's pleased you're here and says hello.'

Freja and Seth were clearly connected in the same way she and Michael were. She had tried to contact him several times, but hadn't been able to track him down. It only seemed to work if the other person knew where they were. Michael was in the dark so she couldn't see him. But she should be able to find Ethne, if only Ethne could hear her.

'Freja, can you send a message to someone who isn't Homo Angelus? Have you ever tried it?'

Freja nodded, her jaw working on a spoonful of muesli. 'Just have to be careful not to surprise them, that's all. I'll show you later if you like.'

Ana smiled and relaxed. She liked this new friend. Freja seemed kind and straightforward, older than Ana by a good ten years, with spiky hair and piercing blue eyes. Ana thought she might be Swedish, so probed gently into her mind and found she was right. Freja was from Stockholm and her husband was divorcing her because she was one of the new humans, with the excuse that she scared him.

Freja put her empty bowl on the coffee table between them and winked. 'He's a coward. Poor thing.'

Footsteps pounded down the stairs and a middle-aged sweet-faced cherub bounced into the room. The cherub was also wearing a fluffy dressing gown, his tight curly hair wet from the shower.

'Hi Ana,' he said, extending his hand in greeting. 'I'm Seth. Fuck me, this is an honour. How long till he arrives?'

Ana shook Seth's hand feeling bewildered.

'Oh, shit,' said Seth. 'You don't know, I mean, obviously you know about it, but not-'

'Stop talking Seth,' said Freja with a fixed smile.

'Me and my gob.' Seth whacked himself on the forehead and bounced into the kitchen. 'Got time for a little smackerel of something before the big meet? Who wants coffee?'

'Me,' said Freja, getting up and grabbing her bowl from the table. She joined Seth in the kitchen. 'Ana?'

'Yes, thanks.'

'You sure?' said Seth. 'What about the effects of caffeine on the-'

Freja pinched him on the arm and shushed him. They exchanged a brief, intense look, and then Seth turned away and put the kettle on. 'Oh,' he said under his breath.

'Joshua will have one too,' said Ana. 'I'll take it up to him.'

Freja and Seth both turned to stare at Ana opened mouthed.

'Tell me you're joking,' said Seth. 'He's here. He's actually in this building. Holy mother of shitting-'

Freja punched him on the arm. 'Please *try* to be civilised.'

After breakfast, Beatrice came to tell them the meeting would be starting soon. Ana walked across the snow-bound square arm in arm with Freja who was giving her a run down of what she had learned in the last couple of weeks. Joshua followed under a barrage of questions from Seth. When they had arrived, Ana had noticed Joshua's mind had turned opaque; the walls had gone back up and the shutters were down. He clearly wasn't happy surrounded by all these souped-up humans and was in full lock-down. Seth was baffled by this and was trying to crash through some of the barriers he was encountering in Joshua's mind. He wasn't getting very far.

They entered the main cabin and squeezed into the crowded meeting room. There weren't enough seats for everyone so most were standing in groups around the walls or squatting on the floor. Ana found herself the centre of attention as the other Homo Angelus all wanted to shake her hand or give her a friendly hug. Seth led the way through the throng, searching for a space to sit.

'We need a bigger boat,' he grinned.

Weary groans and a few chuckles spread through the crowd. Niloufer and Beatrice were standing in front of the fireplace facing the assembled humans. They exchanged a glance and in an instant the room expanded. The walls extended away from those leaning against them, and several extra sofas and armchairs materialised in the centre of the now spacious room. Applause erupted from some of the newly arrived Homo Angelus, while the old hands merely threw themselves into the available chairs and made themselves comfortable.

'Now,' said Niloufer, causing the applause to fizzle out. 'We have two new guests. Anastasia Wilson and Joshua King. Welcome to you both.'

Joshua glanced at Ana sitting beside him on the sofa and fired a question into her mind. He wanted to know if she had given them his real name. She frowned and shook her head.

Niloufer continued, 'We are lucky to have you, indeed. In fact, if you wouldn't mind, I wonder if you would oblige us with some information. You have been on the front line, as it were. Beatrice has given us some of the details, but it would be good to hear it from the horse's mouth, so to speak.'

He looked at Ana, waiting for her response. She didn't want to stand up in front of these people and tell them what she had lived through in the last couple of days. The thought of it brought the nausea back to her stomach and she shrank into the sofa, wishing it would swallow her whole.

Joshua took her hand and squeezed. 'I got this, babes.'

Niloufer smiled and opened his arms wide. 'Thank you, Joshua. You have the floor.'

Joshua was living his ultimate nightmare. He didn't want anyone in this room to know who he was and why he was here. What would they do to him if they knew? He imagined his mind was encased in steel. It probably wasn't enough to keep out an angel, but it should stop any curious Homo Angelus.

He cleared his throat and stood. A mosaic of faces watched, waiting for him to speak. Every one of them was capable of exposing him. He took a deep breath and began.

'Two days ago Ana and I were able to confirm that ARK have been doing experiments on the Homo Angelus. We're not sure what that involves exactly, but several bodies have been found. Two were shot, but the others all died from an overdose of barbiturates. We think ARK are trying to control the mutation to extract its benefits. I've been trying to find out what they're planning and I'm afraid I haven't got far.'

'We thank you for your efforts,' said Niloufer.

'There's more,' said Joshua. 'Another Homo Angelus was taken, right from under Ana's nose. They would've got her too but Beatrice stopped them.'

'Who was it?' said a voice. 'Who got taken?'

'Michael Okeke,' said Joshua. 'We think he's at the lab where these experiments are being done.'

'Michael from the Okeke Gospel?' said the voice. 'His films really helped me. I was lost before I found him. I hope he's okay.'

A murmur of agreement rippled around the room. Joshua watched the attention drift away from him and wondered if he should sit down, but then, as if he had hit a switch, the chatter stopped. All faces turned back to him, silent and waiting for him to continue. It seemed they could read his mind despite the steel shutters. Unnerved, he cleared his throat self-consciously.

'Right, so...what else? Oh, the stones. A friend of ours, Ethne Godwin, a normal human, got called to Greenland. They've found a stone circle or something, in a cave under the ice, and it has a prophecy written on it. She's been tasked with translating it.'

The room burst into excited murmuring again, and Joshua was hit with a volley of urgent questions. 'Has she done it?' 'Do you have the prophecy?' 'What does it say?'

Joshua raised his hands in desperation and silence fell once more. 'I can't answer any of these questions, I'm sorry. We don't know where Ethne is. We need to contact her, but we weren't sure if ARK has her or not. We didn't want to cause her any problems by getting in touch.'

'Very wise,' said Beatrice. 'But we can help with that. Ethne is safe.'

Ana sat forward on the sofa. 'Is she all right? Where is she?'

Beatrice smiled. 'She is in Scotland and has the best help available. She is with one of the Great Ones.'

'We still need to find Michael,' continued Joshua. 'I've been trying to locate the lab, but, no luck so far.' He glanced at Niloufer. 'I think that's all of it.'

'Thank you, Joshua,' said the angel.

Instead of returning to his seat, Joshua moved through the crowd towards the door. From there he could watch the faces around the room more easily. He couldn't understand why they were allowing him to be there. He wasn't one of them. Niloufer continued to talk to the Homo

Angelus about their role in the world to come. The more Joshua listened, the more alarmed he became. The language seemed tame enough, but the intention was clear. Just as Michael had hinted in his film, the Homo Angelus wanted to take over the world.

'The time is close,' said Niloufer. 'Once we have the prophecy, all will become clear. You each have a role to play in the coming transformation, not one of you is insignificant. Some will play larger roles than others. Size is not important.'

Seth guffawed and playfully elbowed his neighbour in the ribs, grinning like it was his job to play court jester. Niloufer smiled faintly at him, then continued.

'You are the forerunners, the way showers. Some of you are the Guardians of old, returning to take up where you left off many aeons ago. You have fallen into amnesia. The prophecy will awaken your ancient memories. The rest are humans evolving as you should. This is the first stage.

'Once you have remembered and the Guardians are in place, stage two will commence. The human race will awaken en masse. There is much danger at this time. The Age of Darkness is about to end, but it will not end quietly. It will not limp off and lie down and cause no fuss. It will rage. It will fight. And we must be ready. The light will prevail.'

Joshua had heard enough. He slithered towards the door, muttering apologies as he inched his way around people towards the exit.

Across the room, Ana listened with rapt attention as Niloufer explained why the Homo Angelus were evolving. She had to find out what was in the prophecy. She needed to speak with Ethne, urgently.

A movement at the door made her look up. Joshua was edging towards the exit looking rattled but doing a good job of hiding it. She watched, dismayed, as he slipped silently from the room.

29

Joshua zipped up his arctic jacket and stepped onto the path, his breath freezing on his lips. He fished his hat and gloves from a pocket and pulled them on, and gazed into the silent stillness around him. He checked his watch. It was approaching eleven o'clock; nearly nine in the UK. He had to make a call.

Beyond the cabins, the frozen air held the pine forest in a deathly embrace. The first weak filaments of sunlight were streaking into the sky, illuminating the cabins and trees in an unearthly twilight. Joshua crossed the square and walked past banks of snow sculpted into undulating mounds of crystal so fine they looked like icing sugar confections created by a flamboyant baker.

To ensure absolute privacy, he continued past the cabins into the trees and then down to the lake beyond, his boots squeaking on the compact snow. On the far side of the lake stood more pine trees heavy with snow. In the twilight their peaks shone like hundreds of lighthouses.

Joshua stepped onto the glassy lake. The ice appeared strong. He rammed his boot against it to test the thickness and a shuddering crack resounded from the depths. He hurriedly stepped back from the edge and pulled out his phone.

'Jack Dexter,' he said, when the call connected.

'How many ducks have you seen this morning?' said a man's voice.

'Two,' said Joshua. 'No swans though.'

'Shame. Go ahead, Jack. This better be good.'

'I don't have the lab, Kendrick. I'm working on it.'

'So why are you in Finland? Fancied a skiing holiday?'

'I'm at Linnunrata,' said Joshua. 'The Homo Angelus are being trained to use their powers, not just here but all over the world. They're planning something big. No details yet.'

'Tell me about Linnunrata.'

'It's an angel boot camp. On the face of it, these Homo Angelus seem harmless, but I have reason to believe they could be dangerous, and groups of them together would be unstoppable. I can keep one of them out of my head at a time, but when they're in a group, it's...well, impossible.'

'What are they planning?' said Kendrick.

'There's a prophecy-'

'Yeah, Greenland cave, stones, got it. What does it say?'

'I don't have that information,' said Joshua. 'They said humanity was going to awaken. I think that means everyone will turn Homo Angelus. Is that right? Is that what we want?'

'Not my place, Jack.'

'What's the play? D'you want to get a team over here?'

'Stand down, Jack.'

'What d'you mean?'

'I mean, stand down,' said Kendrick tersely. 'Let it play out. Keep an eye on them and keep us up to date.'

'What about the lab?' said Joshua.

'I take it you're with Anastasia Wilson?' said Kendrick.

'I am.'

'Stick to her,' said Kendrick. 'I want details of this awakening plan. Dates, places, players. Are we clear?'

Kendrick replaced the receiver and leaned back in his chair. The man on the other side of the desk watched him the way a dog watches its master.

The façade was plausible. Tailored suit, not a hair out of place, and a smile that ranged from charm personified to dead-eyed menace. Men like Gregori were ten a penny. He saw them everywhere in the City and upper echelons of the corporate world. Men who thought they could rule the world, command armies and play at being king. They never lasted long and there was always another pretender waiting in line.

These days the queue would stretch around the world, never mind around the block.

And yet, Gregori had brought stunning intel, the kind of inside information you could work an entire career to uncover. Kendrick's team was following it up, checking every detail and pulling apart the lawyer's personal history. He had run this department for twenty years and had never come across anyone with such a flawless bio. That in itself was suspicious.

Christian Gregori was orphaned age five, then schooled by the Church in Italy. He won a glittering scholarship to the Angelicum in Vatican City, and then studied for a Law Degree at Cambridge in the UK where he was headhunted by Pinecone Freeholdings, an organisation adept at staying below everybody's radar. Kendrick had his suspicions about this company, and the man sitting before him, but he didn't have anything admissible. Gregori seemed too perfect and Kendrick didn't believe in saints.

He spun his chair to gaze out of the window. The Thames was a grey slug crawling through London leaving the foul sludge of decay in its wake. They would have to abandon this building soon if the barrier upriver didn't hold. There had already been two close calls this year and it wasn't yet February.

A delicate cough sounded from behind his chair. The lawyer was eager to conclude his business, but Kendrick was in no rush. He wasn't giving Gregori anything until his bio checked out. He swung back to face him, steepled his fingers and watched him over the top of his glasses.

An age passed with the men locked in a silent war of attrition. Finally, the lawyer lowered his eyes and Kendrick allowed himself a secret smile. Gregori examined his fingernails with focused attention and when he spoke it was with an air of feigned indifference.

'You have great fortitude, Mr Kendrick. I applaud you.'

Kendrick rolled his eyes. Who did this guy think he was? Thankfully, at that moment, the door burst open and a compact woman stepped into the room. She nodded a greeting to Kendrick, and then gave Gregori a quick look up and down.

'He checks out,' she said, and spun on her heel.

'Weber, hang on,' said Kendrick, and she turned to face him. 'You're sure. Hundred percent?'

She nodded. 'Holy See just confirmed.'

'Holy See?'

Weber turned to leave. 'They also confirmed they own Pinecone Freeholdings.'

Kendrick wanted to leap across the desk and kiss her. He nodded casually and buried his jubilation as deep as it would go. So the Vatican was the silent partner in the ARK consortium, and Gregori was their attack dog. Now he knew what he was dealing with. He waited for Weber to close the door, and then scribbled a series of numbers on a scrap of paper.

'You understand,' he said as he wrote, 'what I require in return.'

Gregori pulled a slip of paper from his pocket and unfolded it with exaggerated drama. The men exchanged their slips of paper and each checked what the other had written. Kendrick tapped the numbers into his computer and waited. 'You understand what will happen if this doesn't check out,' he said, watching the screen.

'The Fire Stone is there,' said Gregori. 'You have my word. In return, can you guarantee that Ms Wilson will be found at these coordinates?'

'Jack is one of my best,' said Kendrick. 'That's the GPS on his phone.'

Gregori stood.

'One more thing,' said Kendrick, leaning back in his seat. 'This Fire Stone in Greenland. You haven't made it clear what you expect us to do with it, once we've located it.'

Gregori smiled and the room filled with a cold light that made Kendrick shiver right down to his soul.

'Destroy it, dear boy.'

The lawyer crossed to the door and punched the GPS location into his phone. He was about to leave, but then turned with a look of concentrated fury on his face.

'What is the meaning of this?'

Kendrick remained a blank slate. 'Problem?'

Gregori slung the scrap paper onto the desk. 'These are not GPS coordinates.'

'Really?' Kendrick made a play of checking the scrawled numbers. 'That's curious. Must be satellite slippage. We put a new one up after the storm. Damned inconvenient.'

'I am not a fool, Mr Kendrick. These are random numbers.'

'Are they?'

'We had an agreement.'

'I lied,' said Kendrick. 'Sorry about that.'

'Perhaps I didn't make myself clear,' said Gregori. 'It is imperative that we find Ms Wilson. You could say it is a matter of national security.'

'I agree.'

'Then you must give me her location.'

'I don't have it,' said Kendrick. 'Like I said. Jack is one of my best. Has one of those stealth phones.'

Gregori strode to the door. 'You will regret this moment, have no doubt.' He put his hand on the doorknob, and then turned as if remembering something he wanted to say.

Kendrick stifled a laugh; this guy really was too much. He would be glad to see the back of him.

'One more thing,' said Gregori. 'One of yours has turned.'

'Turned?'

'Joshua King. His mutation has activated. He is Deviant.'

Kendrick finally allowed himself to smile openly and turned to gaze out of the window.

'Weber will see you out,' he said.

30

Lucy stood guard over Ethne's body and watched the two ARK Security men stagger about the marshy grass. She had never heard such bad language. The men were trapped behind an invisible barrier and were determined to break through. They hurled their guns, their blasphemy, and their bodies at the congealed air, to no avail. One even began to dig like a terrier looking for a bone.

As soon as Ethne had hit the ground, Lucy had surrounded the men in a perceptual filter. She could see them, but the men couldn't see out. As far as they were concerned, the women had simply vanished. Lucy watched them exhaust every option and waited for their confusion and fear to drive them away.

As the men retreated to the Lexus, Lucy knelt beside her ward to inspect the damage. Ethne was bleeding heavily from a wound to her shoulder. Lucy gently pressed her hand against the ruptured flesh and searched for the bullet with her angelic vision. Physical forms were mostly empty space so she could see it easily through the bone, sinew and blood, buried deep against the shoulder blade. She concentrated and after a moment, felt the sting of metal hit her palm. She gazed at the mangled slug nestled in her hand and shuddered, then tossed the offending item to one side.

With a single pass of her hands over Ethne's shoulder, the haemorrhage stopped and flesh closed over the hole. Lucy cleaned away the blood with another pass of her hands. She tenderly touched her fingers to Ethne's forehead.

'Come back to us, Ethne, Scribe of the Ancients. Come back to us, Daughter of Thoth.'

Ethne blinked. She was standing on the shore beside an estuary where a wooden ship waited in the dock. Men were loading a red granite menhir carved with her words onto the boat, shouting and manoeuvring the stone with pulleys and ropes. There were seven ships in all, one for each stone.

Ethne glanced down and saw she was wearing the feather cloak from her dreams. She moved to the water's edge and peered at her reflection.

The shock of what she saw hit like lightning. An unfamiliar face gazed back, rippling and distorting with the movement of the river. The woman was older by twenty years and over six feet tall. Her long blonde hair was matted into dreadlocks, dark kohl lines marked her eyes and red ochre was smeared over her forehead. Her feather cape had a large hood and if she raised her arms to open the cloak, she looked like a human vulture. The effect was enhanced by a long face with high cheekbones and piercing blue eyes.

Ethne checked her left wrist and found her own tattoo: a five pointed Akhu star. She had crossed time and was inside another woman's life, inside one of her dreams.

'Guardian,' said a voice behind her. 'The ship is ready.'

Ethne turned to find a small man dressed in a simple tunic cowering before her like she was a queen or a goddess. He wasn't speaking English, but whatever the language, she was having no trouble understanding it. Her dream-self must be set to auto-translate. Rather than risk saying something intolerably modern, she kept her mouth shut and walked along the riverbank towards the boats. They were impressive craft, similar to the drawings she had seen of boats depicted in Egyptian art with high sea-going prows. She knew where they would be going. It would be a long journey.

Further up the bank was an area of woodland where a small crowd had gathered to watch the activity on the river. Half concealed behind a Scots Pine stood a man Ethne seemed to know. Perhaps he was from her tribe or family. He shared the same height and features that made him look like a walking serpent. Their eyes met and a pulse of recognition passed between them. She was his acolyte, but he wasn't watching her with pride. Something terrible had torn her away and a burning resentment crackled behind his eyes.

Two women broke from the group in the trees and descended the bank. Their long capes billowed behind them like wings and radiant smiles lit their faces as they approached. Ethne realised she must know the pair well, and returned their smiles.

The women took her hands in greeting, and with that delicate touch Ethne knew them to be Ana and Michael in different forms. Both were middle-aged women like her, but their skin was a deep brown. They wore elaborate beaded necklaces and long dreadlocks, and carried the same tribal mark on their left wrists: the Akhu star of the Shining Ones.

All three were Guardians of the Light. Ethne had been initiated into the sisterhood and chosen as their scribe. They had travelled to this northern place from the land called Khem to oversee the writing of the prophecy. The Shining Ones took many names around the world, and the sisters had returned many times in multiple guises, and would do so again.

'Seshat,' said the woman who was Ana. 'May your journey be safe.'

'And yours, Isis,' said Ethne, amazed at the words she had long forgotten.

She turned to the other woman and gazed into her dark eyes. She could see the light of the soul burning there, the soul that would become Michael in twelve thousand years. Ethne, as Seshat, wished she could return home with them. She knew they would not meet again on this earth until the Great Awakening, and then her time with Michael would be short.

'Nephthys,' said Seshat, her eyes filling with tears. 'There is never enough time.'

Nephthys laughed joyously and embraced Seshat. She stepped back and gazed into her sister's sad eyes.

'You have seen it, Seshat,' she said. 'It cannot be unseen. We three shall return.'

'Say farewell to the others,' said Seshat. 'I send my love on phoenix wings. I shall not see Rostau again in this life. My end shall come under the ice of Thule.'

Seshat embraced Isis. She didn't want this day to end, but the fates were in motion and she must fulfil her duty. The stones must be in place before the sky began to burn. She must not fail; the future depended upon it.

She had been thirteen when the gods first spoke to her and changed the shape of her life. She would not take a mate. The otherworld called too deeply to her soul for her to give herself to a mere man. She was initiated into the temple and served for many years to uphold the pillar of the world in the Land of the Watchers. But when the Akhu had arrived from the south, she knew her destiny lay elsewhere, in a distant land of ice and darkness.

She had left her home and descended the mountain to join her new friends. The priests of her homeland had foretold calamity if she left, but her choice had been rewarded with a vision. It had lasted a full cycle of the moon, and her mind had filled with images and words of which she had no understanding. Guided by the Bringer of Light, she had been given the letters and their meaning, and over many moons had grown in wisdom and knowledge. Her teacher came to her in the light, sometimes as a man, sometimes a woman, and she had received her anointed name of Seshat.

The vision was a prophecy of the Great Awakening, to be written into seven stones. One stone would remain to act as Key and guide. The rest would stand with the Prophecy Stone itself, the instrument of transformation: the Fire Stone. She did not understand this stone; it came from beyond this world. It was created by the Light-Bringer, using secret and forbidden knowledge, to bring about the end of the Age of Darkness. At the appointed time the Guardians of the Light would return, the stones would be found, and humanity would awaken.

Seshat gazed into the sky.

A skein of swans passed overhead, flying north into the endless night. It was time. She descended to the dock through the rough grass, and took her place on the vessel to carry her to Western Thule. She had seen the cave in her night visions and knew the stones would be safe from the coming darkness.

As Seshat's boat set sail, Ethne watched the land retreat and searched for landmarks that would tell her where she was. The ship sailed north, straight for the wall of ice beyond Thule. This ice had once covered the land but had now receded, opening a route across the Arctic to the far west. A column of smoke and ash rose into the air on the horizon. Ethne realised this must be a volcano erupting on what would become known as Iceland. By a process of elimination, she realised the prophecy had been carved on Orkney.

Seshat settled in for the journey, lulled by the rocking of the boat and the rhythm of the oarsmen beaten out on a drum. Her adopted sisters, Isis and Nephthys, were returning to Egypt. How she longed to be with them, even in such uncertain times. The Black Land was suffering, the crops would not grow. The Beautiful Place of the First Time could no longer sustain their culture and they would be moving on soon, leaving behind the Great Lion by the river.

But Seshat knew she would return to Rostau. Not in this form, but one day, under a different sky.

The ships arrived in Greenland and sailed up river until they could go no further. Ethne's dreams came alive and, as Seshat, she sang to the stones. They rose into the air as if made of nothing heavier than feathers, and were carried to the cave on cushions of sound.

The entrance was narrow and treacherous. Ice and snow still clung to the rocks. It would not be long before the mouth of the cave was hidden under the ice once more.

Inside the cave Seshat warmed herself on the flames of the fire. She gazed across the dark cavern at the stones, silent in their golden spiral. It would be many ages before they would be read. She herself would return. The Key Stone waited patiently in the land that would become Scotland. Encoded in its crystalline structure was all she would need to remember of this time. A spell cast on the stone would protect it from being discovered by destructive forces, whether human or otherwise.

She stood and raised her eyes to the entrance high above her head. The sky blazed in red fury. It was madness to leave the safety of the cave, but she must. She had seen the end.

The air filled with a boiling tempest that turned the rocks to glass. The great double-headed serpent, the source of all life hiding in the smallest of places, must be transfigured. It would lie in wait, like a snake in the grass, waiting for the return of the Shining Ones.

Seshat emerged from the cave onto the ice. Terrifying shapes rippled through the sky and the air crackled with electricity. Voices shouted for her to follow the men down the mountainside. They planned to return to the boats to escape the inferno. They would fail. Pain flared in her skin. In horror, she watched her arms blister in the heat. Sores appeared on her face as the skin ruptured. She was burning.

The horror of what was about to occur brought Ethne thrashing into a twilight state. She could feel the heat tearing through Seshat's flesh as if it were her own. Opening her mouth to scream only brought more pain as the flames rushed to consume her throat from the inside.

A flash of lightning exploded the rocks behind her head, bringing down an avalanche of stone. Ethne cried out as Seshat was buried, still burning, under the liquefied rock.

31

Ana pushed through the bodies packing the cabin. The meeting was breaking up and she had to find Joshua. Smiling faces turned to greet her as she passed. They wanted to be close to her, to touch her, as if her simple presence would enrich and heal them. She returned their smiles and did her best to grasp every hand thrust into hers, but by the time she reached the door she was overwhelmed and desperate for some fresh air.

Niloufer's closing words circled her mind like a taunt: 'We will build a new world on the principles of love even as the old world disintegrates about us. Many will cling to the past. They will try to continue as if nothing has changed. We know better and can lead the way. Do not deceive yourself into thinking this will be easy. It sounds a small matter – to be kind – but imagine the whole world doing such a simple thing. Not just occasionally. Not just when it is convenient. But every day, in every moment, and with all people.'

The angels wanted to create a society of saints. Ana knew it wasn't that simple. She wanted to believe it was possible to become her better self, to let her inner angel lead the way, but for her, love always ended in betrayal.

She emerged from the cabin into the frigid air and watched happy groups of friends chatting and laughing as they made their way through the snow. Across the square stood Joshua, his face pink with cold. He shoved his hands into his pockets and watched the others leave the cabin.

Freja joined Ana and linked her arm with hers. 'You look worried,' she said.

Ana tried to smile as she searched around for Beatrice. She had to tell someone about Joshua. They had to know the danger she had put them in by bringing him here.

Beatrice stepped from the cabin, deep in conversation with Niloufer. Ana rushed over and took her hand.

'Please, I need to speak with you.' She led the angel away from the others and continued. 'I'm sorry, Bea, but I have to warn you. Joshua is MI6. He's a spy. He's been using me to find this place and infiltrate, and goodness knows what they're planning. He's not even Homo Angelus. I'm so sorry. If I'd known I never would've let him...Why are you smiling?'

'Did I not tell you to bring him?'

'But-'

'I know who he is,' said Beatrice. 'It is as it should be.'

Ana stared at the angel in disbelief and a flash of anger sent heat spiralling down her arms. Sparks escaped into the air from her fingers. 'You knew who he was from the moment we met. You knew he wasn't called Jack. You knew he was lying to me. Why didn't you tell me?'

'It was for him to share.'

'And why didn't you tell me about the prophecy?' continued Ana, not even trying to calm down. 'Everybody here seems to know me better than I do myself.'

Beatrice smiled and Ana felt her anger subside. The angel was trying to make her feel better, but she didn't want to be soothed. She wanted the truth.

'What's so important about me?' she said.

'You will remember soon.'

'I don't want to remember. I want you to tell me.'

'It doesn't work like that, Ana. You must discover the truth for yourself. I cannot think for you.'

Ana felt a familiar mental signature buzzing close behind and turned to find Joshua approaching. He smiled and opened his mouth to speak, but she cut him off.

'Don't.'

'What?'

'Are we safe?' she said.

'Ana, I told you-'

'I know you've been on the phone. Did you tell them where we are?'

'SIS know where I am, but they have no reason to tell ARK. As far as I know.'

'As far as you know isn't good enough, Joshua.'

Ana spun to face Beatrice expecting the angel to agree with her, but she was smiling benignly at Joshua as if he were as harmless as a newborn lamb.

Joshua put his arm around Ana's shoulders. 'I won't let anyone get to you, babes.'

She pushed at him and spun away. 'Don't touch me.'

Joshua watched Ana march across the square towards their cabin and sighed. An angelic hand slid into his and squeezed.

'Give her time.'

Ethne woke with a shout and flailed blindly at the rocks covering her inert dream form.

'Breathe,' said Lucy.

Ethne sat up and stared in incomprehension at the landscape around her. She appeared to be sitting on some grass beside a river, a great wall of rock loomed over the valley on the other side. A faint glow emanated from the skin of her angelic companion, who was watching her gravely.

'Did you see?'

Ethne nodded and rubbed her head. She knew the prophecy. She had seen the whole thing. It had poured into her head on fast-forward, whether she wanted to see it or not. She couldn't remember every detail, for that she would need to consult the text, which she was certain she could now read like a native. The only details that had lodged in her mind concerned her friends, Isis and Nephthys.

'We have to find them,' she said. 'I need to see them.'

'Shush now, Ethne. You must rest.'

'I need to tell Ana who she is,' said Ethne. 'They can't get her, Lucy. We have to keep ARK away from her. They'll kill her if they know who she is.'

Lucy pressed her hand to Ethne's forehead. 'You must calm yourself.'

'I can't just sit here.'

She stood on shaking legs and stumbled through the grass looking for the road. Something was missing.

She spun on the spot. 'Did you...? Where...?' There were the two rocky peaks, the road behind and the river in front. Where was the Wandering Giant? She stared at the space where there once stood a giant hunk of red granite. 'Did you move me?'

'No,' said Lucy. 'The stone is gone. It has served its purpose.'

Ethne shook her head. She needed to think but it felt like her brain had been replaced with an assortment of root vegetables. She wanted to argue with Lucy. She wanted to point out, strenuously, that stones don't simply vanish into the air as if they had never existed. But there was no point and she couldn't find the words anyway. She had seen this happen before. She should be used to it by now. She was through the looking glass, she was no longer in Kansas, she had entered the Twilight Zone.

'I have to...' Ethne lurched towards the road. She could see her Softail glinting in the sunshine. The Lexus was gone.

'Michael...I have to find Michael.' She trudged through the marshy ground, her head swimming with ancient words and confusion.

'Ethne, come back here,' said Lucy sternly.

'Michael's going to die,' said Ethne, hardly believing her own words. 'I have to find him. We have to stop them. I'm not sitting around here doing nothing while they kill him.'

She stumbled forward and wriggled inside her jacket and yanked at the leather to make it hang straight. Something wasn't right. She fiddled with the collar and found her clothes were torn. A few spots of blood were visible on her shirt. She pulled it back to check her shoulder.

There was no bullet hole. The wound she remembered receiving had gone.

Ethne reached the road, yanked on her helmet and clambered onto the bike. In a flash of light, Lucy appeared and stood with her hands on her hips looking severe.

Ethne stared at her. 'Did you heal my shoulder?'

'You must rest,' said Lucy. 'You need to eat.'

'You're obsessed with food, you are. And besides, we've run out. I'll have to find a shop. We can pick something up on the way to find Michael.'

'Get off the bike.'

Ethne started the engine. 'I'm not staying here. You can come with me, or not. It's up to you.'

She turned the bike and drove up the road. In her mirrors, she watched Lucy transform into her bird form and fly towards her. She raced into the next valley pursued by an enormous irate eagle. Lucy flew at her head, dive bombed the motorcycle, and flapped her huge wings in

Ethne's face. Finally, after almost driving off the road into a ditch, Ethne stopped and jumped off the bike.

'What the fuck?' she shouted at the eagle. The bird perched on a nearby fence. 'Are you insane? You could've killed me you lunatic.'

The eagle morphed back into Lucy. She stood looking regal and impassive while Ethne shouted at her. 'We have to save Michael. They're going to kill him.'

'Ethne. You can't rewrite the prophecy. It has been seen. It cannot be unseen.'

'Because it's written in stone?' said Ethne. 'Bullshit.' She continued to rage at the angel, who simply stood there and took it. After some time Ethne's spleen ran out of fuel. She crossed her arms and glared defiantly at Lucy.

'Where are you going?' said the angel calmly.

'To find Michael.'

'And where is he?'

'I don't-'

'You don't know,' said Lucy. 'You also do not know who or what you are up against. You have no idea what is going on. Have you understood the prophecy correctly? Do you even understand why he is to die?'

Ethne stared at the asphalt. 'No to all of that. But we have to help him. Will you help me?'

'All right,' said Lucy gently. 'Now will you eat something?'

'We don't have anything.'

Lucy walked to the bike and opened one of the saddlebags. She whipped out a tin of beans and a pack of sausages, as if pulling a rabbit from a hat. She even had a pan to cook them in.

Ethne stared in disbelief. She couldn't deal with any more weirdness. If anything else happened she was sure her head would explode in protest.

Lucy led them to a secluded area beside the river and settled down to build a fire. Ethne suddenly realised how hungry she was and crouched beside the fire to help. In no time, they were tucking into sausages and beans, and Ethne's head began to clear.

'Are you allowed to go around conjuring food out of nowhere?'

Lucy grinned. 'Just eat your sausage.'

After finishing lunch, Ethne rinsed the pots in the river. She sat on the bank and watched the water spin and swirl. A breeze lifted her hair and chattered through the branches of the trees in the woodland beyond the stream. A bird sang lazily in a nearby branch. Lucy joined her beside the water and gazed across the land as if hypnotised.

'This is such a beautiful place,' said the angel.

Ethne smiled to herself. Michael was always saying that. Whenever she got fed up with the tedious routines of her life, or the horror of the news made her wish she had a serious narcotic addiction, he would take her somewhere breathtaking; somewhere like this. Or he would simply point to a flower growing out of the concrete, or a bird singing its head off in a tree. He would smile and remind her:

'Look at it, Ethne. This is Eden, right here.'

She stood and returned to the bike and Lucy joined her. 'I need to get home and get the prophecy written down before I forget it again.'

'Good plan.'

'And you need to teach me telepathy.'

'Do I?' said Lucy, smiling.

'I want to contact Ana and see if I can find Michael. It's a good enough place to start.'

Ethne drove south and after several hours arrived in the Borders. But the closer she got to home, the more anxious she became. One vision filled her mind: her father cowering in the dark clutching a sharpened flint axe. Something was terribly wrong. Even Lucy became agitated. She took to the sky and flew behind the Softail as an eagle, emitting a series of encouraging kaahs.

Ethne pulled into the driveway of Newgrange House, her senses on high alert. She drove slowly around to the back of the house, gazing up at the windows. Everything seemed to be fine, but then she saw the back door was wide open. She parked and jumped off the bike. Lucy fluttered to the lawn and transformed into her usual shape and stood with her hands on her hips to survey the scene.

Ethne ran into the house and called for her dad and Irene. No answer. She pulled her phone from her jacket and switched it on in case she had missed any messages. There were none.

The house was untouched, as far as she could tell. If anyone had broken in, they hadn't taken anything valuable. She ran from room to room, but they were all empty.

She ran outside and almost collided with Lucy, who was smiling. The angel took her hand and led her from the house towards the Neolithic bunker. 'They are safe.'

Ethne went to the mouth of the passageway and peered into the blackness inside. 'Dad?'

A gasp echoed from the chamber and a pale, worried face appeared. Irene emerged from the bunker with tears in her eyes. She threw her arms around Ethne and hung on like a limpet.

'What happened, Renie? Is he okay?'

Irene maintained her grip on Ethne and nodded vigorously. Lucy stepped forward and gently extracted Ethne from the housekeeper's arms. 'It's all right, Irene,' she said softly. 'Come inside and get warm.'

Lucy led the quivering woman into the house and Ethne turned to the bunker. She had never been inside. She hadn't wanted to encourage what she considered to be an unhealthy obsession. But after her trip back to the Ice Age thanks to a bewitched stone, she had a little more perspective.

She shuffled down the passageway into absolute darkness. 'Dad? Are you in here?' She was just thinking she should have brought a torch, when a light appeared at the end of the passage.

'Ethne, is that you?'

She hurried to the end and stepped into the chamber. Her father was huddled against a wall holding an oil lamp high above his head, peering at her through the gloom.

'How long have you been in here?' she said.

'Men came,' he said in a wavering voice. 'They were looking for you. Irene left the door open, but they couldn't get into the house, Ethne.'

She sat beside him and put an arm around his bony shoulders. He was shivering and obviously still traumatised. Empty bowls and plates of crumbs were stacked in a corner. She listened to his teeth chattering and gazed at the walls of the chamber, lit by the glow of the lamp.

Great swirls, circles and labyrinths were etched into the stone vaulting over her head. It was one of the most beautiful things she had ever seen.

'Did you do all this?' she said in wonder.

'A bird took him,' said Conor. 'A bird took him.'

'Took who?'

'The man,' he said. 'He was outside. I blew out the lamp. He was going to come inside. I had my flint. I was going to fight him, Ethne. I never fought anyone in my life. But I would've fought him. I would've killed him. I would. And the bird came.'

'What bird?'

'I heard it call,' he said. 'Like an eagle. The man screamed. I had to see, so I crawled and lay in the passageway in the dark. He was on the ground and the bird...Ethne, it was so big. I never saw a bird so big. It lifted him up. It took him.'

'Okay,' said Ethne, rubbing her hand over his back. 'Shush now. We need to get you back inside, get some food in you and get you warmed up.'

'But-'

'No arguments, Dad.'

Ethne took the oil lamp and cajoled her father out of the bunker and into the house. She left him in the care of Irene before returning outside. Lucy was standing in the back garden listening to the wind dance through the branches of the trees beside the river, a faint smile on her face.

'What have you been up to?' said Ethne.

Lucy beamed at her.

'You were with me the whole time,' continued Ethne. 'How could you watch over me and my dad at the same time?'

'Ah, Ethne. You do like the tough questions, don't you?'

'What did you do with the man?'

'What man?' said Lucy, the picture of innocence.

'The man outside the bunker, and stop pretending you don't know what I'm talking about.'

'I left him up a tree,' said Lucy. 'I think.'

'What?'

'He'll be fine. Once he stops shouting and figures out how to climb down.'

'I don't believe-' Ethne was about to give Lucy a piece of her mind when she was interrupted mid-thought by her phone pinging. She pulled it from her pocket and stared at the screen in shock. The message had been sent two days ago but had only just made it through to her phone.

It was a text from Will.

32

The fire was fading. He had no more fuel, no more wood. The water was gone.

Will glanced at the remaining squares of chocolate. They wouldn't keep him going for long. He had been rationing himself carefully, hoping someone would return and find him. The radio was dead. He had fired out a couple of SOS calls and had received nothing but static in reply. The satellite phone sat next to the chocolate. He had switched it off to conserve the battery and didn't know if his texts had got through.

Somebody had to come. He didn't want to die in this cave.

He picked up the phone with his good arm and switched it on. It seemed an eternity before it sprung to life and his heart flipped over when he saw the message waiting for him.

Ethne had replied: help is coming!

He closed his eyes in gratitude. He knew Ethne would come through for him. He had seen her escape. Amongst the explosions, rock and dust, chaos and screaming, she had flown to freedom. He had thought he was dreaming.

Gunfire had kept him away from the rock face. Every time he had tried to climb he was beaten back. He had made it twelve feet up only to be blown against the cave wall when the rock above him detonated. He had landed badly and shattered the bones in his left arm. His right leg was bleeding from the shrapnel embedded in his thigh. He had leaned against the jagged wall and howled in pain and fought against the fog of unconsciousness that threatened to drag him under.

Then he had seen Ethne. He had wanted to shout a warning, but that strange and beautiful woman with the insane hair had grabbed her. Together they had ascended through the explosions and disappeared into the light of dawn.

He had assumed he was delirious, that the pain was making him hallucinate. His last thought before he had passed out was that she must have been an angel.

Will had no idea how long it would be before Ethne's cavalry arrived. He might have to hold out another day. He pushed the chocolate to one side, determined to wait as long as possible before eating, despite the hunger burning his stomach. He poked at the dying flames of the fire, desperate to extract as much heat and light from the embers as he could. He needed to find more clothes to wrap around himself or burn on the fire.

He picked up his torch. Thankfully the battery still had some life, and he shone it around his immediate area. The bodies of his colleagues and friends lay where they had fallen. He couldn't think about their deaths right now, all his energy was concentrated on surviving the next 24 hours, and the day after that.

He scrambled to his feet, biting down on the pain that seared through his leg, and with the torch in his good hand, limped towards the nearest body. It was Marcus. He bent over his friend and unzipped the jacket, then began to yank it free. It took several moments, and some extreme profanity, but it finally yielded.

'Sorry, mate,' he said. 'I'd do the same for you.'

He hobbled back to the pile of faintly glowing ash. Torchlight bounced around the cavern and the beam flashed across the fire obsidian, sending out sparks of red and green. Will ran the light around the other stones. They were all intact, serene and oblivious to the destruction that had raged around them in the darkness.

He dropped Marcus' jacket beside the fire and continued on to the stones, drawn like a moth to a light. He gazed at the column of obsidian in wonder. The magnetite crystals embedded in the dark glass glowed in rainbow swirls in the light of his torch. He wanted to run his fingers over its surface but the pain in his free arm was too intense. The slightest movement left him lightheaded with nausea.

Will allowed his imagination to do the work of his fingers. He touched the fiery patterns with his mind and let them move through his being.

A gentle fizzing poured around his body, as if the air around him had become electrified. Something shifted inside, as if the stone was rearranging his internal furniture. His ankle began to throb and pulse with a pleasant heat rather than searing pain. He held his breath and tentatively flexed his foot, turning it one way, then another. His leg appeared to be healing.

Something fell against the skin inside his trouser leg. It felt metallic. He looked down and was amazed to find pellets of shattered metal bursting from his thigh. It was expelling the shrapnel from the blast. He shook his leg. Tiny fragments of metal emerged from the bottom of his trouser leg and collected around his boot on the cave floor. Will stared at them like they were visitors from another world.

Without thinking, he grabbed his leg and kneaded the flesh with both hands. The wounds had vanished. He lifted his left arm and stared at his hand. He was moving it without pain. He swung it back and forth, working the shoulder, trying it out. He was healed.

His laugh began slowly and softly, and then gathered strength and erupted in a volcanic outburst of ecstatic euphoria. Will leaned against the obsidian as tears poured down his face in relief and joy. What was this stone? What kind of trickery did it contain?

He gazed across the cavern at the jagged slope rising to the cave entrance high above his head. He wouldn't have to wait for rescue now. If only he had dragged himself to stand in front of this miraculous rock two days ago.

It took only a few moments to gather the necessary equipment: ropes, camming devices, and ice picks. He clipped his crampons onto his boots and ran his eyes over the rocks, searching for the easiest route up.

The sky over his head was dimming. By the time he made it onto the ice, it would be dark. He would fix his ascent line now, while he had the energy, and then rappel down to spend the night in the cave where it would be easier to keep warm. Then tomorrow he would climb out with the rising sun.

Will twisted his headlamp on and shone the yellow light over the rock. He swung to grab his first handhold on a safe ledge and began to climb.

33

Joshua stood at the bedroom window in the cabin and watched the sky turn deep amethyst. Laughter drifted from downstairs. Ana was with Freja and Seth who were sharing their angelic knowledge and teaching her new tricks. Joshua felt like a spare part. All he wanted to do was protect Ana, but it was clear she didn't need his protection. He couldn't compete with Beatrice and Niloufer. Even Kendrick no longer needed him. He had been sidelined.

He pulled Evangeline's drawing from his jacket pocket and unfolded it. A pregnant Ana stood surrounded by burning buildings and chaos. The faint smile on her face made it seem as if she didn't care that her world was in flames, but Joshua knew why she was smiling. He gazed at the picture, transfixed by the look on her face, then realised he recognised where she was.

It was Linnunrata. The burning buildings were the cabins and Ana was standing in the centre of the square.

A noise on the stairs startled him and he hurriedly folded the drawing and tucked it into his jacket. Ana entered the room and caught him looking sheepish.

'What's that?' she said.

Joshua pulled his face into a mask of innocence, but the lie that was too easy to tell died on his tongue. He removed the drawing from his pocket and began to open it again.

Ana brushed past him into the bathroom. 'Never mind.'

'I think you should see it.'

Ana slammed and locked the door. 'Not interested.'

He waited for the toilet to flush. She reappeared and he held the drawing out for her to take. She ignored him and crossed to the door.

'We have to talk, Ana.'

She spun to face him and folded her arms.

'Please,' he said. 'Let me explain.'

'So you can lie to me again?'

'I admit I was using you to get intel on Phanes. I'm sorry. How many ways can I say that I'm sorry? But when I realised how important you were to ARK, I knew I had to protect you. All Gregori wants is you, Ana. He's obsessed. I've given them everything I have. Everything except you.'

Ana shrugged.

'I swear on my life, I will never lie to you again,' he said.

'I know you won't.'

'What does that mean?' said Joshua. 'That you can see inside my head that I mean it, or-'

'It's finished.'

He started towards her. 'No, Ana. Please. This is important. You can't end this.'

'Why does it matter?'

He held out the drawing. 'This. Look at it and tell me it doesn't mean anything.'

Ana averted her gaze. 'You're trying to trick me into forgiving you, like you tricked me into caring about you in the first place.'

'I wasn't trying to trick you, Ana.'

'You used your father's betrayal to make me empathise with you and feel sorry for you so I would fall in love with you.'

'So you do love me?' he said in a small voice.

'No,' she whispered.

'Now who's lying?'

Ana glared at Joshua and her eyes shone with anger. 'Don't tell me what I feel.' She was about to say more, but spun to face the door in surprise. 'I know you're listening.'

The door cracked opened and Freja peeped through the gap. 'Sorry.'

'Never mind sorry,' said Seth, bursting through the door. 'You guys mustn't fight. It's bad karma, or something.'

'Stay out of this,' said Joshua. He quickly folded the drawing and shoved it into his pocket.

'I'm serious,' said Seth. 'If you fight it'll cause a rupture in the fabric of space and time, or some shit like that. Probably. Is there a phone ringing?'

A faint buzzing was coming from the bed.

Joshua grabbed his coat and retrieved his mobile. He checked the screen. 'Lethe?' He tapped answer and put it on speakerphone.

'Thomas, what can I do for you?'

'Jack? Listen. I can't talk...'

The line muffled for a moment. Joshua leaned closer to the phone and the others gathered to listen.

'Are you still there, professor?'

'I'm in the lab. They're shutting it down, Jack. ARK have pulled the plug. They're going to kill the Homo Angelus.'

'How sure are you?'

'One hundred percent. The gene is spreading and they're determined to stop it. They can track it using the DNA database. If you're on file, you're dead.'

'But if it's spreading how can they stop it?' said Joshua.

'They'll act as quickly as possible,' said Thomas. 'Anybody can turn Homo Angelus if they have a lot of contact with someone who has already turned. It could spread exponentially, as Michael predicted. So the faster they wipe them out, the better.'

'Why are you giving me this, Tom?'

'There's something else going on. I don't know what it is. Gregori is planning something. I need your help, Jack.'

'I'll see what I can do,' said Joshua. 'Sit tight. Find out what you can and pass it on to me, okay?'

'I'll try,' said Thomas. 'Thanks, and oh, the lab's at Jedhirst Castle.'

The line went dead.

Ana and Joshua exchanged a glance.

'Why was he calling you Jack?' said Seth.

Joshua sighed. 'Long story.'

'We need to get Beatrice to take us back,' said Ana.

As she spoke, Beatrice appeared in the doorway, closely followed by Niloufer.

'Do not act in haste,' said Niloufer.

'I have to get back to the UK,' said Ana urgently.

'ARK aren't going to sit on their hands,' said Joshua. 'They have the Homo Angelus under surveillance. All it takes is a phone call.'

'We could be wiped out within 24 hours,' said Ana.

'The alarm has been raised,' said Beatrice. 'We will move the Homo Angelus to safe locations.'

'But Michael is stuck in the lab,' said Ana. 'We have to get him out. Lethe mentioned somebody called Gregori. He's ARK's lawyer and I *know* he wants to wipe us out, me especially.'

Ana stared at Niloufer in shock. At the mention of Gregori, the apparently self-possessed angel had lost his cool. A mangled look of anguish and rage had flashed across his face, to be replaced seconds later by the familiar serene countenance.

Beatrice placed a hand on Ana's arm and gently moved her away from Niloufer, as if putting her out of harm's way.

'Alas, Gregori is working against us,' she said. 'We will find a solution.'

'How soon can we get back?' said Ana.

'I will take you in the morning,' said Beatrice.

'Hang on,' said Joshua. 'We need to think about this. Lethe said Gregori has a plan. This is obviously a trap. He'll be sitting there waiting for you to walk in, Ana.'

'What am I supposed to do? Abandon Michael and let them kill him?'

'No, but let me help. I can have a team-'

'I don't want the Intelligence Services involved,' interrupted Ana. 'I don't care if it's a trap. I'm going to get Michael out.'

'Us too,' said Freja.

Seth nodded vigorously. 'We'll be your team.'

'Okay,' said Ana. 'Me, Freja and Seth. Not you, Joshua.'

'Ana-'

'I don't want you near me.'

Beatrice took Ana's hand. 'You must take Joshua. It cannot be done without him.'

'I can't trust him,' said Ana sadly.

'But you can trust me,' said the angel. 'Remember what I told you in error.'

Beatrice crossed to the door then looked at each human in turn. 'Rest. I will come before dawn.'

34

Ethne stared at the ceiling and listened to the distant burble of the river. She couldn't sleep. Under orders from Lucy she had gone to bed, but every time she closed her eyes she found herself back in time watching her words being carved into the stones or screaming in agony as her flesh curled from her bones. So she began to work through the prophecy in her mind, the sections she could remember, and wrestle it into some sort of order. Finally, she slept just before dawn, when the night was at its darkest.

She woke abruptly. A bird was singing right outside her window, like it was trying to tell her something. Ethne listened for a moment, convinced she had forgotten an important piece of information, but it wouldn't come back to her. There was no point staying in bed, so she dressed and tiptoed through the silent house and down to the kitchen.

With a mug of steaming coffee in hand, she went into the garden to listen to the rest of the birds joining the chorus. She wandered down to the riverbank and watched the water tumble by. The chill breeze pierced her jumper and twisted the naked branches of the ash and oak into contortions even the trees must have found uncomfortable.

Last night Lucy had taken Ethne through the basics of telepathic contact and showed her how to open her mind and identify individual mind signatures. After much experimentation, she had concluded that it only worked if she could touch the person with whom she was trying to connect. Her mind couldn't focus unless it had something corporeal to hang onto. So much for her grand plan to link mind to mind with Ana and Michael. Her powers simply didn't work that way.

She shivered and drained her cup, and then dashed back into the house to get warm. There was only one thing she could do to help Michael: decipher the prophecy and hope that her previous incarnation had got it wrong. A lot could change in twelve thousand years.

Ethne made a teetering pile of toast for breakfast and set Will's laptop to charge on the kitchen table. She grabbed a pen and notebook from a drawer, flicked past Irene's notes and shopping lists, and began to translate the symbols. She wanted to get it on paper before she typed it up and shared it around online. It made sense to have as many copies of the prophecy as possible, and not to leave it to the whims of the cloud or hackers or the power supply.

While she worked, Lucy appeared in the doorway, glowing faintly. The angel crossed to the table and peered at Ethne's work, then took the last piece of toast from the plate.

'Is there any jam?'

'Cupboard,' said Ethne, without looking up.

Lucy opened and closed a couple of doors and sighed theatrically. Unable to locate the jam, she resigned herself to munching on the cold toast. 'How can you eat this stuff?' she said, screwing up her face in disgust. When Ethne ignored her, she continued, 'How are you getting on? Are you nearly done yet?'

Ethne put down her pen. 'No, and it'll take a lot longer if you keep interrupting. Or you could stop bitching about the food and actually help me.'

'Whatever happened to the old Seshat?' said Lucy wistfully.

'She was burnt to a crisp and then buried half alive under a mound of rock,' said Ethne, resuming her translation. 'Not the best death, I can tell you.'

'She was so much easier to work with. So respectful. So honourable.'

'Thanks.'

'It's not a judgement,' said the angel. 'It's an observation.'

'Right. You're just keeping it real.'

Lucy plonked herself in the chair beside Ethne and watched her work steadily through the text, and smiled with pride. 'Do not misunderstand. You are the product of a different time. It is as it should be. You have become everything I hoped you would, dearest Seshat.'

Ethne glanced up from her frantic scribbling. 'Then help me find a loophole in the prophecy. So far, everything in it has come true. Everything except the very end. There has to be a way to get Michael off the hook.'

'It is not that simple,' said Lucy. 'All things are connected. If we were to change one thread of fate, the entire rug would unravel. You cannot escape the consequences of your actions.'

Ethne skimmed the text and sighed. The prophecy was unequivocal. There seemed to be no wiggle room, not that she could see. Except for one phrase.

'All is myth,' she said. 'It comes up three times. All is myth. All is myth. Surely that means the story can be changed?'

Lucy nodded. 'All is myth, yes. But there are laws governing how those myths are enacted, or materialised if you prefer. The right threads must be drawn together at the right time, and once in motion the threads cannot simply be cut and rewoven into a new shape. What is in motion will continue. Changes can be made, yes. But not entire reversals. Unless-'

The angel stopped abruptly and gazed out of the window.

'Unless what?' said Ethne.

'Unless it is done with love,' said Lucy, her eyes focused on eternity. 'A truly selfless love. Such a love is, alas, extremely rare.'

'But it's not impossible?'

'It depends upon what you are trying to undo and the forces binding that situation into form. Ethne, please, I know you want to save your friend, but if his fate is his choice then it cannot be undone.'

'Why would Michael choose to die?'

'What does the prophecy have to say on the matter?'

Ethne flicked through the notebook. 'The last stanza is about the return of the Shining Ones. The Daughter of Djehuty, or Thoth, returns.'

'That's you.'

'Yes. Seshat, Scribe of the Gods, delivers these words to mankind. That's what I'm doing now. Then it says the Lady of the Temple returns and tames the serpent. That's Nebthet, or Nephthys, and that's Michael. I know cos I saw him as her in my vision. Earlier it says something about the seed and the serpent, so I thought maybe the serpent was DNA. So that bit refers to Michael and how he figured out what was happening to our DNA.'

Lucy nodded and smiled. 'What else does it say about him?'

'That Nephthys is in disguise,' said Ethne. 'It says Nebthet hides as a Great One. The Great Ones are angels, right? So that must mean archangel Michael. It's just explaining the name change. But then Nebthet becomes the Light and is sacrificed. In other words, he dies. Is that what it means?'

'Can you see your loophole?'

Ethne frowned and scanned the rest of the prophecy. 'It's not clear if his death has to happen in order for the rest of the stuff to happen. I mean, it starts with Seshat, then it's Nebthet, then Aset, Asar, and the Lords. Only after that does the awakening happen. So is there a way to stop Michael dying or will that stop the rest of the prophecy?'

Lucy placed her hand over the notebook. 'You must let him go.'

'But-'

'It will play out. We shall see what occurs. Michael is in command of his own fate, Ethne.'

'He doesn't know what this says,' Ethne stood and grabbed the notebook from the table. 'If he knew, d'you think he would choose to die?'

'Perhaps.'

Ethne stormed from the kitchen. 'I have to speak to Ana.'

Her mobile phone was recharging on the hall table next to the landline. She snatched it up and dialled Ana's number. It rang a couple of times then went to voicemail. Ethne listened to the message and the beep, but then couldn't work out how to begin explaining what she needed to say.

She hung up and frowned at the phone in her hand. 'I hope she's okay.'

Lucy watched her from the kitchen doorway. 'Ana is in the care of one of my absolute best apprentices. We shall not abandon the Queen of Heaven.'

At that moment, Ana was huddled under a blanket and leaning against the low wall that protected Joshua's cottage from the sea. They had arrived an hour ago and she was still dizzy.

Beatrice had come to the cabin while it was dark and gathered the group together. They had stood in a circle in the kitchen and held hands. Beatrice had completed the chain and teleported them from Finland to Howick. The journey was lightning fast. Ana felt as if she had stepped into a vortex of fire. Joshua had thrown up the instant they landed, and Seth had passed out on the grass. Only Freja had seemed unaffected, and had rushed about taking care of everyone and ushered them into the cottage.

The first filaments of orange light diffused into the sky and spread towards Ana hunched behind the wall. She kept her eyes on the horizon, and as dawn poured over the ocean, she knew the future blazing towards her was unavoidable. Today they would find Michael and bring him home. But first she needed to know what was written in the prophecy, and for that she must speak to Ethne.

Freja had reassured her it was possible to communicate telepathically with someone who wasn't a Homo Angelus, but Ana wasn't sure how Ethne would react if she appeared in her mind without warning. What if she was on her motorcycle and Ana sent her spinning off the road? On balance, she decided it was unlikely Ethne would be out and about this early in the day. The worst she could do at this hour was make her friend choke on her breakfast in surprise.

A commotion and raised voices came from the cottage and Joshua burst through the door. He ran to the wall, dismantled a smartphone, and then hurled the parts into the sea.

Seth followed, leaned over the wall and whined. 'You killed my phone. That was vintage. They're not even making iPhones anymore.'

'I said no phones,' said Joshua.

Freja joined them and offered her deconstructed phone to Joshua. He extracted the SIM and flipped it onto the rocks.

'Why does she get to keep hers?' said Seth.

Joshua returned to the cottage. 'I trust her not to use it in secret.'

Seth scowled and followed him back inside. 'I'm making breakfast, if anyone cares.'

Freja crossed to the back door, and then turned to Ana. 'Coming?'

'Give me a minute.'

She gazed across the sea and focused her mind into a laser. Once she located Ethne's mental signature, their minds would lock together and she would be able to speak to Ethne as if she was standing beside her. It was similar to dialling her phone number and waiting for her to pick up, but the truth was it didn't really work like that at all. In reality, you were always connected and the line was always open. All you had to do was pick up and the other person was there.

Ana concentrated and the shape of Ethne's mind drew close. She could see her quite clearly. Ethne was sitting at a table in a kitchen arguing fiercely with an absurdly beautiful woman who had the most extravagant hair Ana had ever seen. Not sure how to proceed, she called out to Ethne as if she was in the room with her. Her friend stopped talking and cocked her head to listen.

'Ana?'

'Hello,' she said. 'Sorry to barge in. Are you all right?'

'I've been trying to contact you,' said Ethne. 'Apparently I'm a contact psychic so I can't do the long distance telepathy thing. I was hoping you'd get in touch.'

'What d'you mean, you're a contact psychic?'

'My mutation switched on. I'm like you now.'

'How did that happen?'

'Long story,' said Ethne. 'But listen, we have a problem. ARK are on the warpath. They're going to kill Michael.'

'Not just him, all of us,' said Ana. 'We have to stop them. He's at Phanes BioTech laboratory in a place called Jedhirst Castle.'

'I knew it,' said Ethne. 'I dropped by a couple of days ago. Nearly got shot in the back by a trigger-happy ape.'

'You know where it is?'

'It's just up the road.'

'From where?'

'Here,' said Ethne. 'I'm at my dad's place. We need to get in there and get him out. Where are you? Can you come here? Then we can plan what to do. We might need more people though.'

Ana grinned. 'I have others with me.'

'Great,' said Ethne. 'The more the better. ARK are seriously tooled up. Are you feeling all right, by the way? I'm not sure you should be getting into a fight, Ana. You need to look after yourself.'

'I'm fine. Have you got the prophecy?'

'Indeed I have,' said Ethne. 'Tell you when you get here.'

'See you soon.'

'I'll put the kettle on.'

Ethne cut off the connection and vanished from Ana's mind. It was a moment before she realised she was gripping the wall so tight her fingers were in danger of being ripped to shreds.

A delicate cough from behind made her jump and spin round. Freja was standing in the open doorway, a blanket draped over her shoulders.

'You'll catch your death out here,' she said.

Ana returned to the warmth of the cottage to find Seth cooking breakfast and filling the living room with delicious smells and hot steam. She joined Freja on the sofa beside the fireplace but couldn't sit still. She turned to check on Seth's progress. 'D'you need a hand with anything?'

'You just relax,' said Seth, grinning. 'My eggs are legendary. You may need to prepare yourself.'

Freja chuckled. 'They are tasty. I think you'll enjoy them.'

'Got to keep your strength up,' said Seth.

Freja squeezed Ana's shoulder and gave her a conspiratorial wink. Ana sprung from the sofa. She wanted to run from the house and scream into the wind. Why was everybody treating her like she was an invalid?

'What's wrong?' said Freja. 'You need to take it easy, Ana.'

'Stop it,' she said. 'I'm not delicate or vulnerable or ill or whatever it is you think is wrong with me. I do not need protecting.'

Seth laughed uproariously and shook his head. 'Classic.'

Freja shot him a fierce look then turned back to Ana. 'It's not you so much, but the little person inside you.'

'The what?' Ana stared at her in disbelief. 'Where did you get that idea?'

'Niloufer said the prophecy is about a child.'

'I am *not* pregnant. I know I'm not because I can feel it, and besides, I can't be. Joshua isn't Homo Angelus.'

'You sure about that?' said Seth, dishing up breakfast. 'I've tried getting into his head and it's locked up like Fort Knox. No normal human could pull that off.'

'Normal humans and Homo Angelus can't breed,' said Ana, firmly. 'And besides, Joshua is MI6. They'd never let him work for the Intelligence Services if he was Homo Angelus.'

'Maybe they don't know,' said Freja.

'Maybe he doesn't know,' said Seth.

35

Evangeline jolted from a dream. She was slumped over her desk with her head resting awkwardly on her arms. She sat up, massaged her sore neck and checked the clock. She hadn't meant to work through the night. The desk was littered with printouts and scrawled lists and sketches for public health warnings. She gathered her notes into a folder and locked it in a drawer.

Thinking about what was coming made her feel sick. She had spent all night looking for an alternative solution, and now she had a new dream to worry about. The vision struck her like a physical pain. She wouldn't be able to draw it. She could barely bring herself to even think about it.

In the dream, Ana had been kneeling in the centre of a circular room. She was cowering from an invisible enemy as the room filled with a blinding light. It had torn through the carpet and dissolved the book-lined walls and irradiated Ana in a firestorm.

Evangeline left the office and made her way through the silent building. She needed to get some proper sleep and clear her head. She stepped outside and slung her ID badge into her bag. The illuminated figure of Phanes hung over her head, wings outstretched. She glanced up and shivered.

Another day was coming and the sky blushed in darkening layers of pink flame. Her daughter was out there, somewhere, standing on the cusp of a new world. If she survived, she would change everything forever.

Evangeline started towards her car, the only one in the car park. Her senses prickled in the pale dawn and she imagined creatures lurking out of sight, waiting to pounce and drag her off.

She quickened her pace and unlocked the Nissan several steps away. Two short beeps echoed and then died in the silence. She reached the car and yanked open the door.

There was no warning and no footsteps. The man appeared behind her out of nowhere.

'Mrs Wilson,' he said casually, as if greeting an old friend.

Evangeline startled and spun round. She clutched her bag to her chest like a shield and backed towards the open door of the car. Perhaps she could jump in and drive off before he reacted.

The man lunged forward. He stepped to one side and swung the door shut with a flick of his wrist. 'You're not going home yet, Evangeline.'

She watched him closely. His receding hair showed flashes of silver but he had a lithe grace that belied his age. The dapper suit and pencil moustache gave him the air of a perfect gentleman, but Evangeline couldn't see his eyes. His thick-rimmed glasses shone in the morning sun, rendering the lenses opaque.

'Who are you?'

'You're going to let me in,' he said, and nodded at the office complex.

Evangeline shook her head. Her heart was beating so fast she could hardly breathe.

'My name is Kendrick,' said the man. 'I work for the Government and I strongly suggest you do as I ask.'

Evangeline stepped back and found herself trapped against her car. The man towered over her. He seemed relaxed, but beneath the surface she sensed he was poised to strike, and she would never see it coming.

She stared at her own frightened face, reflected twice in his glasses. She swallowed and tried to gain control of her voice. 'How do I know you are who you say you are,' she managed.

Kendrick slid his hand into his dark overcoat and pulled out a leather wallet. He flicked it open and held it up for her inspection. When she seemed satisfied, he smiled and returned his ID to his pocket.

'Now. If you don't mind,' he said, inviting her to walk with him to the entrance.

Evangeline hesitated. She desperately tried to remember the details of the Data Protection Act, but was too tired to think clearly. Surely they had to get a warrant for this kind of thing. She decided to play for time. Perhaps Kevin would arrive for work soon and save her.

'Why?' she said, defiant behind her bag shield.

'I do not need to give you a reason,' said Kendrick. 'I have asked politely.'

'And I refuse.'

'In the interests of National Security. Pretty please.'

Evangeline shook her head. 'You need a warrant.'

Kendrick sighed in exasperation. 'I know what happened, Evangeline. I know who your daughter is and what she did.'

'What does Ana have to do with this?'

'I know she killed your husband, Patrick Wilson. And then she disappeared. Tell me, why didn't you report it?'

'She didn't mean...It was an accident,' said Evangeline. 'And I'm grieving, I can't think about anything else.'

'So you let her go free after doing such a terrible thing.'

'I want nothing more to do with her and I can't face dragging it through court. It's too complicated. How would you prove it? It's too much. I just want to forget about it. And her.'

'And what of Patrick?' said Kendrick. 'Does he not deserve justice?'

Evangeline's legs weakened. She had to keep herself together. She clung to her bag with aching arms. She wanted to flee, to jump in the car and drive and never come back, but she couldn't move. She feared if she did, she would fall to her knees and never get back up. She closed her eyes against the lie she was telling and shook her head.

'He doesn't deserve justice?' said Kendrick. 'That doesn't seem right.'

'Please,' said Evangeline. 'I can't help you.'

'Here's what I think,' said Kendrick. 'I think you're protecting Ana. Perhaps it's true that you don't know where she is, but that just makes it easier for you to keep her safe. I think you took this job at Phanes so you could be close to the research, not to punish your daughter, but to help her.'

Evangeline gazed at Kendrick and a single tear ran down her cheek. 'I thought if I knew what they were doing, I could stop them, but...' She began to shake. Gregori's plans were beyond anything she had imagined and she didn't know how to stop him. She buried her head in her bag and sobbed. 'Please don't hurt her. I don't want anything to happen to her. She's too important.'

Kendrick waited until Evangeline had calmed down. He stepped forward and offered his handkerchief. She took it gratefully and smiled faintly at the ornate K embroidered on the corner. 'What will you do?'

'Protect her. If you help us,' said Kendrick. 'Let me in and I'll make sure no harm comes to Anastasia.'

'What do you need?' she said, wiping her eyes.

'Access to the database.'

'Gregori is planning to use it to target the Deviants to wipe them out,' said Evangeline, feeling braver now she had an ally. 'It's monstrous.' She returned the handkerchief to Kendrick.

He smiled. 'Keep it. Will you help me stop Gregori, Evangeline?'

'I don't have access to the database. My pass doesn't work down there.'

'Is there anyone you trust who does have access?'

Evangeline closed her eyes and thought of Kevin. He would move the earth for her, but could he keep a secret? She would have to risk it. She opened her eyes to find Kendrick smiling at her.

'Could you ask Kevin for assistance, perhaps?' he said.

'How did you...?'

'It is my job to know.'

Evangeline nodded and led Kendrick across the car park to the entrance.

The scramble up the rock face was easier the second time. Will had saved his last pieces of chocolate for the morning, and then climbed from the cave using the ropes and bolts he had put in place the night before.

The sun rose as he climbed. The ice at the entrance of the cave shone with such piercing clarity that Will was forced to climb the last few feet with his eyes clamped shut against the glare. He didn't know what he would find once he emerged onto the ice sheet. There would be more bodies, no doubt. Perhaps, if his luck held, one of the snowmobiles would still be operative. There had been a lot of explosions, so he braced himself for the worst.

The satellite phone was strapped to his back. Once he was out of the cave, he would call the Sirius Patrol. That was probably who Ethne had called on his behalf. They might even be waiting for him on the ice.

Will scrabbled for the final hold against the sharp rocks. His mind filled with fantasies of lavish meals: curry, chips, chicken, anything. Hell, he'd even eat a pot noodle if there was nothing else going.

He pulled himself free of the cave entrance and lay for a moment in the crisp, fresh air. The light was dazzling, so he kept his eyes firmly closed. He had been in the dark far too long.

The sound of boots crunching over the ice made him sit up and jerk his head around. He shielded his eyes with one hand and squinted into the sun.

Men were approaching the cave. They appeared to be armed. Further back, he could see a group of snowmobiles. The sound of an engine reverberated off the side of the mountain. A helicopter?

Will stood and turned on the spot, trying to orient himself. He was lightheaded from lack of food and the men's voices were confusing him. They didn't sound Danish. They sounded British.

'William Maxwell?' said a voice.

Will turned and tried to see the owner of the voice. He stepped forward and confirmed his name. 'Did Ethne send you?' he said.

'I do not have that information, sir,' said the voice.

'Who are you people?' said Will.

'British Intelligence Service,' said the voice. 'His Majesty's Government would like a word.'

36

Ethne stood on the doorstep and listened to a car approach over the long gravel drive. Jack's silver Astra swung into view and parked beside the Softail. Ethne could see Ana smiling from the passenger seat, but it looked forced. Her friend wasn't happy. Ana sprang from the car and ran to embrace her and it was a few moments before Ethne realised Ana was weeping. She opened her mind and received a flurry of images, everything that had befallen Ana since they had parted outside Jack's house five days ago.

Over Ana's shoulder, Ethne watched Jack climb from the car and open the boot. He retrieved a large canvas bag and dropped it on the ground with a heavy clunk. Ana's mind teemed with betrayal and loss, and it all centred on Jack.

Slowly Ethne saw what Ana was struggling to reveal through her anguish.

Jack wasn't Jack. Jack was Joshua.

Beside the car, Joshua crouched to check the contents of his bag. From the doorstep, Ethne saw a gun and that was enough. She ushered Ana into the house and left her in Lucy's care, then marched outside to confront the imposter.

Joshua straightened up as she approached and smiled, like an old friend.

Ethne didn't return his smile. Instead, she drew back her hand and belted him hard across the face.

'That was for Ana 'cos she won't do it herself, and you're not bringing that shit in here,' she said, indicating the gun.

'I'm here to help-'

'Shut it,' snapped Ethne. 'My dad has just been threatened by a bunch of bastards with guns. It makes no difference what your stated motives are, you are not bringing it in. Dump it or fuck off.'

She was about to march back into the house when she saw two awestruck people staring at her like she was the queen or god or someone equally important.

'Holy shit,' said the man.

The woman punched him on the arm. 'Seth.'

'Sorry.' Seth stepped forward and offered his hand. 'Really good to meet you. It's been a long time. I'm Seth, obviously. This is Freja.'

'Hello,' said Freja, and gave a little wave.

They all shook hands. Ethne tried to gather more information from their minds while she was touching them, but it was too quick and she couldn't see anything clearly enough for a coherent picture. She would have to do it the old-fashioned slow way and ask.

'Who do you think I am?' she said, as if she didn't know.

'The Prophetess,' said Freja, her eyes wide in admiration. 'Without you, none of us would be here, Ethne.'

'Or should we call you Seshat?' said Seth.

'Gods no,' said Ethne. 'I haven't been her in a long time.'

Seth grinned and Freja swooned. Ethne groaned inwardly. The last thing she needed was acolytes. She waved them into the house and returned to the interloper. 'Have you decided what you're going to do?'

Joshua placed the bag into the boot and locked the car. 'Happy?'

'Euphoric.'

'Look Ethne, I know you're protecting Ana, but-'

'Who the fuck are you, Joshua?'

'I'm still me. Nothing's changed. Except the name. I really am a journalist but I'm also with the Intelligence Service, that's MI6 to you. I shouldn't tell you that, but it's impossible to keep it secret from all these psychic Human Angels and I don't want to lie anymore.'

'That's a pity. You're so good at it.'

Joshua sighed. 'I'm seconded to an SIS special ops team run by Kendrick and I'd be grateful if you don't tell anyone what I've just told you.'

'Who or what is Kendrick?'

'He's my boss.'

'Poor Kendrick,' said Ethne and strode back into the house.

The group gathered in the living room to discuss their next move. The atmosphere was tense and the negotiations almost deteriorated into a punch up several times. This was mainly due to Ethne refusing to believe a word Joshua said. While they bickered, Irene moved silently around them, bringing fresh pots of tea and plates of biscuits. Lucy ate more than the rest put together. Conor remained in bed upstairs, asleep and mercifully unaware of what his daughter was planning.

'So we go in at nightfall,' said Ethne, and everybody nodded grimly. 'That gives us a few hours to kill.'

Ana sat forward on the sofa. 'You said you'd tell me what the prophecy says about me. The others think...' She trailed off and glanced at Freja.

'Niloufer said she's the mother of the future,' said Freja.

Ethne picked up her notebook. 'Who's Niloufer? Another angel?'

Freja nodded. 'Is it true?'

'It can't be,' said Ana. She looked at Joshua.

'I have the wrong genes,' he said. 'So whatever it says, it has nothing to do with me. I'm just here to observe.'

'If you say so,' said Ethne. She flicked to the right page and cleared her throat. Ana was sitting so far forward on her seat she was in danger of slipping onto the floor. Freja and Seth both appeared to be holding their breath, while Joshua had assumed an air of feigned indifference that was fooling nobody.

'No interruptions, okay?' started Ethne. 'Let me read it through. Then, well, I'll probably have to explain some of it and we'll see what we can see.'

Everybody nodded eagerly. Lucy beamed at Ethne and settled cross-legged on the floor. The angel closed her eyes and a soft glow radiated from her skin. The assembled humans relaxed, bathed in the angel's grace.

Ethne began to speak, and her voice echoed through time. In a stone temple in Turkey, twelve thousand years in the past, the prophetess listened as the words were inscribed into her soul.

'This is seen,' began Ethne. 'In the beginning was the darkness and nothing existed. And nothing itself did not exist...'

Thomas paced the corridor outside the lab and watched the equipment being carried out. The security team were stripping the benches clean like a plague of rats devouring a corpse. He stopped at the door and gazed at the desolate worktops strewn with orphaned power cords, shattered test tubes and blank screens. Yesterday he had tried to access his files. He had wanted to upload his research to his old server at home, but HQ had reset all the passwords.

He had given his life to this company and they had locked him out. Perhaps it was no more than he deserved. He should have stood up to Gregori at the start, before he had crossed the line that could never be uncrossed.

The guests had first arrived in late September and he had run through the usual health tests. By October, some of them had been showing signs of strange behaviour: moving objects around and reading each other's minds. He hadn't seen any of this himself and thought nothing of it at the time. He had assumed the staff were telling tales.

But then Gregori had shown him the videos on *The Okeke Gospel*. Thomas had been ordered to isolate the powers or find a way to shut them down. The first vaccine had shown promise, but then one of the guests had started to emit high levels of energy that had caused every machine in the lab to malfunction. Gregori had intervened and suggested, in that way of his, that the man be put to sleep. Too rattled to disagree, Thomas had allowed himself to be persuaded. It was easier than arguing. He was just doing his job.

In December, they had discovered one of the guests was pregnant. She had wanted to leave the lab and return to her family for the holiday. But ARK had refused. The father, Richard, was also a guest and had tried to negotiate on her behalf. They were volunteers, after all. They couldn't be held against their will.

Thomas brought Richard into the lab, sat him in one of the armchairs next to the coffee table in the corner, and gave him a glass of water. He explained that they needed to keep a close eye on his future child. They didn't know if the Deviants could produce healthy children and more tests needed to be done. It would be for the best if all three of them were to remain at the lab.

But Richard refused to listen.

The glass of water began to rattle against the table as if a train were passing underground. Thomas stared at the glass, rigid in his chair, and pleaded with Richard to calm down. Water began to slop over the side of the glass. A second later, it shattered and sprayed shards over the floor.

Thomas jumped out of his chair in shock. The entire lab had begun to vibrate to a high-pitched squall, and behind him, a computer screen exploded.

Thomas flinched and stared at Richard. Something unprecedented was happening to him. Light was pouring from his hands and pulsing around him in erratic waves.

Thomas watched in awe. He tried to back away, but couldn't move. He shouted desperately, 'Please stop this. We can talk.'

But Richard looked as frightened as Thomas felt. He raised his hands and stared at the light pouring from his fingers. 'I don't know what this is,' he said. 'I can't control it.'

The fluorescent light above Richard's head exploded and showered them both with sparks. Through the glass, Thomas saw a security guard running towards the lab, rifle raised.

Richard reached out to Thomas. 'Please, don't let them shoot me.'

The guard barrelled through the door.

For Thomas, time appeared to slow. As Richard's hand made contact with his arm, there was a flash, and he was flying backwards, arcing over the workbench. He even had time to muse to himself that he had never seen the room from that angle before.

A gunshot detonated like an explosion.

Thomas landed on a bench and sent glass vials and computer screens crashing to the floor.

His ears were ringing. The lab was in darkness.

Footsteps crunched over broken glass.

'Got him,' said a satisfied voice.

Thomas rolled off the workbench and stood on wobbling legs. The lab was wrecked. The security guard stared down his gunsight at Richard's motionless body.

The father of the first Deviant child was sprawled over the coffee table, his head resting on the seat of one of the chairs. Thomas shuffled forward for a closer look. Half of Richard's face was missing, transformed into something from a horror film.

Thomas closed his eyes and turned away. He ran to his desk on the other side of the lab and was violently sick into the waste bin.

It didn't take long for the remaining guests to discover what had happened. They were all locked in their rooms. Gregori ordered Thomas to kill the mother and her unborn child. The Deviants could not be allowed to breed, he said. It was imperative that their numbers be controlled. Thomas was too shaken by what he had seen to refuse.

Following the incident, the other guests had been strangely subdued. Thomas had been prepared to sedate them, but they had complied with every request and no longer exhibited any powers.

Looking back, it was obvious they had been planning their escape telepathically. They had simply waited until the guards were distracted, and had walked out of the front door en masse. The guards had pursued them down the drive, and one of the men had been shot. The rest were tranquillised and brought back inside.

Gregori hadn't needed to tell Thomas what to do that time.

And now it was finished. His career was over.

Outside the empty lab, Thomas ran his hand over his face and stared at the waste bin in the corner. He still felt sick every time he looked at it. Robson joined him in the doorway and slapped him on the back.

'You all right, mate? Looks like you could use a drink.'

Thomas managed to nod. The ex-Head of Security was suffering his own fall from grace. His encounter with the Wilson girl had ended with the death of Stan, and Robson's return to the rank and file. His debrief at the hands of Gregori had already taken on the status of legend, and the fact that he had lived to tell the tale had earned him a new respect among the troops.

'There's a bottle in my desk upstairs,' continued Robson. 'If you fancy it.'

'Thanks, Mark. Appreciate it.'

Thomas ducked out of the doorway and wandered to the end of the corridor. Like the lab, all the treatment rooms had been emptied, except for one.

Michael lay on a doctor's couch, sealed behind bulletproof glass.

After Gregori's abrupt closure of the lab, Thomas had been ordered to keep the one remaining guest sedated. He had complied, but he had a plan. He wouldn't take any more innocent lives. He had been reducing each successive dose, and was even able to issue instructions to Michael on his last visit.

It hadn't been easy. A security guard watched his every move. Thomas had been locked in his room and was only brought out when needed. That morning, the guard had appeared at his door and accompanied him down to the lab.

It had been clear as soon as he had entered the room that Michael was feigning sleep. His breathing was too shallow and his pulse was too high. The guard stood in the doorway and watched as Thomas held Michael's wrist and counted. He knew Michael could read his mind, so Thomas broadcast his plan in clear declarative sentences. He didn't expect to receive a response and was amazed to hear Michael's voice speaking directly into his mind:

'There's no need to shout.'

Thomas suppressed a grin. He fussed about and made sure Michael was comfortable, then shooed the guard into the corridor and locked the door.

He didn't know if the plan would work, but he had to try.

Thomas gazed through the glass at Michael and made a silent promise. Down the corridor, two guards shuffled into the hallway carrying a nitrogen tank between them. They disappeared up the stairs, and Thomas turned back to watch Michael sleeping, or perhaps pretending to sleep. It wouldn't be long now. He was waiting for the right moment and it had to come soon.

He glanced up. A security camera blinked in the corner, its single eye trained on Michael's glass prison. Another camera watched from inside the room. The red light on the camera blinked on.

Now would be a good time to begin.

Thomas returned to the lab and crossed to his desk. The CPU was gone, but the screen and keyboard remained. He scooped them up and grabbed a handful of power cords, and then went upstairs.

Robson passed him on the stairs. 'Bottom drawer. Don't tell the others or they'll all want one.'

It took Thomas a moment to remember what Robson was talking about. He had no intention of taking a drink, no matter how hard his heart hammered against his lungs. He would get blind drunk later, if his plan worked. He strode through reception and continued past the banqueting hall to the security wing of the castle.

Thomas entered the guard's lounge and deposited his haul with the rest of the lab equipment. It was stacked in teetering towers ready to be loaded into a van sometime tomorrow. A guard with a clipboard checked the items off a list and Thomas wandered through to the command centre in the next room.

Two more guards sat before a bank of screens filled with greyscale images of the castle, inside and out. Against the wall stood racks of switches and power units with lines of blinking lights. Each floor of the castle had its own set of cameras; there were eight in the basement.

Thomas searched the tiny labels stuck to each unit and located the one for the lab. Logically enough, it was at the bottom of the rack closest to the floor.

He turned to the screens and watched over the guard's heads as the images cycled through the rooms. All of the bedrooms, except for his, were now empty, but nobody had thought to deactivate the cameras. This was good news for Thomas. It gave him more time.

A black and white image of Michael appeared on one of the monitors. It looked as if he was sleeping peacefully, but Thomas knew the tranquillisers must have worn off by now. The image switched to the next in the cycle: Michael sleeping as seen from the corridor. In a moment, he would vanish from the screens until the cycle returned to this point.

Thomas watched the camera switch to a view of the empty laboratory. He checked his watch and began to count.

37

This is seen. In the beginning was the darkness and nothing existed. And nothing itself did not exist.

The Great Light was in darkness. And the darkness dreamed of the Light. And the darkness is the Mother. She spins Light into form.

The twin serpents hold the Light in darkness. And the Light falls.

All is Light. All is myth.

Without darkness there is no light. And without light darkness is unknown.

This is seen. The Eye is in darkness and must be opened.

The Shining Ones are the Guardians of the Light. They bring the fire of wisdom to mankind.

Mankind is a child who plays in the darkness and burns himself on the fire.

Aset, the Queen of Heaven, and Asar, the Powerful, open the Eye and the djed is raised.

The seed sleeps in the serpent. And the Fire is hidden.

This is seen. The djed falls and the way is lost. Darkness rises.

The Mother is desecrated. The air and water bring death. The ones who remember the truth are mocked.

All is myth.

From the greatest darkness comes the true light. The darkness will fight its extinction.

All is myth.

When night becomes day the seed awakens. The true elite shall rise.

The Shining Ones return. The Age of Darkness ends.

This is seen. The Daughter of Djehuty returns. Seshat, Scribe of the Gods, delivers these words to mankind.

The Lady of the Temple returns and tames the serpent. Nebthet hides as a Great One. She becomes the Light and is sacrificed.
The Queen of Heaven ascends her throne. Aset returns and is the Mother of the Lord of Things to Come. He shall be born into chaos.
Asar, Father of Heru, returns. He shall deliver the Fire to mankind.
Heru shall have twelve forms.
When the Fire is returned to Rostau and the Lords are with the Fire, the Eye shall be restored.
The true elite shall rise.

Ethne looked up to be greeted by four stunned faces. They remained silent for so long that Ethne began to wonder if a spell had been cast rendering her friends immobile and speechless. Finally, in a tiny voice, Ana said, 'So I'm who? Aset? The mother of, what was it?'

'The Lord of Things to Come,' said Ethne. 'Aset is Isis.'

Ana looked shell-shocked.

'Sorry,' said Ethne quickly, 'I should've translated it using the Greek names instead of the ancient Egyptian ones. Aset is Isis, Asar is Osiris, Djehuty is Thoth, Nebthet is Nephthys, and Heru is Horus. Clear?'

More astonished silence.

Ethne cleared her throat and continued. 'So, I'm the Daughter of Thoth, Seshat. Michael is Nephthys, which is the one I'm worried about. Ana, you're Isis, so that means Joshua-'

'It's true then?' interrupted Freja. 'You are pregnant.'

Ana glanced at Joshua. 'Not yet.'

Joshua studied his feet. 'I thought we agreed that wasn't possible.'

'Don't tell me,' said Ethne, her voice dripping with sarcasm. 'James Bond is firing blanks.'

Joshua shot her a venomous look.

'Will you two please stop,' said Ana. 'I don't understand how this can be true. We were like...gods?'

'Not exactly,' said Ethne. 'The Shining Ones were human beings. They were shamans, priests and priestesses, the power elite of the ancient shamanic cultures. I suppose they were effectively gods. They were certainly more powerful than other humans, and they spent a lot of time hanging out with spirits and angels and whatnot, and passing on their knowledge, wisdom and healing. Shall I give you a quick interpretation?'

Everyone nodded.

Ethne consulted her notebook. 'Right. The first bit's a creation myth with the light falling into darkness. Then it introduces the Shining Ones and the Fire Stone. The djed is the link between heaven and earth, sometimes called a sky pole, the World Tree, or the axis mundi. Their religion was based on returning to the stars and travelling between worlds along the Milky Way.'

'What's the Fire Stone?' said Freja.

'Big chunk of obsidian,' said Ethne. 'It switches on the Human Angel gene.'

'And it was hidden,' said Seth.

Ethne nodded. 'It mentions the seed in the serpent. I reckon that's the mutation in the DNA, waiting to be switched on. The Fire Stone is stashed in the cave in Greenland, and then the djed falls and it all goes to shit. Humanity loses its connection with heaven.'

'That bit sounds like recent history,' said Ana. 'The poisoned air and water and the loss of truth.'

'I think you're right,' said Ethne. 'When night becomes day is the solar storm which triggered the mutation, and that's the seed awakening. Then the Shining Ones return, and that's us.'

'So who is Osiris?' said Ana.

Everybody looked at Joshua.

'It doesn't say that,' he said hotly. 'Where does it say who is who? We only have your word, Ethne.'

'I was there,' she said. 'I remember. Isis and Nephthys were there and I recognised them as Ana and Michael. You weren't there, but who else would it be? You want another man to knock up your girlfriend?'

Joshua glared at Ethne and spoke through gritted teeth. 'Looks like she won't have a choice.'

'You're going down fighting, huh?' said Ethne.

Ana placed her hand carefully on Joshua's knee. 'Remember, Lethe said it was possible for people to turn Homo Angelus.'

'I haven't turned,' he said firmly. 'I don't have powers. I don't feel any different.'

'You won't,' said Ethne. 'Not at first. It takes a while to kick in.'

Lucy coughed politely. 'This is becoming rather tedious.'

'Couldn't agree more,' said Joshua.

'I am going to say this once,' said Lucy. 'You will either accept it or not. It is up to you. Ana is Isis. Joshua is Osiris. You can, as they say, do the mathematics.'

Ethne smirked behind her notebook.

Ana glanced warily at Joshua. 'And he's the father of the Lord of Things to Come?'

Ethne nodded. 'That seems to be what it's saying.'

Joshua leapt from the sofa and stormed to the door. 'I am not having this conversation again. For the last time, I am not a Homo Angelus.' He bolted from the room and slammed the door behind him.

'God of the underworld and the dead?' said Ethne. 'Sounds about right to me.'

38

Gregori stood at the castle reception and watched the corpulent security guard nibble the end of his biro. He was doing the crossword, squeezed into his chair behind the desk. He had two wrong answers and was about to enter a third when the lawyer decided to put him out of his misery. He coughed.

The guard looked up in surprise and almost dropped his pen. 'Mr Gregori. Where'd you spring from?'

The lawyer smiled and tapped the newspaper on the desk. 'While I applaud your desire to improve yourself, I would suggest that you try something more your speed. A word search, perhaps. Or join the dots?'

The guard stood, his hand going automatically to the gun at his hip. 'I never see you come in. Never seen you walk through that door. You just appear. Bang. Like that.' He clicked his fingers. 'Why is that?'

'Perhaps you should pay attention.'

'Or perhaps you're one of them,' said the guard. 'One of them genetic freaks.'

Gregori ran his fingers through his slick hair. 'I hardly think that is likely, do you? After all, why would I present myself to reception? I assure you, if I were capable of teleportation, which is what you appear to be implying, I would almost certainly skip this part of my day, pleasant as your company is.'

The guard grumbled under his breath and removed his hand from his gun.

'Now,' continued Gregori. 'I was summoned.'

'Meeting,' said the guard. 'Banqueting Hall. They're waiting for you.'

Gregori turned away from the desk, but not before he caught a glimpse of a smirk on the guard's face. The detestable creature was laughing at him behind his back. 'Please, share the joke,' he said, smiling his coldest smile ever.

The guard looked up from his crossword and shrugged. 'They're not happy, is all. I heard Thorsen say he was going to tear you a new-'

'Thank you,' snapped Gregori, 'but I can handle Mr Thorsen.'

The lawyer stormed into the main hall to be greeted by six glowering faces. The chief executives of the ARK consortium were assembled around the table and were clearly in the middle of an almighty row. Silence fell as he entered, but as Gregori crossed to the stone fireplace, the room erupted once more. Most of the barbs were flying at him. He turned away and stared into the flames, and listened to the men shout across each other as they endeavoured to determine the cause of the calamity that had befallen them. It was not long before they all agreed it was most likely the lawyer's fault.

'Are you ignoring us or admiring the view?' said Thorsen.

Gregori spun to face the men, and found them all standing. They had the look of a mob about them and would not be satisfied until they had drawn blood.

'A little of both,' he said. 'Please, gentlemen. Return to your seats. Let us be civilised. We are, after all, on the brink of a new world.'

The men complied in bad humour. Gregori joined them at the table and waited until their animal spirits had relaxed a fraction. The ruggedly handsome Fredrik Thorsen was the last to sit. As CEO of Phanes BioTech, he had been at the vanguard of ARK's growth and development. Without Thorsen pushing for technological innovation and driving his staff beyond endurance, none of them would be sitting around this table now. Employees of Phanes knew not to test his patience. Meetings with Thorsen regularly ended with his characteristic bellow that would send terrified workers fleeing from the room.

Gregori ran a critical eye over the men before him. Given a free hand in choosing those responsible for the future of humanity, he would not have selected these specimens, but he had to work with what was available. His eyes fell on Thorsen. The old Viking was still quivering with rage at the latest setback.

None of these men were accustomed to being denied what they desired. This was going to take careful handling.

'Mr Thorsen,' said Gregori with as much grace as he could muster. 'If you would be so kind as to explain why we are here, and in such a lather.'

'We were on our way to Greenland,' said Thorsen. 'I was going to fly us over there to get switched on by the Fire Stone. That is the point

Gregori. That is why we're here. We were on the runway, we had clearance, and then the call comes through. We can't go to Greenland. We've been grounded and sent back here with our dicks in our hands because the British Government has seized the Fire Stone. Now what I want from you, Gregori, is a fucking explanation.'

Heads nodded around the table. Sebastian Coburn cleared his throat and pulled a handkerchief from his pocket. The Scottish CEO of ReSource, still red faced from shouting, wiped away the sweat trickling from his shiny pate. It had been a tough week. He was being tested; he understood that. The team in Greenland, ostensibly searching for mineral deposits, had delivered victory into his hands, as he believed they would. It was God's will. But then disaster had struck. He would gain the upper hand in time. He always did.

'We want to know who attacked the cave,' said Coburn. 'Was it the Secret Service? I'm having trouble even finding out if my people are alive, let alone what happened to the stones. We need that Fire Stone, Gregori. Without it we are lost.'

'Do not concern yourself,' said the lawyer. 'We will have the Prophecy Stone. It's as good as yours.'

'Meaning what, exactly?' said Coburn hotly.

'Meaning, have faith Sebastian. You will be in a position to transform yourself very soon.'

A tremor of anticipation spread over every man's face. Of course, there was the possibility that they would transform spontaneously through contact with the Homo Angelus, but Gregori considered that unlikely. The Fire Stone was a failsafe device. It existed to ensure the foretold evolution took place as planned. These most self-serving of men would stand before the Fire Stone and it would make them into gods.

'Has it been read yet?' said Akash Devan. 'Has the girl found the translator stone?'

'I am awaiting reports,' said Gregori. 'Have no fear, gentlemen. The Fire Stone will be retrieved. The prophecy will be read and your futures at the forefront of humanity will begin.'

'How will this happen?' said Devan. 'We lost many men in the fight at the cave. I was told the attackers were a Black Ops unit. There are many nations who would wish to stand before progress like a lame elephant and block our path.'

Gregori nodded sympathetically. Akash Devan was the most astute of these men and the first to offer solutions. These usually involved deploying apocalyptic weaponry designed by the man himself. He looked into the Indian's piercing dark eyes and smiled, giving him the full beam, knock your socks off smile that invariably reduced the recipient to trembling submission. Devan didn't even flinch. He wanted answers.

'As you know,' said Gregori carefully, 'I commandeered a small team of your highly trained and expert security staff in order to effect the very things we are now discussing. They-'

'Why have they not informed me of their progress?' interrupted Devan. 'You are just the lawyer. You are not their commanding officer. I demand to know what you are doing with my own people or I will have you replaced. There are many lawyers, Gregori. There is only one Akash Devan.'

'Of that we can be certain,' said Gregori smoothly. 'I simply wished to maintain a clear line of command. I am certainly not trying to replace you, Akash. As if I ever could. The situation is complex, there are many moving parts and volatile players, and I merely endeavour to bring about a speedy and propitious resolution to our little problem. When I asked my team to report directly to me, I was in no way attempting to undermine your authority. Please accept my most humble apology if I have in any way offended or inconvenienced you.'

Devan smoothed his black moustache and eyed the lawyer, and finally accepted his explanation with a curt nod. Gregori smiled graciously in return. It was a shame he wouldn't get to see Akash Devan transform. It would be a rare sight to behold, and never forgotten once seen. It was almost worth allowing it, just to see what would happen. He chuckled to himself, and drew baffled looks from the assembled men.

'We are close, gentlemen,' he said, beaming. 'The future draws near. But first we must prepare the ground. Mr Franklin, you have an update?'

The American straightened up. Richard Franklin had been reclining in his chair as usual. The head of tech giant CogNet mediated every conversation through some sort of technology and was surgically welded to his phone. He rapidly typed something into the handset and cleared his throat.

'Right, so CogNet is ready to lead with this. Sending data now. You'll see the algorithms are robust.'

A series of pings, bongs and daft little tunes shimmered around the table, and the men consulted their phones. Gregori rolled his eyes. This was supposed to be a meeting and they were all staring into their hands.

'Just explain it to us, Richard,' he said. 'In English. Imagine we are your grandmother.'

'Right,' said Franklin. 'We're ready to start seeding information on the Shining Ones and the prophecy. We've got bloggers, dummy websites, Natter feeds, CogNet channels, boards-'

'Yes, all right,' interrupted Gregori in desperation. 'How does it work? Not technically, just generally.'

'We flood the internet with content on the myths. We've also got TV programmes in development. A lot of this data was already out there, but now we can bring it together, create a coherent narrative. By the time we're done, the world will believe the gods are about to return. And then they will. We will. We create the story we want people to believe and then we sell it to them. As long as we control the narrative, it's easy.'

'This is not a story, Mr Franklin,' said Devan gruffly. 'This is reality. It is happening in the real world. The prophecy will prove it to be true. We six men, chosen to lead the world out of disaster at this terrible time, *are* the returning gods. It is not a fiction, young man. We *are* the Shining Ones.'

'Totally,' said Franklin. 'That's what I'm saying.'

'Others will find it hard to believe,' said Wei Zhou. 'They must be helped to see the truth. Many will resist our return, even as we help them. Not everyone welcomes the gods. People fear what they do not understand. And they will fear us.'

'They already do,' said Ian Goldsmith, making it sound like divine providence that it should be so. The Brit was used to thinking of himself as a Master of the Universe, but economic supremacy was a fantasy compared to what was coming.

'Is no one going to ask the obvious?' said Thorsen. 'We six can't ascend until the seventh man is present. I know Pinecone Freeholdings wants to remain a silent partner, but surely it's time, Gregori. We must meet him. There is much to discuss.'

'You will meet at the appropriate time-'

'Come on, man,' interrupted Thorsen. 'Enough of this bullshit. We don't even have a name. You represent him, so tell us. Who is he?'

'As you wish,' said Gregori. 'Pinecone Freeholdings administrates the property empire of the Vatican, as you know. I represent the Holy Father in Rome. Does that satisfy your curiosity, Mr Thorsen?'

Awkward laughter swept around the table. They had spent so long working towards this moment, dreaming of their impending ascension, that not one of the men present had considered the implications of the involvement of the Holy See. Until now.

Gregori took pride in his ability to deflect unwanted interest in the activities of his employer. The Roman Catholic Church was in disarray, its power and influence shattered by years of disgrace and scandal. All the talk of the Vatican squandering its resources was just that. Talk. He allowed it; it suited his purpose. It was up to Gregori to ensure nobody discovered where the Vatican invested its vast wealth and he was extremely good at his job.

'The Pope?' said Franklin, as if the lawyer had suggested a particularly inappropriate addition to their bowling team.

Gregori ignored his incredulity and smiled. 'The Church stands in readiness to guide you in your new role. After all, if anyone knows how to operate in the world as a god, it is the Holy Father.'

'I don't believe it,' said Zhou.

'What you believe is irrelevant,' said Gregori. 'I am simply giving you the facts.'

'It is reasonable,' said Devan. 'Did we really think the Vatican would allow an underling to join the gods? We have been blind, gentlemen, and surely the direct involvement of the papal office explains one more thing.'

Thorsen growled in agreement. 'Your superhuman foresight, Gregori. ARK would not exist without your prompting. You knew the solar storm was imminent. You knew there would be, shall we say, genetic consequences. You knew the Fire Stone existed and where to find it and what it does. We have come this far and have endured your obfuscations for too long. Your source, man. Now will you give it up?'

'It appears I have already done so.'

'The Vatican Secret Archives,' said Goldsmith. 'The largest depository of lies in the world.'

'And yet, here we are,' said Gregori, smiling faintly. 'You owe my employer a debt of gratitude, it seems. And since it was I who found the secrets of the Shining Ones, hidden as they were in a dusty box in a long forgotten corner of the archive, and since it was also I who presented the possibility of transformation to the Holy Father, it is therefore, I to whom you must direct your gratitude.'

A murmur of disapproval rumbled around the table and the men shifted in their seats. Gregori had given these men everything, and in return, they had served him well. It did not matter that the Pope knew nothing of his plans. These men would never meet the Stone and their dreams would come to nothing.

'This may be beside the point without one thing,' said Coburn. 'The mutation is still spreading. What if we can't stop it?'

'There are contingencies in place,' said Gregori. 'The Homo Angelus currently residing in this laboratory is easy to deal with. He is, as you say, a sitting duck. As for what I like to call the free-range Homo Angelus, it is possible to identify them. We have their DNA on file, as Mr Thorsen can attest. As I understand it, when a person turns, the DNA samples also change. It is a simple technological fix.'

'Totally,' said Franklin. 'The database flags samples that have turned. We simply match the samples to the profiles. We've got the meta: addresses, calls, purchases, locations. We can find them like that.' He clicked his fingers.

'What about Anastasia Wilson?' said Thorsen. 'Was she found?'

Gregori took a deep breath. The inestimable Anastasia had eluded capture yet again. He was beginning to wonder what it would take to stop her.

'Ms Wilson is a paramount threat to your ascension, gentlemen. She is proving exceedingly difficult to pin down. We no longer know where she is, but I have a hunch she will turn up.'

Thorsen exploded from his chair and launched himself across the table at the lawyer. 'You have a hunch?'

'Indeed,' said Gregori. 'Please return to your seat, Mr Thorsen, and allow me to explain.'

Thorsen growled, but remained standing. Gregori held his gaze and waited. The quivering Viking threw himself into his chair and folded his arms.

'We have the bait,' said Gregori.

'Which is?' said Devan.

'Mr Okeke,' said Gregori. 'Anastasia will not abandon her friend.'

'You're counting on her friendship?' said Thorsen incredulously. 'There's too much at stake for mere friendship.'

Gregori watched the men around the table, ugly in their confusion and mistrust of each other, glorious in their naked greed and ambition. If only they could see the world as he did. He understood Anastasia better than any of them could imagine. He understood her better than she did herself.

'You can trust me to secure your futures, gentlemen. I have left nothing to chance. Although, I would advise that you leave before she arrives. We wouldn't want you to get caught in the crossfire now, would we?'

39

Joshua drove the Homo Angelus to Jedhirst Castle as the evening light faded from the sky. After trying to squeeze everybody into his Astra, it was agreed they should take Conor's Land Rover instead. Ethne had prised the keys from her father with reassurances that they were just going for a drive and would be back soon. She hoped that it didn't turn out to be a lie.

They parked behind a hedgerow a mile downstream from the castle grounds. Ana and Seth were to wait with the vehicle, while the others conducted a quick recce. They needed to be sure of the castle layout and how many guards they were likely to encounter. Nobody wanted to walk in blind.

Despite her reservations about offensive weapons, Ethne had conceded that they might need backup from Joshua and his arsenal. She kept an eye on him as he checked his gun and strapped on his night vision gear. Lucy was also providing backup. She appeared in a flash of blue light and then wandered into a nearby clump of woodland. Moments later, an eagle swooped from the trees and landed on the grass in front of Ethne.

Freja stared at the eagle in awe, then looked at Ethne. 'I see it now. It's so obvious. Beatrice told us you were protected by one of the Great Ones. In angel language that means-'

'The Light Bringer,' said Ethne.

Joshua looked up sharply. 'Lucifer?' He dropped his eyepiece down and peered at the eagle who was pecking at the grass. 'Um...Are we set? I'm covering the front. The Light Bringer, um...Lucy is covering the back. Any problems and you run.'

'Roger that,' said Ethne sarcastically.

Freja chuckled. Lucy took off and swooped overhead, flying for the castle. Joshua led Ethne and Freja through a field and into the woodland next to the grounds. They trod silently through the trees and made their way to the low wall that surrounded the castle. A gate bisected the wall from where a path ran through the woods behind them and down to the river below. Inside the gate stood a security guard. They watched as he smoked in the darkness, his cigarette glowing through the trees. He was going nowhere.

Joshua signalled to Freja to move right. She was to follow the wall around to the back of the castle from where she could penetrate the walls with her mind and memorise the floor plan. She didn't need to get too close, so she would be safe behind the wall. As long as she didn't make a noise, they would never know she was there.

Since Ethne was a contact psychic, she had to get close. This carried more risk, so Joshua was covering her, whether she liked the idea or not. Ana had protested too. It made more sense for her to search for Michael as she could do it from a distance, but everybody had agreed she should remain as far away as possible until they knew what they were dealing with.

The call of an eagle echoed against the castle walls. Lucy was checking the perimeter. Her call meant the coast was clear for Freja, so she moved off into the trees and followed the line of the wall.

Joshua and Ethne went left, heading for the front of the castle. The entrance, as Ethne knew, was through an archway around the back. That would be where most of the security was concentrated, so she should be able to get right against the wall at the front without anyone seeing her. But first they had to check for patrols.

Ethne followed Joshua through the trees. Her eyes were beginning to adjust to the darkness but she couldn't see well enough to avoid the low hanging branches. She got hit in the face several times and was about to lose her temper in spectacular fashion when Joshua brought them out beyond the tree line.

They ducked behind the wall and he peered over the top through his night vision goggles. Ethne placed her hand on his shoulder and focused, turning his eyes into hers.

The castle transformed in her vision into an emerald fortress, shimmering against the darkness. Bright patches of green showed lights burning in the windows. Several luxury cars were parked on the gravel.

'Wait here,' whispered Joshua.

Ethne saw what he intended in his mind before he disappeared into the gloom. He wanted to check how many guards were at the main entrance. She waited for what seemed like eternity until he reappeared. He took her hand, looked into her eyes and silently broadcast what he had just seen.

There were two guards at the entrance. One was leaning against the wall staring into the trees; the other was playing a game on his phone. There didn't appear to be any patrols. Activity had obviously been scaled back since the lab had been closed down.

Joshua nodded at Ethne and squeezed her hand, indicating she should go for it. She slapped him on the shoulder in acknowledgement, and then slid silently over the wall.

Ethne kept low. She remembered the layout of the grounds from her last visit and hoped she wouldn't have to get too close to the entrance this time. She had been practising her skills and her mastery was improving every day. She ran over the gravel, trying to be as quiet as possible, and slipped between a Rolls and a BMW coupe. No doubt she would discover the owners of these cars inside the castle.

She made it to the wall. Light shone from the windows on the first floor; the banqueting hall, if her memory was correct. The upper floor was in darkness and there were no windows in the cellar. She placed her hands against the stone and concentrated.

The interior life of the castle sprung into her mind without effort. Ethne found she could simply run her mind down corridors, pop in and out of rooms, and move through walls at will. She started at the top and scanned downwards. The upper floor was deserted. Most of the activity was centred around the banqueting hall. There were several guards in reception, and more outside the hall. Perhaps they were waiting for the men inside.

Beyond the hall was a room piled with computers and exotic machines, and another filled with CCTV screens and more guards. A man hovered furtively near the door, watching the screens. Ethne wasn't sure he should be there. He wasn't a guard and he appeared to be counting under his breath.

She moved her mind into the banqueting hall. Seven wealthy men were sitting around a huge dining table having a heated discussion. She recognised some of their faces from Joshua's research into the ARK consortium. The subject of their argument was clearly of great importance to them. Ethne concentrated and tried to hear what they were saying. She pushed for a deeper connection and her mind filled with a cacophony of voices. It was a moment before she realised she was getting everything, not just what the men were saying but also what they were thinking. An anarchic morass of self-glorification and murderous intent swirled through her mind.

One thing was clear: They had to get Michael out, and fast. She had to find him.

She moved on and scanned down into the cellar. Here she found the laboratory, all glass walls and empty benches. The equipment she was expecting had been removed. The lab had been gutted. She continued down the corridor but her vision became cloudy and muddled. Something strange was going on because suddenly she could see the man who was counting upstairs, only now he was standing in the corridor outside the lab. He was arguing with somebody.

Ethne couldn't understand how he could he be in two places at once. She pushed into his mind, hoping then it would make sense. Anger and terror raged through his soul. Without warning, all his emotion centred on one point.

The barrel of a gun.

Ethne jumped back from the wall in shock as the gun shot exploded. Her mind filled with white light and for a moment it felt as if the bullet had penetrated her own brain. Her ears pulsed with the scream of her blood and she sucked down mouthfuls of air to calm herself.

After a few moments, she tentatively put her hands back to the stone. The images sprang to life at her touch. She raced back to the security office. The man was still standing there, counting. Had she just seen a glimpse of the future?

She continued her search for Michael and sent her mind back into the cellar. He had to be down there somewhere. She flew past the lab to the rooms at the end.

A jolt of energy ripped through her body and she fought to keep her hands on the stone. She had found Michael. He was locked behind a reinforced glass wall, and was asleep on a doctor's couch.

She hung in the air watching for a moment, wishing she could wake him to tell him help was on the way. She was about to withdraw when he opened his eyes and looked right at her. He was surprised for a moment, and then smiled.

'Hi Ethne. Long time no see.'

'Can you hear me?'

'What?' said Michael smirking.

'Very funny. We're coming for you, Mickey. Hang in there.'

'Ethne wait,' said Michael, a warning note in his voice. 'Don't move. I'm going, but don't move.'

Ethne's vision cleared. Behind her came the sound of footsteps on gravel and a low whistle. She opened her eyes and carefully glanced over her shoulder.

Torchlight bounced against the wall. A security guard was patrolling the grounds and he was heading her way.

Ethne considered ducking behind one of the cars lined up between her and the guard, but any movement would draw his attention. She pressed herself to the wall and closed her eyes, and watched the guard's progress in her inner vision.

He shone his torch along the line of the wall, moving inexorably towards her. She watched the beam slide across the stone. As it neared, she shrunk into the wall and hid her face. A mantra ran through her mind in desperation: I am not here. I am invisible. I am not here. I am invisible.

She held her breath and listened as the footsteps approached, stopped and then turned away. He was leaving.

Ethne spun on the spot. The guard was disappearing through the archway. She waited until she was sure he was gone, and then belted across the driveway and threw herself over the wall.

Joshua was waiting for her, his eyes wide in amazement. He had watched the whole thing through his night vision, his sniper rifle following the guard.

'He didn't see you,' he said. 'He shone his torch right on you, but he didn't see you. I was going to take him out. One more second and he was toast.'

Ethne stared at Joshua through the gloom. He had flipped up his goggles and his eyes shone with adrenaline and admiration. She didn't believe she had become invisible. There had to be another explanation.

'He must've not been paying attention,' she said.

Joshua shook his head. 'Not a chance. That's one hell of a superpower you've got there, Ethne. Let's get back to the others.'

He dropped his night vision eyepiece into position and prepared to move back into the trees just as voices and running feet erupted from behind the wall. He peered into the grounds.

Ethne placed a hand on his shoulder and watched as the men from the banqueting hall ran through the archway to their cars, accompanied by their personal guards. She had never seen such men in so agitated a state. She placed her hands on the wall.

Car doors slammed and engines revved.

'Let's move,' hissed Joshua. 'We don't want the headlights on us.'

But Ethne was concentrating. She pushed her mind into the cars, determined to find out what was going on.

A gleaming BMW screeched down the drive scattering gravel. It would be on them in seconds. Joshua took Ethne's hand and pulled her towards the trees.

40

Thomas listened to the bosses rushing out of the banqueting hall. Now would be the perfect moment. The security team would be focused on getting the bigwigs into their cars and he could slip into the basement unseen.

He watched the screens and waited for the final lab camera to show on the monitor. He moved towards the wall and located the power supply for the basement and crouched, pretending to tie his shoelaces. Out of the corner of one eye, he watched the laboratory vanish from the screens.

He hit the power switch.

The red line of LEDs blinked off. He had five minutes.

Thomas ran from the control room and past the hall into reception. The CEOs were jostling each other out of the entrance.

Thomas strode towards the stairs and kept his head down. He entered the spiral staircase and glanced back towards reception. It was clear.

He began to run.

Ethne and Joshua rejoined the others at the Land Rover beyond the woods. The Homo Angelus stood in a circle and held hands, and then each transmitted what they had seen. Joshua added his experience into the mix and within minutes everybody was up to date. It was the fastest debrief Joshua had ever witnessed. The others were amazed by Ethne's newfound power of invisibility, although she seemed embarrassed by the whole affair.

'So we go in through the cellar,' she said, deflecting the attention from herself.

'Can you get through that door?' said Joshua.

'Don't see why not,' said Ethne. 'It's a basic fire door, metal bar locking it from the inside. Could you blast through that?'

Ana nodded. 'I've blown doors off hinges before.'

Everybody stared at her in awe.

'By accident,' she added, embarrassed. 'You just have to amp up your power. Two of us could manage it easily.'

'We need a distraction upstairs,' said Joshua. 'I'll go in the entrance. Ana you're with me.'

She nodded. 'Let's go.'

Joshua dropped his night vision goggles again and followed Ana into the woods, his gun cradled across his chest. Ethne, Freja and Seth stayed close behind. Nobody spoke. All minds were on Michael and his safe return.

Into the silence came the shrill ring of a phone and Joshua stopped moving. He retrieved his mobile from his jacket and stared at the screen.

'You're such a *Homo erectus*,' said Ethne. 'Switch it off, pea-brain.'

'It's Kendrick,' said Joshua, and hit answer. He listened for a moment, and then switched to speakerphone. 'Could you repeat that?'

The others gathered round and listened to the tinny voice coming from the phone. 'I have access to the database at Phanes HQ. Where are you, Jack?'

'Jedhirst Castle.'

'You were told to stand down,' said Kendrick. 'I'm on my way. Whatever you're doing, wait for me.'

'Copy that.'

'Also, we've seized the standing stones found in Greenland. Got a tip off from ARK's lawyer, Gregori. What can you tell us about that?'

Joshua glanced at Ana. She looked as surprised as he felt. Why had Gregori given them the Fire Stone? Ethne grabbed his arm and shook her head at him, defying him to tell them anything on pain of death.

He held her gaze. 'Told you before. I know as much as you.'

'We have a William Maxwell in custody,' continued Kendrick. 'Geologist with ReSource. The company's agitating to get him released. Maxwell mentioned an Ethne Godwin. Know who she is?'

Ethne clamped her hand over her mouth to stop herself crying out. Will was safe. He was alive. Part of her wanted to hug Joshua for bringing this fantastic news, but another part realised he might be about to betray her, so she watched him closely and waited.

'Ethne Godwin?' said Joshua. 'Yes, I know her. She's a friend of Anastasia Wilson. They work together.'

'Know where we can find her?'

'Sorry,' said Joshua, his eyes on Ethne's face. 'No idea where she is. All I know is she went to Greenland. If I hear anything, I'll be in touch.'

'One more thing,' said Kendrick. 'Anything else you'd like to share?'

'Such as?'

'I'm looking at your profile on the database.'

Joshua switched off the speaker and put the phone to his ear. 'And?'

'I want to hear it from you. Have you turned?'

'No, sir.' Joshua hung up and switched off his phone. Ethne looked at him steadily, hands on her hips.

'Perhaps there's hope for you yet,' she said.

Michael eased off the doctor's couch and stood. He flexed his arms and worked his shoulders and felt the energy return to his stiff limbs. The barbiturates were gone from his system but his head still felt woozy.

He had dreamed of Ethne. Somehow she was inside the castle, flying through the corridors in the form of a black raven. The bird had found him and perched on his head and pecked at his hair to awaken him. He had jolted from the dream to find a vision of Ethne standing in his glass cell.

His friends were coming. He could feel them moving towards him through the darkness. If he could find a way out of this cell, he could meet them outside and perhaps they could avoid a fight.

He closed his eyes and summoned all his strength. The energy began to build. It poured into his body and cleared his mind as if he had stepped into a power shower.

Frantic footsteps sounded on the stairs down the hallway. Michael opened his eyes and saw Thomas rushing towards him, fumbling with a huge bunch of keys. The professor had told him the plan. Michael wasn't convinced it would work and was just going to blast his way out of the room, but a key would be infinitely better. He didn't want to draw unnecessary attention to himself by making too much noise.

On the other side of the glass Thomas tried a key. It went in but wouldn't turn. He tried another, getting more agitated by the second. His fingers were shaking and the more he tried to stay calm, the worse it got.

Footsteps sounded on the stairs. Someone was coming. They were taking their time, so it was probably a patrol to check on the prisoner.

Michael pressed his hands against the glass and Thomas could see heat radiating from his palms. He tried another key. It turned.

'Hey!'

Thomas startled. The security guard had entered the corridor. Thomas ignored him and pulled open the door.

'Step away,' shouted the guard. 'Turn around, slowly, or I will shoot you.'

Thomas did as he was told and spun to face the guard.

Behind him, Michael stepped out of his glass cell. He moved close to Thomas and spoke quietly into his ear. 'Stand aside. Let me deal with this.'

Thomas refused to budge. 'I won't let them kill you.'

'What about you?' said Michael.

'Doesn't matter. Just stay behind me.' Thomas looked at the guard, the rifle aimed squarely at his head. 'If you shoot me, Michael will deal with you before you can get off another round.'

The guard squinted down the gunsight, as if he could miss from two feet away. He was barely out of his teens and had cut himself shaving that morning. Thomas was surprised he needed to shave at all.

'How old are you son?' he said.

No reply.

Thomas sighed. He was dealing with an obedient dog. The boy was following orders.

'What's your name?' said Thomas. 'I have a right to know the name of my executioner.'

The rifle wavered slightly and the guard blinked rapidly for a couple of seconds before answering. 'Greene. Darren. Sir.'

'Have you ever killed anyone, Darren?'

'No sir.'

'Well, I have, and I can tell you, it's no picnic. You think you can live with it. You think you can justify it. You're just doing your job, after all. If it weren't you, it would be somebody else pulling the trigger. Am I right?'

Darren's hands shook. 'Stop talking, sir.'

'Have you ever been in love, Darren?'

The gun wobbled again and Darren's cheeks flushed a deep pink.

'You have?' said Thomas. 'Wonderful. I expect she's beautiful, really special. What's her name?'

'Sammy...Samantha,' said Darren, an involuntary smile tweaking his lips.

'Here's my question,' said Thomas. 'Would you shoot Samantha? Would you take your HK417 and put a bullet through her beautiful face?'

'Shut up.'

'Can you live with my death on your conscience?' continued Thomas. 'Could you look into Samantha's beautiful eyes knowing what you had done?'

'Right now,' said Darren through gritted teeth, 'I would shoot you just to stop you talking.'

'Killing someone makes you weak,' said Thomas. 'Believe me, I know. It destroys you. It eats away at you until all that's left is-'

A gunshot ricocheted off the reinforced glass beside Thomas making him duck. Michael took hold of the professor and tried to shunt him to one side, but Thomas resisted and moved back into position.

Another shot fizzed past Thomas' ear. He spun round, grabbed Michael and tried to pull him to the floor. A sharp crack. An explosion of pain and confusion, and he fell into darkness.

Michael caught Thomas and lowered him gently to the floor. Blood soaked through his shirt and pooled onto the flagstones, his eyes vacant.

Michael closed Thomas' eyes and stood.

Darren walked steadily towards him, his rifle raised. Light crackled in Michael's hands but he didn't raise them to fire at the approaching gunman. He simply looked him in the eye and said one word.

'No.'

Darren stopped walking. His gun fell from his hands and clattered uselessly to the floor.

'Don't move,' said Michael.

Darren tried to pull his Glock from its holster but couldn't move his arm. He was paralysed. He couldn't even reach his radio to call for backup. The only thing he could do was shout. He began to yell, screaming in the hope that somebody upstairs would hear him.

Michael walked towards the wailing guard. 'Shush.'

Darren fell silent. His eyes opened wide in terror. He could do nothing to defend himself. As Michael moved past him, the petrified guard closed his eyes. A damp patch appeared on his standard issue combat trousers and a choked sob escaped from his mouth.

'Sorry Darren,' said Michael as he passed. 'But you'll recover.'

Heavy footsteps pounded down the stone stairwell at the end of the corridor. The other security guards had responded to Darren's cries.

Michael ran to the fire door opposite the foot of the stairs. He mounted the steps and threw himself at the metal bar. It wouldn't budge.

A gunshot pinged off the wall above his head, and he tried again. The door was locked.

He returned to the hallway to find more guards filling the stairwell. They hung back, too scared to approach. He decided to fire a couple of warning shots and sent the energy from his hands spiralling towards the gunmen. They opened fire and the air around him burned with raining bullets.

Michael focused all his energy into his hands and his fingers crackled with electricity. He fired out a couple of light bombs and managed to disarm two guards, but more were coming up behind. He was outnumbered and outgunned. It was just a matter of time before one of them managed to land a direct hit.

He needed to generate a force field around his body, but every time he sent out a spiral of light it drained his shielding. He could only use one or the other.

He fought on as the bullets flew around him like annoying wasps and backed up towards the fire door, determined to blast it open. It was his only chance of making it out of there alive.

He sent a ball of energy backwards towards the lock, but in the mayhem his aim was off and it exploded against the wall and sent out a cloud of dust. He would have to face the door and channel the energy through both hands together, but that left him exposed. The guards wouldn't hesitate to shoot him in the back.

He was cornered.

An explosion shook the floor. Michael ducked instinctively and even the guards stopped firing. The fire door was wrenched from its hinges. It collided with the wall behind Michael.

Two beaming faces appeared outside the open door. A man and a woman grinned at Michael as light poured from their hands.

Seth ran down the steps into the basement. 'Need a hand?'

Freja followed and sent spirals of light into the hallway from her fingers. She joined Seth and Michael and all three began firing streamers of light and fireballs at the security guards.

Behind them, Ethne entered the cellar. She descended the steps, unsure how she could help. The skirmish fizzed and exploded around the walls. Several guards had fallen in an unconscious heap at the bottom of the stairs. As far as she could tell, they were still alive. Her friends were aiming to disarm, not kill.

Ethne looked at her hands. She had never produced a fireball or thrown energy from her fingers, and doubted she could start now. She felt like a spare wheel watching the others fight for their lives. There must be something she could do. She turned to the wall, placed her hands against the stone, and extended her mind beyond the knot of security guards clogging the spiral stairs.

More guards were waiting at the top, as if forming a polite queue to join the fight. Freja's voice appeared in Ethne's mind.

'Keep doing that, Ethne. I can target them from here if I can see them through your mind. Hold steady for me.'

Ethne did as instructed and watched in amazement as streamers of light whizzed up the stairs over the heads of the stunned troops, only to drop at the last minute and explode over an unsuspecting guard and knock him out. The stairwell quickly filled with unconscious bodies. The remaining guards began to scramble over their fallen comrades in confused desperation as they fled back to the entrance hall.

Once there, they ran into Joshua. He stood just inside the entrance and took out the guards as they appeared from the stairwell. Some had vaulted over the reception desk and aimed shots at him over the top, but they were unwilling to risk raising their heads to check his position so their shots fell wide.

Another guard popped up on the stairs beyond reception. He leant around the corner, fired off a couple of rounds then disappeared again. Joshua watched and counted and figured out his pattern. When he next appeared, Joshua hit him with one precision shot to the head. He was beginning to enjoy himself.

Behind him, Ana entered reception surrounded by a cocoon of energy. It shimmered as she moved closer to Joshua. She stepped in front of him and placed herself directly in the line of fire.

Bullets exploded against her magnetic shield. They sparked in vivid flashes and left trails of light as they fell to the floor.

Joshua grinned and placed a hand on her shoulder and was immediately engulfed by the force field. They stood together, serene and smiling, as the barrage continued. Every guard in the entrance hall emptied their guns directly at the glowing woman. Not a single bullet hit home.

Downstairs, Ethne watched from her spot against the wall. Michael, Freja and Seth had knocked out all the guards on the stairs. They lay in messy piles, slumped over each other like the aftermath of a drunken bender. Freja and Seth worked together to build a magnetic shield at the bottom of the stairs to prevent any more guards entering the cellar.

Ethne sent a message to Ana. 'We have Michael. Heading out.'

Ana relayed the message to Joshua who acknowledged it with a curt nod.

Silence had fallen in the entrance hall. The guards were stunned. They stared at the pulsing light surrounding Ana as if mesmerised.

'Put down your guns,' she said.

Nobody moved.

'Please,' she continued. 'We have Michael. If you let us leave, no one else needs to be hurt.'

In reply, a guard burst from behind the reception desk, yelling like a banshee, and ran straight at Ana. He fired round after round, but she merely smiled.

Joshua aimed and fired. The guard hit the floor.

'I can do this all day,' said Joshua, as he reloaded his gun, safe inside Ana's protective bubble. 'Anyone else want to try?'

Another guard stood up behind reception, his gun raised above his head. He slowly placed it on the desk and held up his hands.

'Thank you,' said Ana.

The remaining guards dropped their guns. Joshua directed them to kick them across the floor, where he gathered them into a pile. He then led the guards out of reception and locked them in their own control room. He returned to reception to find Ana fussing over the unconscious guards.

'Leave them,' he said. 'Kendrick can deal with them when he gets here.'

Ana and Joshua stood side by side and surveyed the aftermath of the fight. They had done it. Michael was safe.

Ana turned to smile at Joshua. 'We did need you.'

'Does that mean you've forgiven me?'

'Perhaps.'

Joshua slipped his arm around Ana's shoulder. 'Let's get out of here.'

She pulled away and shushed him. 'Listen.'

All Joshua could hear was silence. Then into the stillness came the sound of applause and an immaculately dressed man strode through the door beyond the entrance hall, clapping slowly. He smiled at Ana in a way that suggested he was impressed but was pretending he wasn't.

'Bravo,' said Gregori. 'It is an honour to meet you at last, Anastasia.'

Ana stood her ground as the lawyer walked towards her. 'I've often wondered what a genocidal maniac looks like.'

'Takes one to know one,' said Gregori. He stopped to nudge the body of a security guard with his toe. 'How many men have you killed now, Ana?'

'Most of them will live,' she said. 'They're just sleeping.'

Outside on the gravel path, the silence from the castle was making the other Homo Angelus nervous. Ethne and Michael silently agreed to investigate. They ran up the steps into the entrance hall.

Inside they found Ana arguing with an extremely well attired man with scrupulously neat hair. Ethne watched the odd man for a moment and decided there was something seriously wrong with him. He was also vaguely familiar.

'Who is that?' she said to Michael.

'Gregori. ARK's lawyer, so he says.'

Ethne continued to rack her brains. She was sure she had seen him somewhere before. Hiding behind a tree on a hill by the river in Orkney, twelve thousand years ago.

'He's been after Ana all this time,' she said.

Michael nodded distractedly. He was watching Ana. She was furious and getting more enraged by the second. He had seen that look on her face before, on a snowy night at Christmas, just before she blasted her stepfather against the wall outside the Work Farm.

Ana took a step towards the lawyer. 'You were going to kill every Homo Angelus you could find. That's a choice. You don't have to do it. I was defending myself and my friends.'

Michael reached out to take her hand. 'Ana. We stopped him. It's over.'

She wasn't listening. She stepped away from Michael and walked towards Gregori and put her hand on his arm.

On contact, both Ana and Gregori vanished.

Michael stared at the spot where they had been, and blinked. He spun to face Ethne and Joshua. 'You saw that, right? Where'd she go?'

41

At the end of the corridor on the upper floor of the castle was a cramped spiral staircase leading to an abandoned room. Locked behind a heavy oak door, the turret library contained no books. Empty wooden shelves were stacked floor to ceiling, following the curve of the walls. The circular room had been gutted when Phanes BioTech took possession of the building. Even the heavy tapestry curtains had been taken down. Indentations on the carpet revealed the presence of ghostly armchairs and perhaps a table or cabinet.

A flash of light irradiated the room, and then faded in an instant to leave two figures standing face to face.

Ana glared at Gregori. He smiled in return.

'You want me,' she said. 'Well. Here I am.'

The lawyer chuckled softly. 'Do you have any idea to whom you are speaking?'

Ana fired out a blast of energy. She did it fast, hoping to take him by surprise, but it was no good. He merely stepped to one side.

She tried again. He blocked her. They circled each other, turning round and around in the turret, her sending streamers and light bombs, the lawyer dodging or blocking her at every turn.

Ana watched as he moved around her, effortlessly dodging every attack, and his skin began to glow with its own luminescence. It reminded her of Beatrice. He was anticipating her every move as if he was inside her mind, but she couldn't feel him in there. Usually, when somebody made telepathic contact, she could feel their mental signature rubbing against hers. Gregori was invisible.

Ana's skin prickled cold and her stomach hollowed out as the truth dawned: Gregori wasn't human.

She was fighting an angel.

In the entrance hall, Lucy was surrounded by agitated humans. Everybody was shouting at once. She looked at their frightened, confused and defiant faces, and wanted to kiss them all. They were glorious and perfect. Her children, her hope. She raised her hands and silence fell.

'One at a time.'

Michael and Ethne both started talking at once, until Lucy gave Ethne a significant look and shut her up. Michael continued breathlessly.

'We have to find her. She's in serious trouble. She can't fight Gregori. I don't think he's even human.'

'You are correct,' said Lucy. 'He is an angel, but Gregori went rogue some time ago. We have been trying to get him back on side, but he is extremely stubborn and idealistic.'

'How does an angel go rogue?' said Ethne. 'You told me you can't even lie, so how can Gregori be working against us?'

'He is not an angel like me,' said Lucy. 'He was not created angelic. He was born human. Gregori was the first human to become Homo Angelus, and then the first to ascend and master the light.'

'And become an angel,' said Ethne. 'So what went wrong? What's his beef?'

Lucy's eyes danced with amusement. 'His beef, as you so elegantly put it, dear Seshat, is pride. As a human he was tremendous, a powerful shaman and a true visionary. Born long before you were even imagined, he was a leader, a truth-teller, an artist of the human soul. Without him, you would have none of the sublime art of Lascaux.'

'Right, we get it,' said Joshua. 'He was the da Vinci of the Palaeolithic. Why is he obsessed with Ana?'

'Not just the Palaeolithic, the Neolithic too,' said Ethne. 'He was there the day the prophecy was taken to Greenland. I saw him, watching. He didn't look happy. I was his disciple and then I left to join another tribe. He wants to stop the prophecy and that means stopping Ana. Without her you don't get the Lord of Things to Come, and the True Elite, whoever they are, don't rise.'

Lucy chuckled and shook her head. 'Seshat, Ethne, Daughter of Thoth, please do try to be a little less dense and actually use that magnificent brain with which you have been gifted.'

Ethne considered punching Lucy on the arm, but thought better of it. She ran the prophecy through her mind and pulled the details into focus.

'The True Elite are the Shining Ones,' she said, thinking out loud. 'In the past, the Shining Ones were the priests, priestesses, and shamans. So Gregori was the first. You said it, Lucy. He was the first to become Homo Angelus, so he was the first Shining One. The first of the True Elite. They were the only ones who had access to this knowledge. But now anybody can access it. Anyone can become Homo Angelus and be a Shining One. The whole of humanity is awakening. So the True Elite is everyone.'

'And Gregori doesn't like competition,' said Joshua.

'We have to find Ana,' said Michael. 'He won't stop until he's killed her.'

Ethne moved to the nearest wall and placed her hands against the dark oak panelling. She began flying her mind through the rooms, searching for Ana's signature.

'A little help, guys,' she said. 'Ana might not even be in this building.'

Freja and Michael joined hands and extended their minds into the surrounding countryside. Freja gave a yelp of surprise.

'There's a long line of black Range Rovers heading this way,' she said.

'Kendrick,' said Joshua.

The turret library was ablaze. Light rebounded from the empty bookshelves and exploded in showers around the duelling figures in the centre of the room.

Ana was flagging. Every volley drained power from her body. Her magnetic force field had long since fizzled away, leaving her wide open to whatever the angel threw at her. She was determined to stay on her feet. She dodged and blocked his assaults, but fatigue tugged at her mind. If she surrendered, the riptide would pull her under. She wanted to curl up and sleep, just for a moment, but Gregori was relentless.

'You are starting to understand,' he said. 'I mastered the light long ago. I know the heart of the sun. It lights my being. You are mere flesh hiding a flickering spark. What do you know of the light?'

Ana fired a barrage of light bombs at Gregori, spitting them at random from her fingers. He dodged all but one, which hit him square between the eyes. He simply absorbed the light, his body rippling like a visible purr as Ana's light melded with his.

'You are giving me more power, Anastasia. Most kind.'

'Even if you kill me, there are many others,' she said. 'You can't destroy all of us.'

'I don't need to destroy humanity,' said Gregori. 'You are more than capable of doing that yourselves.'

'You know nothing about humanity.'

Gregori laughed. 'Neither, it seems, do you.'

Ethne stood with both hands and her forehead pressed against the wall. Michael stood close by, watching her with a fierce intensity. He saw everything her mind touched. Her fingers burned. She was pushing herself too hard, too fast. If she didn't find Ana soon, her skin would begin to melt, but she couldn't flake out now.

Michael placed his hand on her shoulder and she felt a surge of power. He was feeding her energy, keeping her moving.

She sensed something Ana-esque on the periphery of her awareness and felt a tingle of recognition from Michael.

'She's close,' he said. 'Go up.'

Ethne flew down the hallway outside the bedrooms and up the spiral staircase at the end, and burst through the door into the turret library.

'She's there,' she said. 'Michael be careful. The prophecy says you-'

Before she could finish, Michael was already halfway up the stairs. Ethne rounded on Lucy, frantic with worry.

'Please,' she said. 'We can't let this happen.'

In reply, Lucy vanished in a flash of ice blue light.

Michael took the stairs two at a time, careened around the corner into the guest corridor and then powered up the steps to the library. Light flashed in pulses through the gap under the heavy oak door. He yanked at the handle, but it was locked. A ball of energy formed in his hand without him needing to even think of it. He threw it against the lock and it blasted open.

The door swung back to reveal nothing but dazzling light. Michael shielded his eyes and stepped into the room.

Vast streamers of light spiralled around the room, weaving themselves into intricate patterns as they zipped around the turret. Michael squinted into the light. Somebody was kneeling on the floor in the centre of the room.

It was Ana.

He took a step towards her but a streamer of light lifted him and threw him against the wall. He crashed into the bookshelves and crumpled to the floor.

'Ana!' he shouted. 'Door's open. Run!'

She didn't move. She couldn't stand.

Michael crawled across the floor. He lifted her face and poured his energy into her. 'Come on, Ana. One last push.'

Behind him, Ethne and Joshua appeared in the doorway and watched the electromagnetic storm crackle around the turret. Joshua ducked beneath a light streamer and crawled towards Ana. Ethne followed. They joined Michael, and between them, lifted Ana to her feet.

Across the room, Lucy stood behind Gregori and wrapped her arms around the rogue angel. He squirmed, desperate to free himself, but she held him fast and spoke into his ear. She fired words like bullets to break his will. He crumpled momentarily, but then rallied and sent out another wave of light. It shattered into fragments and cascaded around the room.

Michael, Ethne and Joshua were lifted from their feet and pinned against the walls. They struggled against the magnetic currents circling the room, but couldn't move. They were stuck.

Ana remained standing. She was gaining strength. Her friends had revitalised her and long forgotten memories flashed into her mind.

Her battle with Gregori had begun eons ago, at the end of the Ice Age. She had taken Ethne from him and he would never forgive her.

'You cannot defeat me,' he shouted.

Lucy grasped him around the neck. 'I can dissolve you into nothing but radiation.'

Gregori laughed. 'Not without destroying the humans.'

Lucy watched Ana. She was holding up well against the charged air, but the others were immobilised. They couldn't escape. If Lucy took her true form, Gregori would be destroyed, but Ana and the others would be killed.

'Make your choice,' shouted Gregori. 'Destroy me or defend your precious humans.'

Lucy released Gregori and stepped back. She could not prevent what would happen next. Ana would be protected. The prophecy would be fulfilled.

'You have too much faith in humanity,' said Gregori. 'You think they can be like us.'

'They will be more than us.'

'Impossible,' said Gregori.

'This is nothing but a jealous rage,' said Ana. 'Twelve thousand years is a long time to hold a grudge, Gregori.'

'So you remember?'

'My tribe were called the Akhu,' said Ana. 'The Shining Ones. We discovered how to become Human Angels and Lucy helped us to create the Fire Stone. We kept it secret and only a select few were allowed to ascend. After the comet hit and the ice melted, our land began to die, we searched for a new home and found you.'

'I ascended without your technology,' said Gregori. 'The Fire Stone is unnecessary. An abomination.'

'When we first found your people in the Land of the Watchers, we were impressed,' said Ana. 'You had found your own method to ascend. You had a talented acolyte, but she was afraid.'

'She misunderstood,' said Gregori.

'She came to me with her concerns,' continued Ana. 'She gave me your secrets and I understood how you had ascended. You are the abomination, Gregori.'

'You took her from me,' he shouted. 'You seduced her and poisoned her mind against me.'

Ethne struggled against the light pinning her to the bookcase. 'I left of my own free will, you raving egomaniac.'

Ana smiled. 'She left because she understood what you couldn't see. That civilisation couldn't be built on death and violence. You cannot build on rotten foundations. The blood sacrifices sickened her soul, and mine.'

'Fine words, coming from you.'

'Why did you bury the temples?' said Ana.

'That was not my doing.'

'It was your command. You built the temples of Gobekli Tepe and then you abandoned them. I suppose they had served their purpose. You had ascended and you no longer needed them. You went further than anyone else dared and became an angel. And then you abandoned humanity.'

Gregori glowered at Ana. 'Yes, I had the temples buried. Humanity was corrupted. I watched as darkness filled every mind. Humanity is too weak to ascend. I have fought against the prophecy ever since. If humanity were to awaken now, the world would be filled with monsters.'

'Like you?' said Ana.

'Humanity isn't ready for this power. You are a case in point, Anastasia. You were one of the first to awaken during the solar storm. Bravo. Take a bow. Put out the bunting, as they say. But what was the first thing you did? You killed.'

'It was an accident.'

'The excuse of the coward,' said Gregori. 'Take responsibility for your actions, human. You killed Patrick Wilson. More importantly, you wanted to kill him.'

'No!' shouted Ana.

'You must have done, my dear, otherwise he would not be dead.'

'You're lying.'

'Did you not see him dead in your mind's eye before you attacked?'

'I just wanted him to stop.'

'Stop living,' said Gregori.

'No. Stop hurting my mother,' said Ana. 'You're twisting everything.'

'You have not answered my question,' said Gregori. 'What did you see before you blasted your stepfather with the full force of your power?'

Ana choked back a sob and shook her head. He couldn't make her say it. She closed her eyes and buried the memory as deep as it would go.

'Ah,' said the angel, his voice softening. 'You cannot live with yourself, Ana.'

She looked up. Gregori was gazing at her with what looked like compassion, but it couldn't be, not from him. He had turned away from love a long time ago. He was trying to trick her into saying the unthinkable.

'Your mother is a remarkable woman,' said Gregori. 'She has denied herself the joy of your company and convinced others that she despises you, just to keep you safe. She has locked her heart in a cage so that you may be free. A noble gesture. What have you done with that gift?'

'You have no right to talk about my mother.'

'You have no right to deny what you are,' said Gregori. 'You are lost in a darkness so obscure that you have no idea you are even lost.'

Ana sagged with exhaustion. She wanted to lie down on the worn out carpet and sleep. Perhaps the angel was right. Darkness crept into her mind and wrapped itself tightly around her soul.

'I did see him dead,' she said softly. 'I was so angry. He betrayed me and my mother. He lied to both of us. He sold me to ARK and expected me to forgive him. He broke my mother's heart. So, yes. I wanted him to suffer. I wanted him to die.'

'And you got your wish.'

'It doesn't make me a monster,' she said, wiping the tears from her face.

'What does it make you?'

'Human.'

Gregori smiled. 'My point exactly.'

Ana nodded sadly. 'You're right. We're the same, you and I.'

Gregori's smile faltered, and Ana continued.

'When I blasted Patrick, I felt so powerful. It was delicious. I could've raised the entire street to the ground, I could've tracked down everyone who had ever hurt me, or said an unkind word, and reduced them to ash and bones. I have tasted bloodlust and it is glorious. I can certainly see the attraction.'

'This is not bloodlust,' said Gregori. 'This is a matter of principle.'

'What principle? That only you should have this power?'

'Only those who deserve it, as it was before the ice melted and before the world became mad.'

'Why are you so much better than me, Gregori?'

He smiled. 'I am an angel. Need I explain?'

Ana sighed. 'Being human is such hard work, isn't it? I mean, I was given these powers and I didn't understand them. I lost control and killed Patrick. I didn't know about his weak heart, but that doesn't excuse what I did. I am responsible for my actions. I didn't have to kill Patrick and I'm sorry that I did. I'll have to live with that. But you're an angel. You should know better.'

'I do know better, my dear.'

'And yet, you kill.'

'I am protecting humanity from itself,' said Gregori. 'They cannot be allowed to ascend. The power would destroy them. It is cruel to push them out of the nest too soon. They are not ready. The plan has failed, as I knew it would. No more interventions. Humanity is a failed experiment.'

Ana shook her head. 'You don't want humans to be as powerful as angels. You're scared of losing your privileged position at the top of the tree. You need to believe you're better than us because, in reality, you know you're not. I bet you couldn't wait to become an angel.'

'I was honoured and humbled to be offered the opportunity.'

'Humbled?'

'Niloufer recognised my gifts even if you didn't, Ana.'

'You hated being human. You wanted to be special and powerful because it was better than being ordinary. That's all I am, Gregori. Ordinary. These powers aren't mine and I no longer want them. If that means the prophecy is never fulfilled, then so be it. You win.'

'What are you doing?'

'Surrendering.' Ana opened her arms wide and lowered her protective bubble.

Gregori stared at her in confusion. 'You realise what I will do.'

Ana smiled and showered the angel with compassion. 'I forgive you, Gregori. Just as I forgive my stepfather for hurting my mother and betraying me. Just as I forgive myself for wishing Patrick harm.'

Her love poured forth and merged with the angel's light, pulling him into an embrace. It spread through the room and dissolved the magnetic lines of force holding her friends against the walls. They fell to the floor, and lay for a moment, stunned and disoriented.

Ana held Gregori close. He resisted and struggled, but the force of her love was too strong. Finally, she released him and stepped back.

'Thank you,' said Ana. 'You showed me who I am and for that, I'm grateful. Everybody carries the darkness within them. Even you. You're more human than you realise, Gregori. Whatever happens now is in your hands. You must choose.'

'You will not resist me?'

Ana smiled and the room blazed with a light so sublime it reminded Gregori of a world he had long forgotten. She was right, twelve thousand years was a long time to hold a grudge. A single tear ran down his cheek and he wiped it away in astonishment. What had she done to him?

Gregori closed his eyes and lowered his head in surrender.

Joshua breathed out in relief, then clambered to his feet and rushed to Ana's side. He pulled off his jacket and draped it around her shoulders. Behind them, Michael and Ethne helped each other to stand on wobbly legs.

'Is it getting colder in here?' said Ethne.

Michael turned to check on Ana, and what he saw made his knees weak with shock.

Gregori was shaking with rage. His face rippled with venomous hatred and he looked as if he might tear everyone in the room limb from limb with his bare hands. His eyes burned gold and light began to blaze from his body in great arcs.

Everybody ducked as the air around them filled with flames.

'I cannot allow it,' said Gregori. 'It must be allowed to fail.'

Ethne realised what the angel was about to do and shouted, 'He's going nuclear. Cover your eyes.'

She ripped off her jacket, threw it over Michael's head and pulled him to the floor with her. She ducked underneath. 'Mickey, don't look.'

He squirmed and tried to stand. 'Ana-'

Ethne grabbed him. 'There's no time.'

Joshua watched in horror and awe as Gregori's light magnified. The room filled with so much light it no longer resembled a room. The bookshelves, the floor and the ceiling all vanished into liquid fire. He pulled his jacket over Ana's head and wrapped his arms around her. 'Close your eyes. I've got you covered. I won't let you go.'

Joshua put himself between Ana and Gregori and closed his eyes, but it wasn't enough. The angel's light pulverised through his body and irradiated his soul.

Ana clung to Joshua, but when the light faded and his arms fell limply to his sides, she knew he was gone.

She didn't move for a long time. Her tears ran down Joshua's neck and soaked into his collar.

Outside the castle, Freja and Seth watched a firestorm erupt from the window at the top of the turret. They stood side by side, their eyes on the shattered window, as the angel's light dissipated harmlessly into the atmosphere.

An unnatural silence fell over the castle grounds. Nobody dared to move or speak. The sound started low and then grew in strength until Ana's wail of grief filled the air with desolation.

42

She remained in the turret for a long time, unable to stand and unwilling to move. She lowered Joshua to the floor and sat with him in her arms and listened while the others moved around her. An argument broke out among the angels, but Ana didn't listen. She felt the touch of hands and a soft voice spoke close to her face, but she had slipped into another dimension. It was too hard to bridge the gap so she closed her eyes and listened to the roar of her own breathing in her ears.

Joshua couldn't be gone. The universe was ruptured. The entire glorious and sickening mess of existence would implode without him, and it would begin with her. She could feel herself collapsing inwards, like the closing of the aperture of a camera. The stars would burn out and nothing would live.

Eventually, Michael carried the body out of the turret and placed it in one of the bedrooms. Ana followed him down the spiral staircase, then sat on the bed beside Joshua and refused to move.

Michael hovered in the doorway and watched Ethne try to coax Ana from the bed. He didn't understand what had happened. He had tried to wriggle free and had squinted into the light from under Ethne's jacket, but he couldn't see anything except the fire.

He played it over and over in his mind. There wasn't enough time. He couldn't reach her.

'It should've been me,' he said.

'Don't be daft,' said Ethne softly.

'But the prophecy-'

'Damn the prophecy,' said Ethne. 'It makes no sense for you to die, Mickey.'

'What about Jack?' he said. 'He didn't deserve this either.'

Ana turned to look at her friends. 'He's called Joshua. And this is my fault, Michael, so you can stop feeling guilty.'

'What happens now?' said Ethne. 'Without Joshua, the prophecy is finished. Gregori has won.'

Ana turned back to Joshua. 'I want to be alone.' Ethne took a step towards the bed and walked into a force field. Ana had encased Joshua and herself in a protective bubble. 'Please. Go and help the others.'

They did as directed.

Freja and Seth were running around downstairs helping the security guards to recover and apologising for knocking them out. Those who were well enough helped to carry the bodies of their fallen comrades outside, where they were laid out on the gravel in a pitiful line.

Nobody noticed when a convoy of black Range Rovers swung into the driveway and the castle grounds filled with the shouts and efficiency of a well-oiled military machine. Kendrick joined the Homo Angelus in the banqueting hall and Ethne did her best to explain what had just happened.

'Has Gregori gone?' he said.

She shrugged. 'Waiting for angelic news on that front. They all vanished pretty sharpish.'

Three tiny pops sounded from the corner of the room, followed by a flash of blue light, and three angels manifested in front of the fireplace. Niloufer and Beatrice appeared subdued, as if they had been admonished in the headmaster's office. They kept their eyes averted and stayed in the background while Lucy stepped forward to greet Kendrick.

She took his hand, flipped it over and kissed his wrist in one fluid movement. He seemed unfazed and merely repeated his question.

'Yes, he is gone,' she said.

'You sure about that?' said Ethne

'Niloufer has dealt with him,' said Lucy. 'It was his error to recommend Gregori for advancement too soon, and now we pay the price. And before you ask a million and one questions, Ethne, I cannot explain how he was dealt with in a way you would understand. Understand?'

Ethne was in no mood to be fobbed off. 'Try me.'

Lucy sighed and considered for a moment. 'He will no longer be able to take form. Niloufer has disrupted his energy signature. It's the angel equivalent of the naughty step.'

Normally, Ethne would have laughed at that, but she was too angry. 'Could you not have done that earlier? Y'know, before Joshua got killed.'

Lucy placed her hand on Ethne's cheek and smiled sadly.

'No, we could not. Gregori was hiding his true nature and we could not locate him accurately. As long as he retained human form, he was one among billions. Niloufer hatched a plan to flush Gregori out, and correct his earlier mistake. We knew Gregori wouldn't be able to resist coming after Ana, so-'

'So you used her as bait?'

'Actually, I was the bait,' said Michael. 'Niloufer gave me the choice. He told me the prophecy and, yes Ethne, I knew what it said, don't look at me like that. They weren't sure how it would play out with Ana and Joshua, so I was like a backup plan. We knew Ana would come for me, and then Gregori would reveal himself.'

'Gregori had planned this day for a long time,' said Kendrick. 'He didn't just create a false trail for his cover story. He actually lived it. That's why it was so hard for us to see through him. Gregori controlled everything from behind the scenes. He suggested ARK form a consortium and then guided their acquisitions and development. He planted the idea of the Shining Ones and told the CEOs they were the chosen ones.'

'So who attacked the cave in Greenland?' said Ethne.

'ARK,' said Kendrick. 'Gregori subcontracted his own team via ARK and they attacked their own people. You can get people to do almost anything if you pay them enough. He never intended to let the bosses meet the Fire Stone. He asked me to destroy it.'

'You won't, will you?' said Ethne. 'Please tell me you're not a barbarian.'

Kendrick laughed. 'Something like that? Not a chance. We'll be keeping a close eye on it. The Fire Stone is one dangerous piece of kit.'

'But without Joshua...' Ethne trailed off and stared at her boots.

'The future is more resilient than you imagine, Ethne,' said Lucy. 'The next step is already in motion.'

'And what is the next step?' said Kendrick. 'With or without the prophecy, the mutation is still spreading, right?'

'Correct,' said Lucy. 'The Fire Stone is an accelerant. It will trigger the *Homo angelus* gene of anyone who stands before it. Many more will turn through contact with the Shining Ones, such as those present here. Eventually, the Homo Angelus will outnumber the rest. It is a matter of time.'

'So it'll just take longer?' said Ethne.

'Correct.'

'But that gives ARK time to fight back,' continued Ethne. 'They still want to control this gene. They're not going to retreat just because their lawyer turned out to be a lunatic angel with a twelve thousand year old grudge.'

Lucy nodded thoughtfully. 'Gregori did make things easier for us in that regard.'

'Easier?'

'He gave us the Fire Stone,' said Kendrick. 'Plus, I have someone on the inside at Phanes BioTech. ARK are on the run.'

Lucy beamed. 'Have a little faith, dearest Seshat.'

'All part of the plan?' said Ethne.

'You'd be surprised,' said the angel. 'Nothing is as it appears.'

They took Joshua back to the cottage at Howick. In the absence of any other family, Ana decided he would like to be buried near the sea and the rocks he had played on as a child. Michael carried him into the cottage, laid him out on one of the sofas in the living room, and crossed his arms over his chest.

Ana stood close by and watched. She could hear Ethne rattling around in the kitchen making hot chocolate for the others. Freja and Seth had offered to help dig the grave at first light. Somewhere deep in her soul, Ana was grateful to be surrounded by her friends, but she just wanted to be left alone with Joshua. She wasn't ready to let him go. Every time she imagined throwing the dirt over his body she had to stop herself crying out in pain.

Ethne appeared at her side and held a mug of steaming cocoa under her nose. Ana shook her head.

Ethne gazed at Joshua for a long time, then sighed. 'He even looks like Osiris now.'

'Don't,' said Ana.

'I'm just saying, if he is Osiris, then he could come-'

'Ethne please. Forget the prophecy. It's a stupid story, nothing more.'

One by one, they left her in peace. She perched on the sofa beside his body and her tears fell in silence. The cottage creaked in the darkness and the wind shook the chimney, howling strange melodies that sung of Ana's grief. She was hollowed out and lost to this world.

In her imagination, she wandered a desolate wilderness searching for Joshua. If she could find him, she could bring him back. Or else, she could join him in the desert. She remembered, too late, what Beatrice had told her in error: that she could trust in Joshua's love. The lies he told were small compared to the truth of his sacrifice.

She didn't deserve his love, she knew that. She had misused her power and this was the consequence. Her love was destroyed and now the prophecy would remain unfulfilled.

It would soon be dawn and she would have to say goodbye. She leaned forward and kissed Joshua on the forehead.

'I'm sorry,' she whispered.

She ran her fingers over his hands and across his chest. Something crinkled under her touch. There was a piece of paper in his pocket. She carefully pulled it free. It was the drawing he had tried to show her in Finland.

She had been too proud to look at it. He had told her it was important, but what would it matter now. She opened the paper and stared numbly at the picture.

It showed her surrounded by burning cabins at Linnunrata. In the drawing she was smiling, with one hand on her round and very pregnant belly.

A sob escaped and she clamped a hand to her mouth. He knew. He had known all along. Perhaps he denied that he could be Homo Angelus because he was scared of the future he knew was coming. He had carried this drawing next to his heart for days.

Ana wrapped a blanket around her shoulders and went outside to the wall overlooking the sea. She leaned against it and gazed across the ocean into the darkness. Waves splintered over the rocks and churned in heaving cycles.

A thin sliver of light broached the horizon. She wanted to believe there could be a new beginning but all she felt was regret. There would be no future. When she looked forward, she saw nothing but darkness. She closed her eyes against the dawn and listened to the ocean boil.

Her imagination was playing tricks on her. She knew it was because she heard Joshua speak as if he was standing right behind her.

'I finally managed to sneak up on you.'

'Only in my dreams,' she said into the wind.

He laughed, a muted chuckle, and she felt his breath against her neck and his lips on her skin where he kissed her. A kiss that felt real and warm and not remotely imaginary.

Ana opened her eyes and spun round. Joshua smiled ruefully at her, his hair falling into his eyes.

'But you...you're...' Ana stumbled forward and touched his face. His skin felt warm. She ran her hands over his body and stopped at his heart. It pounded within his chest, a little fast, but undeniable.

She began to laugh and Joshua smiled.

'I think my powers just kicked in.'

*

Spread the word!
If you enjoyed this book, please tell your friends and write a review.
Thanks for reading!

About the Author

Jessica Davidson is a writer of visionary fiction and non-fiction that explores the power of the human mind and imagination. She started life as a musician and sound engineer, and has toured Europe with an orchestra, produced demos for rock bands, and recorded a talking newspaper for a local council. She began to write in an effort to make sense of it all.

She lives in her head but can usually be found in the UK.

Visit her website for loads more stuff: **www.jessicadavidson.co.uk**

Made in the USA
Las Vegas, NV
30 May 2021

23918858R00174